JAMES TWINING

James Twining was born in London but spent much of his childhood in Paris. After graduating from Oxford University with a first class degree in French Literature, he worked in Investment Banking for four years before leaving to set up his own company which he then sold three years later, having been named as one of the eight 'Best of Young British' Entrepreneurs in *The New Statesman* magazine. Married and living in London, James is currently completing the second Tom Kirk adventure.

The 1933 Double Eagle is the world's most expensive coin. In July 2002 it sold at auction for $8 milllion, marking the end of an incredible seventy year journey that had its roots deep in Depression-era politics and involved a daring heist, an Egyptian King and a dramatic government sting operation.

For automatic updates on James Twining visit HarperCollins.co.uk/jamestwining and register for author tracker.

Praise for *The Double Eagle*

'This would make the perfect Tom Cruise movie'   *The Independent on Sunday*

'A carefully constructed tale straight out of the Dan Brown mould of thriller writing'
                                        Sunday Sun

'*The Double Eagle* will leave you breathless, but never dizzy . . . Solid debut work'
                                        Ladsmag

JAMES TWINING

The Double Eagle

HarperCollins*Publishers*

HarperCollins*Publishers*
77–85 Fulham Palace Road,
Hammersmith, London W6 8JB

www.harpercollins.co.uk

This paperback edition 2005
11

First published in Great Britain by
HarperCollins*Publishers* 2005

Copyright © James Twining 2005

James Twining asserts the moral right to
be identified as the author of this work

ISBN 0 00 776663 7

Set in Meridien by Palimpsest Book Production Ltd,
Polmont, Stirlingshire

Printed and bound in Great Britain by
Clays Ltd, St Ives plc

For automatic updates on James Twining visit
HarperCollins.co.uk
and register for author tracker.

To Victoria, always

Là, tout n'est qu'ordre et beauté,
Luxe, calme et volupté

Charles Baudelaire, L'Invitation au Voyage

Acknowledgements

My thanks to Roy, Claire and Sarah Toft, Bruce Ritchie, David Sale, Jeremy Green, Jeremy Walton, George Hammon, Sean Corbett, Julian Simmons, Charlotte Cameron, Mark Gill, Samantha Axtell, Maria Barrett, Nico Schwartz, Florian Reinaud and most especially of all Rod Gillett, for their invaluable comments, suggestions and help. The book is immeasurably better because of it.

Thank you too, to my agents, Jonathan Lloyd and Euan Thorneycroft at Curtis Brown in London and George Lucas at InkWell Management in New York, for plucking me from the depths of their in-tray, spotting the potential of my early drafts and for believing in me.

Thank you to Wayne Brookes, my fantastic editor, for his unfaltering championing of this book and his infectious enthusiasm and to Alison Callahan at HarperCollins US for her insight and belief. Thanks also to Lynne Drew, Debbie Collings and the whole sales, marketing and creative team at HarperCollins who have been absolute stars from start to finish.

For their assistance in researching this book, I would like to acknowledge the Smithsonian Institution (National Museum of American History and National Numismatic Collection), The US Mint, The Department of the Treasury, US Army Armor Center – Fort Knox, Christie's, Sotheby's, The Turkish Ministry of Tourism and The French Ministry of Culture.

And finally, my boundless love and thanks to my parents, Ann and Bob, to my sister Joanna, to my wife Victoria and to our beautiful new baby daughter Amelia.

London, September 2004

For more information on the author and on the fascinating story behind the 1933 Double Eagle, please visit:

www.jamestwining.com

Executive Order No. 6102

By virtue of the authority vested in me by Section 5(b) of the Act of October 6, 1917, as amended by Section 2 of the Act of March 9, 1933, entitled 'An Act to provide relief in the existing national emergency in banking, and for other purposes,' in which amendatory Act Congress declared that a serious emergency exists,

I, Franklin D. Roosevelt, President of the United States of America, do declare that said national emergency still continues to exist and pursuant to said section do hereby prohibit the hoarding of gold coin, gold bullion, and gold certificates within the continental United States by individuals, partnerships, associations and corporations and hereby prescribe the following regulations for carrying out the purposes of this order.

All persons are hereby required to deliver on or before May 1, 1933, to a Federal Reserve bank or a branch or agency thereof or to any member bank of the Federal Reserve System all gold coin, gold bullion and gold certificates now owned by them or coming into their ownership on or before April 28, 1933.

Upon receipt of gold coin, gold bullion or gold certificates delivered to it, the Federal Reserve Bank or member bank will pay thereof an equivalent amount of any other form of coin or currency coined or issued under the laws of the United States.

Whoever wilfully violates any provision of this Executive Order or of these regulations or of any rule, regulation or license issued thereunder may be fined not more than $10,000, or, if a natural person, may be imprisoned for not more than ten years, or both; and any officer, director, or agent of any corporation who knowingly participates in any such violation may be punished by a like fine, imprisonment, or both.

This order and these regulations may be modified or revoked at any time.

Franklin D. Roosevelt
President of the United States of America
April 5, 1933

PROLOGUE

What do you not drive human hearts into, cursed Craving for gold!

Virgil – The Aeneid (iii.56)

Pont de Grenelle, 16th Arrondissement, Paris
16th July – 9:05pm

They were late.

They'd said quarter to and it was already five past. It made him uneasy to be standing out in the open for this long. If they weren't there in the next five minutes he was leaving, a million dollars or not.

He patted his pocket nervously. It was still there; he could feel it through the black woollen material, its warm weight pressing against his thigh. It was still safe.

A teenage couple, arms interlinked, strolled towards him, snatching kisses every few steps in the dying light. Mid-embrace, the girl caught sight of him and broke away with an embarrassed shrug. Her fingers flew unconsciously to the small silver crucifix that hung around her neck.

'Bonsoir, mon père.'

'*Bonsoir, mon enfant.*'

He smiled and nodded at them both as they walked past him to the other side of the Pont de Grenelle, noting that it was only then they allowed their guilty laughter to echo up through the fading heat. Against a crimson sky, the lights on the Eiffel Tower sparkled as if it was on fire.

He rested his arms on the parapet and looked out at the Statue of Liberty. Identical to her much larger sister across the Atlantic, she dominated the Allée des Cygnes, the narrow island in the middle of the River Seine upon which she had been erected in 1889, according to the inscription on her base. She had her back to him, smooth bronze muscles of crumpled fabric and taut skin, eternally youthful despite the green patina of old age.

As a child, his grandmother had once told him that many members of their family had made the long and difficult journey from Naples to America in the 1920s. When he looked at the statue, he felt somehow connected to those faceless relatives, understood something of their sense of wonder at their first sight of the New World, their unshakeable faith in a new beginning. So he always chose this place. It felt familiar. Safe. Protected. *Caso mai.* Just in case.

Two men appeared out of the shadows of the bridge below and looked up at him. He sketched a wave, crossed to the other side of the road and made his way down the shallow concrete steps towards them, walking under the bridge's low steel arch. He stopped at the edge of the wide area encircling the statue's massive stone pedestal, careful as always to keep about twenty feet between himself and them.

They must have been there all the time, he thought to himself; watching him, checking that he was alone, hiding in the lengthening shadows like lions in long grass. That figured. These were not people to take chances. But then neither was he.

'*Bonsoir*,' the large man on the left called clearly through the night air, his long blond hair melting into a thick beard. An American, he guessed.

'*Bonsoir*,' he called back warily.

A large Bateau Mouche swept down the river past them, its blinding lights reaching into the darkness, probing, feeling. The heavy folds of the statue's robe seemed to ripple and lift gently under their touch as if caught in some unseen draught. As if she was teasing them.

'You got it?' The bearded man called out in English when the throb of the ship's engines had faded and the burning lights had shifted their relentless glare further along the bank.

'You got the money?' His voice was firm. It was the usual game, played out more times than he cared to remember. He looked down, feigning indifference and noticed that his polished black shoes were already dusty from the dry gravel.

'Let's see it first,' the man called back.

He paused. There seemed to be something strange about the bearded man's voice. A slight tension. He looked up and checked over his shoulder but his escape route was clear. He blinked his concern away and gave them the standard response.

'Show me the money and I'll take you to it.'

There. He saw it this time. Most wouldn't have noticed but he had been around long enough to read the signs. The stiffening of the shoulders, the narrowing of the eyes as the lone antelope strayed just that little too far from the rest of the herd.

They were preparing themselves.

He looked around again. It was still clear, although it was difficult to see beyond the trees as night closed in. Then he realized. That's why they'd been late.

So it would be dark.

Without saying a word he spun on the gravel, running, running as fast as he could, his slick leather soles spraying stones behind him like tyres accelerating on a dirt track. He couldn't let them get it. He couldn't let them find it. He snatched a glance over his shoulder and saw the two men bearing down on him, a gun barrel glimmering in the orange glow of the lights that lined the bridge overhead like a sharp claw.

Instinctively, he snapped his head back round just as he ran onto the point of the knife. Now he understood. The dark shape that had appeared in front of him, arm outstretched, face masked by the night, had been hiding in the shadows until he had come within striking distance. He'd been herded into the arms of death like an animal.

With a short, sharp punch, the six-inch serrated blade carved up into his chest and the shock of the impact made him swallow hard. He felt its coldness slicing through the soft cartilage at the base of his sternum, cutting into his heart.

It was the last thing he felt.

In the orange light, the blood that had leaked over the starched whiteness of his dog collar glowed green as Lady Liberty's weathered skin. But unknowing, unseeing, unfeeling, her steady gaze was fixed instead towards America.

Towards New York.

PART I

Gold conjures up a mist about a man, more destructive of all his old senses and lulling to his feelings than the fumes of charcoal

Charles Dickens – Nicholas Nickleby

ONE

Fifth Avenue, New York City
16th July – 11:30pm

Gracefully he fell, his body arcing in one smooth movement out from the side of the building and then back in, like a spider caught in a sudden gust of wind as it dropped on its thread, until with a final fizz of the rope through his gloved hand he landed on the balcony of the 17th floor.

Crouching, he unclipped the rope from his harness and flattened his back to the wall, his dark, lithe shape blending into the stained stone. He didn't move, his chest barely rising, the thin material of his black ski mask slick against his lips.

He had to be sure. He had to be certain that no one had seen him on the way down. So he waited, listening to the shallow breaths of the city slumbering fitfully below him, watching the Met's familiar bulk retreat into shadow as its floodlights were extinguished.

And all the while Central Park's dark lung, studded with the occasional lights of taxis making their way between East and West 86th Street, breathed a chilled, oxygenated air up the side of the building that made him shiver despite the heat. Air heavy with New York's distinctive scent, an intoxicating cocktail of fear, sweat and greed that bubbled up from subway tunnels and steam vents.

And although a lone NYPD chopper, spotlight primed, circled ever closer and the muffled scream of sirens echoed up from distant streets through the warm air, he could tell they were not for him. They never were. Tom Kirk had never been caught.

Keeping below the level of the carved stone balustrade, he padded over to the large semi-circular window that opened onto the balcony, its armoured panes glinting like sheet steel. Inside, he could see that the room was dark and empty, as he knew it would be. As it was every weekend during the Summer.

A few taps on each of the hinges that ran down the side of the right-hand window and the bolts popped out into his hand. Then carefully, so as not to break the alarmed central magnetic contact, he levered the edge of the window away from the frame until there was a gap big enough for him to slip through.

Once inside, Tom swung his pack down off his shoulder. From the main compartment he took out what looked like a metal detector – a thin black plate attached to an aluminium rod. He flicked a switch on the top of the plate and a small green light on its smooth surface glowed into life. Keeping completely still, he gripped the rod in his right hand and began to sweep the plate over the arid emptiness of the floor in front of him. Almost immediately the light on the back of the plate flashed red and he paused.

Pressure pads. As predicted.

Moving the plate slowly over the spot where the light had changed colour, he quickly identified an area that he circled with white chalk. Repeating this procedure, he worked his way methodically across the room, moving in controlled, precise movements. Five minutes later and he had reached the far wall, a trail of small white circles in his wake.

The room was exactly as the photos had shown it and had the distinctive smell of new money and old furniture. A large Victorian partners' desk dominated, a masculine marriage of polished English oak and Italian leather that reminded him of the interior of a 1920s Rolls Royce. Behind the desk, the wall was lined with what looked like the remnants of a once substantial private library, now presumably scattered across the world according to auction lots.

The two sidewalls that ran up to the window were painted a sandy grey and symmetrically hung with a series of drawings and paintings, four down each wall. He did not have to look closely to recognise them – Picasso, Kandinsky, Mondrian, Klimt. But Tom was not there for the paintings, nor for the decoy safe he knew lay behind the third picture on the left. He had learned not to be greedy.

Instead, he picked his way back through the chalk circles to the edge of the silk rug that filled the floor between the desk and the window, its colours shimmering in the pale moonlight. With his back to the window, he gripped one corner of the rug and threw it back. Underneath, the wood was slightly darker where it had been shielded from the bleaching sun.

Kneeling, he placed his gloved hands flat on the floor and slid them slowly across the dry wooden surface. About three feet in front of him, the tips of his fingers sensed a slight ridge in the wood. He moved his hands apart along the ridge, until he reached what felt like a corner on both sides. Placing his knuckles on these corners, he leant forward with all his weight. With a faint click, a two-foot square panel sank down and then sprang up about half an inch proud of the rest of the floor. It was hinged at the far end and he folded the panel back on itself so that it lay flat, revealing a gleaming floor safe.

The safe manufacturing and insurance industries cooperate on the security ratings of safes.

Manufacturers regularly submit their products to independent testing by the Underwriters Laboratory, or UL, who in return issue the safe with a Residential Security Container Label that allows the insurers to accurately determine the relevant insurance premium.

The safe that Tom had revealed had, according to its freshly affixed label, been rated TXTL – 60. In other words, it had been found to successfully resist entry for a net assault time of 60 minutes. It was one of the highest ratings that UL could give.

Even so, it took Tom just eight and a half seconds to open it.

Inside there was some cash, around fifty thousand dollars he guessed, jewellery and a 1920s Reverso wristwatch. But he ignored all these, turning his attention instead to a large wooden box, its dark mahogany lid inlaid with a golden double-headed eagle, an orb and sceptre firmly gripped in each of its talons. The Romanov Imperial crest.

He eased the box open, carefully lifting the precious object it contained out from the luxuriant embrace of its white silk lining.

He felt his pulse quicken. Even to him, who had seen myriad objects of breathtaking beauty, this was an exceptional piece. So much so that he took the unprecedented step – for him at least – of sliding his mask up off his face so he could see it properly. His uncharacteristic imprudence was almost immediately rewarded. As the moonlight caught its jewelled surface, the delicate object came alive in his hands, glowing like firelight through the hoarfrosted window of a remote wooden cabin.

The words on the roughly torn page from the Christie's catalogue that had been included with his briefing notes immediately came tumbling back into his head.

'The Winter Egg was made by Carl Fabergé for Tsar Nicholas II to give to his mother, the Dowager Empress Maria Feodorovna, for Easter 1913. The Egg, cut from Siberian rock crystal, is encrusted with more than three thousand diamonds, with another one thousand three hundred diamonds adorning the base.

As with all Fabergé's Eggs it contains an Easter 'surprise', in this case a platinum Easter basket decorated with flowers made from gold, garnets and crystals. The basket symbolises the transition from winter to spring.'

Alone, he gazed at the Egg. Soon, he could hear nothing except the steady rise and fall of his own chest and the ticking of an unseen clock. And still he stared, the room melting away from the edge of his vision, the diamonds sparkling like icicles in a midday sun, until he was certain he could see right through the Egg, through his gloves and his fingers to the bones themselves.

Suddenly he was back in Geneva, standing at

the foot of his father's coffin, candles sputtering on the altar, the priest's voice droning in the background. Some water had dropped off the circular wreath onto the coffin lid and was trickling off the side and onto the floor. He had stood there, fascinated, watching the red carpet change colour as the crystal drops shattered again and again on its soft pile.

Unexpected and unwanted, a thought had occurred to him then – or rather, a question. It had slipped into his head and tiptoed around the edges of his consciousness, taunting him.

'Is it time?'

Afterwards, he had dismissed it. Not given it much thought. Not wanted to, perhaps. But in the two months since the funeral, the question had returned again and again, each time with more urgency. It had haunted him, undermining his every action, investing his every word with doubt and uncertainty. Demanding to be answered.

And now he knew. It was so clear to him. Like winter turning to spring, it was inevitable. It was time. After this, he was going to walk away.

He slid his mask back on, packed the Egg up, shut the safe door and closed the wooden panel. Stealthily retreating across the room, he made his way back out through the window onto the balcony.

The sirens far below him seemed louder now, and he found that his heart was beating in time with the thumping blades of the police helicopter that was almost overhead, its spotlight raking over the trees and street below, clearly looking for someone or something. Crouching, he attached the rope to his harness and timed his jump for when the helicopter had made its next pass. In an instant he was gone.

Only an eyelash remained where it had fluttered down from his briefly unmasked face to the floor. It glinted black in the moonlight.

TWO

FBI Headquarters, Washington DC
18th July – 7:00am

She knew what would happen as the door opened and the dark shape came through it. She fought to stop herself, but it was no use. It never was. She raised the gun in front of her in a classic Weaver stance. Her stronger left arm was slightly flexed, pushing the gun away from her. Her supporting arm was bent and pulling the weapon in to create a properly braced grip, her feet apart with her weak-sided right foot slightly forward.

She fired three shots right in the kill zone – a perfect equilateral triangle. He was dead before he hit the floor, his white shirt billowing red like a bottle of ink spilt onto blotting paper. It was then, as the light hit his face – only then, that she saw what she had done.

Jennifer Browne woke with a jump, peeled her

cheek, sticky with sweat, off the desk's laminate surface and fumbled for the clock. Blinking hard, her eyes adjusting to the glare of the overhead neon, she checked the time. Seven am. Shit. Another all-nighter.

She stretched and flexed her neck, her back clicking into place. Yawning, she reached down and pulled out the bottom desk drawer, felt inside and took out a cellophane-wrapped white blouse identical to the one she was wearing. It was resting on two others. Placing it on her desk, she began to unbutton the one she had on, her fingers stiff as she worked the buttons. Eventually, when it was undone, she stood up and slipped it off, dropping it into the open drawer which she then nudged shut with her foot.

She was strikingly beautiful in that effortless, double-take way that some women are. Five feet nine, smooth brown skin, slender yet curving where it counted, rounded cheeks and curly black hair that just kissed her bare shoulders. She wore no jewellery – never had – apart from the Tiffany's twisted heart necklace that her sister had given her on her 18th birthday that nestled in the smooth curve of her breasts.

As she buttoned the blouse and tucked it into the waistband of her black trouser suit, she looked around at the windowless painted breeze block walls that encircled her and smiled, the dimples creasing into her soft brown cheeks. Even though it was small, she had still not quite got used to having her own office. Her own space. Her own air. After only three months back in DC, the novelty had certainly not worn off yet. Not by a long way. Not after three years down in the Atlanta field office, afraid to breathe out too far in case the cubicle walls collapsed. She was glad to be back; this time she was planning on staying.

There was a knock at the open door and Jennifer's thoughts were interrupted. She looked up reproachfully but relaxed her frown when she saw that it was Phil Tucker, her Section Chief, right on time. He'd told her yesterday that he wanted her in early, that he needed to talk to her. Wouldn't say why though.

'Hey there,' she called.

'You okay?' He walked up to the desk and squinted down at her through frameless glasses in concern, his double chin flattening over the top of his tie. 'Another late night?'

'Is it that obvious?' Jennifer self-consciously smoothed down her hair and rubbed the sleep out of the corners of her eyes.

'Nope.' He smiled. 'Security told me you hadn't gone home . . . Just so you know, I appreciate it.'

That was Tucker all over. He wasn't one of these bosses who just expected people to stay late and then never noticed when they did. He kept track of his team and made sure they knew it. She liked that. It made her feel like she was part of something again, not just an embarrassment that had to be explained away.

'No problem.'

He scratched his copper-coloured beard, then the top of his head, his scalp pink and raw where the hair was thinning.

'By the way, I spoke to Flynt, and the Treasury boys are going to handle everything from here on in on the Hammon case. They were very grateful for your help. He says he owes you one. Good job.'

'Thanks.' She gave an awkward shrug, never having been good at accepting compliments and changed the subject. 'So what's all this about? Why the early start? Some Congressman lose his dog?'

Tucker levered himself into a chair, his hips grazing its moulded plastic arms.

'Something came up yesterday. I volunteered you.' He grinned. 'Hope you don't mind.'

She laughed.

'Would it make a difference if I did?'

'Nope! Anyway, you won't want to. It's a good opportunity. Chance to get back on the inside track.' He paused and looked suddenly serious. 'A second chance, maybe.' His eyes dipped to the floor.

'You still trying to earn me my redemption?' With her dream still fresh in her thoughts, something bitter rose to the back of her mouth and made her swallow hard.

'No. You're doing that all on your own. But

you and I both know that it's hard to change people's minds.'

'I'm not looking for any hand-outs, Phil. I can make my own way back.' Her eyes shone with a fierce pride. Tucker nodded slowly.

'I know. But everyone needs a break once in a while, even you. And I wouldn't have suggested you if I didn't think you'd earned it. Anyway, I told him to swing by here about now, so it's too late to back out.'

He checked his watch, shook his wrist, held it to his ear and then checked it again.

'Is that the right time?' he asked, pointing at Jennifer's desk clock. She ignored the question.

'Told who to swing by here?'

There was a knock at the open door before he could answer and a man walked in. Tucker leapt up.

'Jennifer – meet Bob Corbett; Bob – meet Jennifer Browne.' All three of them stood motionless for a few seconds and Tucker's eyes flicked anxiously to Jennifer's, as if he was worried she might do or say the wrong thing.

They shook hands. Tucker breathed a sigh of relief.

'Here, take my seat.' Tucker pointed eagerly at his chair before perching unsteadily on the edge of Jennifer's desk. Corbett sat down. 'Bob heads up the Major Theft and Transportation Crimes Unit here.'

'We were introduced in the elevator once,' Jennifer nodded with a curious smile. From the times she'd seen him around the building, she knew that Corbett always looked immaculate, from his smoothly shaved chin to his polished black shoes, thin laces neatly tied in a double knot. But now she immediately noticed that something was different. The knot on his woven silk tie was much smaller than usual, as if he had loosened it and then re-tightened it several times. As if he was worried.

Corbett frowned and looked at her quizzically before nodding slowly in sudden recollection.

'Sure. I remember. Hi.' He spoke in short, sharp bursts and there was something in the precise urgency of his machine-gunned words that suggested a military background. They shook hands again.

Corbett often passed for a man ten years younger than his forty-five years, although the deepening creases around his eyes and mouth suggested that time was at last beginning to catch up with him. Next to Tucker certainly, he looked fit and healthy although that was possibly an unfair comparison. There was something stream-lined about him, from his slicked back steel-grey hair to the rounded contours of his chin and cheekbones that gave him the chromed elegance of one of those 1930s Art-Deco locomotives that look like they are powering along at two hundred miles an hour even when they are standing still. Above the sharp angle of his nose, the cold light of his close-set grey eyes suggested a very clever and very determined man. He reminded her, in a strange way, of her father. Hard but fair.

'You know, Bob's got the best clean-up rate in the Bureau?' Tucker continued. 'What is it now? Only five unsolved cases in twenty-five years? That's outstanding work.' He shook his head, as if he couldn't quite come to terms with it.

'Actually, Phil, it's two. And I haven't given up on them yet.' Corbett smiled, but Jennifer could tell he wasn't joking. He didn't look like the sort of man who did.

'Bob needs someone to work on a new case for him. I suggested you.'

Jennifer shrugged awkwardly, her face suddenly hot as two pairs of eyes focused in on her.

'Thank you, sir. I'll do my best. What's the case?'

Corbett slid a large manila envelope towards her and motioned with a wave that she should open it. Warily, Jennifer lifted the tab and pulled out a series of black-and-white photos.

'The man in that photo is Father Gianluca Ranieri.'

She studied the picture carefully, taking in the man's contorted face and the large gash in his chest.

'They found him in Paris yesterday. River cops fished him out the Seine. As you can see, he didn't drown.'

Jennifer flicked through the rest of the photos, her mind focused. Close-ups of Ranieri's face and the knife wound flashed past her large hazel eyes. A quick scan through the translated autopsy report at the back confirmed what Corbett had just told her – stabbed and then presumably thrown in the river. A single blow through the xiphisternum, aimed up towards the left shoulder blade, had caused a massive, almost instant heart attack.

As she read, she flashed a quick look at Corbett. He was studying her office with a faint smile. She knew that some of her colleagues found it strange that she kept the stark green concrete walls bare. Truth was, she found the lack of clutter helped her keep her mind clear.

'Any thoughts?' Corbett asked, his eyes snapping back round to meet hers.

'Judging from the injury, it looks like a professional job. Some sort of hit.'

'Agreed.' Corbett nodded, his eyes narrowing slightly as if he was re-appraising Jennifer in the light of her quick diagnosis.

'And it was public. The body dumped where they knew it would be quickly found.'

'Meaning?'

'That they're not worried about getting caught.

Or that maybe they wanted to send someone a message.'

Corbett nodded his agreement.

'Perhaps both. Best guess is that he was killed round about midnight on the sixteenth of July, give or take three or four hours either way.' He got up and padded noiselessly over to the filing cabinet, Jennifer noticing now that he seemingly kept his pockets empty of change and keys or anything else that might give away his position, like a cat who had had the bell on its collar removed so that it might be better able to stalk its unsuspecting prey. She continued to leaf through the file.

'From what we know, Ranieri trained as a Catholic priest and then worked at the Vatican Institute for Religious Works.'

Jennifer looked up in surprise.

'The Vatican Bank?'

'As it's also known, yes.' Corbett raised his eyebrows, clearly impressed now. 'He was there for about ten years before going missing about three years ago, along with a couple of million dollars from one of their Cayman Island accounts.'

Jennifer swivelled her chair round towards him, her forehead wrinkled in anticipation. She sensed that he was building up to something. Tucker, meanwhile, sat enthralled with his arms crossed and resting on his belly, his mouth slack and half open. Corbett ran his finger along the top of the filing cabinet as if checking for dust. She knew there wouldn't be any. Not in her office.

'He must have spent all the cash though, because he turned up in Paris last year. The French say he set himself up as a low-level fence. Nothing big. A painting here, a necklace there, but he was making a living; a good living, judging from the size of him.'

All three of them laughed and the tingle that Jennifer had felt slowly building inside her chest vanished like steam rising into warm air. Corbett moved back round to the chair and sat down again, Jennifer just getting a glimpse of the top of his shoes where over the years the constant rubbing of his suit trousers had buffed the leather to a slightly deeper shade of black than the rest of them.

'I don't get it.' Jennifer replaced the file on the desk and sat back in her chair, confused. 'Sounds to me like he got whacked by someone he ripped off. Or maybe he had some sort of deal go sour. Either way, it's got nothing to do with us.'

Corbett locked eyes with her and the tingle reappeared and instantly sublimated into a cold, hard knot in the pit of her stomach.

'Our angle, Agent Browne – and you won't find this in the autopsy report – is that when they opened him up, they found something in his stomach. Something he'd swallowed just before he died. Something he clearly didn't want his killers to find.'

Corbett reached into his pocket and, leaning forward, slid something sealed inside a small clear plastic bag across the desk towards her. Against the desk's veneered expanse an eagle soared proudly, its majestic flight etched in solid gold.

It was a coin.

THREE

Clerkenwell, London
18th July – 4:30pm
Outside, the afternoon rush hour traffic rumbled past, a never-ending river of rubber and steel that surged and stalled in tidy blocks to the beat of the traffic lights.

Inside, the shop windows glowed yellow as the sunlight fought to shine though their white-washed panes. In a few places, the paint had been scratched off and here narrow shafts of light pierced the gloom, the dust dancing through their pale beams like raindrops falling across car head-lights.

The room itself was a mess – the orange walls blistered, the rough wooden floor suffocating in a thick down of old newspapers and junk food wrappers, while bare wires hung down menacingly from the cracked ceiling like tentacles.

At the back of the room, almost lost in the

shadows, two tea chests rested on the uneven floor. Hunched forward on one of them, Tom Kirk was lost deep in thought, his chin in his hands.

Although he was just thirty-five years old, a few grey hairs flecked the sides of his head, becoming more noticeable in the several days of rough stubble that covered his face, the hair slightly darker in the shallow cleft of his square chin.

He reminded everyone of his father, or so everyone told him, much to his annoyance. Certainly he shared his delicately angular face, messy brown hair and deep-set blue eyes that nestled under thick brown eyebrows.

He was more athletic than his father though; a lithe, sinewy five foot eleven physique that suggested someone both quick enough to steal second base and strong enough to crack a shot into the bleachers if he had to. The irony, of course, was that he'd never been much of a big-hitter in high school, his signature play instead being a split-fingered fastball that had batters swinging at thin air as it broke violently downward. It fooled them every time.

Perched on the chest opposite him, a large backgammon board threatened to slide onto the floor at any moment. It was an intricately inlaid set that he'd picked up for next to nothing in some dusty side street off the Grand Bazaar in Istanbul years ago. It still smelled of glue and grease and spices. When he couldn't sleep, he would some-times play against himself for hours; checking the probabilities, shifting the pieces around the board, studying how different moves and strategies evolved. The half-empty bottle of Grey Goose on the floor next to him suggested that it had been a long night.

But Tom wasn't even looking at the board. Instead he was considering the black ski mask that lay in his lap, carefully cradled as if made from the finest Limoges porcelain. With a half smile, he slipped his right hand into the neck opening and then stuck a finger out of each of the eye holes, wiggling them playfully up and down like fish chasing each other in and out of a skull's eye sockets.

He had long, elegant fingers that made graceful, precise movements, each joint flexing like indi-vidual links in a chain, large white half moons at the bottom of each neatly clipped nail. And yet the back of his knuckles were covered in small white scars and his palms were rough and worn. It was almost as if he was a concert pianist who moonlighted as a bare knuckle fighter.

Tom knew that he couldn't avoid making the call any longer. He'd been out of contact for three weeks now and didn't have a choice. But would Archie understand? Would he even believe him? Abruptly his smile vanished and he flung the mask as far as he could across the room, willing it to shatter into a thousand pieces against the opposite wall.

He took his phone out of his back pocket and dialled, the high-pitched tones echoing back over the traffic's low rumble. It was answered almost immediately, but there was silence from the other end. Tom coughed and then spoke, his voice smooth and soothing, his slight American accent more pronounced than usual as it often was when he was nervous.

'Archie, it's Felix.'

'Jesus Christ, Felix!'

Felix. A name that he'd been christened with years ago when he had first got going in the game and one that he was stuck with now.

'Where the hell have you been?'

'I got . . . held up,' Tom answered.

'Held up? I thought you'd been nicked.'

Archie. The best fence in the business. Tom had often wondered whether his was an invented name too, a shield to hide behind. On balance, he thought that it probably wasn't. Somehow it seemed to fit.

'No. Just held up.'

'Spot of aggro?'

For once Archie sounded genuinely concerned.

'No, but I'm not doing the States again. I've told you, it's too risky doing jobs back there. I know I'm the last person they expect to see but one day they might get lucky.'

'How did it go?'

'Pretty much like we planned. Except they were having some construction work done and I was worried about extra security until it was finished. So I staked it out for about three weeks in the end before I went in – you know, just to be sure. I dealt with the pressure pads and the combination hadn't been reset, so it was all pretty simple.'

'Nice one. Usual place, then?'

'My stuff already there?'

'What do you think?' Archie almost sounded offended.

'Fine. I'll drop it off in a few days.'

'You're going to have to get your skates on for the second one, though. You've not left yourself much time.'

There was a pause and the line crackled with static as Tom sat down on the tea chest, massaging his temple with his left hand. As he'd thought, Archie wasn't going to make this any easier for him. But he'd made his decision and he was going to stick to it.

'I wanted to talk to you about that.'

'Oh yeah.' Archie's tone was immediately suspicious.

'Thing is, I'm not going to do the other job.'

'You what?'

'You heard me. I'm calling it off.'

'You having me on?'

'The truth is Archie, I'm done with this shit. I

just don't want to do it any more. I can't do it any more. I'm sorry.'

'Sorry?' The word was hammered back into Tom's ear. 'Sorry? What the hell's that supposed to mean? You do me over and then you apologise? You must be having a laugh. Well, I'm sorry too, sunshine, but sorry just doesn't bloody cut it. You're sorry and I'm buggered because I've got to deliver two Fabergé Eggs to Cassius in twelve days time or I'm a dead man. Capeesh?'

'Cassius?' Tom's lips formed around the word. He stood up again, his feet sinking into the trash-strewn floor like it was quicksand, his voice a whisper. 'That was never the deal. You said it was for some guy called Viktor. A Russian client. You never mentioned Cassius. You know I don't work for people like that. For him especially. What the hell are you playing at?'

'Listen, when I took the job I didn't know it was for him either.' Archie's voice was calm, soothing even. But to Tom it sounded as if he'd practised this speech many times, knowing how he would react. 'And by the time I found out, it was too bloody late. We were already on the hook. You know as well as I do that you don't muck Cassius about. Not now, not ever.'

'Especially if the money's good, right?' said Tom bitterly. 'Has a way of making you forgetful, doesn't it?'

'Oh, do me a favour!'

'What's your take, Archie? Did he promise you a few extra points for keeping quiet?'

'The money don't come into it. It's a sweet deal for both of us and you know it. Straight in, straight out with a buyer lined up. You never even needed to know it was for Cassius.' Tom stood with one hand against the wall, his head bowed, the phone pressed to the side of his head. 'Felix, I know it's bang out of order but maybe we should meet.' Archie's voice was gentle, almost pleading. 'You know, go for a pint or something. We can plan the second job, deliver both Eggs to Cassius and then move on. If you want to call it a day after that, fine, but we got to do this one thing and we got to do it right.'

What surprised Tom most was how quickly his answer came. He would have expected perhaps some silent deliberation, some internal dialogue as he considered Archie's position and the implications of Cassius's involvement on them both, weighed up the pros and cons of doing nothing or agreeing to follow through on this last job. But his answer was instinctive and immediate and had required no debate.

'I'm sorry, Archie,' Tom stood up straight, his voice hard. 'You should have told me the truth. This is your problem now, not mine. You can have the Egg I've got as agreed but then that's it. I'm out.' He snapped the phone shut and breathed out. There, it was done.

He looked up and flinched. When he had
thrown it earlier, the ski mask had snagged on a
nail. Now, as it hung there, the empty eye sockets
seemed to be mocking him.

FOUR

Louisville, Kentucky
18th July – 2:23pm

It was the sound of the engine that finally woke him. It had broken into his dreams and gotten louder and louder until the noise had shaken him awake. The strange thing was that he had this dizzy, floating sensation as if he was still asleep. Then he remembered. The knock on the back of the head, the sudden flash of pain. Then nothing.

Blinking through the smoke, his head throbbing and awkwardly slumped forward onto his chest, his streaming eyes could just make out a steering wheel, a window, a red tube jutting into the car. The truth slowly dawned on him and his eyes opened wide with fear. Not like this, surely not like this. This wasn't how it was meant to end.

He realized then that he was coughing, struggling to catch his breath, gasping for air as the blood raced around his head, the dull pumping of his heart echoing in his ears, the tie and collar of his uniform tight around his neck. He felt sick and random thoughts began to tumble through his head as he strained to remain conscious, fireworks of memory that exploded brightly and then immediately dimmed only for another to go off.

His Auntie May, drunk at Thanksgiving when he was eight. Kissing Betty Blake at the Prom. Falling off his bike at college and cutting his chin open. His retirement party when Police Captain O'Reilly had clapped him on the back and whispered that if he ever wanted his old job back, then it was his. The time he'd picked the phone up to do just that, but then slapped it back down in the certain knowledge that Debbie would say no. Debbie and the kids waving to him from the porch, smiling and happy and oblivious.

Debbie. At the thought of her he had started to cry, tried to wrap his guilt in grief, but found that the tears wouldn't come now, that his arid body had begun to ignore him and his throat merely constricted further with the effort.

Sweet Lord Jesus, he prayed through the drumming in his head, let me live long enough to tell her what really happened; why I really did this; why they killed me.

Even though he couldn't feel his legs, somehow he managed to summon the strength to beat his hand weakly against the glass, scrabble at the door handle. The handle moved, but the door wouldn't open. The seat belt was hugging him, pressing into his stomach, crushing his chest, stopping him from breathing.

He tried to scream, but his red lips barely parted. And then, despite everything, despite the heat and the smoke and the fear, he smiled at the beautiful simplicity of it all. Gently, the sound of the engine lulled him back to sleep.

FIVE

'You still here?'

Dr Sarah Lucas paused in the doorway to the laboratory as she pulled her jacket on, lifting her blonde hair out from under the collar. The room was dark apart from the pool of light around the computer at the far end, the outline of the person hunched in front of it silhouetted against the flickering screen.

'Yeah,' the outline grunted back. 'I promised some cop in New York I'd run something through the system before I left tonight. Kinda wishing I hadn't.'

Sarah smiled. David Mahoney was a rookie fresh out of Quantico, full of zesty enthusiasm and uncomplicated ambition. He still had a lot to learn; knowing when to say no was right up there. But that would come with time and experience. Then again, she mused, it was past eleven and she was still there. Maybe some people just never learned to say no. She put her briefcase down and stepped into the room.

'What have you got?'

Mahoney was tapping furiously into the keyboard, his stubby fingers complementing his round, fleshy face, greasy brown hair parted on the left hand side and scooped behind his ears. He barely looked up when she peered over his shoulder, adjusting her tortoiseshell glasses on her face.

'Get this. Some guy abseiled down to the 17th floor of a Park Avenue apartment block, stole a nine million dollar Easter egg and then vanished. NYPD forensics found an eyelash on the floor next to the safe. They figure it's probably unrelated but wanted us to run it through just in case something showed up. It'll only be another few seconds.' He looked up at her, the spots on his shiny forehead glowing purple in the flickering blue light. 'What about you? What are you still doing here?'

'Keeping my promises, like you.' She smiled back. 'Here you go.'

The screen flickered red, a boxed message flashing intermittently.

'*Restricted Access – Security Clearance must be sought before viewing this file.*'

Beneath it, a name and a phone number.

'Shit.' She swore as she read the message and stood up straight.

'What just happened?' Mahoney was clicking furiously on his mouse as he tried to get the previous page back. 'What does that mean?'

'It means you forget you ever saw this.' Her voice was grim, her jaw set firm. 'You call up the NYPD tomorrow and tell them that you didn't get a match. This never happened, understand?'

Mahoney nodded dumbly, his eyes wide and bewildered. She reached past him for the phone and dialled the number at the bottom of the message on the screen.

'Yes – hello, sir,' she said when the phone was answered. 'This is Dr Lucas over at the FBI Lab in Quantico. I'm sorry for calling you so late. It's just that NYPD sent across a sample taken from a crime scene two days ago. When we put it into the computer the system locked us out and said to call you . . . yes, sir . . . no, sir, just me and a new recruit . . . yes, sir, I've told him the drill.' She fixed Mahoney with a cold stare. 'I think he knows the consequences . . . thank you, sir. You too, sir.'

She put the phone down and turned to a confused-looking Mahoney with a tight smile.

'Welcome to the FBI.'

SIX

Washington DC
19th July – 08:35am
The car was new and the smell of faux leather and moulded plastic hung heavily in the air. A silver crucifix hung on a thin chain from the driver's mirror and spiralled gently, its flat surface catching the light every so often.

Looking up from her notes, Jennifer lowered the window and let the hot breeze massage her face as the car crawled through the downtown traffic on Constitution Avenue towards the Smithsonian, as first the Lincoln and then the black hulk of the Vietnam Memorial inched past. A lone veteran was on patrol, two small Stars and Stripes taped to the handles of his wheelchair like pennants on a diplomatic stretch. Up ahead, two huge coaches spewed Japanese tourists onto the sidewalk, cameras unholstered as soon as their feet hit the concrete.

Unconsciously she smoothed the left lapel on the jacket of her black trouser suit. She always wore black. She looked good in it and besides it was one less decision to make in the morning. Noticing the time on the dashboard clock, Jennifer shook her head in irritation. She was late for her appointment and she hated being late. Five minutes later, seeing that she was only level with the Washington Monument, she opened her purse.

'I'll walk from here,' she said thrusting twenty dollars past the driver's right ear.

She opened the door and stepped out onto the street, the tarmac already soft under the heel of her shoes as the temperature climbed. She squeezed between two government-issue black sedans, their air-conditioned passengers shielded behind smoked glass, and stepped onto the sidewalk. A bit further on, a hot-dog seller had already installed himself on the corner of 16th Street and the smell of frying onions and reheated sausage meat made her stomach lurch unsteadily. Gritting her teeth and breathing through her mouth, she walked on.

The Smithsonian Institution is the largest museum complex in the world, comprising fourteen separate museums and the National Zoo in DC itself and two further museums in New York. Taken as a whole, the museum's collection numbers over one hundred and forty-two million separate objects.

The Money and Medals Hall of the National
Numismatic Collection is housed on the third floor
of the National Museum of American History, a
low-slung, white stone 1960s building on the
National Mall at the junction of 14th Street and
Constitution Avenue. The Collection numbers
over four hundred thousand items although only
a tiny fraction of these are ever on display.

Ten minutes later, Jennifer was ushered into a
dark wood-panelled office, her feet sinking into
the thick green carpet. A Stars and Stripes loomed
in the corner. Framed by two large windows at
the far end of the room, Miles Baxter, forty-two,
the curator of the National Numismatic Collection,
was sitting behind a massive desk covered in files
and papers. He wore a dark blue sports jacket over
a button-down white shirt and beige chinos and
the air was heavy with the scent of freshly applied
aftershave. He didn't get up.

'They didn't tell me they were sending a
woman.'

'I'm sorry to disappoint you.' Jennifer felt
herself tensing automatically.

'Quite the contrary, *Miss* Browne. It's a very
pleasant surprise. It's just that if I'd known I'd
have made more of an effort.'

He smiled and two rows of piano-key perfect
teeth flashed back at her from a tanned and confident face. They shook hands and his palm felt
moist. Almost subconsciously she registered that

his hair was less fluffy where it parted on the left hand side. She knew instinctively that he had licked his hand and then smoothed his hair down just before she had been shown in. So much for not making an effort.

'It's Special Agent Browne, actually,' said Jennifer, taking out her ID and passing it to him.

His smile faded.

'Of course it is.'

He studied her ID carefully, diligently comparing her face to the picture with several searching glances. She took the opportunity to wipe her palm, still damp where he had clutched her hand in his, against her trouser leg. He snapped her wallet shut and handed it back to her.

'Of course, I've dealt with the FBI before, although if I may say so never with someone quite so . . . attractive. Unfortunately I'm not at liberty to discuss those cases with you.' His eyes narrowed. 'A small matter of national security; I'm sure you understand.' He gestured towards the right hand wall which she could see was decorated like a small shrine with photos, carefully calligraphed certificates and gilt-lettered diplomas. She nodded and hoped that he didn't notice her stifle a smile.

'Do you know Washington well?' She gave a slight shrug which seemed to be all the encouragement Baxter needed. 'You know, if you want

someone to show you around, I'd be very happy
to act as your tour guide one weekend.'

A couple of years ago, when she had still
believed that intelligence and hard work would
be enough for a black woman to make it as an
FBI agent, Jennifer would have met that sort of
offer with an acidic smile and a dismissive laugh
as a matter of principle. But that was before the
dull blade of experience had taught her to use all
the tools at her disposal. If that meant telling Miles
Baxter what he wanted to hear so that she would
have something good to go back to Corbett with,
then so be it.

'I'd like that.' She brushed her hand coquet-
tishly through her hair.

'Great.' He beamed. 'Please sit down.' He
nodded towards the leather armchair opposite
him. 'And you must call me Miles.'

'Thank you Miles.' She smiled warmly. 'You
must call me Jennifer.'

Baxter placed his hands together as if in prayer,
his fingers sore and ripped where he had bitten
his nails.

'So, Jennifer, how can I help?'

She reached inside her jacket.

'What can you tell me about this coin?' She
held the coin still sealed inside its protective plastic
envelope, out to Baxter, who slipped on a steel-
rimmed pair of glasses and angled it underneath
the green shade of his desk light so that he could

make out the embossed detail. He looked up, his eyes wide with amazement, his voice halting and for the first time uncertain.

'Where . . . what . . . how did you get this?' He shook his head in disbelief, the slack skin under his chin tracking his head movements like a small pendulum. 'This is incredible. It's impossible.' His breathing was ragged, his hands trembling slightly as he turned the coin over and over in his fingers as if it was too hot to hold still.

'What do you mean?'

'Well . . . it's a 1933 Double Eagle, of course.'

She shrugged.

'I'm not a coin expert, Miles.'

'No, of course not. Sorry. Well, you see, the US government has been minting gold coins since the mid 1790s and twenty dollar coins, or Double Eagles, since the 1849 Gold Rush.'

'Why Double Eagle? There's only one eagle on the coin.'

'Just one of those things, I guess.' He sniffed. 'Ten dollar coins were known as Eagles, so when the twenty dollar coins appeared, they were called Double Eagles. Most people can be very unimaginative if they try hard enough.'

'I see.'

'It's all down to the date,' he said, with a thoughtful look on his face.

'You mean on the coin? Why, what happened in 1933?'

'It's more what didn't happen in 1933,' said Baxter, tapping the side of his pink nose enigmatically as the colour began to return to his cheeks and his voice grew more confident. He placed the coin on the desk and sat back in his chair. 'The interesting thing about a gold coin minted in 1933 is that at the time America was in the grip of the Depression. And as a result, days after assuming the Presidency in March 1933, Roosevelt took the country off the gold standard and banned the production, sale and ownership of gold.'

Jennifer nodded as a long-forgotten high-school history project bubbled back to the top of her mind. The Wall Street Crash in 1929. The Great Depression that followed. A quarter of the nation out of work, the country in chaos. And in that hurricane of human misery, with stocks and bonds worthless and life savings wiped out, people had clung onto the only thing that they believed had any real value. Gold.

'The President wanted to stop the hoarding and calm the markets by shoring up the Federal gold reserves,' Baxter continued, illustrating this with a series of increasingly animated hand gestures. 'Executive Order 6102 prohibited people from owning gold and banks from paying it out.'

'Leaving coins like this stranded, I guess.'

'Exactly. By the time FDR passed this law, 445,500 1933 Double Eagles had already been minted and were just sitting in the Philadelphia Mint, ready to be put into circulation. Suddenly there was nowhere for them to go.'

'So they couldn't issue them?'

Baxter smiled. 'They couldn't do anything with them. Except melt them down, of course, which they eventually did in 1937. Every single one.'

He lowered his voice to a dramatic whisper.

'You see officially, Jennifer, the 1933 Double Eagle never existed.'

SEVEN

Clerkenwell, London
19th July – 2:05pm

He'd had the shop's frontage painted a treacly
black, although the windows themselves were still
obscured from the street by the thin coat of white-
wash. Against this background the shop's name,
freshly painted in large gold letters in a semicircle
across both panes, seemed to stand out even more
prominently. Tom read it proudly: 'Kirk Duval'.
His mother would have liked that. And then under
it in a straight line and smaller letters: 'Fine Art
& Antiques'.

He checked both ways and then crossed the
street, stopping halfway as he searched for a gap
in the traffic, eventually reaching the shop door.
It opened noiselessly under his touch to reveal a
jumble of hastily-deposited boxes and half-opened
packing crates, their contents poking resolutely
through straw and Styrofoam. In one, an elegant

Regency clock. In another, a marble bust of Caesar or Alexander, he hadn't checked yet. Across the room, an Edwardian rosewood card table had been completely unpacked and a large Han Dynasty vase filled with dried flowers stood in the middle of the dark green felt. It was going to take weeks to sort it all out.

Still, that didn't bother Tom. Not now. For the first time in as long as he could remember he had time on his side. He had thought about stopping before, of course, or at least toyed with the idea. After all, he hadn't needed the money for years. But he'd never been able to stay away for more than a few weeks. Like a gambler ushered back to their favourite seat at the blackjack table after a brief absence, he had been sucked back in every time.

This time was different though. Things had changed. He'd changed. The New York job had proved that to him.

And yet one name lurked beneath the thin veneer of normality that Tom had tried to build for himself over the past few days. Cassius. He wasn't sure if Archie had been lying or not, using Cassius's name perhaps to try and force Tom's hand to follow through on the job. If so he was taking a big risk. But if it really was Cassius that had commissioned the theft, then Archie was rolling the dice without even properly under-standing the rules or how Cassius played the game. Or even perhaps what was at stake.

But Archie wasn't his responsibility. That's what Tom kept reminding himself. Not now, not ever. If he had gotten himself into this mess then it was up to him to get himself out of it. Tom wasn't being heartless. Those were just the rules.

He continued through the shop, the wooden floor freshly cleared of the debris that had coated it, until he reached the two doors at the rear of the room. Opening the one to his left, Tom stepped through onto the narrow platform that ran along the back wall of the large warehouse.

On the left hand side, a metal staircase spiralled tightly down to the dusty floor some twenty feet below. A steel shutter in the opposite wall opened onto the street that ran down the hill and around the back of the building. There was a faint buzzing from the neon tubes that lined the warehouse ceiling and their primitive light made the flaking and stained white walls come out in a sickly sweat.

'How are you getting on?' Tom called out as he came down the stairs, the cast iron staircase vibrating violently with each step where it had worked itself loose over the years. The girl looked up at the sound of his voice, brushing her blonde hair aside.

'There's still a lot to do,' she took her glasses off and rubbed her blue eyes. 'How does it look?' Her English was immaculate, although spoken with the slight tightness of a Swiss-French accent.

'Great. You were right, the gold does look better than silver would have.'

She blushed and put her glasses back on. Still only twenty-two, Dominique had worked for Tom's father in Geneva for the last four years. After the memorial service, she'd volunteered to help him move all his father's stock back to London and get the business up and running there. She'd done a great job. He was hoping she would agree to stay on.

'Is everything here?' Tom nodded towards the piles of crates and boxes that were stacked across the warehouse floor.

'I think so, yes. I just need to check those last few boxes off against my list.'

'These?' asked Tom walking over towards the three crates she had pointed at.

'Uh-huh. Read off the numbers on the side will you?'

'Sure.' He went to the first one and bending his head slightly, read the numbers back to her.

'131272.'

She turned back to the laptop she was sitting in front of.

'Okay.'

Tom moved to the next crate.

'1311 . . .'

He was interrupted by a clipped, nasal voice that sank heavily from the platform above.

'My, my – we have been busy, Kirk. You must

have knocked off Buckingham Palace to get your hands on this little lot.'

'Detective Constable Clarke,' Tom said flatly without bothering to look up. 'Our first customer.'

Clarke robotically lit another cigarette from the one already in his mouth before flicking the sputtering butt over the railing and wedging the new cigarette between his teeth. It landed harmlessly at Tom's feet.

'It's Detective *Sergeant* Clarke now, Kirk,' he said as he took a drag on his cigarette and made his way down the stairs to the warehouse floor, the staircase strangely silent under his lazy step. 'While you've been away, there's been a few changes around here.'

'Detective Sergeant? They really must be desperate.'

A muscle in Clarke's neck began to twitch. He was quite a tall man, although his rounded shoulders made him seem shorter. He was also distressingly thin, his grey skin drawn tightly across his sharp cheekbones, his mouth pulled into a permanently grudging grimace, his hair fine and brushed forward to disguise how far it had receded. His wrist bones, especially, jutted out under translucent skin and seemed so delicate that they might snap if you shook his hand too firmly. The only colour came from the broken blood vessels that danced across his sunken cheeks.

'I heard you were back, Kirk. That you'd

crawled out from whatever hole you've been hiding in for the last couple of months.' His watery eyes flashed as he spoke. 'So I thought I'd come and pay you a visit. A social call. Just in case you thought I'd forgotten about you.'

'Well, if it's any consolation, I'd certainly forgotten about you.'

Clarke clamped his mouth shut and Tom could see from the colour rising to his face that he was focusing all his energies on not losing his temper. Eventually he turned away from Tom and indicated the room around him with his head.

'So, all this shit yours then?'

Tom stole an anxious look at Dominique, but she was staring at the computer screen as if nothing was going on behind her.

'Not that it's any of your business, but yes.'

'You mean it is now,' said Clarke laughing coldly. 'But God knows which poor sod you nicked it off.' He kicked the crate nearest to him, his clumpy, thick-soled shoes at odds with his delicate frame and making his feet seem huge. 'What about this one. What's in here?'

'You're wasting your time, Clarke,' said Tom, his own mounting frustration giving his voice a slight edge now. 'I've moved my father's business from Switzerland and I'm re-opening it here. I have import papers in triplicate from both the Swiss and British authorities for everything.'

Clarke turned back to face him and smirked.

'Tell me, was it the drink or the shame over having you for a son that finally did him in?' Tom's body stiffened, the muscles in his jaw bulging as he clenched his teeth together. He could see Clarke savouring the moment, his eyes narrowed into fascinated slivers of grey.

'I think it's time you left,' said Tom, taking a step forward.

'Are you threatening me?'

'No, I'm asking you to leave. Now.'

'I'll go when I'm ready.' Clarke thrust his chin out in defiance and folded his arms across his chest, the material of his grey suit, shiny on the elbows, acquiring a new set of creases.

'Dominique,' Tom called out while keeping his eyes firmly fixed on Clarke's. 'Could you please get me the Metropolitan Police on the line and ask to speak to Commissioner Jarvis. Tell him that Detective *Sergeant* Clarke is harassing me again. Tell him that he has illegally entered my premises without a warrant. Tell him that he's refusing to leave.' She nodded but didn't move.

Clarke stepped forward until he was so close that Tom could smell the smoke on his breath.

'You'll slip up, Kirk. Everyone does eventually, even you. And I'll be there when it happens.'

Flicking his cigarette to one side, sparks scattering in its wake, Clarke marched back up the stairs and through the door.

Dominique fixed Tom with a questioning stare.

He cleared his throat nervously. Although he had known that he would have to have this conversation at some stage, he had planned to do it on his own terms when he was good and ready. Certainly not like this.

'I'm sorry you had to sit through that,' he began. 'It's not what it looks like.'

'Sure it is.' She gave him a half smile and then looked away.

'What do you mean?' His eyes narrowed.

Silence.

'Your father used to talk a lot, you know, when he drank,' she said eventually. 'He said some things about you. I got the picture. Your policeman friend just filled in a few gaps.'

Tom sat down on the crate nearest her and rubbed the back of his head.

'Well, if you knew that, what are you doing here?'

'You really think I expected you to be the only honest person in the art business? Everyone's got some sort of angle. Yours is better than others I've seen.'

'That's it?'

'Partly.' She smiled and tilted her head to one side. 'You know, I put a lot of time into this business with your father. By the time he died, things were going really well. When we first met, you said you were serious about trying to keep it going. I guess I wanted to believe you.'

'I am serious about making it work. More now than when we first spoke about it.' He looked at her earnestly.

'So what about . . . ?'

'That's over. This is all I've got now.'

'Okay.' She nodded slowly.

'Okay?' He raised his eyebrows. 'You sure?'

'Okay.' She put her glasses back on and turned back to the computer.

EIGHT

The Smithsonian, Washington DC
19th July – 09:06am

'And unofficially?'

Baxter leapt up from his desk and gripped the back of his chair.

'Unofficially, ten coins survived.' He breathed excitedly, his upper lip beginning to bead. 'It turned out they were stolen from the Mint by George McCann, the former chief cashier there, before the melting. He denied the accusations, of course. But it was him.'

'And the coins?'

'A couple started surfacing at numismatic auctions in 1944. A journalist alerted the Mint who brought in the Secret Services. It took them ten years, but eventually they tracked them all down and destroyed them. All apart from one.'

'They couldn't find it?'

'Oh, they knew where it was. Only problem

was that they couldn't get to it. You see, it had been bought by King Farouk of Egypt for his coin collection and the United States Treasury, not realising what it was, had issued him with an export license. There was no way he was going to hand it back just because they'd screwed up their paperwork.'

'Even though he knew it was stolen?'

'As far as he was concerned, that probably just added to its value. In any case, after the Egyptian Revolution in 1952 he was out of the equation. The new government seized the collection and auctioned it off, including what had by then become known as the 'Farouk coin.'

'So somebody else bought it.'

'No.' Baxter's eyes flashed, mirroring the excitement in his voice as he seemed to relive the events he was describing. 'The coin just disappeared.'

'Disappeared?' Jennifer found herself edging forward on her seat, excited by Baxter's fevered account.

'Vanished.' Baxter bunched his fingers into a point and then blew onto them, stretching his hand out flat as he did so. 'For over 40 years. Until 1996, when Treasury agents posing as collectors seized the coin from an English dealer in New York and arrested him.' Baxter's eyes glistened. 'Only he then sued the Treasury, claiming that he'd bought the coin legitimately from another dealer. It went to court and eventually the

Treasury agreed to auction the coin and split the proceeds with him.'

'How do you know all this?' Jennifer asked, puzzled at the level of detail that Baxter seemed to have at his fingertips. 'This is just one coin – you must have hundreds of thousands here.' Baxter threw up his hands.

'Because this isn't just any old coin, Jennifer. This is the holy grail of coins. It has been stolen from the Philadelphia Mint, owned by a king, vanished and then reappeared in dramatic circumstances. This is the forbidden fruit, the apple from the garden of Eden. It is totally unique.'

'So how much are we talking?'

'Twenty dollars for the paperwork to make it official US coinage,' Baxter paused dramatically. 'And just under eight million for the coin itself.'

Jennifer's eyes widened. Eight million dollars for a coin? It was a crazy, reckless amount of money. It didn't make any sense. Except that perhaps it did. It was certainly enough to kill for and, in Ranieri's case, maybe even to die for.

'You know, the National Numismatic Collection automatically receives examples of all American coins. We actually have two 1933 Double Eagles on display over in the Money and Medals Hall. They and the Farouk coin are the only 1933 Double Eagles in existence, although as museum exhibits they are clearly not available for private ownership as the Farouk coin is. We

can go and take a look if you like.' Baxter
suggested eagerly.

'Sure.' Jennifer nodded. 'That way we could at
least compare them to this one.'

Baxter slipped out from behind his desk and
over to the door which he held open for her.

'After you.'

'Thank you, Miles.'

It was only a short walk to the Hall which
revealed itself to be a long narrow gallery, flanked
on each side by wall mounted rectangular display
cases, their contents glittering under the lights.
Baxter headed to one of the cabinets in the middle
of the room and stopped next to it. Two coins
were set apart from the others and lay side by side
in a specially constructed chemically inert plastic
container, each displaying a different face against
the green felt.

'They're beautiful, aren't they?' Baxter's hushed
voice rippled through the empty room. Jennifer
bent forward until she started to fog the glass, the
ghostly fingerprints of earlier visitors materialising
with each breath and then immediately vanishing.

'The actual design was commissioned by
President Theodore Roosevelt in 1907 from the
sculptor Augustus Saint-Gaudens. You can see his
initials there, just below the date. He wanted to
try and capture something of the majesty and
elegance of the coins of the Ancient World. I think
he succeeded, don't you?'

She sensed Baxter lowering his face and staring at her as she gazed at the coins, moving his head closer to hers, almost whispering in her ear.

'As you can see, one side features a large eagle in flight, while the obverse depicts Lady Liberty, a torch in her right hand and an olive branch in the left, symbolising peace and enlightenment. She's beautiful isn't she?'

She felt Baxter's hand brush against her neck and instinctively drew away with an annoyed shrug of her shoulders. She immediately wished she hadn't. The hurt look on Baxter's face showed his realisation that this, rather than their earlier flirtatious exchange, perhaps better reflected her true feelings for him. When he spoke next, his voice was tinged with anger.

'What is this *really* all about, Agent Browne?'

'This is about whether my coin is a fake, Mr Baxter.' Jennifer made no attempt to be friendly now. It was too late for that.

'Well, it's impossible to say without running some tests. It's clearly the same design and looks real enough, but we would need to analyse the coin, take some samples, compare it to our originals. It could take days, weeks even.' He tailed off.

'I understand.' Jennifer nodded. 'Thank you for your time, Mr Baxter. It has been very useful. The lab will be in touch about those tests.' She turned to leave but Baxter reached out and grabbed her shoulder, his fingers scrabbling against the black material.

'Jennifer – wait.' His voice was strained, pleading. 'You can't just go like that. Where did you get that coin? I have to know.'

She smiled.

'I'm sorry Mr Baxter, but that information is classified. A small matter of national security; I'm sure you understand.'

NINE

FBI Academy, Quantico, Virginia
19th July – 12:30pm
'So we still don't know if it's a fake or not? This guy, Baxter, he couldn't help with that?'

Corbett sat down on one of the wooden benches that lined the shaded banks of the Potomac in this part of the FBI compound and placed a polystyrene cup full of thick black coffee down on the ground between his feet. Jennifer sat down next to him, her sandwich still in its plastic wrapper. Lunch could wait.

'Not without sending it to the lab for tests which I'll do this afternoon. But he did mention something else.'

'What?'

'Well, it's probably nothing . . .'

Jennifer noticed Corbett's forehead creasing. Although he probably had many qualities, she suspected that patience was very definitely not one of them.

'It's just that Baxter said that all nine of the coins recovered by the Secret Services in the 1940s were destroyed. But I spoke to someone I know over at the Treasury on the way out here who owed me a favour. He told me, off the record, that although four of the nine coins recovered by the Secret Services in the 1940s were destroyed, the other five were put into storage back at the Philadelphia Mint before being moved to Fort Knox about ten years ago when they re-inventoried the place. As far as he knows, they're still there.'

Corbett nodded slowly and settled back into the bench, the sunlight seeping under the branches of the overhanging tree. Jennifer studied his face and noticed the total lack of surprise at this latest piece of information. Her eyes widened in realisation.

'But then, you already knew all that, didn't you?' she said slowly.

'The French doctor who performed the autopsy on Ranieri happened to be a bit of a coin freak,' Corbett admitted, his eyes fixed on the river, the occasional splash and glittering ripple showing where a fish had risen to the surface and then powered its way back down to the river bed, bending the water with a flick of its tail. 'He recognised the coin. That's why we got it back so quickly. I pulled the file. You just pretty much confirmed everything in it.'

'So what's this all been about, sir?' Jennifer fought to control the anger in her voice. She'd thought she was being given a clear run, but Corbett was treating her with the same suspicion as everyone else. 'Is this some sort of test? Because if it is, I resent . . .'

Corbett cut her off, his eyes boring into her.

'You know, there's a lot of people who think you're damaged goods. That you're a liability. That you should have been retired three years ago after the shooting.'

She paused before answering and returned his stare, trying not to let her voice sound too defensive.

'I can't help that.'

'No. But it bugs you.' He shrugged and turned to face the river again. 'Me, I think that everyone makes mistakes. It's how they deal with them that sets them apart. Some just go to pieces and never recover. Others move on and come back twice as strong.'

'Which do you think I am, sir?'

He paused.

'It took me two days to get the Treasury to confirm what happened to those other coins. You did it in one phone call. Let's just say that you don't strike me as a quitter.' The hint of a smile crossed his face for the first time that afternoon. 'The case is yours.'

'Thank you, sir,' Jennifer stood up, a slight

tremor in her voice. This was the sort of chance she had been hoping for. Praying for. 'I'll get right on it.'

'Good.' He flicked his eyes back round to hers. 'I want you down in Kentucky first thing in the morning, checking on those coins. I'll get a plane booked for you.'

'Yes, sir.' Jennifer got up and turned to leave, but Corbett called after her.

'By the way, who bought that Farouk coin in the end? We're probably going to need to talk to them too.'

Jennifer reached for her notebook and flicked through the first few pages until she found the right entry.

'According to my Treasury contact several people bid for it. But it went to a Dutch property developer, a private collector.' She found the name she was looking for and looked up as she said it to see if Corbett recognised it.

'Darius Van Simson.'

TEN

The Marais, 4th Arrondissement, Paris
19th July – 6:00pm
'Vous savez pourquoi on appele ce quartier le Marais?'

His French faultless, Darius Van Simson was sitting behind the large mahogany desk that dominated the right hand side of his office. Circumflex eyebrows over a chopped angular face, his sandy hair and the firm arrow of his goatee were flickering slightly in the stiff breeze from the overhead air conditioning unit. He was sipping whisky from a heavy crystal glass.

'Presumably because it used to be a swamp.'

The man sitting opposite him was short and round, with a puffy red face and small brown eyes. He had long since outgrown his suit and the fabric creased violently around his shoulders and across his arched back. His cracked black leather belt could not hide the fact that he wore his trousers with the top button undone.

'Bravo, Monsieur Reinaud!' Van Simson slapped the table in appreciation. 'Quite so. The Knights Templar drained it in the 11th Century. Who would have thought then, that in the Middle Ages it would emerge at the epicentre of French political life? That aristocratic families would build their houses on its narrow streets so as to be near their King?'

Reinaud nodded awkwardly, as if unsure if he should say something. Van Simson put his glass down, stood up and crossed to the other side of the room so that Reinaud had to shuffle around in his chair to see him. He was wearing a blazer over dark grey flannel trousers, his white shirt open at the neck. He wore no socks, his bare feet clad in a pair of brown suede moccasins.

Four large windows had been set into the wall and in between each one was a different Chagall painting, each illuminated by a single recessed spotlight that made the colours glow as if the image had been projected onto the space, rather than merely hung there.

'Of course, over the years, most of those grand houses were carved up into apartments or shops or offices or simply knocked down.' Van Simson continued, gazing out the window at the courtyard below. 'Why, this very house was a ramshackle assortment of restaurants, craft shops and dance studios before I bought them all out and had the place reconverted.'

'Monsieur Van Simson, this is all very interesting, but I fail to understand how this is relevant to . . .'

'Have you seen this?' Van Simson walked over to the white architectural model that stood in a glass display case in the middle of the room. Reinaud heaved himself to his feet with a sigh and walked over.

'What is it?'

'Surely you recognise it?'

Reinaud frowned as he studied the layout of the streets. A shopping mall, a car park, office buildings, luxury apartments around an artificial lake. Suddenly, his eyes narrowed.

'Never! I've told you, I'll never allow it!'

Van Simson smiled.

'Things change, Monsieur Reinaud. A swamp can grow to become the site of a royal palace; an aristocrat's home decay into a slum. It is time for this land to evolve. You're only fooling yourself if you think you can stand in the way of progress.'

'No, you're the one fooling yourself with your lawyers and accountants.' Reinaud fired back, taking a step closer to him. 'There will be no sale. Not now, not ever.'

Van Simson sighed. Nodding slowly, he reached into his inside jacket pocket and drew out a large chequebook which he laid flat on the display case. Unscrewing the lid of a silver fountain pen, he looked up at Reinaud with a smile.

'You are a tough negotiator, Monsieur Reinaud, I'll give you that. But come now, enough of this . . .' He searched for the appropriate word. '. . . posturing. I have the planning permission. Everyone else has accepted my terms. My men have already broken ground on the first phase of this project. Yours is the only outstanding plot. How much do you want?'

'The price is not the issue,' Reinaud spluttered. 'My family have lived on this land for six hundred years. My ancestors lie buried in its soil as I and my children and their children will one day. To us, this is more than just land. It's our birthright. Our inheritance. Its spirit runs through our veins. It's not a cell on a spreadsheet, not a footnote in your annual report. We will never sell it. I would rather die than see this . . . this monstrosity come into being.'

Van Simson's smile faded, his face creasing and narrowing into a point, furrows of anger carved in neat, vertical lines across his cheeks. Under his blazer, he could sense his shirt beginning to stick to his back. He walked over to his desk, had another sip of his whisky, the ice tinkling against the crystal.

Suddenly, he spun round and in one violent movement hurled the glass across the room as hard as he could. It shot through the air, whistling past Reinaud's head and crashing into the wall. The heavy base smashed on impact, an exploding petal of glass shards. Just for a moment, as the light caught them, hundreds of tiny rainbows fluttered through the air before falling to the floor.

'That tumbler was one of a pair salvaged from the first class lounge of the Titanic. The only ones to have survived. Your stubbornness has just cost me a hundred thousand dollars,' Van Simson hissed, advancing towards a now white-faced Reinaud. 'You mean nothing to me, Reinaud.' He snapped his fingers. 'Certainly less than that glass. Defy me and you will find out what it means to stand in my way. Now for the last time, what is your price?'

On the other side of the room, whisky ran down the wall in dark rivulets, pooling amidst the shattered glass. Against the pale brown carpet, it looked like blood.

ELEVEN

Highgate Cemetery, London
20th July – 3:30pm

Tom made his way through the gravestones, the cracked and threadbare path snaking its way down the hill. In a couple of places the tarmac had worn away completely and here the surface of an earlier, cobbled path shone through, the stones brightly polished where generations of heavy-hearted feet had stumbled over them.

There was a time when he could have recited from memory the names on most of the tombstones between the upper gate and his mother's grave. They jutted out from the fleshy earth like teeth, some overlapping, others separated by wide gaps, decaying according to the seasons in the wind and the sun and the cold. Here and there, plastic flowers leered from rain-filled jam jars. In the distance, the distinctive sceptre of the BT Tower rose above the city's concrete ooze.

The solid black marble slab nestled snugly in the grass, sheltered by the drooping branches of a willow and the tangled undergrowth that concealed the crumbling cemetery wall. The gilding that had been painted into the carved inscription still shone brightly and Tom ran his fingers over the letters, silently tracing her name. Remembering. She would have been 60 that day.

Rebecca Laura Kirk
née Duval

Everyone had told him at the time that it wasn't his fault, that it was just one of those things. An accident, a terrible tragedy. Even the coroner had played it down, blaming mechanical failure, before suggesting that his mother had been at best reckless for letting a thirteen year old boy drive, even if it was just a short distance down a normally quiet road. For a moment he had almost believed them.

But the look in his father's eyes at her funeral, the anger that had shone through the tears when he'd hugged him, convinced Tom that he, at least, thought otherwise. That if she had let him drive, then it was because Tom had begged and bawled until she had relented. That he had as good as killed her. When he was much older, he often wondered whether when his father had hugged him so tightly that day, he had really been trying to suffocate him.

Tom closed his eyes subconsciously toying with the ivory key-ring his father had given him a few weeks before he'd died. He breathed in deeply through his nose finding the smell of freshly turned earth and cut grass comforting. It reminded him of long lazy summer afternoons in the garden, before all that. Before he had been abandoned to his loneliness. And his guilt. Because after that day, his father had never hugged him again.

'There's a bloody fortune in marble here.' A familiar voice broke into Tom's thoughts. 'I know a bloke who'd take all these off our hands.' An impossible voice. 'He just splits the top layer off and re-engraves 'em. Punters never know the difference.' A voice that had no right being there.

'Archie?' Tom spun round. 'How . . . why . . . what the hell are you doing here?'

Over the years, Tom had often wondered what Archie looked like, tried to mentally sketch a face to match the voice, an expression to suit the tone. With every conversation, a little more detail had been added to this picture; an extra crease around the eyes, a slight bump in the nose, a sharper edge to the jaw. At times, Tom had almost managed to convince himself that they must have met. But with Archie, the real Archie, actually standing there in front of him for the first time, his careful reconstruction instantly crumbled and now he found that he could not salvage a single memory of it.

Instead he saw a slim man – in his mid-forties, Tom guessed – about five feet ten. He had an oval face, his hair clipped very short and receding, so that it formed a fuzzy point right at the tip of his forehead. His three-buttoned suit was clearly bespoke, possibly Savile Row, a 10-ounce dark blue pinstripe that wouldn't have looked out of place on any City trading floor.

His blue Gingham shirt was unbuttoned at the neck and Tom guessed that he was probably wearing a set of red braces to match his socks. These were expensive clothes with the right labels in the right places, subtle tribal markings that allowed Archie to circulate unchallenged through the smart and fast-moneyed world he inhabited.

And yet despite this, there was something rough and ready about him. His face was slightly crumpled, his chin dark with stubble, his ears sticking out slightly from the side of his head. He had the easy confident manner of someone who knew how to handle himself and others. But his dark brown eyes said different. They said that he was afraid.

Tom looked around anxiously, wary that Archie might not have come alone.

'It's all right, mate. Cool it.' Archie held his hands up. 'It's just me.'

'Don't tell me to cool it,' Tom's voice was stone. 'What's going on? You know the rules.'

'Of course I know the rules – I bloody well invented them, didn't I?' Archie gave a short laugh.

It had been Archie's idea that they should never meet. Ever. It was safer that way, he had said, so that all they would have on each other was a name and a phone number. By coming to find him, Archie had broken his own, most important rule. It was an act of desperation, a cry for help. Or maybe a trick?

Tom leapt forward and fired off two quick punches, a right to the stomach and a left to the side of Archie's head. The first winded him, the second dropped him to the ground.

'Are you wearing a wire? Is that it, you bastard? Have you cut a deal with Clarke to ship me in?' Tom knelt over Archie and patted him down roughly, feeling around his chest and groin to see if he was concealing some sort of transmitter. He wasn't.

'Fuck you.' Archie heaved Tom off him and rubbed the side of his face, coughing as the air seeped back into his lungs. 'I'm no fucking grass.' He hauled himself back to his feet and gave Tom an angry look, brushing his jacket down.

'Yesterday Clarke shows up promising to put me away. Then after ten years of our avoiding each other, you break cover. What am I meant to think? That it's all a coincidence?'

'Clarke, that hairy-arsed wanker? Do me a

favour. You think I'd risk you, risk me for him? You should know me better than that.'

'Should I? The Archie I know doesn't break the rules.'

'Look – I followed you here from your gaff. I'm sorry. I should have warned you or something.' Archie had his breath back now, but was still patting his cheekbone gingerly.

'You know where I live?'

Tom shook his head in disbelief, his anger mounting at this latest revelation.

'Yeah, well, after our last little conversation I got a bit worried, didn't I? So I did a bit of home-work. There aren't that many Tom Kirks in London. Your place was the third I tried.'

'Christ, you even know my name.' Tom looked around him in concern and lowered his voice to an angry whisper.

'I hate to tell you this, mate, but I've always known. Ever since the first job you pulled for me. You don't like taking risks and neither do I. Till now, I've never had any reason to need it.'

'Well you're wasting your time because this isn't going to change anything. I've told you, you'll have to find someone else to do the job.'

Archie had an awkward look on his face.

'It's not that simple.'

'Sure it is.' Tom's eyes narrowed. 'I didn't sign up for Cassius. That was your call. Now you deal with it.'

Archie flashed Tom a guilty look.

'I didn't sign up to Cassius either. He signed up to you.'

'What?' It was Tom's turn to sound concerned.

'I got the usual visit from one of his people.' Archie stared down at the floor as he spoke. 'Another bloody foreigner. Sometimes I think all the English people have left this country.' He shook his head. 'Anyway, he said you were the best, that only you would do for the job, usual spiel. I told him that there'd been a death in the family, that you'd gone abroad for a few months to sort everything out and to find someone else. But he said he'd wait. When you came back it all sort of fell into place.'

'So you *did* know that Cassius was behind this job right from the start. You lied to me.'

'So what?' said Archie, suddenly defensive. 'What did you expect me to do? Turn him down?'

'After all the jobs we've done, all the years we've worked together, I'd expect you to tell me the truth.'

A mobile phone rang, an annoying, rambling tune that bounced jarringly down a high-pitched scale like a child sliding down stairs. Archie reached into his jacket's left inside pocket, the lining flashing emerald as he pulled a phone out, checked the number that had flashed up on the screen and killed the call. He looked up.

'And I'd expect you to follow through on *your*

promises. You signed up to both jobs. You can't just back out because you feel like it. What do you think this is? A bloody game? I'm trying to run a business here. A business that has made you a very rich man. I find the buyers, you do the jobs. That's how it works. That's how it's worked for the last ten years. Did I deliberately not tell you that the job was for Cassius? Too fucking right I did. A buyer is a buyer. His money is as good as anyone else's.'

'It's always the money with you, isn't it?' Tom retorted. 'Except now you've realized that his money isn't the same. It comes with conditions attached.'

They were both silent and Archie moved closer to Tom, his black brogues sinking into the grass's soft pile.

'What's really going on, Felix? Let's go for a pint and sort this out.'

'Felix is gone now. Finished.'

'It's just another job. Pack it in after that if that's what you want.'

'How long have you been doing this now, Archie? Twenty, twenty-five years?'

Archie shrugged.

'About that.'

'You never wonder how you got to this point in your life?' Tom spoke with a low, urgent voice. 'About how a different decision here or action there could have totally changed things?

Sometimes I think my life has been like a row of dominoes that I knocked over fifteen years ago. I can't even remember how the first one got toppled and suddenly I'm here.'

Archie gave a short laugh.

'A thief with a mid-life conscience? Pull the other one.'

A phone rang again, this time with a series of frantic beeps that grew louder and more frequent the longer the phone rang. Archie reached down into his other jacket pocket and drew out a second phone, a thick gold bracelet glinting momentarily as his sleeve rode up his arm. Again he checked the number. This time he answered it.

'Hello . . . not right now, no . . . about five hundred . . . no . . . no deal, not unless he takes the lot. All right, cheers.'

Tom waited for him to return the phone to his pocket and look up before continuing.

'You know what? I'm thirty-five years old and I've never spent more than four weeks in the same place since I was twenty.'

Archie snorted.

'What, am I meant to feel sorry for you or something? That's how they trained you. It's part of what makes you so good. It's part of the job.'

'There's more to life than this job, Archie.'

Archie's eyes flashed with impatience.

'Sorry mate, but I'm fresh out of tissues.'

'All good things come to an end. Even this. Even us.'

Archie sighed.

'I'm just not getting through to you, am I? Unless we deliver a week today, we're both dead men. Period.' Although his voice sounded casual, Archie's eyes were burning brightly. 'There's a rumour about that Cassius is hard up, that he lost everything in some deal. So he won't let it slide, won't take no excuses. And if I can find you, then he certainly can. If we're going to sort this, we're going to have to do it together. I'm sorry, Tom, but this ain't just my problem. It's *our* problem.'

TWELVE

Fort Knox, Kentucky
20th July – 10:05am
A black Ford Explorer had picked Jennifer up from her apartment that morning and driven her to Reagan Washington National, where, in one of the side hangars, a tan Cessna Citation Ultra had been prepped and was waiting for her. Corbett clearly did not kid around when it came to getting things done.

The jet had looked brand new, and apart from the pilot and lone cabin attendant, she was the only passenger. Sinking back into the soft leather seats, she had stretched her legs right out into the narrow aisle, basking in the cabin lights. Twenty minutes later and the plane was arrowing through the clear Washington sky.

Flying had always made her slightly nervous. Once a plane she was on had hit an air pocket and dropped almost five thousand feet. As if they'd hit a glass wall in the sky and slid down it. Take-off and landing were the worst and she unconsciously alternated between gripping the arm rests and bracing herself for possible impact against the seat in front of her, depending on what stage of the journey they were at. This time though, tired from the early start, she had found herself falling into a deep sleep until the gentle bump of the undercarriage coming down shook her awake.

Blinking, she turned her head to the window. The elliptical porthole framed a quilt work of differently coloured fields, each one bounded by a dark line of trees. A single, cotton thin strip of blacktop ran in an unbroken line right to left and disappeared in both directions into a shimmering heat haze. Lonely farmsteads and barns stood marooned in the flat landscape like small wooden islands. Then, as the plane dropped lower, a low-slung galvanised fence on the military airbase's outer perimeter surged up to meet her.

'Welcome to Kentucky, Agent Browne.' Jennifer stepped down off the steps that had concertinaed out of the jet's gleaming fuselage and shook the hand of the man waiting to greet her. 'I hope you had a pleasant flight. I'm Lieutenant Sheppard. I'm to escort you to the Depository.'

'Thank you,' she answered, unable to mask her smile. It was quite an outfit. Pink plaid trousers, white polo shirt and yellow sun visor all competed for her attention. Beneath the visor the man's face was creased into a broad grin as he pumped her hand up and down enthusiastically.

Although Jennifer was mindful never to form opinions of people too quickly, a trait she had inherited from her mother who maintained that time was the only reliable lens through which to view someone's true character, she instinctively liked Sheppard. He had a breezy, cheerful confidence and an uncomplicated and genuine manner that his gaudy wardrobe reinforced rather than undermined.

Sheppard looked down at himself and then flashed her a guilty smile, brown eyes twinkling in his smooth, sun-tanned face.

'I'm real sorry about the clothes, Ma'am. I was just heading out for a round when I got word to come and meet you here. I didn't have time to change.' Jennifer nodded back, her tone understanding.

'That's quite all right, Lieutenant. I appreciate you taking me over. Is it far?'

'No, ma'am. Not in this baby.' He pointed to a white golf cart, his clubs firmly strapped to the back.

'In that?' She looked at him questioningly as they walked over to it.

'In this.' He swung himself into the driver's seat and then reaching up, fixed a red light to the roof. 'I had a buddy in the Corps of Engineers make a few alterations. You into cars?'

'I used to fix up and race Mustangs with my dad if that counts,' she replied with a smile.

'Hey – then maybe you should drive,' Sheppard suggested eagerly, sliding across to the passenger side. 'Then you can tell me how you think this baby handles.'

'Sure.' She shrugged and slipped in behind the wheel, turning the key in the ignition. 'You holding on?'

'Hell yeah.'

As well as being the site of the US Bullion Depository, Fort Knox is also the tank capital of the United States, its 109,050 acres home to 32,000 men and women of the US Army Armor and Cavalry which has its headquarters there. It was not long, therefore, before they were speeding past barrack buildings, mess halls, training blocks and groups of soldiers running in tight formation, their chanted cadences blending with each other to form a muscular, sweaty symphony.

Her foot flat to the floor, Jennifer slalomed through the troops and the buildings, the red light flashing, oncoming vehicles sounding their horns as Sheppard called out the directions, his hand fiercely gripping the grab handle to stop himself from sliding across the shiny white vinyl seat as she dived in and out of the traffic. She sensed he was enjoying the ride.

Ahead of them, the granite-clad shape of the Depository loomed closer. From a distance,

Jennifer thought that it seemed fairly ordinary; not much bigger than a small office block really, like one of those low-rise bank buildings you get in local malls. But as she drew closer she saw that it had, in fact, the squat solidity of a small white mountain.

Set in a wide compound, it was a two storey building, the upper storey smaller than the lower one, its roof slightly tiered like the first few steps of a ziggurat. Steel-framed windows had been evenly set into the walls of both storeys like embrasures in a castle wall. The only access came through a single gate in the fifteen-foot high steel fence that encircled the compound, itself flanked by two armoured sentry boxes. Once inside, a service road with neatly cut grass verges on each side ringed the building, which had four concrete bunkers surgically grafted onto each of its corners. A lone lawnmower patrolled the outer verge, its engine buzzing.

'It was built in 1936 and the first gold shipments arrived in 1937.' Sheppard shouted over the whine of the cart's electric motor, angrily gesticulating soldiers scattering in front of them like ninepins. Jennifer nodded. She couldn't imagine it having ever actually been built. It seemed to have been there forever, as if it had erupted out of the solid bedrock millions of years ago and then been shaped and polished by tens of thousands of years of sun and rain and frost.

'Usage peaked in 1941 when it held about 650 million ounces,' he continued. 'Course these days, the main reserves are held at the Federal Reserve in New York, about five stories down. You should go and check it out sometime. I'm told the security there makes this place look like Disneyland.'

She slowed the cart as it approached the gate and then accelerated hard again as they were waved through. The sentries saluted Sheppard, their arms juddering to a rigid halt at the side of their head, their hands stiff, thumb tucked in, seemingly unfazed by his clothes and the sight of Jennifer at the wheel of the careering golf cart.

Up close, the building was even more formidable. The sheer mass of its granite walls seemed to weigh down on everything around it – a dark, dense, oppressive energy that compressed and squeezed and stifled. Jennifer found herself strangely conscious of the sound of her own breathing, of the sheer effort of moving, as if underwater.

Surveillance cameras, positioned high on the granite walls like glass eyes on white steel stalks, covered every inch of the building's walls. Twin floodlights perched atop black poles gazed out at the surrounding compound on all four sides. A huge Stars and Stripes snapped in the wind outside the main entrance. The golden seal of the Treasury Department carved into the lintel glinted like a small sun.

'Stop here,' Sheppard shouted. Jennifer immediately threw the cart into a tight skid, the tyres
biting the tarmac as it slowed to a stop.

'Wow,' Sheppard breathed. 'I think you just set
a new record.'

'It sure is quick.' She jumped out and tossed
the keys over to him. 'What did you do? Change
the gearing?'

'Trade secret.' Sheppard smiled. 'What d'ya
think of the handling?'

'Slight understeer. You want to tighten up the
front left suspension.'

'I'll do that.' He winked at her. 'Come on. Rigby
will be waiting and boy does he hate that.'

Turning on his heel, Sheppard disappeared
through the Depository's massive black doorway
into the cold marbled darkness of the building.

THIRTEEN

10:27am

As Sheppard had predicted, the Officer in Charge, Captain Rigby, was standing in the large entrance atrium ready to greet her. He gave her a brief handshake and what looked to Jennifer like a forced smile as Sheppard introduced them.

He was tall, perhaps six foot four, his uniform immaculate, his hair clipped short, his eyes bristling with well-drilled efficiency. From his snatched glances, Jennifer could tell that he was struggling to reconcile Sheppard's garish golfing outfit with his well-ordered world. She decided to keep it short and businesslike, sensing that anything else would fail to show up on Rigby's internal radar.

'Thank you very much for agreeing to see me today, Captain.'

'That's quite all right, Agent Browne,' he said stiffly. 'We all have a job to do.' The way his pale eyes narrowed a fraction over his thin nose and high cut cheekbones suggested what he was really thinking. That he thought this was a waste of time. That he didn't want her or any other federal pains in the asses anywhere near his facility, asking him questions, disrupting his routine, marking his polished floor with their gumshoes. He just wanted her out, ASAP. That suited her just fine.

'Have you received the instructions from Washington?'

He nodded.

'Yes, they came through this morning. As requested we have left the items in situ.'

'Good. Then before we go down, I wonder whether you could answer a couple of questions.'

'What sort of questions?' Rigby's tone was immediately suspicious.

'Any questions I choose to ask, Captain,' Jennifer answered firmly.

'This is a classified installation,' Rigby countered forcefully. 'If you think I'm just going to reveal sensitive intel without specific authorisation, then I suggest you get back on your plane, Agent Browne.'

'And if you think I'm going to leave here without everything I want, I suggest you take another look at your orders, Captain.' Jennifer's voice was hard and her eyes flashed defiance. Normally, she would have preferred to use reason rather than raising her voice, but in Rigby's case she sensed he had been conditioned not to react to anything else. 'They specify full and unconditional cooperation with the FBI for the duration of our investigation, including disclosing relevant security procedures. If you've got a problem with that, then I suggest we step into your office right now and call your and my superiors in Washington. I think we both know what the answer would be.'

There was an awkward silence, punctured only by the rasping of the studs on Sheppard's golf shoes against the marble floor as he nervously shifted his weight onto his other foot. Rigby had gone a deep shade of red and he seemed to be rolling something around between his thumb and forefinger, the tips of both fingers white from squeezing so hard. Jennifer, lips pressed together, returned his glare until, eventually, he managed a grimace that she assumed approximated to a smile.

'Very well,' he conceded, his voice slightly strangled.

'I have no intention of prying, Captain,' Jennifer said, adopting a more conciliatory tone now that she had made her point. 'Just a bit of background about the installation to go into my report. For instance, is this a military or a Federal installation?'

'Oh,' Rigby sounded relieved, although there was still an unmistakeably impatient edge to his voice. 'A bit of both. The buildings are on an army base so they have some responsibility for the security and defence of the facility. But it is run by the US Treasury and staffed by officers from the Mint Police. There are twenty-six of us in all.'

Jennifer frowned.

'Buildings? I only see one building.'

'No.' Rigby shook his head firmly. 'It's two buildings. The one that you see around you now is just a single story outer shell built from granite and lined with concrete. But the vault itself is an entirely separate building on two levels built from steel plates, I-beams and cylinders, all encased in reinforced concrete.'

'So how do you get in?'

'Through a twenty-ton steel door.'

Jennifer nodded, satisfied.

'Okay. Then let's get started.'

'Yes ma'am.'

He set off, with Jennifer next to him and Sheppard bringing up the rear. She soon saw what he had meant about the two buildings. The atrium led to a corridor running left and right that encircled the vault with offices and storerooms giving off its outer edge. It was a narrow, constricted space and Jennifer recognised the same ruthless anonymity she had witnessed in other Federal installations, the Bureau included. She was glad when they emerged, having turned right and then followed the corridor round until they were on the other side of the building, into another large space.

Here, the large steel shutters that had been set into the outer granite wall and the loading bays and ramps suggested that this was where bullion and supplies were moved in and out. Opposite the shutter, built into the vault wall, was the gleaming steel bulk of the vault door.

'No single person has the combination to the vault,' Rigby continued. 'Instead three separate combinations are required, each held by different members of my team.'

As he spoke he approached a console to the right of the door. Beyond a plate glass window to the side of them that looked onto the atrium, Jennifer saw another two men step towards similar consoles. Ten seconds later there was a series of loud clunks as the restraining bolts retracted. With a steady mechanical drone the massive door began to swing back towards them, steel pistons gleaming and hissing like a steam train.

'It's certainly an impressive set-up.'

At these words, Rigby came as close to smiling as she imagined he had ever done in his life and she sensed that their earlier disagreement had temporarily, at least, vanished from his mind.

'Ma'am, I'm proud to say this installation is more secure than most of our missile silos. We're in the middle of a fully manned Army base. We have our own power plant, water system and strategic food reserves. We have twenty-four seven, three hundred and sixty degree surveillance. Nothing gets in or out of here that isn't meant to.'

They stepped inside the vault and walked along a narrow metal platform to the elevator that took them with a low-pitched whine down to the basement vault floor. Rigby held the gate open for them. Jennifer looked slowly around her.

The room was like a massive warehouse, consisting of two floors built around the central space in which they were now standing. Each floor was divided into compartments with thick steel bars separating and enclosing the top of each compartment, so that they looked like a series of huge cages. Within each compartment, stacked from floor to ceiling, were thousands upon thousands of gold bars. It took her a few seconds to realise that she was unconsciously holding her breath; fearful, perhaps, that the sound of her breathing might rouse the slumbering dragon who must surely be guarding such a fairy-tale treasure.

'Impressive, isn't it?' Sheppard winked. 'It still hits me right here every time I see it.' He clutched a clenched fist to his chest as Jennifer nodded silently. The gold was everywhere she looked, glowing and alive, a huge dull mass pulsing rhythmically in the flicker of the lights like the beat of a powerful heart.

'We have small shipments going in and out of the facility all the time,' Rigby cut into her thoughts, pointing at three large silver containers standing in the middle of the room, each about four foot long, two feet wide and three feet high with the US Treasury seal emblazoned across the front. 'This is what the bullion is transported in. These are due to go out this afternoon.'

'Right.' She nodded, smiling. Complimenting his facility seemed to have transformed Rigby into the very model of inter-agency cooperation.

'But the items you requested to see are over here.' He led her towards a compartment on the far left of the room. As she drew closer, she could see that it seemed a little less full than the other cages and contained boxes and briefcases and files.

'As you can see,' said Rigby, holding up a large metal tag that was fixed to the door of the compartment, 'each of the thirty four compartments is sealed. When any seal is broken, the compartment's contents are re-inventoried and resealed by the US Mint.'

He snapped the seal off and reaching into his pocket for a key, unlocked the cage and stepped in. He emerged a few moments later holding a thin aluminium briefcase that he held out to Jennifer with a nod.

'I believe that this is what you came for.'

'I'll open it down here.'

'As you wish.'

Rigby carried the case over to one of the containers and placed it down flat on its side, its catches facing Jennifer. She reached forward and flicked the catches open, the noise echoing through the room like rifle shots. Imperceptibly, Sheppard and Rigby moved around to stand either side of her.

She opened the case, only to find another smaller box, about 8 inches long and 6 inches wide, inside it. It was covered in dark blue velvet that had worn away around the corners, leaving them bald and frayed. The top had been stamped with the gold seal of the US Treasury, now faded and dull.

Jennifer gently removed the box from the case and pressed the small gold catch that released the lid, her throat suddenly dry and tight. The lid snapped up, revealing an interior lined in creamy white silk that had been fashioned to snugly house five large coins, two along the top, three along the bottom.

But the box was empty.

FOURTEEN

Amsterdam, Holland
21st July – 4:40pm
Cindy and Pete Roscoe were enjoying themselves. London had been impressive, Paris beautiful, but Amsterdam was fun. The coffee shops, the girls in the windows, the canals. It was as different from Tulsa, Oklahoma as it was possible to be. Hell, the concierge at their hotel had even tried to sell them some pot. They'd both pretended to be shocked but secretly they were pleased. It had made their trip seem somehow more authentic.

Amsterdam was also a special place for Cindy, whose grandparents had fled from Holland in the 1930s. She had endured an emotional visit to Anne Frank's house the day before.

'That poor sweet girl,' she had sobbed into Pete's strong arms, her mascara dissolving into spidery streaks across her face as the other tourists thronged around them.

Today was their last day and after a fortnight of trekking round museums and across cites, they had agreed that a relaxing guided tour around the canals was the perfect way to round off their trip before the long flight home. Ten minutes in, clad in matching Dallas Cowboys jackets with the open-topped canal boat slicing through the city and the tour guide pointing out the various sights, they knew that it had been a great idea.

Cindy, as usual, was armed with a guidebook of biblical proportions, a parting gift from her emotional mother at the airport that she now believed to be the gospel on all things European. Such was her faith in its pronouncements that she had developed an annoying habit of matching any guide's commentary to that of her book and then whispering to Pete if they got something wrong, or even worse, omitted some crucial fact.

Pete, meanwhile, had mastered a knack of nodding and making the appropriate noises while only half listening to his wife. His priority, instead, was to capture as much of their trip as possible on film. So while Cindy had her nose buried in a book, Pete had his eye firmly glued to the viewfinder of the tiny digital video camera that nestled in his broad hands.

He had even developed his own dizzying cinematic style, his camera swooping up and down buildings, or suddenly panning in or out, the image uncertain and jumpy. This time, as they went under a bridge, Pete attempted a particularly ambitious shot, zooming out from the detail at the top of a building down to a wide angle shot of the canal. He then tracked slowly across, until he had framed the rows of seats ahead of him and the tour guide standing right at the front of the canal boat. He smiled. She was cute.

Suddenly, something at the edge of the viewfinder caught his eye. An ex-cop, Pete had learnt to recognise when things did not look quite right and instinctively he moved the camera to the right so that the tour guide's face now only took up half the screen.

It was not the agitated man with the tanned face and the shaved head in the phone box just before the next bridge who looked out of place, but rather the two men in dark suits that had just stepped out of the large black Range Rover and were walking towards him. There was a repressed energy in their walk, an assured confidence in their manner that reminded Pete of a dog walking at the very limit of its leash, tugging on its owner's arm. These two were about to cut themselves loose.

He zoomed in on the phone box, past the tour guide's face, just as the man in it saw the two approaching figures. The phone instantly fell out of his hand and his head jerked from side to side, as he weighed his options. But Pete could see that he'd noticed them too late. Hemmed in by the phone box on one side and the men on the other, he clearly had nowhere to go.

As the two men approached him, their backs came together like heavy black curtains, blocking Pete's view. He kept the camera trained on them, hardly daring to blink in case he missed something. Suddenly their shoulders parted and Pete got a glimpse of the man, his eyes wide with terror, a hand pressed over his mouth to stifle his screams. An arm was raised and a long serrated blade flashed in the sun, hovering for a few seconds, its shiny surface silhouetted against the cobalt sky, before swooping down and diving into the man's chest. He collapsed, lifeless.

The boat was almost level with the two men now and Pete widened his shot as they hunched over the body and went through his pockets. But just then, at the very moment that he was going to get slightly ahead of them and catch their actual faces, the boat went under a low brick bridge and they were lost from view. When Pete emerged the other side, his camera poised, the two men and the car were gone.

'Holy shit. D'ya see that?' Pete whispered to his wife, his mouth dry with fear and excitement. He kept the camera trained on the receding image of the corpse that lay slumped in the embrace of the phone box's shadow.

'Oh I know honey, isn't it bad?' Cindy said shaking her head disapprovingly. Her hooped earrings bounced merrily against her orange cheeks. 'That was where Van Gogh used to live and she didn't say a thing!'

PART II

Plate sin with gold
And the strong lance of justice hurtless breaks;
Arm it in rags, a pigmy's straw doth pierce it.

> *William Shakespeare –*
> *King Lear (Act IV, Sc. vi)*

FIFTEEN

FBI Headquarters, Washington DC
22nd July – 2:07pm
The desk fan was on its highest setting. The vibrations had caused it to skip across the conference table's slippery surface until it was balancing against the thin rim of metal that ran around its edge and threatening to throw itself over the side.

'Okay – let's just go through them one more time,' Jennifer suggested, slurping the dregs of her now warm and flat coke. She dropped the empty cup into the overflowing trash can that sat on the floor between them. Special Agent Paul Viggiano raised his dark eyebrows wearily.

'What for? We've been through every single guy like a hundred times. Cross-checked them with the CIA and the NCIC databases. Been through their bank records. Checked their wives, their parents, even their kids for Chrissake. There's nothing here. They're all clean.'

Jennifer got up and moved around the conference table, the overhead halogens reflecting here and there in the polished walnut.

'Because we're not leaving here till we find something,' she said firmly, her eyes flicking between the piles of paper and files and boxes that had been strewn along the table's length, the rubble of her two day investigation so far.

Viggiano stood up, a trim, muscular figure, his dark hair slicked back, his chin covered in a seemingly permanent five o'clock shadow. Shaking his head angrily, he tucked his white shirt back into his dark blue suit trousers – shiny fabric with a faint red thread running through it – as he spoke.

'You know what? This whole thing stinks. It's a goddamned mess.' He slammed his fist down in front of him, the fan wobbling unsteadily before finally toppling off and plunging helplessly to the floor, the flex trailing behind it like a bungee rope that had been tied too long.

Jennifer had to agree. The whole thing was a mess. She knew that Corbett had fought to control the number of people in the loop over the last two days, but cases like this wouldn't stay quiet for long. It was too good an opportunity for a fundraiser, a chance to put the boot in on some of the other departments and agencies and grab a bigger slice of the Federal budget in the process. It was the sort of story Washington lived and prayed for.

'Yeah, it's a mess, but it's our mess,' she retorted. 'So you're just going to have to deal with it.'

She replaced the fan on the table while Viggiano shook his head again and loosened his military-looking tie a little more. Jennifer knew that he was finding this harder going than she was. He was about ten years older than her and two years ago she'd worked on a case for him for a few months. He'd even made a clumsy pass in a bar that she'd brushed off as politely as she could. Now she was in charge and it clearly hurt, although his feelings were the last thing on her mind. She'd worked too hard for this opportunity to let Paul Viggiano screw it up for her. And although she hated to admit it to herself, she'd had to put up with so much crap over the last few years, it actually felt good to be on the other end for a change.

'Look, I've been there, okay. I've seen the place,' she continued, her voice hard and urgent. 'We're not talking about Macy's here. You don't just walk in and help yourself. Whoever did this had detailed knowledge of the vault's layout and security systems. Very detailed.'

Viggiano snorted.

'Big deal. Everything's for sale at the right price. If someone wanted the plans for Fort Knox they could have got them. Money talks.' Viggiano rubbed his thumb and forefinger together and held it up to Jennifer's face with a thin smile.

'You think they keep the details down at the local planning department? Layout, alarm systems, access codes?' Jennifer asked sarcastically. 'Everything about that place is classified. Jesus, they probably incinerate the grass clippings. It's wrapped tight. I'm telling you, someone on the inside must have been involved. So we're going to go through all of them again. Now.'

'Fine. Whatever.' Viggiano ran his hand through his thick quiff of dark hair in frustration and picked up the file where he'd thrown it down on the table earlier. 'Where do you want to start?' His eyes flashed at her, brimming with resentment.

'Right at the beginning. With how many people have had access or actually been into the vault in the last twelve months. If we need to go back further we will, but let's focus there first.' Viggiano muttered under his breath as he counted the numbers again, consulting various sheets of paper that he picked up from in front of him.

'Like I said before. Forty-seven people.'

'Plus me. That makes forty-eight.'

'What, you think I'm an idiot? You're in the forty-seven,' he said, his chin jutting in indignation.

'I am? How do you work that out?' Jennifer flicked through her hieroglyphic notes, adding numbers in her head.

'Twenty-five guards from the Mint Police,

fifteen military personnel, five Treasury officials and two Federal agents, one of which was you. Not that many people get down there.' Viggiano held up the sheet of paper on which he'd done his sums and waved it in the air as if to prove his point.

'That's strange. Rigby told me there were twenty-six guards. That's why I made it forty-eight,' said Jennifer, her smooth brown forehead momentarily creased by a slight frown.

'Who?'

'Rigby. The Officer in Charge, remember?' she said impatiently, although the corners of her mouth twitched at the memory of Sheppard's pink trousers and Rigby's ashen face.

'Well according to the Treasury, it's twenty-five. I got all the names here.' He held up several sheets of paper by their corners between his thumb and forefinger. 'They faxed them over this morning.'

'Let me see those,' she demanded. Viggiano shrugged and passed them over to Jennifer who scanned through the names carefully. She paused on the final sheet and then frowning, held it up to the light.

'What?' Viggiano's tone was immediately defensive. Jennifer didn't say anything but just gripped the sheet between her thumb and forefinger and rubbed them together. A second sheet peeled away from the first with a faint sucking noise. Viggiano went white.

'Like I said, twenty-six guards,' Jennifer said quietly, inspecting the single name at the top of the newly revealed sheet with a grim look on her face.

'I don't understand,' Viggiano spluttered.

'I guess the ink must have stuck them together.' She knew that if their roles had been reversed, Viggiano would have come down on her hard for that sort of oversight, but that wasn't her style. They both knew he had screwed up and as far as she was concerned that was that. There was certainly no point in rubbing his nose in it. What was important was seeing whether this new piece of information led them somewhere.

'Tony Short.' She read from the piece of paper, 'DOB 18 March 1965. Deceased.'

'Deceased? So he's irrelevant,' said Viggiano with relief.

'He had access to the vault.'

'But he's dead.'

'Only just.' She laid the sheet on the table and pushed it over to Viggiano so he could read what it said for himself. 'Four days ago.'

'A coincidence.' Viggiano sounded like he was trying to convince himself as well as her.

'Maybe. But he's the only one we haven't checked out. What do we know about him?' Viggiano turned to the laptop to his left and typed in the name. A file flashed up a few seconds later.

'Ex NYPD. Medal of Honour. Transferred to the

Mint Police five years ago. Married with kids. Usual boy scout shit. It's all here. Deceased*.' He looked up. 'What's the asterisk for?'

'Suicide,' Jennifer replied. 'The asterisk means suicide.'

SIXTEEN

Clerkenwell, London
22nd July – 7:42pm

It had been a hat factory when it had first been built in 1876, according to the inscription chiselled into its once proud façade. Then, during the Second World War, production had been given over to the manufacture of buttons for RAF uniforms. By the time Tom had bought it, the building had fallen into disuse, the store and warehouse level empty, the three upper floors carved up into office space in the 1960s.

Tom had chosen the, by comparison, palatial surroundings of the Managing Director's office as his bedroom. Inexplicably it came complete with its own marbled *en suite* bathroom, as if the former boss's managerial mystique would have crumbled had the staff ever suspected that he used the toilet much like the rest of them.

Eventually, Tom's idea was to have this top floor

as a huge open plan living room complete with kitchen and dining area. The second floor would be bedrooms and bathrooms while the first . . . well he still hadn't quite decided what to do with the first. More showroom space perhaps?

It didn't matter. That was all in the future anyway, after the store was up and running. For now, he had to make do with the cracked mirror on the back of the bathroom door as he adjusted his tie, picking his silver cufflinks off the chipped filing cabinet that now doubled as a chest of drawers and deftly threading them through the double cuff of his Hilditch & Key shirt.

'I'll see you later,' he shouted to Dominique as he clattered down the concrete steps, his footsteps echoing back up around the stairwell's empty carcass.

'Okay.' She had appeared at the doorway to the second floor where she had taken up residence amid the tea-stained walls of the former finance department. 'Have fun.'

Tom stepped out into a cherry sunset, the sun scrolling down through an orange sky, a warm whisper of air shushing through the streets. He liked seeing the city at this time. It was a strange transition period, when one set of users melted away and another appeared.

He soon reached Smithfield, Europe's oldest meat market, a low slung amalgam of a refurbished cast-iron Victorian market hall and a post-war brick and concrete hangar. It was surrounded on all sides by a crenulated roofline of alternately short and tall warehouses, a jarring convergence of red brick and white stone, of Gothic windows and industrial steel shutters. Five minutes later he was in Hatton Garden, the centre of London's diamond trade.

It was nearly empty. Gone were the eager shop assistants enticing you to enter, offering you their very best price, suggesting a pair of earrings to go with the necklace. Gone were the courier bikes and the security vans and the anxious soon-to-be-weds, comparing ring prices in gaudy shop windows. Their shutters had been drawn down, their contents safely stowed for the night, their neon lights extinguished.

And yet the street projected a latent energy. Rather than be asleep it was merely resting. A few Hasidim with pale faces and dark suits still stood in doorways, plunged into shops and buildings, swapped anxious glances from under their dark fedoras. Behind the scenes, the work went on, stones were cut, deals were done, hands shaken, money counted.

Perhaps because his own life had been so lacking in order, so devoid of any fixed reference points or rules, Tom was fascinated by this place. As in Smithfield, he drew an almost spiritual reassurance from the continuity of these streets, their daily cycle, the comforting embrace of their familiar routine. In a way, he craved their predictability.

Stepping in off the street, Tom presented his pass to the security guards on duty in the dingy fluorescent lobby of the Hatton Garden Safe Deposit Ltd. Sitting behind their barred window they inspected it carefully, flickering screens in front of them covering every angle of the lobby and vault and staining their faces blue. Satisfied, they buzzed him through the first door and then, when that had closed behind him, the second door with metal bars running through it.

The reinforced vault there, at the foot of the dark green linoleum stairs, is about seventeen foot square, its walls lined from floor to ceiling with 950 identically-sized tungsten and steel doors that gleam silver under the lights, each individual box numbered in black. Unusually for that time it was empty. That suited Tom perfectly.

He took a key out of his pocket and indicated to the guard who had followed him into the room which box he wanted opened. They both put their keys into the two separate keyholes and turned them. With a click, the door opened; Tom drew out the long black metal container it concealed and placed it on the metal tray that slid out from between two layers of boxes at about waist height. It was empty apart from another key which he removed. Turning to a second box on the opposite wall, he and the guard again inserted their keys. This time, Tom waited until the guard left the room before opening the black container.

He already knew what was in it but opened the small leather pouch it contained anyway, emptying its contents into his gloved hand. Just over quarter of a million in cut diamonds, his share for the Egg he'd stolen in New York. Much easier to move than cash and, if you knew who to ask, accepted in more places than American Express. He tipped the diamonds back into the pouch.

Reaching into his jacket pocket, he removed the Egg and placed it in the second box. He'd wrapped it in his ski mask, a small symbolic act that he knew wouldn't be lost on Archie when he came to collect it. He slid the box back into the wall and locked the door. He then dropped the pouch and the key to the second box into the first box, returned it to the wall and again locked it shut.

He passed through the security gates again, nodded at the guards and then stepped out onto the street just in time to see the street lights buzz on.

SEVENTEEN

Louisville County Mortuary, Louisville, Kentucky
23rd July – 11:37am
Jennifer had always believed that there were no such things as coincidences, just different perspectives. From one perspective, a series of individual events could appear totally random with nothing binding them together other than their actual existence. A coincidence.

From another, however, events could evolve, become more complex, deepen in significance until they ultimately emerged as constituent parts of an overall pattern of cause and effect that could never have been dreamt of originally, let alone guessed at.

These were the facts as far as she could tell: Short had worked at Fort Knox. He was young and healthy. He was happily married with three children he adored. He was a regular churchgoer. And he was liked and respected at work. So from one perspective, the fact that he had committed suicide just a few days before the discovery that five gold coins had been stolen from Fort Knox, was just a terrible coincidence. And yet, when viewed from another, more cynical perspective, it was no coincidence at all. It was downright suspicious.

Corbett had agreed when she had finally managed to track him down the previous afternoon on his way to another internal meeting, a look of grim-faced resignation stamped across his face. He had greeted her with a tired smile.

'Five minutes, Browne, that's all I got. So you'd better make it quick. Let's talk and walk.'

She had rapidly explained what she had found out about Short, choosing to omit Viggiano's mistake, although she knew he wouldn't have done the same for her. Corbett had clearly been impressed, even pausing to give her a pat on the side of the shoulder that had made her swell with pride.

'So he didn't leave a note?'

'No.' She had given a firm shake of her head. 'All the witness statements say it was totally out of character. He was happily married and doing well at work. He just doesn't fit the profile.'

'I agree.' A brief pause. 'And you say he was one of the guards down at Fort Knox?'

'Yeah. One of their star performers apparently. Whatever that means.'

'And tell me again when this happened?'

'Four days ago. That's just two days after Ranieri was murdered in Paris.'

'Hmmn.' Corbett's forehead had creased in thought.

'The autopsy hasn't happened yet. I spoke to the Louisville coroner's office earlier and they've agreed to delay the procedure until tomorrow so I can observe. I've booked a flight.'

'Good,' Corbett had nodded as he reached the meeting room door he'd been heading for. 'You're right, it doesn't add up. Let me know what you find. Oh and Browne . . .' He had said as she turned away. 'Nice work.' She could almost have kissed him.

The mortuary was an anonymous white slab of a building on the outskirts of town, only a short drive from Louisville International Airport and screened from the road by a wall of cedar trees. Jennifer stepped gratefully out of the humidity's dank embrace into the building's refrigerated reception area.

There was a hint of desperation to the way it had been decorated, the walls painted a jarring concoction of pinks and blues, orange moulded plastic seating lining one wall. The Beach Boys was being piped through a lone ceiling speaker, the noise muffled where the protective mesh had been painted over by mistake.

An expressionless woman, funereally dressed

behind a rectangular access hatch punched into the far wall, acknowledged her with a shrug, dialled a number and announced her arrival in a whisper. A few minutes later and a short balding man – about fifty years old, Jennifer guessed – bustled into the room, gold pocketwatch chain spanning his stomach before vanishing into the depths of his waistcoat pocket.

'Agent Browne? I'm Dr Raymond Finch, the pathologist here. We spoke earlier on the phone.'

'Hello.' Jennifer shook his hand warmly, holding out her ID in her other hand, although she noticed that he barely gave it a glance. 'Thank you for inviting me down here.' He'd had no choice really but she knew that it never hurt to show a little humility, especially with the locals.

'No problem. We're pretty much good to go if you are.'

'Great.'

He led her through a door, along a narrow corridor, down some stairs and then through a set of heavy double doors that swung open in front of them to reveal a small, white tiled ante-room. The temperature had dropped down here and her throat had a slight burning sensation from the cocktail of disinfectant and formaldehyde that seemed to grow stronger as she penetrated deeper into the building's entrails.

'You ever done one of these before?' Finch handed her a long white gown that she slipped on over her black jacket and long skirt, taking one for himself to cover the pale green scrub suit he was pulling on. He then placed a set of plastic shoe covers over his brown deck shoes.

'No.'

'Well, it's pretty straightforward. Ugly but straightforward. You're welcome to sit out here until we're done, if you like.'

He smiled sympathetically but Jennifer gave a firm shake of her head. She hadn't travelled all this way to miss the action.

'I've seen a lot of dead bodies, Doctor. One more won't hurt.'

'Okay. Then let's get started.'

Finch led her through another set of double doors to the autopsy room. It was quite a wide space, perhaps twenty foot square and blindingly white. Powerful lights beat down on the spotless tiled walls and floor and reflected off the stainless steel worktops and glass fronted cabinets that wrapped themselves around two of the walls. In the middle of the room stood a stainless steel table, a waist-high slanted tray that had been plumbed for running water. A chrome hanging scale rocked gently in the air conditioning's hum like a medieval gibbet.

'So what's the Bureau's interest in this case?'

'It's just a routine enquiry. Nothing to get excited about,' she lied, hoping that she had disguised the deceit in her answer better than

Finch had disguised the curiosity in his original question.

'Ah.' She could tell he didn't believe her. 'Well, it may be routine for you but we don't get too many suicides round these parts. And when we do, they tend to have put a gun to their head. So this is about as exciting as it gets.'

He laughed and in different circumstances, Jennifer knew that she would have found Finch quite soothing, kind grey eyes peering warmly over the top of half moon spectacles, a grandfatherly white moustache bristling under his beaked nose. But she was cold and her eyes stung from the whiteness of the room and she just wanted him to get on with it.

'So where's the body?'

Finch didn't seem to notice the slight impatience in her voice.

'My assistant should be along with Mr Short any minute now. Ah, here he is.'

A gurney rolled in, a white sheet covering the body lying on it, closely followed by a bored-looking youth sporting a disconcerting blaze of peroxide hair and matching tongue stud and nose rings. He was dressed like Finch in medical scrub suit and protective gown.

'You've read the police report, I expect?' asked Finch as the assistant scraped the gurney along the side of the autopsy table with a metallic screech. Jennifer nodded, flinching at the noise.

'Of course. His son saw smoke coming from the garage and found his father in the car. The police tried to administer first aid on the scene but it was too late.'

'Yes. They found him on the back seat.'

'Did they? That wasn't mentioned anywhere.'

The assistant levered the body onto the autopsy table with a brutal series of pushes and shoves that made Jennifer wince. Short lay awkwardly, like a hastily arranged doll. His skin was waxy and bleached, the face flat with dark rings under the eyes, the flesh slack and gloopy.

'Buckled in.' The way Finch said it suggested that he thought this had a deeper significance and Jennifer picked up on it immediately.

'Buckled in? You think that might mean something?'

Finch shrugged.

'It's certainly unusual.'

'As is finding him in the back, if you ask me. I mean, if it was your car, wouldn't you normally sit in the driver or passenger seat?' Finch nodded his agreement as he pulled first one, then another set of surgical gloves onto each of his hands, releasing each wristband with a loud thwack.

'I guess people do strange things when they're about to kill themselves,' he ventured. 'Who knows what he was thinking. A cry for help? An unconscious reference to a troubled childhood? There are any number of possible reasons.'

Finch pulled a mask over his face and moved round to confirm that the toe tag matched the autopsy permit handed to him by his assistant together with detailed X-rays of the whole body that had been taken earlier in the day. Having satisfied himself that he had the right body, he began the procedure.

First, he checked the body for any abnormalities – puncture marks, bruises, cuts. His voice droned on mechanically as he dictated what he saw into the small microphone clipped to his lapel, the only other sound the shutter-click of the assistant's Nikon as he followed him round the table, Finch stepping back every so often to allow him to get a better shot.

Even though the room burned with the intimacy of death, it was the terrifying impersonality of the procedure which struck Jennifer most. The laboratory-like surroundings, the faceless uniforms, the official forms and photographs and case numbers that reduced what had once been a man, a person, to an anonymous file entry, a lonely statistic. She felt suddenly very sorry for Short.

The initial examination confirmed that carbon monoxide – or, as Finch would have it, CO poisoning – was the most likely cause of death – Short's fingernails and lips were stained a tell-tale cherry red, a sure sign of asphyxia from lack of oxygen in the blood. Apart from a small tattoo on his left shoulder, there was nothing else.

This phase complete, the assistant placed a 'body block' under Short's back, a rubber brick that caused the chest to protrude outward and the arms and neck to fall back, allowing the maximum exposure of the trunk for incisions.

Finch selected a scalpel from the instrument tray on his right and cut into Short's chest, a deep Y-shaped incision that ran from each shoulder to the base of the breast bone and then down in a straight line to the pubic bone, deviating slightly to avoid the navel. He peeled the skin, muscle, and soft tissues away from the chest wall and then pulled the chest flap up over Short's face so that the front of the rib cage and the strap muscles of the front of the neck lay exposed. Then he used a bone cutter to clip through the bones on each side of the front of the rib cage as if he was cutting through a wire fence. This allowed him to peel off the sternum, although he had to hack away at some of the soft tissues that stuck stubbornly to the back of the chest plate.

Jennifer looked on with horrified fascination, part of her wondering whether she should have accepted Finch's offer to wait outside rather than let her fear of missing anything get the better of her, part of her unable to look away. He used what Jennifer recognised from some class or other back at the Academy as the standard 'Rokitansky' method, not unlike field-dressing a deer where, starting at the neck and moving downwards, he cut all the organs free and then removed them from the body in one block.

Finch carried the blood-soaked mass to the dissecting table, a stainless steel surface mounted at the foot of the autopsy table, while his assistant moved the body block to behind Short's head as he prepared to remove his brain. Finch spread the organ block out and then cut the chest organs away from the abdominal organs and the oesophagus with scissors, dictating all the time. But his monotonous delivery was suddenly interrupted.

'Doctor Finch.'

Finch looked up as the assistant beckoned him over.

'What's up, Danny?'

'Can you take a look at this?' Finch put the scissors down and walked round to where his assistant was standing behind Short's head.

'What have you got?'

'Check it out.' The assistant pointed at Short's head. Finch ran his hands over the base of Short's skull, feeling it with his fingertips.

'That's strange,' he said.

EIGHTEEN

Sotheby's, New Bond Street, London
23rd July – 5:00pm

'I have 330,000 pounds to my right. 330,000 pounds for this unique piece. The sword awarded to Admiral Lord Nelson by Sultan Selim III after the Battle of the Nile. Do I have any improvements on 330,000 pounds? Going to the gentleman on my right for 330,000 pounds. Going once. Going twice. Sold to the gentleman on my right for 330,000 pounds.'

The auctioneer's hammer came down with the resounding crack of ivory on oak and a dignified round of applause echoed off the gilded ceiling.

Tom slipped unnoticed from the room, hoping to beat the inevitable crush as the auction drew to a close. The lobby was already busy and a couple of journalists brushed past him as they ran outside to ring the afternoon's events through to their desks. The sword had made nearly five times its estimate and that, together with its illustrious provenance, was good copy.

It felt good to be back. Auctions had been a fertile hunting ground for him over the years, providing ready-made targets, especially the private collectors who seemed to have a more cavalier approach to security. But he found he was enjoying it even more now he wasn't on the lookout for his next possible score, like walking along a street and taking time to look up at the buildings on either side rather than always concentrating on the sidewalk and where he was next going to tread.

'Thomas? Thomas, is that you?' Tom heard his name, strangely unfamiliar in its lengthened form, scrambling over the heads of the people now flowing out of the auction rooms – thick catalogues in one hand, the other poised to grab a glass of white wine from one of the eager waiters strategically positioned to meet the onrushing crowds head-on. Turning, Tom immediately recognised the man in the white linen suit elbowing his way through to him and broke into a broad smile.

'Uncle Harry. How are you?' Tom held out his hand, but the man brushed it aside and instead threw his arms around his shoulders. He was about fifty-five now, Tom estimated, tall with powerful arms and a strong, square cut face that he held high with military stiffness. Although it was fading to grey, he still had a full head of hair that parted neatly on one side and his dark green eyes twinkled merrily under thick eyebrows. He reminded Tom, as he had always done since he was a boy, of a large bear.

Up close, many might have described him as scruffy, the obvious quality of his clothes not compensating for their now faded glory. The years had certainly taken their toll on the linen suit, for example, repeated launderings dying it a pale grey, a few tell-tale wine stains still visible on the left lapel and the right trouser leg. The fold in the double cuffs of his blue Turnbull & Asser shirt had long since frayed, strands of white cotton hanging loose, the points of the collar blunted and worn. Against this muted background, the loud orange and yellow stripes of his MCC club tie stood out, the yellow echoing the squat gold signet ring that engulfed the small finger of his left hand. He carried a Panama hat rolled in his right hand.

'Thomas my boy, I thought it was you.' His voice was diamond sharp, centuries of carefully-controlled social breeding revealing itself in his clear, hard and uncompromising vowel tones.

'Hello, Uncle Harry.'

'Where the dickens have you been? Good God, man, it's been years.'

'I'm sorry. It's been a busy time, what with the funeral and everything.'

'Yes . . . yes, of course.' The man's voice was

suddenly serious. 'How insensitive of me. I'm so sorry I couldn't be there.'

'That's fine. Thanks for your letter. It meant a lot to me.'

'How have you been since . . . ?' He tailed off and looked away.

'Fine,' said Tom, placing his hand reassuringly on the man's upper arm. 'It's been five months now and, well, you know how bad things were between us anyway. It was just a bit of a shock, that's all.'

'I know. We were all shocked.'

The man's face sagged in sorrow.

Tom couldn't actually remember ever meeting Uncle Harry for the first time. He just knew that he'd always been around. Of course, he wasn't really his uncle, although over the years he'd been much more than that to him. No, Harry Renwick had been his father's best friend, to the extent that his father had had any friends. During the school holidays when he'd been packed off back to Geneva, Uncle Harry had been the one to offer to take him skiing, or to the movies. When he'd been sent down from Oxford and moved to Paris, it had been Uncle Harry who had set him up in a place and lent him some cash.

He was still the only person to call him Thomas, though. Tom had never known him to use diminutives. No contractions or slang or jargon, no nicknames or acronyms or verbal shorthand of any sort. The irony, of course, was that he insisted on calling himself Harry rather than Henry. Tom had never been able to figure that one out.

'Did you hear I decided to move the store back to London?'

'Really? That's great. No, really it is. He would have been happy that you've kept it going.'

'Well, I'm doing this for me, not for him,' said Tom, his chin jutting in defiance. Renwick nodded and there was an awkward pause. 'So what are you doing here?' asked Tom, changing the subject. 'I didn't know you were interested in naval history?'

'Well, I'm not really,' Renwick leant his head forward conspiratorially. 'But I have a client who collects this sort of stuff, so I thought I'd have a look. Keep my finger on the pulse of the market and all that rubbish you're meant to do.'

'Do you still come to a lot of these, then?'

'No,' Renwick shook his head. 'Used to. It's not the same these days, you know. I liked it more when people were allowed to smoke. Gave the place a bit more atmosphere, a bit of an edge. You could see it, smell it. It was exciting. Not all caviar and canapés like it is now.'

He gave a dismissive wave at the finger food that was circulating through the room, the silver trays glittering under the chandeliers' cold light like small icebergs. A man barged his way between them, shouting over the noise into his phone.

'So are you still based in London? I thought you'd moved abroad,' Tom asked as they came back together.

'No still here, although I've just moved into a new place. You should come round for dinner.'

'That's very kind but . . .'

'Now, let me see. I can't do tomorrow, or the day after that. Can you do Monday the 26th?'

'Well, it's just that . . .'

'No, I insist. 8 o'clock, 74 Eaton Terrace. Here's my card. Don't be late.'

'Okay,' Tom conceded. 'Thank you.'

'My pleasure. Now if you'll excuse me, I've just seen someone who owes me a favour.'

With a wink, Renwick unrolled his Panama hat, wedged it onto his head and disappeared back into the crowd, while Tom navigated his way out into the open.

Harry Renwick. Tom couldn't believe it. Still the same after all these years, even wearing the same ridiculous suit.

He wasn't sure if it was because he hadn't seen him for a while and had a fresh perspective on things, but thinking about it now, the suit niggled him a little. It was only a small thing but it occurred to Tom for the first time that there was just a hint of the deliberate to it. It had a sort of studied raggedness that seemed somehow false, like new furniture that had been painstakingly distressed to make it look old.

Tom flicked the edge of Renwick's card a few times, thick ivory with a heavy copperplate script. He slipped it into his top pocket, dismissing his thoughts with a rueful shake of his head. Uncle Harry was Uncle Harry, just the same as always.

NINETEEN

Louisville County Mortuary, Louisville, Kentucky
23rd July – 12:01pm

Finch's eyes narrowed as he massaged the back of Short's lifeless and pale head.

'What have you found?' asked Jennifer, stepping forward towards the table.

'It's soft.' A spark of interest was now in Finch's voice for the first time since he'd started the procedure.

'Are you saying it's been fractured?'

'Certainly feels that way.' Finch nodded. There are bits of bone moving around under my fingers, right here at the base of the skull.'

'Which would suggest he was assaulted, wouldn't it?' Jennifer breathed excitedly.

'Possibly. Or dropped by one of the orderlies. There's only one way we can be sure.'

Finch reached towards the instrument tray

beside him and picked up a fresh scalpel. Pressing hard, he cut deeply from behind one ear, over the crown of the head, to behind the other ear, the thin blade scraping against the skull like a knife over unglazed pottery. At the noise, Jennifer bit down hard on her lower lip.

The cut had effectively divided the skin on Short's head into a front flap and a rear flap. Tugging hard, Finch pulled the front flap down over Short's face as if he was peeling an orange, exposing the top and front of the skull. He then peeled the back flap towards the nape of the neck, the flesh ripping away in one entire section.

Jennifer's resolve finally snapped. Without saying a word she spun on her heels and walked swiftly out of the room. Finch smiled but didn't look up. He picked his Stryker saw up off the tray and with a piercing screech tested that it was working, before lowering it to the now perfectly exposed hemisphere of Short's skull.

Ten minutes later Finch emerged from the autopsy room, his white gown covered in a fine film of blood and bone, small flecks of cartilage hanging off his mask. He carefully took the mask off and threw, it and his blood streaked rubber gloves into the yellow surgical waste bin next to the door.

'You feeling okay?'

'Sure.' Jennifer was sipping water from a disposable plastic cup. 'It just got a bit too much, you know . . .' She nodded towards the mutilated cadaver that lay silently in the adjoining room. She was annoyed with herself for not lasting the distance, seeing it as exactly the sort of frailty that her male colleagues were always pointing out as evidence of the unsuitability of female agents for certain lines of work. That said, she would have been even angrier with herself if she'd thrown up. 'I'm sorry.'

'Hey, don't beat yourself up about it,' said Finch, sitting down on one of the seemingly ubiquitous orange chairs next to her. 'To be honest, I didn't expect you to last as long as you did. That last bit gets everyone, even cops who've pulled body parts out of car wrecks. Frankly, I'd have been more worried if you'd stayed. I filed for divorce shortly after my first wife sat through the whole procedure for the first time. I figured if she could sit through that, then it was only a matter of time before she made sure I ended up on the table myself.'

Jennifer laughed and suddenly felt a lot better.

'So what's the verdict?'

'First impressions? He died of acute CO poisoning. I need to finish off the examination of the other organs to be sure, but the lips and the fingernails are a giveaway.'

'So you're saying there was no head injury?' She didn't even try to pretend she wasn't disappointed.

'Quite the opposite. If the fumes hadn't killed

him, the head trauma would have. He's got a massive comminuted fracture.'

'Caused by?'

'A baseball bat, an iron bar . . . something blunt and heavy because the skin isn't broken.' Finch shrugged his shoulders. 'Somebody left-handed in any case.'

'How do you know that?'

'Oh, it's an old forensic trick. Right-handed people tend to strike down on the right side of their victim's head. Otherwise it's awkward and they can't get any real force into the blow. Short's skull has been crushed on the left hand side. It's a guess, but it's an educated one.' She stored that piece of information away, although she knew it would hardly narrow the search.

'So are you saying the suicide was faked?'

'You want my professional opinion? There's no way he could have even climbed into the car in that state. He was knocked out and put there and the exhaust fumes just finished him off. It was just window dressing. He was already a dead man.'

'You're sure that he was hit before the fumes got to him? There's no way that he could have got those injuries after he died?'

'No way.' Finch shook his head firmly. 'The cerebral vessels had bled into the brain causing a massive subdural haematoma. That could only have happened prior to death while he still had a pulse.'

Jennifer nodded. So it was murder. This would have Corbett bouncing off the walls. She felt herself smiling and guiltily tried to suppress it.

'Thank you, Doctor.'

'Not at all. Now if you'll excuse me, I have to go and finish up.' He shook her hand, his skin cold and rubbery from the gloves.

'Doctor,' Jennifer called after him, trying to sound as casual as she could. 'At this stage I think it would be better if you don't release the autopsy results to the family. You know how it is. Until we are sure exactly what happened, I don't want people jumping to the wrong conclusions.'

Finch shrugged his shoulders.

'Sure. No problem.' He helped himself to a fresh set of gloves and then strode back into the autopsy room, leaving Jennifer staring pensively at the tiled floor. This opened up a whole new angle on the Fort Knox theft – an angle she was determined to pursue.

Finch suddenly stepped back into the room, his gloves half-on, and interrupted her thoughts.

'By the way, Agent Browne – you did say Short had a kid, didn't you?'

'Yes, three of them. Why?'

'It's just that one reason you might put someone on the back seat is that you can't open the rear doors from the inside if the child-lock is turned on.'

TWENTY

Prospect, Kentucky
23rd July – 1:33pm

Liberty Street in the optimistically-named Louisville suburb of Prospect had been given a particularly vicious dose of anonymity by the local planners. Cookie-cutter clapboard houses, caged off from their neighbours by a galvanised wire fence, lined a wide road that spooled drearily into the distance. Ash trees struggled awkwardly from the ragged sidewalk at municipally specified intervals, gaps visible every so often where they had finally given up their struggle to eke out an existence from the thin soil. Trashcans were chained to gateposts; cars sagged mournfully on concrete driveways.

In the distance a large water tower supported by four improbably spindly steel legs reared into the sky like a huge insect. It had once been painted red, although the paint had long since blistered and peeled, rust now chewing into every joint and rivet. A single name, ECKLEBERG, painted in three feet high white letters, circled the tank, an early advertising gimmick whose purpose had long since been forgotten. Down the road, a few kids were practising skateboard tricks.

Jennifer stood outside the house and waited, fanning her face with her FBI badge as the sun's rays ricocheted off the ground. According to Short's file, he'd joined the Mint Police after five years with the NYPD. He'd been an exemplary officer, winning the Medal of Honour when responding to a reported break-in at an Upper West Side pharmacy.

His partner had been shot and while trying to save him, Short had returned fire, killing one suspect and wounding another. He'd been set for big things, maybe even Captain one day, some had said. But apparently this incident and the unpredictable hours required of New York's finest had finally taken their toll on Mrs Short who had demanded that he either find a new job or a new wife.

Her brother was already in the Mint Police and had arranged the interviews. With his record, Short had sailed through the selection process, although it had been noted that Short had been heard to complain to some of his colleagues that he was being made to swap his gun for a nightstick. He'd been given a choice of postings and had chosen Fort Knox so they'd be near his wife's family. That was pretty much it.

To understand why Short had been killed, she had to try and understand him; who he was, where he lived. She could see from the outside that the Shorts had done their best with the little they had. The symmetrical window frames had been painted light blue to match the mailbox at the end of the driveway, the wood bubbling now with age in a few places. The porch had been recently swept, while round the side she could make out a toy-strewn back yard.

The front yard was neat and low maintenance. No trash. The kerb stone had been painted with the house number, yellow against the grey concrete – 1026. The garage stood to the left, a separate building with a pitched roofline and white wooden walls to match the main house. She remembered with a half-smile that she had played in a very similar yard of a very similar house with her sister Rachel when she was a kid. There was love here amid the ugliness.

A white patrol car with a blue stripe emblazoned down its side pulled up onto the kerb and a short uniformed man with wiry ginger hair got out and nodded at her.

'Agent Browne?' he asked uncertainly, leaning over the roof, one leg still in the foot well of the car. Jennifer didn't answer, instead just flipping her ID open and waving it at him impatiently.

'You're late.'

'Yes ma'am. My apologies.' He walked up to her, his hand extended, a concerned look on his freckled face. 'I was way over on the other side of town when they told me that . . .'

'That's okay, Officer . . . ?' Jennifer looked down to his name badge as she was shaking his hand. '. . . Seeley. You're here now.'

'Bill Seeley. Louisville Metro Police Department,' he said earnestly, his large blue eyes widening, thin lips flattening across uneven teeth, ears like a car that's had both its doors left open. Jennifer smiled, his fresh-faced eagerness making her feel suddenly old. She knew the type. Diligent, conscientious and kind but unlikely ever to set the world on fire. For this part of the world, ideal. She looked up at the house behind her.

'So this is it?'

'Yes ma'am.'

'How long had Short lived here?'

'These past five years. Nice kids and wife. Real friendly with me and the other boys. He was an ex-cop himself, you see. Used to speak about it all the time. I reckon he missed the big city.'

'Tell me again what happened.' Jennifer's eyes were drawn to the garage and she had to force herself to snatch them away and concentrate on Seeley's voice.

'The eldest, Tony Junior, found him in the garage. TJ's a smart kid. On the football team too.

He dialled 911 and when the call came through I drove straight over.'

'What about Mrs Short?'

'Debbie? At work. Tony worked shifts and they took it in turns with the kids in the summer.'

'Any other witnesses see anything?'

'Nope.'

'So what d'you do when you got here?'

'Well, the kids were screaming and crying. One of the neighbours came by and she took them home with her. I opened the garage door and turned the engine off real quick, you know, to get the smoke out. Tony, I mean Mr Short, had run a hose or something from the exhaust in through the window.'

'And you're sure he was buckled in?'

'Oh yeah. In the back seat like I said. I got him out the car and tried to give him CPR, but he was gone. I did what I could.'

She could see that Seeley was still upset, perhaps thinking that if he'd got there sooner he maybe could have saved him. She knew that it was always harder if you knew the victim. It gave death a personal edge, as if you'd betrayed some unspoken agreement to look out for each other.

'Don't worry, Officer,' said Jennifer as she turned to face him, 'you did the right thing. Believe me, by the time you got here, he was already dead. There was nothing you could have done.'

He smiled gratefully.

'Well . . . then I radioed back in and they sent the coroner to collect the body. I would have gone to tell Debbie myself, but I had to deal with the fire, so one of the other guys went over. I heard she took it pretty bad.' He shook his head, his lips compressed in sympathy. Jennifer shot him a questioning look.

'The fire. What fire?'

'Oh you know these damn kids,' he nodded down the road where one of the children was nursing a sprained wrist where he had just fallen. 'We get a lot of problems round here. There's not a whole lot for them to do apart from hang round the malls or make trouble. There's a field out back and someone had set fire to a bunch of trash.'

'On the same day?' Jennifer fired the question at Seeley, her eyes locking with his.

'Yeah.' He cleared his throat nervously. 'The neighbour was worried about it spreading, what with the hot weather we've been having an' all. Why? I do something wrong?'

Jennifer didn't answer. She was already making her way past the side of the house, through the yard and the upturned pink bicycle lying in the middle of the path and out through the back gate. She didn't believe in coincidences.

Seeley had been generous when he had described it as a field. In reality it was a desolate scrap of wasteland, a lunar landscape of yellowing weeds and dry brown earth dotted with rusting refrigerators and burnt out cars that separated the houses from the ugly weal of the interstate in the distance.

To the left of the gate she had just come through, in the shadow of a cypress tree, a crater perhaps ten feet across and five feet deep, one of several, scarred the earth. A large pile of ashes, charred wood and twisted metal rose from within it like a grotesque funeral pyre. Seeley came running up behind her.

'What did I say?'

Jennifer stared at him, hands on her hips.

'Don't you think it's strange, Officer, that on the very day that Tony Short committed suicide, someone lit a fire twenty yards from his house?' Seeley looked at her blankly.

'Folks light fires all the time.'

'Don't you think it's possible that before killing himself, he decided to burn something?' Jennifer stabbed her finger forcefully in the direction of the hole. Understanding flooded over Seeley's face.

'Oh, I geddit. It's just that the kids here, you know, they're always foolin' around. But yeah sure, why not?'

Jennifer approached the remains of the fire and looked into it carefully. Despite what she'd just said, she had to admit that Seeley was probably right. But then again, if someone had murdered

Short, it was just conceivable that they had started the fire to destroy the murder weapon or some other piece of evidence. Either way, she had to be sure.

'Give me a hand.' She jumped down into the hole and stepped into the ashes, grey and white flecks rising around her ankles like flies around fruit on a summer's day. Seeley scrambled down to help and together they moved several large pieces of wood out the way, until Seeley breathed in sharply.

'What the hell's that?' Out of the ashes, a large metal object had appeared, its sides blackened, rusted and twisted where it had buckled under the heat.

'I have no idea,' said Jennifer. 'Here, help me move it.'

They dragged the object out of the middle of the crater, clouds of dust and ashes billowing around their heads, making them cough and their eyes stream.

It seemed to be some sort of large metal container. It had two compartments, the upper one being nothing more than a shallow tray accessible under the top lid, while the much larger lower one was reached from a panel on the side. Both compartments were empty.

And then she noticed it.

On one side, where the silver paint had almost all peeled away, she could just about make it out;

a ghostly signature that the heat had not quite been able to erase. The US Treasury seal.

The sight triggered a memory of where she'd seen a similar container before. Inside Fort Knox.

TWENTY-ONE

Saint-Germain-en-Laye, Northwest of Paris
23rd July – 7:00pm

The ground had already been beaten into a muddy pulp by a steady procession of heavy trucks and earth moving equipment. The air reverberated with the roar of diesel engines, the whine of hydraulics and the steady chatter of an unseen pneumatic drill. In the distance a crane was being assembled, while closer to the road, temporary accommodation units were being hoisted into place, the operation overseen by a group of three men wearing fluorescent jackets.

Catching sight of the yellow Bentley as it drew up, one of the men broke away from the group and hurried over to the car, holding onto his hardhat as it wobbled on his head. He waited for the chauffeur to step round and open the door before peering in.

'Mr Van Simson. We weren't expecting you until tomorrow.'

'Next time I'll book an appointment,' said Van Simson as he stepped out the car, black Wellington boots over his pale brown trousers, a light blue jumper tied around his shoulders over a white shirt. The chauffeur offered him a bright yellow hardhat which he ignored. 'Where's Legrand?'

'Overseeing the foundation work in sector three.' The man pointed behind him. 'I can take you over.'

'No need. Get back to work.'

Van Simson indicated with his head for his chauffeur to follow him. He set off up the hill, stepping carefully over the treacherous tyre furrows that in some places were over a foot deep.

His phone rang.

'Charles?' Van Simson snapped. 'I hope you've got good news.'

'I'm afraid not. Ranieri's dead. Has been for over a week. Murdered. Cops have been trying to keep a lid on it.'

Van Simson stopped and six feet behind him the chauffeur stopped too and waited.

'So where's the coin?' Van Simson hissed.

'I don't know,' came the nervous reply.

'You don't know? What about the priest's apartment?'

He set off again and the chauffeur followed.

'We already did that. There was nothing there.

He must have stashed them somewhere else. The cops are all over it now.'

'Damn you, Charles,' Van Simson spat. 'This is your fault. You were too slow. Someone else got to him first.' He kicked a clod of earth and it sailed through the air ahead of him.

'Darius, don't you think you've taken this far enough? This coin business has got out of control.'

'When I want your advice, I'll ask you,' Van Simson snapped back. 'I'll have taken it far enough when I have those coins.'

Van Simson stabbed the off button on the phone and stuffed it angrily into his trouser pocket.

'Damn!' he muttered to himself.

Ahead of him, two men were holding up an architectural drawing, one at each end. A large cement mixer behind them was pouring cement into a deep trench that had been cut into the soil.

'Legrand?' Van Simson called over the clatter of the mixer's revolving drum. One of the men dropped his end of the plan and it scrolled shut as if on a spring.

'Monsieur Van Simson. I wasn't expecting you until . . .'

'I know, I know,' Van Simson interrupted him with a wave. 'Are you still on schedule?'

'Ahead, even,' Legrand said proudly. 'We'll have completed Phase One by the end of the month. By Christmas, we'll be ready to start erecting the steelwork.'

'And that other thing?'

'Taken care of.' Legrand nodded towards the trench.

Van Simson walked towards it, the concrete oozing against the brown earth, steel rods surging out of the glutinous grey mass. He stood at the edge for a few seconds, then bent down and scooped up a handful of soil. He paused, then scattered it onto the wet concrete, the dark earth speckling the surface.

'Well, he did say he wanted to be buried here with his ancestors.'

TWENTY-TWO

Dept. of the Treasury, Washington DC
25th July – 08:52am
People walked past them, their footsteps echoing down the brightly-lit basement corridor like a long, slow handclap. Important-looking people with badges and passes and files, walking to and from secret meetings with secret people discussing secret things.

Jennifer knew she should feel nervous. After all, they had both spent the whole of the previous day and most of the night since she got back from Kentucky preparing for this meeting and she was stepping right into the firing line. But in a strange way she was actually looking forward to it. They had some answers. For the first time since this had all began, they actually had some answers.

'Okay, now remember what I told you,' Corbett broke the silence. 'Keep it short and stick to the script. No heroics.' He spoke quickly and quietly, his voice slightly anxious.

'Don't worry,' she said, smiling. 'I got it.'

While Jennifer had been down in Kentucky, Corbett had had a team down at Fort Knox itself going over every scrap of paper and every inch of the security system. Rigby, still in a state of shock, had let them in, unplugged his phone, locked his office door and left them to it. Their time had been well spent, since what they had discovered tied into Jennifer's own findings.

'Do you mind?'

'What?'

She reached forward and smoothed his collar down where it had bent back on itself.

'Thanks,' he smiled. 'This is going to be a tough crowd. I just want you to put on as good a show as I know you can, that's all. These people, they don't do excuses, just results.'

'Oh shit!' Jennifer rolled her eyes. 'Come on, you might as well tell me. What are we dealing with here? Major League assholes or Minor League bureaucrats?'

'As far as I know a bit of both. Director Green, Mint Director Brady and apparently that two-faced son-of-a-bitch John Piper from the NSA.'

'The NSA?' Jennifer was startled. This was way below their normal radar. 'What's it got to do with them?'

'I guess we'll find out,' said Corbett grimly. 'You

come across Piper before?' Jennifer shook her head. 'He's a real piece of work. Twenty years with the Agency going nowhere. Then his family donated five million bucks to the new President's election campaign, and suddenly he's rubbing shoulders with the Pentagon top brass and making up for lost time.'

'Do you think they want to muscle in?'

Corbett gave her a reassuring look.

'No. They just want to hear what we know. D'you get some sleep last night?'

'A bit.'

Corbett's eyes softened just a fraction.

'You know, if this is all too much I can always reassign someone to help.'

She shot him an indignant look.

'No way. I'm doing just fine on my own. When I need a monkey on my back I'll let you know.'

He smiled.

'Just checking.'

The door opposite them opened and a man appeared, his brown hair slicked into a vertical salute, his eyes squinting out from a sunken, pallid face. He was in shirt sleeves, his charcoal pants pulled too high around his waist so that his nylon-clad ankles could be seen peeking out between his shoes and trouser legs. He smiled thinly at Bob and ignored Jennifer.

'Corbett.'

'Piper.' Corbett nodded back.

'Looks like you're on, sport.'

Swapping a look, they both plunged into the room behind him.

TWENTY-THREE

09:00am

It was not a large room – but at fifty feet underground, it was one of the most secure in the building. The sound-proofing gave it a strange, deadened feel, while the acrid smell of industrial disinfectant caught in the back of Jennifer's throat and immediately brought back graphic memories of Dr Finch's mortuary down in Louisville.

Four people were sitting around three sides of a rectangular glass table, from where they had a clear view of the white projector screen that took up most of the furthest wall. Two vinyl and steel chairs had been set aside for them next to FBI Director Green. The lights had been dimmed, giving everyone's face a slightly haunted look.

'We have just been joined by Special Agents Corbett and Browne,' said Green. 'As you know,

Bob heads up our Major Theft and Transportation Crimes Unit. He and Agent Browne have been working this case from day one.'

Piper flashed Jennifer an uninterested look as Green said her name.

'Okay, now we're all here, let's get started.' A bald man with a thick neck and a boxer's hard, worn and squashed face was clearly in charge. He stood up and leant across the table on his fists, the sleeves of his striped shirt rolled up above his elbows, his biceps bulging, the catch of his gold Rolex straining. He was chewing a piece of gum as he talked, pausing every so often as he spoke to work his jaws around it.

'For those of you who don't know me,' he continued in his lazy Texas drawl, looking directly at Jennifer and Corbett as he spoke, 'Ah'm Treasury Secretary Scott Young.'

Jennifer had recognised him immediately, of course. A recent Presidential appointee, Young had moved from the boardroom of one of Wall Street's most aggressive investment banks to his new position – his plain-speaking, no-holds-barred reputation going with him.

'The President has personally asked me to chair this meeting,' he continued. 'To put it politely, he is mighty pissed.'

Jennifer looked at the silent faces around the table. Green was sitting on Young's left hand side, stuffed as normal into an ill-fitting three-piece suit, sausage fingers twirling a pen, dyed brown hair over a round red face.

Piper was to Young's right and although Jennifer didn't recognise the person sitting next to him, she assumed that he must be Mint Director Chris Brady. He had a wide, oval face with hollow cheeks and sagging skin and wore an ill-fitting wig. His staring brown eyes sheltered behind thick tortoiseshell glasses. He, too, had removed his suit jacket and his dark blue polyester tie ballooned over a paler blue shirt.

As he sat there, nervously twisting the remnants of a polystyrene disposable cup between his nicotine-stained fingers, he kept reaching up and tapping his knuckles against his forehead as if trying to remember something. As the official with immediate responsibility for Fort Knox, she guessed he was feeling the heat more than the others.

'Fort Knox has been robbed, ladies and gentlemen.' Young continued, still chewing away. 'Not the local five and dime. Fort Knox. One of this nation's most heavily guarded facilities. And we didn't even know about it!' He slammed his fist down on the table. 'Now Mr Piper's colleagues are telling the President that it's only a matter of time before someone snatches one of our nukes. Ah have to say, for once Ah find it hard to disagree.' He stood up straight now, a stocky five foot nine with his shoes on. 'Hell, after this, Ah wouldn't be surprised if the President walks into the Oval Office and finds the goddamned Resolute Desk gone.'

Green looked down and shuffled his papers so as to avoid Young's accusing stare.

'Now, Ah've convinced the President that this is a Treasury matter. He's agreed to leave it to me to resolve internally with FBI help given that they were the ones who popped the lid on this in the first place. And he's told the military and the CIA to back off. For now. But from what Ah've seen so far, everyone's more concerned with covering their own asses than finding out what happened and we're all running out of time. What Ah need now are some answers and Ah need them fast. Jack, what have your people got?'

Green nodded at Corbett, who flashed Jennifer an encouraging look. She stood up in front of the large white screen and cleared her throat.

'Gentlemen. As you know, nine days ago a rare 1933 Double Eagle was discovered in the stomach of an Italian priest in Paris.' The photos of Ranieri that Corbett had shown her a few days before flashed up on the screen behind him, together with close-ups of both sides of the coin.

'Subsequent forensic tests have shown that the coin is original and in all likelihood is one of five coins stolen from Fort Knox where they had been secretly kept in storage for the last ten or so years.'

Piper, who had been studying her performance with a smile on his face, gave a dismissive wave, picked up one of the many files spread out in front of him and shook it.

'We know all this, Browne, it's right here in the file. Tell us something new.'

Jennifer glanced at Corbett, who winked. She knew him well enough by now to know that he was thinking the same thing as her. John Piper. Major League asshole.

'Our investigation has pinpointed the likely time of the theft as between three and four am on Sunday the fourth of July,' she continued, staring defiantly at Piper as she spoke, almost willing him to take her on.

'What, just three weeks ago?' Piper shot back. 'How can you be so sure?'

Corbett took over.

'An analysis of the Depository's IT systems has shown a power surge at zero three hundred hours on that date. The power levels then remained erratic until zero four hundred hours when they returned to normal.'

The power systems check had been Corbett's idea and after consulting the Bureau's IT people, they had been in no doubt what the likely implications of their findings were.

'The tech guys are still looking into it, so at the moment it's still just a theory, but according to them the power surge seems to suggest that some sort of computer virus was loaded directly into the Depository's mainframe. It was probably programmed to wipe itself, but we've found some traces of code that suggest that it was designed to temporarily disable the security systems in the vault, without this being visible to the guards on the outside.'

'So my guys are in the clear then?' said Brady with audible relief. 'There was no way they could have known what was going on inside, right?'

Piper had a thin smile on his face, as he turned to face Corbett.

'A theory? One week on and that's all you've got, a theory? Cm'on, sport, tell me you got more than that.'

'John, let's just hear what they've got to say,' said Young cautiously.

'I know, Scott. I'm just curious, that's all. You know, like what about the cameras? Why didn't they pick something up?' Piper asked, the same aggressive tone in his voice.

'Because there are no cameras in the vault itself, sir, just around the outside perimeter,' replied Jennifer calmly. 'I believe that information is also in the file.' Piper flushed bright red. A smile flickered around the corner of Corbett's mouth.

'The vault's primary protection is to deny physical access although inside it has been equipped with a combination of infra-red beams, pressure pads, movement and heat sensors and electronic contacts.' She continued, addressing her comments almost exclusively to Young and Green now, as if Piper wasn't there. It was a dangerous game, she knew, but then she had never been very good at playing the safe, diplomatic option. If Piper was as determined to score points off her as he seemed to be, she was not going to make it any easier for him.

'None of these systems were directly tampered with and yet the coins are gone. Our view is that someone gained access to the vault, had some sort of virus temporarily disable the electronic systems and then stole the coins before the systems came back online.'

'But how did they actually get in and out?' Young had edged right forward in his seat. 'Ah heard the Treasury boys went over every inch of that facility and didn't find so much as a chip in the concrete.'

Brady nodded in agreement.

'That's right. No one could have got in or out that vault without someone or something picking them up.'

'Well . . . if no *one* could have got in, then perhaps some*thing* could have,' Corbett suggested carefully.

'What are you saying, that one of my guys let something in? That's ridiculous,' snorted Brady. 'These are highly-trained men. All of them security cleared and closely monitored. There's no way any of them would knowingly let anything in that shouldn't be there.'

Jennifer approached the screen again and a photograph flashed up onto it. It showed a confident, smiling man, about forty years old, appealingly large brown eyes set into a strong, angular face. When she'd first seen this photo, she'd found it hard to believe that this was the same man she'd seen helplessly pinned out on Finch's steel table like a butterfly on a card. Even now, she turned away, finding his accusing stare hard to stomach.

'This is Tony Short, one of the guards down at Fort Knox. Short was working the night of the fourth and had access to the security systems and the vault. We believe he was murdered seven days ago. Were he alive, then no doubt he could explain the sudden appearance of two hundred and fifty thousand dollars in his bank account three weeks ago, one day after we think the robbery took place.'

Jennifer had run a standard bank account search using Short's Social Security number and discovered the account in California. It had only been opened the day before the deposit was made. Short's wife certainly hadn't known anything about it when asked. For Jennifer, this had been the final, damning link in the chain of evidence.

'This is bullshit!' Brady exclaimed jumping to his feet. 'Why wasn't I told any of this? I'm being set up.' Young grabbed his arm, his short fat fingers levering Brady back down into his seat.

'Sit down, Chris. No one's blaming anyone. We

just want to know what happened.' He nodded at Jennifer to continue as Brady muttered angrily.

'We also found this round the back of Short's house.' A photograph of the metal container she had recovered from the bonfire flashed up on the screen and Young twisted his head onto one side as he tried to make out what it was. The image gave way to a close-up of the scarred and faded Treasury seal on its side.

'We think that this was how the thief got inside. A sort of Trojan horse.'

'Trojan what?' asked Piper. Jennifer ignored him.

'We've gone through the inventory records and it seems that on the night of the fourth, a small gold shipment turned up at the Depository at about seventeen hundred hours, just before it closed. Short was the duty officer. In fact, he'd volunteered to have his shift changed to that day. He signed it in and placed it down in the vault.'

She paused to take a sip of water from the glass on the table in front of her before continuing.

'We think that this,' she indicated the photograph again, 'was the container in which the gold was delivered. As you can see, when painted it would have looked very similar to the containers typically used for moving bullion around.'

Another photograph flashed up alongside the first one showing a silvery container of identical proportions.

'However, the container we recovered from near Short's house is different in one vital way. It contains a separate compartment accessible from the side, here.' She pointed out the side panel on the screen. 'It would have been very uncomfortable, but it is large enough for someone to get into. A small amount of gold was presumably placed in the upper compartment to make it look like the container was full in case the lid was opened.'

'This is all bullshit,' said Brady, a pleading tone in his voice now as his jacket slipped off the back of his chair and onto the floor. 'It's standard procedure to inventory every shipment in and out to make sure it's all there.'

'And the procedure was followed to the letter,' Jennifer said firmly. 'Only it was Short who was following it. According to statements from the other guards on duty that night, he insisted on personally inventorying the shipment. As the ranking officer, that was his prerogative. Once he'd okayed the contents, he had it taken down to the vault. Given that it was the Fourth of July, he told the guys who took it down that they could unpack it in the morning, so they could get home early. Short was like that, apparently. They thought nothing of it.'

'We believe,' said Corbett, picking up on Jennifer's line, 'that whoever was hiding in the container waited until a pre-agreed time when the virus had kicked in, stole the coins, re-sealed the cage they were in and then got back inside the container. The next day, again according to the inventory records, another truck turned up at zero nine hundred with a new set of paperwork claiming that a mistake had been made and that they had to take the container back to where it had come from. It all checked out and no one gave it a second thought.'

'And Short?' asked Green.

'Short? A loose end. Presumably killed to make sure he couldn't talk, the money they paid him an acceptable loss. We found the truck burnt out in a field about 80 miles away. No forensics, not even a serial number on the engine block. Whoever we're dealing with here, sir, they're not taking any chances.'

'What about the gold?' asked Young. 'There's billions of dollars down there. Why didn't they take any of that?'

'Mainly because if these coins are really worth forty million, then the equivalent amount of bullion would weigh about three and a half tons,' Corbett replied. 'These people, whoever they are, they're professionals. They knew exactly what they were looking for and where to find it and they didn't let themselves get distracted.'

'Thank you, Agent Browne,' said Young. Corbett nodded at Jennifer to sit down next to him. 'Okay, so we may have an idea of how they did it. But that still leaves the who. Who could have done this to us? . . . Any ideas? . . . Anyone?' He looked expectantly around the table.

'The Mafia?' Green ventured. 'Or someone in the Far East, maybe the Triads?'

'Or Cassius?'

As Corbett had spoken there had been a sudden lull in the conversation and his voice had echoed across the room's sudden calm. Young looked at him blankly.

'Who?'

'A man; more of a shadow really,' Corbett explained slowly. 'He allegedly heads up an international crime syndicate that is involved in almost every aspect of the art and antiques underworld. We never get any closer than rumours. Every time we do, somebody dies.'

'I thought all this talk of a Captain Nemo figure, of some controlling mastermind in the art world had been ruled out,' Green interjected.

'None of the experts will talk about it, the insurance companies least of all. It would be too much for them to admit that one man can manipulate and influence the global art market. But people forget that art crime is a three billion dollar a year business.'

'Three billion dollars?' Young was clearly shocked by the number.

'It's the world's third largest area of criminal activity after drugs and arms dealing,' Corbett confirmed with a nod. 'And the really big scores don't come from stealing a work and selling it to a *new* buyer, but in stealing it and ransoming it back to the original owners. The insurers call it a finder's fee, of course, but they'd rather offer ten per cent to the thieves than pay out the full value to the owners. It happens all the time. From the consistency in how and where these jobs are financed and structured, our view is that there is a sophisticated and coordinated global operation behind the vast bulk of the high-end heists.'

'So do you think that this Cassius is involved or not?' Young leant forward in his chair. He was clearly used to dealing in Yes or No, in Buy or Sell. He wanted an answer. Corbett's answer, though, was non-committal.

'A job like this would have needed a lot of planning and funding. Not many people would have the resources to pull it off. He's definitely one of them. But even if he is behind this, he wouldn't have actually done the job himself. People like him hire others to do their dirty work. Most often, they probably don't even know they're working for him. What we need to find is the person actually in the vault. They'll lead us back to whoever set the job up and hopefully the rest of the coins.'

Piper leant towards Young and whispered something in his ear. Young, for the first time since Jennifer had been in the room, stopped chewing. He looked at Piper and whispered something back.

Piper nodded and, getting to his feet, walked to the back of the room. Here, Jennifer noticed for the first time, a large mirrored panel was set into the wall. Piper tapped on the glass and then drew his hand across his throat twice. The signal made it clear to Jennifer that this whole meeting had been taped. Now, for some reason, Piper wanted it off the record. Why?

'I think perhaps it would be appropriate for Browne and Brady to leave at this point,' Piper suggested to Young. Corbett shook his head firmly.

'Whatever is about to be said, Browne should be here. She's point on this case. Whatever I know, she knows.'

Piper looked at Young questioningly who nodded slowly. Jennifer flashed Corbett a grateful smile, her curiosity mounting.

'Wait for me outside, Chris,' said Young.

'How come she gets to stay?' whined Brady. 'I'm being set up. I know it.'

'Just wait the hell outside,' Young snapped back. 'And leave that file here.' Muttering under his breath, Brady slapped the file down into the table, scooped up his jacket and stumbled to the door.

'Okay, John. This had better be good,' said Young. Piper blew slowly through his lips before speaking.

'On the 16th July there was a break-in at an Upper West Side apartment block. The thief abseiled down from the roof to the 17th floor, broke in and stole a nine million dollar Fabergé Egg. NYPD got lucky and found a hair sample next to the safe. They sent it to the FBI Lab in Quantico to run it through their system just in case it wasn't the maid's. They got a hit and following the on-screen protocol alerted me immediately.'

'You'd put some sort of security trigger on this guy's file?' Corbett asked.

'Yeah. Because as far as we knew, he died ten years ago.'

'But why you? What's your connection?' asked Green.

'My connection? I recruited him into the CIA fifteen years ago. His name's Tom Kirk.'

TWENTY-FOUR

09:21am

Piper reached into the slim leather briefcase that was resting against his chair leg and drew out four files, one for himself and one each for Young, Green and Corbett.

'You two will have to share.' He nodded in Jennifer's direction.

Jennifer edged her seat closer to Corbett's as he took the file and broke the paper band that was wrapped round it with his hand, the seal ripping right between the words 'TOP' and 'SECRET'. Corbett opened the file, revealing some loose-leaf black and white photos and a thick wedge of bound documents.

'These photos were taken yesterday in London by the CIA. They show Tom Kirk, or as we knew him, Thomas Duval. Caucasian male, thirty-five years old, five foot eleven, no distinguishing features.'

Jennifer studied the photos. Even though the images were slightly blurred, she could see that Tom was an athletic looking man, with a strong jaw and striking, intelligent eyes.

'He has dual British and US citizenship from his parents Charles and Rebecca Kirk. Both parents are now deceased, the mother in an MVA when Kirk was thirteen and the father earlier this year in a climbing accident in Switzerland.'

Jennifer looked up and saw Corbett eyeing Piper with a strange look, as if he suspected that this was leading some place that he'd rather not go.

'Following his mother's death, Duval was sent to live with his mother's family in Boston, while his father moved to Geneva.'

'Boston?' Green queried. 'Any relation to Trent Duval?' Piper nodded.

'He's Senator Duval's nephew. That was another factor in his favour when we recruited him. After high school he won a scholarship to Oxford but was kicked out after a year and moved to Paris. That's where I met him.'

'You were stationed in Paris?' asked Corbett with surprise.

'Three years. Normal diplomatic cover.' Piper confirmed with a nod. 'I met Duval through a guy we had on the staff of the Sorbonne. He had signed up to an Art History course. He was ideal material for us. Young, single, highly intelligent, no real family ties, looking for something to believe in. It took a while but I reeled him in. We put him through the Farm and then gave him some more specialist training for the program we'd recruited him for.'

'Which was?' asked Green.

'Industrial espionage. Codename Operation Centaur.'

'Industrial espionage?' Green repeated in disbelief.

'Computer files, blueprints, photos of prototypes, chemical formulae – you name it. The Europeans have been accelerating their efforts to reduce their reliance on US and Japanese defence, technology and biotech suppliers for years. Their investment was beginning to tell, costing us billions of dollars of lost revenue a year, not to mention potentially undermining our own national security. Duval and others like him were the cutting edge of our efforts to ensure we didn't lose out.'

'Jesus Christ,' muttered Green. 'I thought they were meant to be our allies.'

'Duval was the best agent we had. There wasn't a safe or a security system he couldn't deal with. And he blended in. He spoke five languages, had read the right books, knew the right people, could get an "in" to anywhere he wanted. None of the agents we'd recruited in the States could do that. It gave him a real edge.'

'So what happened to him?' Green again.

'About five years in, he went bad.'

'What do you mean, bad?' Corbett now.

'Refused to take orders, started behaving errati-cally, backed out of jobs. We tried to bring him in but he refused. Said he was working for himself from now on. Then he went right off the reser-vation and murdered his handler. After that, he just dropped off the grid.'

'But you said you thought he was dead.' Green again.

'A year later Interpol provided a DNA sample of a man the French police had shot dead trying to break into the Ministry of Finance. It matched Duval's. By then the whole operation had been shut down anyway, so we just closed his file and stopped looking.'

'But you still tagged his DNA profile,' said Corbett. 'You weren't convinced?'

'Let's just say I had my doubts. Duval was too good to get caught out in the open by a bunch of cops. But that's all they were. Doubts. I tagged his profile just in case and then forgot about it until a few days ago.'

'So what the hell happened to him?' Young replaced the gum in his mouth with a fresh piece, folding it between his teeth with a single, podgy finger.

'Interpol suspect that Duval, or Kirk as he apparently now calls himself again, has been oper-ating as an art thief for the past ten years based out of London. Goes by the name of Felix. They rate him as the best in the game.'

'What makes him so good?' Young again.

'*We* trained him for a start. And let me tell you, the guy's a real pro. Believe it or not, most art thefts are carried out opportunistically by small-time criminals who don't really know what they're doing. They just see something on a wall and grab it.' Corbett nodded in a rare show of agreement. 'Kirk's smart. He focuses on jewellery which can be re-cut or on B-list artists that don't attract so much publicity and so can be more easily sold on. And over the years either he, or someone working with him, has somehow assembled a network of private collectors who are prepared to pay big money for the right items and don't ask questions about where they've come from.'

There was a pause as everyone let this new information sink in. Then Young asked the question that was in all their minds.

'Knocking off a museum is one thing. Hitting a government installation – well, that's a whole different ball game. What makes you think he's involved in the Fort Knox job?'

Piper shrugged.

'I know this guy. He always liked the difficult, spectacular jobs. A job like this has got his name all over it.'

'I think we're going to need a bit more than

gut feel,' Corbett observed dryly. 'You got anything solid to back this up?'

Piper nodded firmly.

'Canadian INS have a record of a Mr Felix Duval flying into Montreal from Geneva on June 28th, one week prior to the date you've just given us. You think that name and the timing and the fact that his DNA showed up in New York is all a big coincidence? He hit Fort Knox, then stopped off on Fifth Avenue for a bit of shopping. He's laughing at us.'

'Jesus, how could you guys let something like this happen? One of our own people ripping us off!'

Piper responded swiftly.

'As far as anyone outside this room is concerned none of this did happen. So we're going to have to handle this investigation very carefully.'

'What are you hiding, John?' Corbett asked, his head angled quizzically to one side. 'What aren't you telling us?'

'Oh, fuck!' Young, who had been frowning into the desk for the past few minutes as if trying to remember something, gasped, the colour draining from his face. 'You said you recruited this guy fifteen years ago, didn't you?'

'Yeah,' Piper answered.

'Wasn't . . . ?' Young raised his thin blond eyebrows into a question.

'That's my point,' said Piper with a nod of his head.

'Wasn't what?' asked Jennifer looking from Young to Piper and then back again.

'Wasn't the President the Director of the CIA back then?' Corbett said tonelessly.

'Good God.' Green had gone an even deeper shade of red than normal.

'You can imagine the diplomatic shit storm if this gets out. He wouldn't survive. I doubt many of us would.' Piper made eye contact with every person around the table, even Jennifer. 'I can't allow that to happen.'

For the first time, Jennifer saw a flicker of fear in Piper's eyes. His family had bet big on the President winning the election and Piper was already reaping the benefits. Now, he was faced with the possibility of it all crumbling away underneath him. She savoured the moment.

'So what are you suggesting?' asked Green. 'That we just drop the whole thing?'

'No, of course not.' Piper shook his head emphatically. 'We can't just drop a criminal investigation. Not without making the situation a whole lot worse. I'm just saying we gotta be real careful. If the coins lead to Kirk then Kirk could be traced back to Centaur. We need to find a way to make sure that doesn't happen.'

'So what *are* you suggesting?' Corbett insisted.

'That we offer Kirk some sort of deal. Return the four coins he still has, tell us who commissioned the theft and promise to keep his mouth shut and we'll wipe his file clean, and forget what he did to us all those years ago. From then on, as far as we're concerned, Thomas Duval or Kirk or whatever he wants to call himself never existed. The whole issue of the President's involvement just won't come up.'

'Think he'll go for it?' Green asked sceptically.

'Kirk plays the percentages. Always has. He must have spent every day for the past ten years wondering if the next knock at his door was going to be us finally catching up with him. This is a one-time offer to start over. Yeah, he'll go for it.'

'Well, it sure works for me,' Young confirmed with a nod and a smack of gum against teeth. 'This way, everyone wins. This administration's looking good for a second term. Ah don't want to be the guy who screws that up.'

'Then there's no time to lose, Mr Secretary,' said Corbett, his voice strained and urgent. 'We recovered one coin by chance. The longer we leave it, the harder the others will be to track down. We need to get someone over to London to get Kirk onside.'

'Agreed.' Young nodded. 'Who do you have in mind?'

TWENTY-FIVE

Dulles International Airport, Washington DC
25th July – 9:30pm

As the plane taxied out to the runway, Jennifer settled back into her seat and closed her eyes. She had a long flight ahead and knew she ought to try and get some sleep, but her mind was racing. The moment that Corbett had suggested to Young that she be the person sent to strike a deal with Kirk kept coming back into her head.

'We should send Agent Browne, Mr Secretary.'

There had been a moment's silence before Piper had punctured it with a hollow laugh. Jennifer had been tempted to join in but the look on Corbett's face had told her he was deadly serious.

'Browne. I don't think so.'

'Why not?' Corbett had fired back.

'You want me to spell it out?'

'If you've got something to say, then I think we should all hear it.'

Piper had swallowed and his eyes had flicked to Jennifer's and then down to the table before he answered.

'We all know what happened three years ago.' He tapped his finger on one of the three files spread out in front of him. Straining to read their covers upside down, Jennifer could just about make out her name on one of them. Clearly Piper had done his homework. 'We need someone we can rely on. Someone who won't crack under pressure. We can't take the risk of another . . . accident. There's too much riding on this.'

'Mr Secretary,' Corbett snorted. 'We also all know that the inquiry into the shooting that Browne was involved in absolved her of any blame. Her performance since then, and in this investigation in particular, has been faultless.'

'It's too much of a risk,' Piper had insisted. 'She's too inexperienced.'

Jennifer willed herself not to blurt out something she might regret, although it was against every instinct she had to let Corbett fight her corner for her.

'Besides,' Piper continued, 'this is Agency business, nothing to do with the FBI.'

'My view, Mr Secretary,' said Corbett, again ignoring Piper and speaking directly to Young, 'is that tactically it would be better to adopt a low-key approach. We want to win Kirk over, not scare him. Using the FBI shows that our focus is on the

Fort Knox robbery, not his past misdemeanours. Using Agency personnel might suggest a broader agenda and link back to Centaur. I maintain that Browne would do an excellent job.'

'Jack?' Young had nodded towards Green.

'If Bob's happy that's good enough for me,' Green said shrugging.

Young suddenly turned to Jennifer, his question startling her.

'What do you think, Agent Browne?'

'I . . . I think that Mr Piper's right,' Jennifer said slowly, measuring her words carefully. 'I made a mistake and somebody died and that's something I'm going to have to live with for the rest of my life. But I'm a good agent, sir. I get results.' She threw Piper a defiant look. 'You put me out there and you won't be disappointed because I'm not a quitter. I'm a fighter.'

'Ah do believe you are,' Young had turned towards Jennifer, stretched out his hand and smiled for the first time since she had been in the room. 'Make us proud, Agent Browne.'

With a final lurch, the plane leapt into the air, breaking into her thoughts and she shifted uncomfortably in her seat, gripping the armrests with both hands as the customary wave of panic washed over her. It was funny, this was the sort of chance she'd been dreaming about, fighting for these last few years, and now she had it, she felt almost as apprehensive as she was excited. It was a big chance and she couldn't afford to screw it up.

Kirk's file was on her lap and was primarily made up of pooled intelligence reports from Interpol and various national police forces. Overall it was pretty sketchy. Rumours of jobs he'd done, details of people he had allegedly worked for or with, but nothing certain. From one perspective it all added up to nothing, a flimsy web of innuendo, half-truths and gossip that collapsed as soon as it was subjected to any form of detailed scrutiny.

And yet from another perspective, when viewed as a whole, it all knitted together to form the damning and compelling biography of a master criminal, a true professional, who used a choking glut of misinformation to shroud his movements and cloud the judgement of his adversaries. But how to separate the fact from the fiction, the myth from the man when a constant haze of rumour and suspicion dogged his every step?

Corbett, though, was trying to set up a meeting with somebody he thought might help cut through the fog. Someone who'd cooperated with him before on a previous case. Her mind reached for his name. Harry something. Harry Renquist? No, Harry Renwick, that was it. According to Corbett, not only was he a coin expert who could help with the case, but as Piper had confirmed, he also happened to know Kirk well through having worked with his father. If Corbett could try and engineer a meeting between them all, it would be a chance to confront Kirk on home turf and hopefully catch him off his guard. He certainly wouldn't see that one coming. She smiled at the thought.

As the plane levelled out and the fasten seatbelt signs pinged off, she glanced around the cabin, taking in the usual assortment of diplomats, journalists and lobbyists that formed the bulk of the daily DC to London business class traffic.

She closed her eyes again and her mind circled back to the one thing that had been troubling her and that no one, to her surprise, had thought to ask. If this robbery had been so meticulously planned and executed, if Kirk really was so good, how had one coin ended up in a corpse on the other side of the world two weeks later?

Clearly something had gone very wrong.

TWENTY-SIX

St James', London
26th July – 11:28am

Normally Jermyn Street, perched between the hustle of Pall Mall and the bustle of Piccadilly, peddled its own unique sepia-coloured version of a long-vanished England. It spoke of country house picnics, of interminable games of cricket played out on village greens by players dressed in whites, of blazers and bowlers and tweeds, of a dry sense of humour and wet summers, of warm beer supped around a blazing pub fire. Of a green and pleasant land.

On this hot and dusty afternoon, however, it had been transformed into a sweaty bazaar of tourists and lunchtime shoppers that shouted and haggled and cursed and spat as convincingly as in any Middle Eastern souk. Shop windows beckoned the passing crowds like pushy merchants, proclaiming their wares with mosaics of outrageously coloured and patterned shirts. Carefully arranged fountains of ties shot up into the air only to fall into still pools of silk handkerchiefs.

On the right, a beggar, slumped in the doorway to a personal shopping agency, sung and swore, his upturned hat outstretched. Most chose not to see him. On the left, the chauffeur of a large black Jaguar waiting patiently outside Wilton's was bartering with an unsmiling traffic warden, the ticket already half written.

Walking through this evocative pageant, his jacket slung over his shoulder, Tom turned, almost without thinking, into the Piccadilly Arcade, a marbled oasis of delicately curved windows crammed with shoes, waistcoats and ties, until he found himself outside his favourite shop, on the right, about half way up.

Tom loved watches. It had always been a passion of his. Most often, like today, he wore the 1957 Jaeger Le Coultre Memovox that his mother had left him. It was not the most valuable watch he owned, but to Tom it was certainly the most precious. That was where his fascination had started, he now knew.

He leaned forward, looking through first the left hand, then the right hand window, his eyes running jealously over their carefully arranged contents, laid out on green velvet like precious jewels. No prices, of course. He stood, oblivious to the people swarming past behind him, until the sudden musky smell of a woman's perfume shook him out of his reverie.

'Beautiful, isn't it.' Her voice was soft, the American accent unmistakeable, and out of the corner of his eye he could see her motioning with her head towards the Rolex 'Paul Newman' Daytona that he was looking at.

'But if you want a Rolex, you're much better going with one of the Princes. Smoother movement and far less . . . obvious.' She again made a small movement with her head, pointing out the sleek lines of the Prince's 1930s oblong stainless steel case.

Tom stood up straight and turned to face the woman. She was beautiful. Slender with a delicate brown face and full lips, lustrous hazel eyes framed by a close cut mass of black curly hair. The woman smiled back. He wondered for a second whether she was a pro trying to pick him up. But her shoes seemed too new, her skirt too formal. No. She was something else altogether.

'Are you a collector?' he asked warily.

'No.' She smiled. 'I worked on a case once where I had to learn a bit about them.'

'A case? You're a lawyer then?'

'Not exactly. I work for the government. The US government.'

In a way, Tom had been preparing himself for this moment for the last ten years – for when they finally found him. Occasionally, during that time, he had almost managed to convince himself that they might never come. He realized now that he should have known better. 'I take it then, that this isn't a chance meeting, Miss . . . ?'

'Browne. Jennifer Browne. And no, it isn't.' She held out her hand to shake his but Tom ignored it. 'Perhaps we could go some somewhere and talk? I need to ask you some questions.'

'What about?'

'Not here.'

The initial shock passed, Tom's mind was racing as he considered what to do. Run perhaps, although the two bulky figures pretending to window-shop at either end of the arcade and blocking his escape route would complicate that option. Or maybe, if he really was going to move on, try and settle this once and for all. He couldn't keep running forever.

'I know a place,' he muttered eventually. 'It's not far.'

TWENTY-SEVEN

11:42am

Tom and Jennifer walked down Piccadilly in silence, allowing themselves to be carried along by the smooth muscle of the masses, red buses trundling cheerfully past. Here and there, black umbrellas, incongruous in the summer sun, were held above the crowds by tour reps, makeshift buoys for their youthful charges to navigate to their next 'must-see' destination.

Tom had a much more willowy and delicate build up close than in the photos Jennifer had seen – he walked with careful steps his movements precise and controlled like a cat negotiating a narrow ledge, expending the exact amount of energy and control to get where he wanted. He was also, she had to admit, a handsome man, his high cheekbones and square jaw giving his face a slightly sculpted look, his eyes alert and an incredibly deep blue.

Reaching the Criterion restaurant at Piccadilly Circus, hamburger wrappers and Spanish school kids swirling around their feet, they cut themselves adrift from the crowds and plunged inside. Here, the noise of the traffic gave way to an animated babble that bounced gaily off the restaurant's gaudy mosaic walls and ceilings in five different languages. A harassed-looking Italian waiter showed them to a table and took their order – a vodka tonic for Tom, a mineral water for Jennifer.

There was a silence until Tom spoke.

'So, Agent Browne? It is *Agent* Browne, isn't it?' The waiter reappeared with their drinks.

'*Special* Agent Browne, actually. FBI.' Tom tilted his head as if he hadn't quite heard right.

'FBI?'

'Uh-huh.'

He sipped his drink, looking pensive. The ice settled, caressed by the soft fizz of the bubbles.

'Aren't you a bit out of your jurisdiction here, Special Agent Browne?'

'Oh, when it comes to the big fish we stretch the net pretty wide these days.'

'Is that right?'

'You see, I'm here to help you,' she said firmly.

Tom sat back and pushed his glass away from him.

'I didn't realise I needed helping.'

'Most people don't until it's too late. You're in a lot of trouble, Mr Kirk.'

'That's news to me.'

'There are some old friends of yours back at Langley who are just dying to catch up with you.'

Tom shrugged.

'Langley? Sorry, that's not ringing any bells.'

'And I'm sure the NYPD would love to discuss how one of your hairs ended up on the floor of that apartment you dropped in on ten days ago.'

Jennifer studied his face for a reaction, some glimmer of realisation, of guilt, however slight. But she saw nothing.

'You're wasting your time.'

'Don't screw around.' Jennifer raised her voice ever so slightly. 'I know what you do, who you are . . . Felix or Duval or whatever you call yourself these days.'

There was a pause as Tom looked at her, his face inscrutable, his right hand moving his glass around in tight wet circles where the condensation had run down onto the table.

'Why are you really here, Agent Browne?'

'I've come to offer you a deal.'

Tom gave a wry smile.

'That's easy, then. Whatever you're selling, I don't want it.'

'You sure? If they've sent me all the way over here it's because they're serious. Maybe you should hear me out.'

'What for? More lies? You've got nothing I could ever want. Have a good flight home.'

'I'm talking about a fresh start, Mr Kirk. I'm talking about wiping your file clean.' Tom had stood up to leave but Jennifer's urgent tone seemed to stop him in his tracks. 'The CIA forget about you. We forget about you. The last fifteen years just never happened. Think about it.'

Tom studied her for a few moments and then sat back down.

'What's the catch?'

He frowned.

'No catch. We just want the coins back.'

'The coins?'

'And the name of whoever paid you to steal them. You do that and you'll never hear from us again.'

Tom nodded thoughtfully and resumed the circling with his glass, slowly extending the edges of the wet patch on the table.

'There's only one problem with your deal,' he said eventually.

'What's that?'

'I haven't got a clue what you're talking about.'

'Don't play games.' Jennifer spoke with an icy edge to her voice now. 'You want me spell it out for you? Fine. We know you took the coins and we know how you did it. We want them back and the name of whoever sent you. Stand in our way and now that we've found you again, we'll make life very difficult for you. That's a promise.'

'No, let *me* spell it out for *you*.' The people at

the neighbouring table looked over disapprovingly from under their baseball caps as Tom's voice rose until he was almost shouting. 'I don't know what you're talking about. And let me give you an update. I'm out of the game now. Permanently. That's the way it is, whether you believe me or not. Now you think you got something on me, you go ahead and play that card. But I'm not taking the fall for something I know nothing about. Screwing me over will not help you find whatever it is you're looking for.'

Jennifer considered him for a moment. She had always been able to sense when people were lying. She looked for small things; involuntary twitches, hand movements, the eyes mostly. To Jennifer's surprise, all the signs that she could read pointed to Tom telling the truth. How could that be right? Even so, she continued along the lines Corbett and she had agreed.

'So you're refusing our deal?'

'What deal? I don't know what you're talking about. There's nothing to deal.' There was a pause as he stared at Jennifer angrily. 'Are we done here?'

Jennifer nodded. She'd rattled him. That was probably all they could reasonably expect at this stage. As to whether he would come round as the consequences of what she'd just outlined and the attractiveness of the deal sank in, only time would tell.

'For now. But I'll be seeing you soon.'

'You know what, Agent Browne? Don't bother.'

Tom got up, drained his glass and marched towards the exit. As he approached the revolving door the same two men who'd been loitering in the arcade earlier stood up from where they had been sitting and squared up to meet him. Tom looked from one to the other and then swivelled round to face Jennifer. They stared at each other for a few moments over the heads of the crowded restaurant, before she signalled with a wave of her hand that they should let him pass. The two men parted like a set of iron gates.

As Tom disappeared out onto the street, Jennifer reached for her phone. Corbett answered on the second ring, in his usual terse manner.

'How did it go?'

'As we thought. Deny, deny, deny. He's certainly convincing.'

Corbett snorted.

'Oh yeah? Well, I figure it's time to light a fuse under Kirk's lying ass.'

Jennifer frowned.

'What do you mean?'

'I mean you've got a date tonight.'

Her eyes widened in understanding.

'You've managed to set something up with your contact?'

'I didn't even have to ask. When Renwick heard that one of my people was in town he mentioned that he was having someone over for dinner tonight and then asked whether you'd like to join them. Guess who the other guest is?'

'Kirk?' Her voice betrayed her excitement. This was even better than they'd hoped.

'That's right. Turns out he invited him over last week. Let's see how convincing Kirk is when you show up right in his back yard.'

'Does Renwick know why we're here?'

'No. I told him that we were investigating something and needed his help again. I want you to take the coin along with you tonight. If anyone can help us narrow down the list of people who are behind the Fort Knox job, it's him. Tell him what you need to, but try and keep the specifics to a minimum.'

'Okay.'

'Oh, and we've set something up with Van Simson tomorrow at his place in Paris. Two thirty. It's the only slot he could do. Can you make it?'

'Sure. I'll get the embassy people here to sort some transport out. It won't be a problem.'

'Great. Call me in the morning and let me know how tonight goes.'

She returned her phone to her purse, smiling. Times like this reminded her why, despite all the John Pipers in the world, she still loved her job.

TWENTY-EIGHT

Belgravia, London
8:00pm

Harry Renwick lived on a wide, elegant street. Broad brick houses with tall windows and high ceilings climbed four storeys into the sky. Station wagons and SUVs nestled bumper to bumper with weekend Ferraris and Porsches.

Tom had pulled on his best suit for the occasion, a merino and cashmere mix that was light and yet sat well on his square frame. In the end, knowing Renwick as he did, he had decided to wear a tie, although the unfamiliar collar rasped against his neck. Suits weren't really his thing.

He stepped out of the cab and checked his wrist, a Tank from the 1920s which Tom still regarded as Cartier's best period. It was gold and solid and squat, the roman numerals elegantly spaced out on the oblong face. It was eight o'clock. He was right on time.

'Come in, come in,' exclaimed Renwick as he threw the door open, Tom's face reflecting in its gleaming black paint and polished brass.

Renwick was still wearing the same white linen suit, although he had taken the jacket off, revealing his shirt's threadbare elbows. Tom shook Renwick's hand and then handed over the bottle he was holding as he stepped onto the hall's marble chequerboard floor.

'My dear boy!' Renwick exclaimed, his face beaming as he unwrapped it. 'A Clos du Mesnil and an '85 too. You really shouldn't have.'

'I know,' said Tom smiling. He was feeling much more composed after the initial surprise of that morning's events. More than anything now he was intrigued. The FBI's involvement suggested that the Agency were not behind this approach which had to be good news. And the fact that they hadn't just had him picked up suggested that they needed something from him which might give him some room for manoeuvre. Even if he still didn't really have a clue what they wanted.

'Well, let's get this opened right away,' Renwick continued as he led Tom through to the sitting room. 'Now I hope you don't mind, but I invited someone else to join us tonight. Thomas, meet Jennifer Browne, Jennifer meet Thomas Kirk.'

Tom had frozen in the doorway as he had glimpsed Jennifer rising from her chair on the other side of the room. He glared at Renwick angrily. What was going on? Was Harry working with the Feds?

'Good evening, Mr Kirk.' She glided towards him as if they'd never met before, a cloud of Chanel No 5 in her wake.

Tom gave her a tight smile as they shook hands.

'Miss Browne.'

'Come, come. No need to be so formal. We're all friends here,' Renwick chided. 'Jennifer works at the FBI in America for a friend of mine. Apparently he thinks I might be able to help on a case they're investigating. It's awfully exciting.' Renwick grinned. 'Anyway, she's only in town for a few days and I thought you two might get on.'

'That's very thoughtful of you, Uncle Harry,' said Tom forcing a smile and feeling slightly guilty. Perhaps he'd been a bit too quick to judge Renwick. It was more likely that he was an unwitting pawn in whatever game the FBI was playing rather than their willing accomplice.

'Drinks, anyone?' Renwick exclaimed. 'How about you, my dear, what will you have? A glass of champagne? Excellent.' Renwick removed the foil wrapper and the wire cage from the bottle and gently levered the cork out until it came free with a repressed hiss.

'Glasses. Bugger. Hold that will you, Thomas, and I'll go and get some. And an ice bucket, of course. Never forget the ice bucket.' Handing the open bottle to Tom, Renwick swept off to the kitchen.

'Even for you guys this is pretty low,' Tom hissed, rounding on Jennifer.

'You think this is some sort of game?' Jennifer shot back indignantly. 'Just so you know, this is your life from now on. Wherever you go, wherever you turn, we'll be there. Your world's about to get a whole lot smaller.'

'You got a problem with me, fine. But Harry's on the outside. He's got nothing to do with any of this. I won't let you drag him into my life.'

'He's not really your uncle, is he? Your whole life is a lie.'

'That's irrelevant.' Tom took a step towards her until they were only a few feet apart. 'I'm warning you, keep him out of it.'

'Well, if you play ball with us, it won't ever get to that, will it?' Jennifer glared defiantly into Tom's eyes.

Renwick strode back into the room clutching glasses and a champagne bucket.

'Well, you two certainly seem to have broken the ice.' He chuckled. 'Excellent.'

At the sound of his voice they both jumped apart and stood awkwardly as Renwick poured them each a glass. He then ushered them to the right-hand sofa while he sat on the one opposite. In between them, a low blue silk divan covered in auction catalogues served as an impromptu coffee table, while the large marble fireplace had been filled with dried flowers.

'Business must be good,' said Tom straining to make his voice sound relaxed and normal, indicating the room around them.

Although simply furnished with modern mushroom-coloured sofas and seagrass matting, the sandstone walls had been carefully hung with a collection of paintings and sketches. An Old Testament prophet, a beatific Madonna clutching a cherubic Christ child, a papal portrait, its subject frozen in martial pose, and a mythical scene of Bacchanalian abandonment to name but a few. Not to mention, of course, that Tom had immediately recognised the hand of van Eyck, Rembrandt and perhaps even Verrochio in several of the works. It was a staggering collection that would have sat well in the Renaissance gallery of any major museum.

'What, this? Most of it's new to me, actually,' Renwick said looking around him dispassionately. 'I inherited the house from a relative a few months ago, gave it a lick of paint and bought some new furniture. He was in shipping or something. Made a fortune after the war. Anyway, I don't know how he lived here because it was full of junk. I sold most of it but some of it was worth keeping.'

'I can see that,' said Tom appreciatively.

'In fact I've got a chap coming round here tomorrow to look at that one there.' He pointed at the Papal portrait at the far left side of the room. 'It's always been attributed to the School of Titian. But I have a suspicion that it may have been painted by Titian himself.'

'Really?' Tom stood up and approached the painting with an appreciative look.

'And what are they?' Jennifer pointed at the luridly painted masks that had been hung over the mantelpiece.

'Ah. Now they *are* mine,' Renwick's voice was immediately energised. 'I collect them. They're Japanese Nō masks.'

'I'm sorry, I don't . . .'

'Nō was a form of Japanese theatre that emerged in the Muromacho period,' Renwick explained. 'The plots are always simple and serious and very symbolic, the costumes elaborate. The masks are worn to show stylised characters or emotions, much like in ancient Greek theatre, and also to let the same actor play several characters. I've been collecting these since I was a boy.' Renwick's eyes shone brightly, his voice vibrant.

'How old are they?'

'Well, the oldest one I have is that one.' He stood up to point at a white mask decorated with golden horns and bulging eyes, its mouth drawn into a white-teethed demonic grin. 'That's from about 1604 when Nō was adopted as the official theatre of Japan under the protection of the ruling samurai class and the shogun. The others date from the late 17th and 18th centuries.'

Tom let his eyes flick over some of the other masks. A smiling mandarin, eyes scrunched in laughter, a neatly clipped beard and moustache decorating his dimpled chin. A worried-looking Japanese youth, forehead creased, hair thinning, eyes narrowed in surprise.

'Now I hope you don't mind, my dear,' Renwick boomed to Jennifer. 'But we're eating in the kitchen. The dining room still looks like a bomb site.'

He showed them into the kitchen, a wide stone-flagged room with a rustic-looking wooden table in the middle of it, set for three. French windows along the right-hand wall gave out onto the garden and these were slightly ajar, allowing the smell of the honeysuckle that grew up the side of the house to seep in. Granite-topped cherrywood units ran along the left and facing walls, punctuated by a gas range, a huge mass of cast iron and dials and pipes and a deep Belfast sink which was already piled high with pans and dishes.

They sat down, Renwick at the head of the table, Tom and Jennifer opposite each other. Tom looked at Jennifer angrily. He knew that this intrusion into his life was some trick, some underhanded way of showing him just how far they could go, would go, to get what they wanted.

'If I'd known you were coming earlier I would

have done something special,' Renwick apologised.

'This looks wonderful,' Jennifer protested.

She was wearing a fitted black jacket over a white blouse, her long legs sheathed in flowing black silk trousers, the material fluttering around her ankles. Tom noticed that as she talked the tip of her nose twitched in sympathy to the movement of her lips, like a small rabbit.

Despite everything, that made him smile, which only infuriated him further.

TWENTY-NINE

10:09pm

Several hours later, Jennifer's cheeks glowing a little from the wine and the heat from the stove, they went back through to the sitting room for coffee. Once they had all helped themselves, Renwick settled back into the sofa and smiled benevolently at Jennifer who had parked herself next to him and opposite Tom.

'So, Jennifer. Robert said that I might be able to help with something? Confidentially, of course.' Jennifer nodded gratefully and put her cup down. She had been careful to drink only one glass of wine in anticipation of this moment and although she had spoken to Renwick for almost the whole meal, she had felt Kirk's angry eyes on her throughout.

'Agent Corbett, I mean Robert, said you were *the* person to talk to about numismatics in Europe.' Her tone was businesslike now.

'He did, did he? Well, that's very kind. I suppose it is true to say that it's my area. I was a dealer for years and years. That's how we met, you know, on another of his cases several years ago now. I've diversified a bit recently into other areas but one of my clients is a fanatical collector, so I still have to keep up with things.'

Jennifer hesitated. This was a careful balancing act. While she wanted the benefit of Renwick's insight, Corbett had reminded her she couldn't afford to give him, a civilian, all the details on the theft. And yet this was also an opportunity to crank up the pressure on Kirk by showing him that they knew exactly what had happened and then seeing how he reacted. It was a fine line to tread. She reached into the zipped compartment of her purse and extracted the protective envelope containing the gold coin, handing it to Renwick.

'Good God,' Renwick gasped. The coin dropped from his hand to the floor and disappeared out of sight. He fell to his knees, apologising to Jennifer as he reached under his chair.

'I'm terribly sorry . . . please forgive me . . . don't know what came over me.' He stuttered. Jennifer smiled, noticed Tom looking on with curiosity. He had barely moved in his seat.

'It's fine. Don't mention it.'

'It's just that it was such a shock,' he explained, once the coin was safely back in his hand and he had settled back down. 'I've never seen one before.'

'Not many people have,' Jennifer said helpfully.

'Seen what?' Tom asked, his forehead wrinkled, straining to see what he was holding.

'A 1933 Double Eagle. A phenomenally rare coin,' Renwick explained to Tom, handing him the coin.

'A twenty dollar coin,' Tom said examining it. 'Gold. Is it valuable?' He flipped the coin in the air, caught it and then placed it down on the blue silk divan.

Jennifer snorted her disbelief at Tom's question.

'Only about eight million dollars,' Renwick said excitedly.

'Christ!'

Tom sat forward and picked the coin up again, a respectful look on his face now. Jennifer's brows furrowed. Either Tom was a very convincing actor or else . . . ? Renwick interrupted her thoughts.

'My client, you know the one I mentioned earlier, he has one. Bought it at auction recently. I've never seen it, of course. He keeps it locked up in Paris. I thought that his was the only one though.'

'If your client is Darius Van Simson, then officially, it still is.'

'And unofficially?' He looked at her quizzically over the top of his coffee cup.

'Unofficially, the US Treasury did hold onto a

few other coins. Only they have been . . . mislaid.'
She stared at Tom as she said this and again was
confused by his reaction. Sudden understanding
swept across his face as if the pieces of a puzzle
had just fallen into place. As if he'd only just realized what this was all about.

'Mislaid?' Renwick took his glasses off and
flashed her an indulgent smile. 'Where were they
last seen?'

'This coin was found in Paris. We are assuming
that the others are also in Europe.'

'I see.' Renwick rubbed his chin thoughtfully.
'You know, Van Simson will be furious when he
hears about this.'

'I thought we'd agreed that he won't,' said
Jennifer, sharply. 'Or at least if he does it'll be from
me. I've an appointment with him tomorrow.'

'My dear girl, I won't breathe a word. But the
art world is a very small place, just ask Thomas.
Van Simson likes to keep on top of things and he
pays a lot of money to get this sort of information first. If he doesn't know already, he soon will.
And believe me, when you pay eight million
dollars for a coin that is supposedly unique, you
don't react too well to people pulling one out of
their handbag like confetti.'

'Do you know him well?' asked Tom.

'Not really. As I said, he's a client. I look out
for coins for him. And I got him some paintings,
modern stuff mainly. But that's about it.'

'What I need to know,' Jennifer asked, mindful of steering the conversation back to the coin, 'is who the likely buyers might be here in Europe. Who would pay to own such a piece.' Tom was studying Renwick as if he was as interested in his answer as she was.

Renwick sucked his cheeks in.

'I really couldn't say. Your best bet is probably to identify the winning bidders at the large coin auctions over the past few years and focus on them. The most active buyers in the market tend to be institutional. You know – museums, trusts, corporates. Van Simson is the only private collector I know of who could come close to affording something like that.'

'So how would you sell something like this, if you were to have . . . let's say . . . stolen it?' Jennifer fixed Tom with a stare as she said this but he returned it unblinkingly.

'Stolen it?' Renwick paused. 'Hmmm. Well, something like that would almost certainly have a buyer lined up before it was stolen. It's not the sort of thing you can just sell on the open market.'

Jennifer considered the thought that had struck her on the plane flying over. For the coin to have ended up back in FBI hands, somewhere along the line the plan had clearly gone wrong. Maybe this explained it.

'But what if you didn't have a buyer? What would you do then?'

Renwick shook his head.

'It's unlikely, but the obvious step would prob-ably be to try and find a fence. You know, someone who would take it off your hands and then try and sell it themselves through their own network.'

A fence? Jennifer nodded slowly. It made sense. Ranieri was a fence. Maybe that was how he'd ended up with the coin? For some reason there'd been no buyer and Ranieri had been brought in to help. But by whom?

'Or an off-site?' Tom suggested.

'Yes, that's possible too, I suppose,' said Renwick, rubbing his chin again. 'It's possible, but very risky. Especially these days.'

'An off-site?' Jennifer looked questioningly at each of them. 'What's that?'

'It's a sort of black market auction,' Tom explained, Jennifer noticing a slight edge to his voice as if he was forcing himself to be civil. She was glad. She wanted him to feel uncomfortable.

'What do you mean?'

Renwick answered for him.

'Any major artist has a *catalogue raisonné*, a book put together by experts showing photos and descriptions of every work by the artist in ques-tion together with details on the rightful owners. The first step for any respectable gallery owner or auctioneer when asked to sell an item would be to consult these books to see where the piece in question had originally come from. The second step would be to consult the Art Loss Register in London which records all reported art thefts on its system. Together, they make an open sale of a stolen quality piece almost impossible.'

Nodding, Tom took over.

'One alternative is an off-site, an opportunity to get some of the benefits of an auction without the publicity. There's a very selective list of approved buyers who get told when and where it's happening at the last minute. Used to happen a lot, but less so now. The cops have wised up.'

Jennifer nodded and then turned to Renwick.

'What would be really useful is to run through who the likely buyers might be, both at regular auctions and these off-sites.'

'Yes, of course. I'd be happy to help. When would you like to do that?' Jennifer gave a sheepish smile. 'Now?' He asked with surprise.

'I'm still running on US time.' Her tone was apologetic. 'It's only . . .' She snatched a look at her watch. '. . . five thirty in the afternoon back home. I'd sure appreciate it if we could make a start tonight. I'm on a pretty tight schedule my end.'

'Fine. Of course, if that's what you want. I'm somewhat of a night owl myself so I'm more than happy to stay up and knock it on the head.'

'Well, in that case, I'm off,' said Tom yawning. 'I've got an early start tomorrow. Another shipment coming in. And you two clearly don't need me any more.'

Renwick phoned for a taxi. It arrived five minutes later and he showed Tom to the door, Jennifer standing behind him.

'Goodbye, Agent Browne,' said Tom, 'and I hope you find your coins.'

'Oh, don't worry, we will.' She smiled tightly. 'And whoever took them.'

Renwick walked Tom to the taxi.

'Bye-bye, Tom – do keep in touch.'

'I will, I promise.' The two men hugged each other.

'By the way, isn't she a great girl?' Renwick whispered quietly. 'Full of fire. And beautiful, too. Maybe you should make a move.'

'Make a move? She's really not my type,' said Tom laughing. 'And in any case, it was you she wanted to meet. You're the coin expert.'

Tom shook his hand again and climbed into the taxi.

Waving him goodbye, Renwick closed the front door and turned to face Jennifer.

'Right. Let's get cracking. If you go back into the sitting room and help yourself to a drink I'll pop upstairs and get my files. This should only take an hour or so.'

'Great.'

Renwick walked upstairs and into his book-lined study, sitting down heavily in the leather chair that he pulled out from under the front of the large desk. For several minutes he sat there, thinking, until he pulled the phone towards him, lifted the receiver out of the cradle and dialled a number.

'Yes?'

'It's me.'

'What is it?'

Renwick sat back in the chair and put his feet up on the desk.

'You'll never guess what I've got downstairs.'

THIRTY

10:40pm

'Did you find the port?'

Renwick had reappeared at the sitting room door and Jennifer turned round to face him, reluctantly tearing her eyes away from the oil painting she had been studying.

'Water's fine for me, thanks.' She held up her glass to show she had helped herself.

'Very sensible. Let's do this in the kitchen, shall we? Give us a bit more room to spread out.' He nodded towards the dark blue folder he was clutching under one arm.

Jennifer followed him through to the kitchen and helped him clear a space on the table, piling plates and glasses high on the worktops, the sound of expensive china and cutlery echoing around them.

'Leave all that, my dear,' Renwick boomed as Jennifer began to clear some of the plates into the trash. 'The housekeeper will clear it away in the morning. Now, why don't you sit yourself down there and I'll pull a chair up next to you.' He pointed at a chair on the left-hand side of the table and dragged another over next to it. Jennifer sat down.

'So what is all this?' she asked as Renwick began to empty the contents of the file onto the table's coarse wooden surface.

'Press cuttings, newsletters, sale reports. Anything relevant to the European coin and medal markets. I have a company that collates them all for me as well as for other areas I work in. Helps keep me up to speed. Anyway, between all this we should be able to come up with a list of names and companies you can look into.'

'You know, I really appreciate you helping me on this. Especially this late.'

Renwick beamed at her.

'My dear, it's my pleasure. Really it is.'

He sat down and then immediately stood up.

'I'm hot. Are you hot?' Without waiting for an answer he moved over to the French windows that gave onto the garden and threw them open. A cool breeze slid into the room. Renwick sat down again.

'I hope you didn't mind Thomas being here as well?' he said with a smile.

'No, not at all,' she replied, careful not to sound too enthusiastic. The last thing she wanted was

Renwick realising that they were just using him to get to Tom.

'It's just that Robert told me that you were only in town for a few days and I'd already invited Thomas over last week. He didn't think you'd mind. And it did occur to me that Thomas might have some useful input for your investigation as well. I hope that wasn't presumptuous.'

'Of course not. Although I'm intrigued. What is it that Mr Kirk, I mean Tom, does for a living that made you think he could help?'

'Ah!' Renwick laughed. 'Many people have asked themselves that same question. From what he tells me, and that's not much, he's some sort of antiques dealer. They've always been his thing, ever since he was a child. I suppose he got that from his parents. Anyway, he knows the business inside out, hence why I thought he could help.'

'Have you known Tom for long then?'

'Since he was fourteen at least. I met Charles, his father, after he moved to Geneva. Tom would turn up every so often in the holidays.'

'He didn't live at home?' Jennifer already knew the answer to this question, but then she couldn't let Renwick realise that the CIA had a file on Kirk an inch thick.

'No. His mother, Rebecca, was killed in a car accident when he was about thirteen. It turned out that Tom was driving at the time.'

'Oh,' Jennifer nodded in understanding. Her

father often used to let her sit on his knee and drive the short distance from their house to the first main intersection. A game that in this case had clearly gone horribly wrong.

'Charles took it very badly – never really recovered, if truth be known. Thomas was sent to live with his mother's family. I think Charles found it too painful to have him around.'

'That must have really screwed him up. Losing one parent and then being rejected by the other.'

'Yes.' Renwick paused. 'You know, he never really talks about his childhood now but he did once tell me a story that always stuck with me. One day at junior school, or whatever it is you Americans call it, Thomas saw two boys stealing a purse belonging to one of the teachers. He didn't say anything because he'd only been there a few months and it was hard enough for him as a new pupil at a new school in a new country without attracting even more attention to himself. Apparently these two pupils somehow knew that Thomas had seen them and decided to put the money they'd taken in his locker before tipping off the teacher. She opened his locker in front of the whole class and there was her purse, right where these two boys had put it.

They suspended him for a few weeks and no matter what he said, no one ever believed he was innocent. Charles least of all. Not even when the same two pupils were caught shoplifting and the police then found a stash of stolen items in one of their rooms. Thomas was always guilty in his father's eyes and I'm not sure he ever forgave him for that.'

'I'm not surprised,' said Jennifer arching her eyebrows. How ironic that having been wrongly accused of theft, Kirk had actually become a thief.

'Anyway, that was all a long time ago now.' A pause, 'We should get cracking. Let's split this up.' He roughly divided the wedge of papers into two equal piles. 'You go through that one, I'll go through the other.'

For the next forty-five minutes they both read through their piles, the silence broken only by the noise of their pens as they took notes and the occasional question from Jennifer or comment from Renwick as he pointed something out to her. He had been right. It was a small market, the same names, some institutional, some private individuals, showing up several times over. Jennifer kept score, adding a little line next to each name every time it was mentioned. Van Simson had already scored twelve, double his closest competitor. Looking over, she could see that Renwick had amassed a similar score for him.

She paused mid-scribble.

'What was that?'

Renwick didn't look up.

'What was what?'

'That noise. It sounded like it came from the garden.'

'Oh.' Renwick looked up, smiling. 'Probably the neighbour's cat culling the local mouse population.'

Jennifer nodded, looked out the window and then back down at her notes. A few moments later her head snapped towards the open window again.

'That's no cat.'

'What?'

'I said that's no cat.' Jennifer had got up and moved over to the window. 'Too big. And there's more than one too.'

'Are you sure?' Renwick stood up, a concerned look on his face.

'Quick, turn the lights out,' Jennifer whispered. Renwick stumbled over to the light switch and flicked it off, his forehead crumpled into a worried frown. Jennifer edged her head round the window's edge so that she could see into the garden.

She immediately jumped back, pressed herself to the wall.

'Two men,' she whispered. 'Making their way towards the house.'

'What the blazes do they want?' Renwick whispered back, his voice suddenly afraid.

'I don't know but I figure we shouldn't wait around to find out. Let's get outside and call the cops.'

'What about all my paintings?'

'You're insured, aren't you?' Renwick nodded. 'So leave them. These guys look like they mean business.'

They both tiptoed out of the kitchen and made their way to the front door. Jennifer unbolted it.

'Now remember . . .' she said as she pulled it open.

She never finished the sentence.

'Watch out!' shouted Renwick.

Instinctively, she raised her arms in front of her face and a fist glanced harmlessly off her elbow. She could tell from how quickly it had come that whoever it was had been waiting for the door to open – and she knew then that the other two must have been deliberately sent round the back to flush them out onto the street.

She only had time to register that her assailant was a short, stocky, white man before she had to dodge his follow-up punch, his knuckles slamming instead into the door's polished surface and making him yelp. She seized the opportunity, chopping him in his throat with the edge of her hand and then kicking him hard in the groin. He immediately dropped to his knees with a groan and sagged forward, his face bright red as he choked and gurgled, unable to catch his breath.

''nuff, bitch.'

Jennifer jerked her head round to see the two men who'd come in through the garden standing in the hallway, the one on the left holding a gun to Renwick's head. Like the other man, they were also white, although their forearms were dark with matted hair and swirling tattoos. Both wore jeans, shiny black bomber jackets and bright white trainers.

'Pull another move like that and we off grandad. Got it?' Renwick stared at her, his head tilted to one side where the man was pressing against his temple with the gun's muzzle, clearly terrified.

'Fine.' She raised her hands. 'Take what you want.'

The man on the right stepped forward, his mouth thin and purple from poor circulation, his right ear pierced in three places, his nose bent like a boxer's.

'Oh we will, sweetheart, don't you worry.'

'Get out of my house, you scum,' Renwick shouted, his eyes fierce and proud. 'I know who sent you and you can tell him from me that . . .'

The man pulled a gun from the waistband of his jeans, turned round, aimed the gun at Renwick's chest and fired.

'Harry!' Jennifer called out as Renwick collapsed onto the stone floor, his tongue lolling out the side of his mouth.

The man she had knocked to the ground struggled to his feet behind her, still wheezing, the fingers of his right hand now gripping a thick brass knuckle-duster.

'You fucking bitch,' he snarled as he struck her with a big looping punch to the back of her head.

Jennifer saw the marbled floor accelerating towards her as she fell, but blacked out before she hit it.

THIRTY-ONE

Clerkenwell, London
27th July – 05:30am

The sun had barely risen when the first van pulled up, the street still empty apart from the two grey pigeons chasing each other across the sidewalk. The driver jumped down to the ground. Pulling on his black helmet, he tapped twice on the van's side. Almost immediately the side door slid back on its well-oiled runners and the seven men inside stepped out, their gloved hands clasping their gleaming Heckler and Koch MP5s. Nobody spoke.

They were all dressed identically, multi-pocketed combat trousers tucked into ankle-high boots, the long laces zigzagging up their shins before being wrapped several times around the top of the boot and then tied off. A Glock 17 self-loading pistol was velcroed to each person's left leg while handcuffs, extra ammunition and CS gas canisters hung around their waist. Their black bullet-proof vests made their chests bulge.

A second van drew up and a further six men erupted onto the street, helmets and goggles already on. A tall man in civilian clothes with rounded shoulders and thin wrists stepped slowly out of the passenger seat of the second van. He looked down the street at the armed men standing with their backs pressed to the sides of the vans with quiet satisfaction. His moment had finally come.

'Daniels,' Detective Sergeant Clarke whispered through his teeth. One of the men peeled off from the others and walked over, the insignia of the Metropolitan Police's elite SO19 armed response unit clear on his shoulder.

'This man is probably armed and certainly dangerous. You go in and you go in hard. Shoot him if you have to. And remember, I want to make the arrest in person. This is my collar, not yours.'

Mike Daniels grimaced.

'Why don't you let us worry about who we shoot and you worry about the paperwork and not getting in our way.' Daniels turned and walked back to his men who gathered round him in a tight circle. Clarke stood fuming, only grateful that no one had overheard their exchange.

In a low voice Daniels gave some quick instructions, before looking over at Clarke and nodding.

Two men took up position opposite the building, leaning on the bonnet of each van. The other twelve men trooped silently over to the shop entrance in close formation.

'Right,' said Daniels as they crouched in front of the large windows, 'you know the layout. You five with me up the stairs to the living quarters on the top floor. You four secure the ground floor and warehouse. You two, round the back. He's not expecting us, so this should be simple, but he might try something, so stay alert. Smith, get the door. Go! Go! Go!'

THIRTY-TWO

05:35am

Tom threw himself out of bed as the alarm went off. He had rigged the system up himself; the computer screen perched on the tea-chest at the foot of his bed lit up with a floor plan of the building, the flashing red section showing where the alarm had been triggered. Someone was in the shop downstairs. A sickening crash as something fragile was knocked to the ground echoed up the stairwell and confirmed it.

Tom grabbed a shirt and a pair of jeans off the floor and pulled them on, wriggling his feet awkwardly into a pair of trainers that still had the laces done up. He could hear them coming up the stairs now, their moulded rubber soles squeaking on the concrete, doors slamming, shouts of 'clear' and 'on me' rolling ever closer as they made their way through the maze of offices towards him.

Finally the door crashed open and six black shapes tumbled into the room.

'Armed Police! Don't move!'

Tom put his hands up. No point in arguing, not with these odds.

'Tom Kirk?' asked Daniels. Tom nodded sullenly.

'Of course it's Tom fucking Kirk,' gasped Clarke. He had appeared in the doorway breathing heavily, his face flushed with the effort of running up the stairs, his tie askew. The armed men stepped back to allow him into the room, still covering Tom with their guns.

'Tom Kirk,' said Clarke between breaths. 'I'm arresting you for the murder of Henry Julius Renwick.' Tom's eyes widened with bewilderment. 'You do not have to say anything, but it may harm your defence if you fail to mention, when questioned, something which you later rely on in court.'

Clarke walked right up to Tom and stood with his nose only a few inches away from Tom's.

'Anything you do say can be given in evidence against you.' His lips stretched over his teeth in a thin smile. 'I'd told you you'd slip up eventually, you smug bastard.'

Tom was stunned, uncomprehending. Uncle Harry? Dead? *He* had murdered *Harry*? It was ridiculous. It was insane. It was too awful to even begin to take in. He didn't believe it. Refused to believe it.

'Clarke, even you know that this is bullshit. I may be many things but I'm no killer. Harry Renwick and I are almost family.'

'People like you don't have family.'

'I saw Harry last night, had dinner with him and a friend of his. When I left he was alive. Just ask her.'

'Is that right?' sneered Clarke, walking behind Tom. 'Funny that the table was only set for two, then.'

'For two? There must be some mistake.'

'No mistake, Kirk, at least not by us. Because guess whose prints we found all over the place? That's right. Yours. Yours and Renwick's. No one else's.'

Tom could feel Clarke's wet breath against the back of his neck as he reached into his pocket and took out his handcuffs. 'I've waited a long time for this. And believe me, it's been worth it to see the expression on your face,' Clarke hissed.

Tom knew that he should just go quietly. He was out-numbered and out-gunned. But the table only set for two? Only his prints at the house? This was an old fashioned set-up and somebody had gone to a lot of trouble to get it right. And Clarke had clearly fallen for the bait. Every instinct that Tom had developed and trained and refined over the years was screaming at him to get out of there and get out of there fast. But if he was going to make his move, it would have to be now.

Clarke grabbed one of Tom's wrists and began to twist it upwards behind his back. Rather than fight him, Tom relaxed his arm so it gave away easily under Clarke's rough grip. Clarke, who had braced himself in expectation of Tom resisting him, overbalanced slightly. Tom immediately snapped his wrist out of Clarke's grasp and in an instant had spun round behind him, grabbing his arm and pinning it to his back.

The armed men, caught unawares by the sudden blur of Tom's movement, took a step forward and raised their guns as they realized what had happened. Tom sheltered behind Clarke and twisted his arm viciously, causing him to shout out in pain.

'Don't move. He's breaking my sodding arm.'

'I've got a shot, sir,' one of the men called out to Daniels, aiming just past Clarke's head.

'Are you fucking crazy?' Clarke screamed at him. 'You'll shoot me, you dozy bastard.'

Daniels lowered his gun and motioned with his hand for the others to do the same, fixing Tom with his eyes.

'Don't be an idiot, Kirk. We've got the place surrounded. Give it up. No one needs to get hurt here.'

'No one will get hurt if you stay back,' Tom responded.

He backed across the room and into the bathroom, kicking the door shut behind him and bolting it. He pushed Clarke to his knees and bent him forward over the toilet, handcuffing his hands together, so that his arms were stretched forward and joined at the wrists under the soil pipe. He couldn't move. Clarke was white with fear and rage.

'You bastard, Kirk,' he said, his voice muffled and hollow as it echoed out of the toilet bowl. 'You're dead. I'll fucking kill you myself. You hear me?'

Tom opened the bathroom window and checked outside. It gave onto a narrow, empty alleyway, a thin ribbon of pigeon-soiled tarmac some fifty feet below. There was hammering on the door.

'Open up, Kirk. You've got till the count of ten and then we're coming in for you.' Daniels started to count. 'One . . . two . . .'

Tom jumped up onto the windowsill.

'Three . . . four . . . five . . .'

He reached out and flushed the toilet before clambering out and sliding down the drainpipe.

A few seconds later and the bathroom door splintered open as three men, led by Daniels, flew in, their guns poised. Seeing that the room was empty, Daniels rushed to the window and looked out, taking in the drainpipe and the now empty alleyway.

'He's gone out the window. Get everyone outside. We'll need to lock down the whole area.'

The men trooped obediently out of the room, but as Daniels turned to leave, he heard a coughing and spluttering noise from behind the battered door. Pushing it aside, he saw the back of Clarke's head, his hair and shoulders soaking wet, his body shaking violently.

'Daniels. Is that you? Get me the fuck out of here!' roared Clarke, the water still swirling only inches from his nose. Daniels bent down towards him and whispered in his ear.

'Nice collar, Clarke.'

THIRTY-THREE

05:45am

Tom had planned out this escape route when he had first moved in. Old habits die hard. The alleyway led him to a maze of back streets and passages that eventually brought him out down by the river nearly a mile from his building.

The Embankment was still quiet when he reached it, the odd car and taxi heading towards the City and Canary Wharf, traders keen to catch up with the overnight news from the Asian markets or steal a march on the European ones. A few joggers panted past him, nodding to the music playing through the MP3 players strapped to their waists.

As he slowed to a walk, he tried to make some sense of what had just happened. Uncle Harry dead. Himself framed for it. Why?

'Kirk,' a woman's voice called out. 'Kirk, over here.' He looked up and saw Jennifer waving him

over from the open door of a black cab. Tom
stopped and stared at her accusingly. First
Piccadilly, then Harry's, now here. She was
persistent if nothing else.

'Get in,' she said, more urgently now. 'They're
sealing off the whole area. You've got to get out
of London. Let me help you.'

Tom stood there, certain that whatever she
wanted, helping him was not her prime concern.

'Listen,' she continued, stepping out of the cab
now and shouting over the occasional traffic.
'You've been set up. I know you didn't kill Harry.
I can prove it. Just get in and I'll show you.'

Whatever suspicions Tom had of Jennifer's
motives, he knew that it was risky for him to stay
out in the open. The sound of an approaching
siren made his mind up for him. He jogged over
to the cab and climbed in. Jennifer stepped in after
him and slammed the door shut.

'Are you okay?' she asked breathlessly, folding
down the seat opposite him. Tom looked past her
to the taxi driver sitting behind his plastic screen.

'I think you met Max yesterday. Don't worry,
he's one of our people here. The taxi just helps
us blend in a little.'

Max winked at Tom in his rear-view mirror and
Tom recognised him as one of Jennifer's minders
from the day before. The square-jawed driver with
his blond crew cut and thick muscular neck could
hardly have looked less like a London cabbie if he

had tried. But then the cab was not standard issue either. The windows were clearly bullet-proof; the bodywork, judging from the meaty clunk made by the closing door, armour-plated and in all likelihood cork-lined as well for sound insulation. Most noticeable of all, the usual diesel whine had been replaced by the throaty roar of a transplanted V8 to cope with the extra weight.

'No, I'm not okay,' said Tom, taking in Jennifer's packed bag on the floor next to her, clothes poking out from the zip fastening. 'Why are you here? What's going on?'

For the first time since he had met her, Jennifer looked uncomfortable – sad, even.

'I'm sorry about Harry. We should never have got him involved.'

'You can apologise later. Just tell me what happened.'

She paused before answering.

'About forty-five minutes after you left, three men broke into the house and attacked us. They shot him – shot him right in front of me.'

'Shot him? . . . And you? How come you got away?' His voice was loaded with suspicion.

'I don't know. I tried to help him. Tried to fight them off. But there were too many of them. They were armed. They knocked me out and when I came round there was no sign of Harry, just blood all over the hall floor. But I smelt burning and followed the blood trail to the basement. They'd set fire to him. They shot him, dragged him to the basement and set fire to him.'

'Shit.' Tom bit his lower lip, his brain feverishly conjuring up an image of Renwick's charred and twisted corpse before immediately straining to banish the ghoulish scene from his mind. Harry was gone. Harry who had always been there, who had been more of a father to him than his own father. His grief struck him like a sudden wave, leaving him disorientated and gasping for breath, uncertain whether to swim up or down to get back to the surface. Even so, he wouldn't allow himself to cry, not in front of her. Not in front of anyone.

'Then I called Max here to come and fetch me. He called the cops after we'd left.'

The taxi crossed the river and made its way past the poured-concrete mass of the South Bank and the delicate steel web of the Millennium Wheel, its now-stationary pods shining like pearls in the morning sun.

'How did you know where to find me?'

'We've had people here following you for several days. They were watching you last night to make sure you didn't disappear or make a move for the coin. Luckily one of them saw you jumping out that window.'

'Where's the coin?' he asked, his throat swollen.

'Gone.' Jennifer's voice was hollow and she turned her head to stare out the window as she answered. 'It was the only thing they took. It's what they came for.'

'You mean it was some sort of professional hit?'

'Looks that way.'

'But how did they even know it was there?'

'Two possible explanations. One, that I was followed there by someone who knew I had the coin on me. Two, that someone else tipped them off. We know you didn't make any calls on your cell or from home last night so that puts you in the clear.'

'So you think that Harry . . .'

'We're analysing his phone records.' There was a pause until Jennifer spoke again, regret in her voice. 'Look, Kirk, I don't know how to tell you this but we ran some checks on Harry Renwick last night. There was no rich relative, no inheritance.'

'What are you saying?' Tom was instantly on the defensive.

'Think about it. Those paintings, that huge place. He must have paid for it all somehow. Maybe he just got greedy?'

Tom bit his lip. He refused to believe it. Harry on the take. It just didn't make sense.

'And whoever murdered Harry and stole the coin made it look like you did it. When I went back to the kitchen I saw that they'd removed my place setting and just left yours and his. I guess they just had to look for the lipstick.'

'Why?'

'That's what I want to know.' Jennifer's eyes glinted with determination. 'I guess you make a pretty convincing suspect.'

Tom nodded, reliving that morning's events in his head.

'You should have seen Clarke's face when he came to arrest me.'

'Clarke?'

'A cop. Been trying to nail me for years. He must have thought he'd finally hit the jackpot.'

There were a few moments silence as Tom's mind raced over everything he had just heard.

'So let me get this straight,' he said eventually. 'You've got people who can prove that Harry was alive when I left him, that I didn't move from my place all night long and that I didn't call anyone.'

'Uh-huh.' Jennifer nodded.

'So what do you want? What's the catch?'

'Did you steal those coins, Kirk?' Her eyes searched his out as she asked the question. Tom returned her gaze unblinkingly and answered in a firm, confident voice.

'No. Before last night I'd never even heard of them. I wish I still hadn't.'

She nodded and Tom sensed that she was wrestling with a decision that she didn't really want to make. The cab had reached Vauxhall, and the glass and stone castellated mass of the MI6 building dragged past them.

'The catch is that if I help you, you have to help me.'

'What do you mean?' asked Tom warily.

Jennifer sat back in her seat and again gazed out the window as she spoke.

'That coin was one of five stolen from Fort Knox three weeks ago.'

'Fort Knox!' Tom interrupted. 'Christ! How did they do that?'

'That's not important right now. What is important is that one of them turned up in Paris two weeks later. The same coin I showed you last night and which I've now lost. So we think the other coins are in Europe too, possibly being sold to a private collector. The question is, if you didn't steal them, who do you think did?'

Tom looked away from her angrily.

'I'm no grass.'

'What about Harry?'

'What about Harry? What's he got to do with it?'

'You think the Fort Knox job and his murder are unrelated? My money says that whoever stole the coins, somehow lost one, found out that Harry had it and killed him to get it back. Help me find who was behind this job and you'll be helping catch Harry's killers.'

Tom was silent as he considered what she had just said.

'I've got to go to Paris,' she continued. 'I've got

a meeting set up with Van Simson this afternoon. Afterwards, I want to have a look around. It's where the coin was found. You know the city, understand the way things work over there. I'm talking about a couple of days of your time at most.'

'You're kidding, right?' He almost laughed his question.

'Why not?'

'Are you crazy? For a million different reasons. You think I trust you guys? I got screwed over once. I'm not falling for the same trick again.'

'I don't know what happened to you before, I don't want to know. But this is the real deal, I promise.'

'We both know your promises aren't worth shit.'

Jennifer nodded slowly.

'You're right. It's not my call. But come to Paris and I'll speak to my boss. If he refuses the deal then I'll let you go, say you gave me the slip or something. That I can promise.' Jennifer continued, leaning back in her seat and looking out of the window. They were heading out towards Clapham now, the office buildings and plush riverside developments having given way to rows of neat Victorian terraced houses. She knocked on the screen and the taxi slowed to a halt.

'Otherwise, it's up to you to take your chances

here and now.' She opened the taxi door and waved towards it. 'But I can tell you that the US government will not be in a position to back up your story. There will only be your word that I was at that dinner, that Harry was alive when you left and that you didn't leave your place all night. Frankly, I don't fancy your chances.'

Tom started laughing in spite of himself.

'Just so I know, is this you helping me still?'

'I'm not trying to make any friends here. I'm talking about a truce. You help me find the coins and whoever took them. I help you to find Harry's killers, square things up with your friend Clarke and wipe your file clean. It's up to you, but it's a good deal.'

Much as Tom hated to admit it, she was right.

'Fine, I'll come to Paris and you talk to your boss. If he doesn't like it I'll disappear before you can say extradition treaty. But I'm doing this for Harry, not for you and certainly not for the FBI.' He raised his voice slightly to emphasise his point. 'And when we find them, whoever they are, don't stand in my way. I want the people who did this to him. I want them to pay.'

THIRTY-FOUR

Kent, England
08:05am

It took them two hours to drive down to the airstrip. The black taxi made its way incongruously, once they had left the city, down narrow roads and steep country lanes, its domed roof just visible over the top of the thick hedgerows, until they reached the plane that was waiting for them at one end of a large sloping field deep in the Kent countryside. Obtaining it had required a quick change of plan by the ever-helpful Max since, with the police looking for Tom, the chartered flight that Jennifer had been booked on was now out of the question. Good old Uncle Sam clearly did have very long arms, thought Jennifer proudly.

'Climb on board,' she said to Tom as they approached the plane. 'I'm going to make that call.'

Nodding, Tom hauled himself through the

hatch as Jennifer reached for her phone. It was only just after three am in DC, but she figured Corbett would want to be woken for this. Her stomach tightened the second he picked up. 'It's me, sir.'

'Browne? What time is it?'

'About eight am London time, sir. I'm sorry to have woken you.'

'No, that's fine.' She heard a yawn from the other end. 'How did it go last night? Everything okay?'

'No sir, everything's not okay.'

'What happened?' The tiredness evaporated almost immediately from his voice.

'Renwick's dead.'

'Dead?' She could picture Corbett jumping to his feet as he said this, his eyes flashing.

'Murdered. Shot. I saw it.'

'Slow down. What happened?'

She took a breath, tried to steady herself. When she spoke it was in calm, deliberate sentences.

'Kirk was there as planned. We had dinner and then he left. I stayed to talk the case over with Renwick. Then three men broke in. They attacked us, shot Renwick and knocked me out. When I came round the coin was gone.'

'It was *what*?' Now she saw him sinking onto the bed, his fist clenching and then relaxing against his side. There was a pause. 'Shit. Young will have a heart attack when he hears this.'

'I'll get it back, sir.'

'Do you think they were there for the coin or was it coincidence?'

'No coincidence. Renwick had millions of dollars of paintings hanging on his walls. They didn't touch them. They were in and out. And they didn't just shoot Renwick, they practically executed him. Because he knew who'd sent them.'

'But how did they know the coin was there?'

'Max is checking Renwick's phone records for me. It looks like he made a few calls after Kirk left.'

'So we got a dead civilian and a missing eight million dollar coin?'

'The Brits think Kirk killed Renwick and tried to arrest him for it this morning. I had him under surveillance all night and there was no way he was involved. He was set up. His prints were deliberately left at the scene while mine were wiped.'

'What are you saying?'

'Sir, I think we may be chasing the wrong guy. I can read people and my gut tells me he knew nothing about Fort Knox and nothing about the coins until I told him.'

'So what are you suggesting? We just let him walk away?'

'I want to take him to Paris with me to see Van Simson. He knows the game better than anyone and he knows the territory over there too. He refused to strike a deal yesterday but now we're his only alibi and he's got no choice. He's agreed to help if we put the cops here straight. It makes sense to use him while we can.'

'I'm going to have to talk to Green and Young about this. It's too big a call for me.'

'Fine, just let me take him with me now. If it comes back a no, we can decide what to do with him then. But the more time we lose, the colder the trail.'

'You're way out on a limb here Browne – you know that, don't you? There's no way you can be a hundred per cent that Kirk's not involved. It's a big risk.'

'You'd take it . . . sir.'

Corbett gave a short laugh.

'You know what? I probably would.'

THIRTY-FIVE

Deauville, Coast of Northern France
11:40am
The small Cessna Skylane bounced its way across the English Channel's shifting wind currents like a stone skipping across a pond. Her eyes shut to steady her stomach, Jennifer barely said a word from the moment she stepped on board. But it didn't seem to matter because Tom had not been particularly talkative, staring silently out the window instead.

Several hours later, the plane touched down at Deauville airport where a dark green Renault Mégane was waiting for them, together with a few changes of clothing for Tom and a new American passport in the name of William Travis, that he accepted with a grudging nod of respect to Max's obvious efficiency.

'So what was your boss's verdict, Agent Browne?' asked Tom, as they turned onto the A13 and headed for Paris.

'You know, if we're going to be working together, perhaps we should try first names.'

Tom shrugged.

'Sure. Jen.'

'Jennifer, if you don't mind,' she said curtly. First names was one thing. 'Jen' suggested a degree of familiarity they weren't close to having. Tom made a dismissive noise and turned away. Jennifer shook her head ruefully. This was clearly going to be a long journey. 'He said that he'd think about it.'

'Well, that fills me with confidence.'

They were both quiet and the wheels thumped rhythmically over the joints in the tarmac like a needle reaching the end of a record. The flat countryside slid by, huge rectangular sheets of gold and bronze that the combine harvesters had yet to dent. After a while, Jennifer looked over at him.

'So you used to be in the CIA?'

She accelerated into the outside lane as she spoke, noticed Tom clutching the grab handle over the door. She had insisted on driving, knowing that the familiar feel of the pedals under her feet and the wheel in her hands would help her unwind after the flight.

Tom stared out the window as he answered.

'Yeah.'

'Operation Centaur?'

'Yeah.'

'What happened?'

'It's a two-hour drive to Paris,' Tom snapped. 'If it's all the same to you, I'd rather talk about something else.'

'Fine.' Jennifer dropped a gear and sped past a huge truck, its plastic sides whipping the air, before changing up again, the car lurching forward as she stamped the accelerator down to the floor. She sensed Tom flinching next to her and smiled. She could see he was not used to being a passenger, but then neither was she.

Another ten minutes went by, until it was Tom's turn to break the silence, his question betraying the thought that had clearly been circling through his head.

'How do you know about Centaur?'

'Oh, so you want to talk about it now?' Tom glared at her. 'You dropped a hair in New York when you stole that Egg,' she explained. 'We got a DNA match and the system triggered an alert to the NSA. They briefed us about it. That's how we made the connection between you and the Fort Knox job.'

'What else did they say?'

'I can't tell you that.'

'Did they tell you about me? About what happened?'

'They said you went off the reservation.'

'Christ!' Tom started laughing. 'John fucking Piper.'

'How did . . . ?' Jennifer asked in surprise.

'Because only he would have said that.' He laughed again. 'So John Piper's managed to crawl his way out of the Agency into the NSA now, has he? I bet he's terrified this whole Centaur thing will come out and bite him in the ass.'

'Like us, he just wants the coins back.'

'Let me tell you something about John Piper. All he's ever wanted is what's good for John Piper. What did he say about me?'

'That you were a good agent who went bad. Their best agent. He said you killed someone.'

'Did he now?' Tom's voice was hard, his eyes narrowed.

'Did you?' Jennifer asked, briefly flicking her eyes away from the road.

'Yes.' He nodded slowly. 'But he would have killed me if I hadn't.'

'That's original.' She sniffed dismissively.

'They'd decided to shut Centaur down.'

'Who's they?'

'Piper and his CIA buddies. They asked me to do one last job – break into a Swiss biotech company, steal some files, torch the place and then put a bullet in the chief scientist's head so that he couldn't recreate the research. I didn't do wet work, they had other people for that, so I refused. They threatened to bring me up on charges. You know, refusing to obey a superior officer, that sort of crap. When I told them I was leaving they sent my handler to retire me. That's what they call it, by the way. I just did what I had to do to stay alive.'

'Why the hell would they do that?' She shrugged disbelievingly, although she had to admit the little she'd seen of John Piper lent some credibility to Tom's story, however much she mistrusted him.

'Because by then they'd realized that if Centaur ever got out they'd all be in the firing line. I figure they asked us all to make a hit to see how far they could control us. Maybe even planned to use it as blackmail to make sure we all stayed quiet. I don't know what happened to the others but when Piper realized I wasn't going to play ball he made his move. It's how they work.'

'It's how you want me to think they work,' she snorted.

'They don't play by the normal rules. You get caught on the wrong side of them and they come down on you hard.'

'So what happened in Paris?'

Tom smiled.

'I cut a deal with the French.'

'What sort of deal?'

'I got something back for them that they'd lost and they helped me disappear.'

Jennifer glanced at Tom.

'And then you became a thief?'

'What did you expect me to do? You think that I was ever going to be able to hold down a regular nine till five sort of job? Work in an office? Push paper around?' A faint shadow of Tom's face reflected in the glass as he smiled at the thought. 'I didn't choose this life. The Agency left me swinging in the wind. I lost everything I had. In the end I had no choice.'

'But you enjoyed it, didn't you?' she asked in an accusing tone.

'Why was that wrong of me? Stealing was what I was good at, what I was trained to do. Yeah, I enjoyed it. Still do, I guess. The planning, the job, the escape. After a while, the adrenalin's addictive. I stopped needing the money years ago.'

'So what made you decide to stop?' she asked sceptically, knowing that her tone would reveal that she still thought it highly unlikely he actually had.

Tom shook his head.

'No one thing. My father's funeral, maybe. I guess sometimes things come together in your head and you just know it's time.'

The reflections of white chevrons, painted onto the road to indicate how close cars could safely drive behind each other, strobed across the front of his sunglasses.

THIRTY-SIX

1:37pm
They drove on in silence, tower blocks and squat warehouses joining the land to the sky in a grey mist of steel and concrete as they reached the grimy underbelly of Paris, the glittering new soccer stadium in St Denis an unexpected break in the dark suburban fog.

'What do you know about Darius Van Simson?'

'Only what Harry told us last night,' Tom replied. 'About him having bought the Double Eagle that came up at auction. The name's familiar, though. I think I read about him somewhere.'

'You probably did,' Jennifer nodded. 'He turns up in the Fortune 500 every year. They think he'll break the top fifty this time.'

'Why do you want to go and see him?'

'Until a few weeks ago as far as anyone knew there were only three Double Eagles in existence – Van Simson's and the two in the Smithsonian.

Now, with the theft of the five secret Fort Knox coins, it seems there are eight. Van Simson shouldn't know that yet. I want to see how he reacts when I tell him that his coin might not be quite so unique as he thought it was when he bought it.'

'You think he might be involved?'

'He's certainly rich enough to have put the job together. And he's a big player in the coin market as well as one of Harry's biggest clients. I think it's possible he may know something about what's going on, yes.'

'Where did he make his money?'

'Real estate. You know, office buildings, shopping malls, residential developments, that sort of thing. He seems to have a gift for buying cheap and then miraculously getting a road moved, or planning permission to add an extra three floors.'

'So he's smart?'

'Smart and if you believe the stories, brutal.' Jennifer checked her mirror as she carved smoothly across two lanes to get out from behind another truck. Tom gripped the grab handle over his head.

'What stories?'

'They say he got his first break when he bought a retirement home and then forced all the residents to leave so he could knock it down and build something else. When they refused, he set fire to it. All told, thirteen people died. Of course, there was nothing to link him to it, but he got his apartment block.'

'You see, that's the problem with you people. Always so willing to think the worst of everyone. Have you any idea how easy it is for these rumours to start?'

'Sure,' she cut in. 'And sometimes those rumours start for a reason. Most of the time, there's no smoke without fire.'

Tom shook his head.

'What do you know about it? I'll bet you've never even had a parking ticket.'

Just for a moment Jennifer contemplated revealing how wrong he was. But the thought vanished almost as quickly as it had occurred to her. Much better to keep things strictly professional between them.

'Tell me about this Fort Knox job, then,' Tom asked eventually. 'What do you think happened?'

Taking a deep breath, Jennifer briefed Tom on her investigation so far. The murder of the Italian priest Ranieri, the discovery of the coin, the FBI's theory about the break-in and Short's involvement and subsequent murder. Tom listened intently, especially to the technical details of how the job had actually been pulled.

'They were pros, that's for sure,' Tom nodded slowly when she had finished. 'Looks like they had every angle covered.'

'You do think it's possible then. Breaking into Fort Knox in the way I've described?'

'If they had a guy on the inside, then it's possible, sure.' Tom shrugged. 'All it takes is one person to disable a security system or not check something that they should and you leave yourself wide open.'

'And the computer virus? You ever see that before?'

'More and more. The world's moving from keys to computers. A virus like that is just a very sophisticated lock pick. That was the easy part. It was getting the container inside that took some real planning.'

'Yeah.' She nodded thoughtfully. 'I guess so.'

'You don't sound convinced,' Tom said with a smile. 'What's the matter? You don't believe your own theory?'

'No, it's not that, it's just . . . well it's probably nothing really, but something's been bothering me that last couple of days. Something I didn't really think about at the time.'

'What?' Curiosity in Tom's voice now.

'You don't think that discovering the murder and finding the container so quickly was all a bit . . . convenient? All a bit easy.'

Tom shrugged.

'Just because everything points to the same thing doesn't necessarily make it convenient. It could just make it consistent.'

'Maybe.' She paused before continuing. 'But then what I can't figure out is why go to all the trouble of faking a suicide when you've already smashed the guy's skull to pieces? I mean an autopsy is standard for all suicides. Someone was bound to pick it up sooner or later.'

'Unless they figured that no one would realise the coins were gone until years later and so never link the two?'

'Sure, but it's not just the suicide. If you really wanted to destroy a vital piece of evidence, would you throw it onto a fire at the back of the house of the person you'd just murdered?'

'Maybe they got disturbed. Maybe it was a mistake.'

'No, these people don't make mistakes. The job was perfectly planned from beginning to end. You said so yourself.'

'Well, then,' Tom clasped his hands together. 'The only other explanation is that the reason they left the container there is the same reason they made it obvious that it was a faked suicide.'

'Which was?' Jennifer asked the question, already knowing in her own heart what Tom's answer would be – and wishing that she had another.

'So someone like you would find it.'

THIRTY-SEVEN

8th Arrondissement, Paris
2:04pm

As they hit central Paris, they were soon immersed in the mid-afternoon traffic. Scooters and roller-bladers weaved randomly in and out of the cars and buses which in turn fought their way through the steady waves of tourists washing over the road, seemingly oblivious to the traffic lights. Tom navigated them down to the Quais where a stiff breeze chased them along the riverbank.

Jennifer was struggling to concentrate on the road as the city scrolled past, her eyes shining at her first glimpse of the Eiffel Tower, its skeletal frame soaring over distant rooftops. Tom took on the role of the dutiful tour guide by pointing out the sights as they streamed past – the Place de la Concorde, the Louvre, the Hôtel de Ville, Nôtre Dame – until they reached the Marais and Tom directed her to the symmetrical elegance of the Place des Vôsges.

'What a beautiful square,' she breathed.

'It should be. It's the oldest in Paris. It used to be called La Place Royale because Henry IV built it so that he could live on one side and his wife on the other. But he never moved in. Some say it was a property scam, that he never had any intention of living here and just used his name to sell it on at a huge profit.'

Jennifer gave a short laugh.

'I guess every age has its Van Simsons.'

Tom pointed at a space that had just opened up on the left hand side of the square outside a café. 'Let's park here. It's only a few minutes walk.'

'Fine.'

'And I guess I'd better get changed.'

Jennifer parked and Tom quickly slipped on the shirt, suit and shoes that had been left for him in the car. He was not surprised that they had got his sizes exactly right. He left the tie off.

'Don't forget, you're here as an observer,' Jennifer warned over her shoulder as she waited for him to finish dressing. 'So just observe. I'll do the talking.'

'Let's just get this over with,' Tom shot back.

They walked down the Rue des Francs Bourgeois, the cars parked bumper to bumper, occasionally even mounting the kerb to squeeze themselves in, before turning left down the Rue du Temple. Jennifer walked with long fluid strides, the material of her skirt stretching around her knees with every step and then loosening again.

The doors to Van Simson's house soon loomed above them, a glassy cliff of polished oak and brass. Unsurprisingly, they were bolted firmly shut and it took several minutes of leaning on the bell before the approaching sound of crunching gravel indicated that someone was in.

'Agent Browne?' A large man had opened the gate that was set into the left-hand door, his skin bleached, his hair white and thin. His eyes, unprotected by any natural pigmentation, glowed red and sore as he glanced at Tom questioningly. One of his hands was bent awkwardly behind his back as if tucked into his waistband, and Tom knew instantly that his fingers were almost certainly wrapped around a gun.

'Yes,' Jennifer stepped forward, 'and an . . . associate of mine, Mr Kirk. We're here to see Mr Van Simson. I believe we're expected.'

'You, yes.' The man looked accusingly in Tom's direction. 'Him, no.' Suddenly, he put his index finger against his right ear and nodded quickly. A clear plastic wire snaked from his ear, round the back of his head and into his collar.

'Mr Van Simson will see you both.' He grunted, his Dutch accent clear. Taking a quick look up and down the street behind them, he opened the gate wide enough for them both to slip through into the courtyard before crashing it shut behind them.

'Please raise your arms,' said the man. He frisked Tom and then ran his hands over Jennifer to her obvious discomfort. Seemingly satisfied, he nodded in the direction of the house.

They walked silently across the gravel, Tom noticing that two other men were watching them from an upstairs room, the barrel of what looked like a high-powered rifle poking its nose out of the window. Van Simson's yellow Bentley was parked casually across the middle of the courtyard, the heavy skid marks in the gravel indicating that it had been thrown there at some speed.

'The two side wings are offices for Van Simson's property business,' Jennifer whispered. 'He lives on his own in the main building and has his office on the top floor.' Tom nodded. 'Apparently it's an entirely separate construction within the original building, built to Israeli military specifications to withstand a direct missile strike.'

Tom raised his eyebrows but said nothing. He had met people like Van Simson before and had long since ceased to be either surprised or impressed by the countless bizarre ways such people seemed to find to spend their money.

The front door buzzed open automatically as they approached and they stepped into the building's cold echoing emptiness. The vaulted ceiling soared perhaps thirty feet above their

heads, while the walls, and the wide square staircase that swept regally up into the darkness of the
upper floors, were sheathed in a sombre collection of paintings and portraits. One in particular
caught Tom's eye. In it a mother pleaded for her
son to be spared, as around her Roman soldiers
indiscriminately slaughtered women and children.
The street ran with blood.

'Please go straight upstairs.' Another man, also
clad in a black suit, had appeared out of the
shadows on the left and indicated what looked
like a door ahead of them. They walked towards
it until it suddenly split open down the middle,
revealing an elevator. There were no buttons, just
a keyhole on the left, but it started up without
them pressing anything.

They looked at each other in silence, a small
red light on the overhead camera flashing intermittently, almost invisible under the laboratory
glare of the overhead lights. With a gentle shrug,
the elevator stopped and the door opened onto a
large rectangular room, windows along one wall.
Van Simson was behind his desk, open-necked
white shirt over blue jeans, bare feet encased in
soft brown suede. He stood up as soon as they
came in.

'Hello, I'm Darius Van Simson.' Jennifer took
his hand and shook it firmly.

'Mr Van Simson, it is very kind of you to see
us at such short notice.'

'Not at all, not at all,' said Van Simson, smiling generously. 'And you must be Tom Kirk?' He thrust his hand out again. 'Charles' son.'

'Yes,' said Tom, surprised.

'I thought I recognised your face. I was a great admirer of your father's – a regular customer, in fact.' He indicated the four Chagalls that hung between the windows with his other hand. 'He chose all these for me.'

'Really?' Tom flashed Jennifer a knowing glance. If his father, that bastion of puritanical thought and deed, had dealt with Van Simson, then he couldn't be as bad as Jennifer had suggested in the car. 'It's a fantastic set.'

'I've been very happy with them.' He smiled at Tom. 'You have my condolences.' He sounded sincere and Tom was grateful.

'Thank you.'

'Let's all sit down.' He led them past the large white architectural model in the centre of the room to the two sofas on the other side and turned to Jennifer.

'Can I get you a drink? No? You Mr Kirk?'

'A vodka tonic please.' Tom relaxed back into the sofa.

'I think I'll have the same,' said Van Simson as he busied himself over a small drinks cabinet. 'And you must call me Darius.' He handed Tom a glass and sat down in the sofa opposite them. 'Cheers.'

As he raised his glass, Van Simson's left sleeve

rode up slightly and Tom caught a glimpse of his watch's black face and pink gold case. He recognised it immediately. A limited edition Lange & Söhne 'Tourbillon de la Merite', a masterpiece of German craftsmanship and at over one hundred and fifty thousand dollars a shot, as expensive as it was rare.

'Beautiful watch,' said Tom, tilting his glass respectfully towards it.

'Thank you,' said Van Simson warmly. 'Most people don't notice but it's always nice when someone does.'

He looked at it lovingly, centring it on his wrist before lifting his eyes back towards Jennifer.

'Ambassador Cross mentioned that you wanted to ask me some questions when he called up yesterday and demanded I see you.' A smile crossed his lips, as if the thought of someone demanding something of him was an amusing novelty. 'So, now you're here, how can I help?'

'It's a . . . delicate matter,' Jennifer began, under Tom's watchful eye. He was curious to see how she handled this. 'Approximately two weeks ago the French police recovered a coin here, in Paris.'

'Go on.'

'It was a 1933 Double Eagle.'

Van Simson gave a short laugh.

'Well, it must be a fake, then. As far as I know there are only three 1933 Double Eagles. It's certainly not mine and I doubt very much Miles Baxter has let one out from under his claws.'

'No, Mr Baxter is as vigilant as ever.' Jennifer smiled. 'But we don't think it's a fake. In fact, the forensic analysis showed an almost perfect match with the two Smithsonian coins.'

'Can I see it?' asked Van Simson, placing his glass down on the table in between them. It was a thick circle of glass resting on what looked like the shredded rubber remains of a racing wheel, evidence of Van Simson's sponsorship of a Formula One racing team, Tom guessed.

'I'm afraid not. I don't have it on me.' Tom smiled. She didn't have to lie about that, at least.

'So where do you think this coin is from?' Van Simson folded his arms across his chest.

'At this stage, we're not sure.'

'Then I'm sorry, but I fail to see how I can help,' said Van Simson, rubbing his hand across his goatee. 'If you can't show me the coin, how can I give you an opinion on it? That is why you're here, isn't it?'

'Partly, yes. But it did also occur to us that the coin we have might be yours. That would at least explain where it was from and the match to the Smithsonian coins.' Van Simson laughed.

'I'm sorry to disappoint you, but the security system I have here is watertight. There's no way that you have my coin.' Tom sensed that Van Simson flashed him a quick look as he said this. Perhaps he knew more about him than he was letting on?

'When was the last time you saw the coin?' Jennifer persisted.

'Four, maybe six months ago.'

'That long?'

Van Simson smiled.

'Some people love to endlessly gaze and touch and toy with whatever it is they collect. For me, I do not feel compelled to revisit my collection again and again. It's enough to know that I own it. That *I* own it and no one else does.'

'Can I make a suggestion, then?' Jennifer asked.

'Of course.'

'If we can confirm your coin is safe, then – as you said – won't that prove that the one we have is a fake?'

Van Simson got up and walked over to the window, his left arm folded behind his back, clearly considering Jennifer's proposal. Outside, a distant church clock chimed the hours. There was silence as each strike resonated, then settled.

'I could wait for you outside,' Tom suggested to Jennifer, mindful of Van Simson's earlier glance. If he did know who Tom was, then he would be the last person he would let down there.

'No need,' said Van Simson, turning round to face them, a broad smile on his face. 'Let's just go down and check on my coin and then we'll both know what's what. And I insist you come too, Mr Kirk. I think we'll all find it very interesting.'

THIRTY-EIGHT

3:01pm

Van Simson inserted a small key into the keyhole on the left-hand side of the elevator and a rectangular section of the stainless steel wall retracted smoothly, revealing a keypad and a glass panel. He punched a short code into the keypad; the glass panel lit up and he placed his hand against it. For a few seconds a bright blue light leaked out from under his hand as a scanner rolled over his palm and read his handprint. A few seconds later the doors kissed and the elevator started down.

'You know, not many people have seen what I am about to show you,' Van Simson said, turning round to face them, a hint of excitement in his voice.

The lift came to a smooth stop and the doors slid open to reveal a wide corridor, lit with recessed lights. The walls and floor were made of smoothed concrete sections and the clean smell of steel and fresh mortar was in the air.

'The vault's new. I had it built especially to house my collection,' said Van Simson proudly. 'We're about twenty-five feet underground now. But don't worry. The walls are made from reinforced concrete and have been lined with two-inch steel plate. We're quite safe.'

Instinctively, Tom was assessing the set-up. He couldn't help himself. The corridor was about twenty feet long with the lift at one end and the vault door at the other. There was no other way in or out that he could see. Halfway down a huge steel gate had been embedded into the wall and beyond that he could make out small holes in the stonework, housings for laser trip beams. Video cameras tracked every single inch of the corridor.

As they approached the steel gate, Van Simson withdrew a card from his pocket and swiped it along a reader set into the wall. This opened a panel in the wall behind which was a speaker and a small screen. Van Simson leant forward.

'This is Darius Van Simson. Initiate challenge procedure.'

A processed voice came back:

'Please confirm today's password.'

'Ozymandias,' said Van Simson firmly and the

small screen flickered with a series of long oscillating lines as it captured and analysed his voice.

There was a brief silence and then the robotic voice spoke again:

'Password and voice match. Please step away from the gate.'

A light next to the speaker flashed green as they stepped back and with a loud clang as a restraining bolt slid home, the gate slid up into the roof.

'It's a very impressive set-up, Darius,' said Tom. Van Simson glanced back at Tom and Jennifer, his voice animated.

'Thank you. I designed it myself.'

They walked through the gate and up to the vault door where Van Simson swiped his card along another wall mounted reader. A similarly disguised panel slid back, this time revealing a small screen and numerical touch pad. The screen flashed:

Please enter pass code.

Van Simson leant forward and deftly tapped out a long sequence of numbers. The screen went blank and then flashed back:

Entrance sequence authenticated. Please stand by.

A light over the door turned red and to a low mechanical whine, the vault bolts were smoothly retracted, a satisfying metallic clunk echoing through the corridor as each one came to rest within its housing. The red light began to flash and the massive door swung back on its thick hinges. With the door fully open, the light turned green.

'I'm sorry about the wet floor,' said Van Simson stepping through the doorway. 'When the vault is sealed the room is flooded with a couple of inches of water which I then run a high voltage current through. Just another little precaution.'

The vault was a low, rectangular room perhaps 50 feet long and 30 feet wide. Large waist-high stainless steel display cabinets were scattered through the room, the black rubberised floor meandering between them like a narrow path through a maze. The floor was wet, as Van Simson had predicted and a channel perhaps half a foot wide ran all around the room between the floor and the wall where the water clearly drained away.

'Welcome to the Van Simson collection,' he said grandly. 'This is now the largest private collection of gold coins and ingots in the world. It's taken me almost my entire life to assemble it.' He led them gleefully past the first few cabinets like a child showing off his favourite toys.

Each cabinet had a clear glass top and six or

seven narrow drawers beneath them. Above each cabinet was a thick sheet of glass, suspended between the ceiling and the cabinet below with steel wire. Each was dimly lit by an individual spotlight. Apart from these small islands of light, the room was quite dark.

'Look at these,' Van Simson said, bending down over one of the glass tops. 'Greek Staters from around 54 BC.' He looked up, his eyes shining. 'These were struck to finance Brutus and the Republican army in their struggle against Octavian and Marc Anthony after the assassination of Julius Caesar. They were discovered on the very battle-field where the Republicans were finally defeated.' He sprang to another cabinet, sliding one of its drawers open.

'And look here,' he pointed down into the velvet-lined drawer. 'Nazi ingots recovered from Lake Lunersee.' Tom and Jennifer leant forward and saw the unmistakeable stamp of an eagle surmounting a swastika, circled by oak leaves. 'The gold came from Dachau.' Van Simson went on, lovingly picking up one of the deep yellow bars and cradling it in his hands, 'From teeth and wedding rings.'

Tom chose to ignore Van Simson's gruesome trophy. Instead he focused on the sheets suspended over the cabinets that he could now see actually contained coins that had been sand-wiched between two panes of glass so that both sides could be seen, while ensuring they remained chemically sealed from the atmosphere.

'Come,' said Van Simson, slamming the drawer shut and sounding suddenly impatient. 'Over here.' He led them to the far end of the room where there was a small raised platform, with a desk and various pieces of computer equipment and television monitors. The display cabinet nearest the platform was lit with a slightly brighter light than the others and Tom guessed that this contained the highlights of the collection. As they approached, Tom recognised the now familiar detail of the Double Eagle suspended over the cabinet.

'Here it is, then,' said Van Simson triumphantly, 'as I promised. The only 1933 Double Eagle in private ownership, safe and sound. These sheets are bullet-proof. I can assure you, my coin's not going anywhere.'

'I would have to agree with you,' said Jennifer, studying the coin closely.

'So why are you really here, Agent Browne?' Van Simson's voice was suddenly cold and distant. She returned his stare.

'I think I've explained that.'

'I heard what you said, but I don't think you've told me everything. What are you going to do about this fake Double Eagle?'

'What do you mean?'

'I mean that I had a deal with the Treasury.'

Van Simson had raised his voice and it was echoing off the low ceiling. 'They promised that mine was to be the only coin on the market. That there were no other coins.'

'That deal still stands, as far as I know.' Jennifer's voice was calm and assured.

'Except that you've found a coin that you and presumably your experts believe to be real, otherwise you wouldn't be here. That was not what was agreed. A fake fundamentally undermines the value of my investment and creates a huge amount of uncertainty in the market. You must destroy the coin.'

'I can assure you,' said Jennifer soothingly, 'that as soon as we find out exactly what we're dealing with here we'll let you know. And I'll make sure your views are known.' Van Simson's face lifted.

'That's very kind.' He smiled. 'I hope you don't think me rude but I feel quite passionately about this. A lot of money is at stake.'

'I understand.'

'Well then, if you've seen enough, can I ask you to make your own way back to the lift. It will take you upstairs and Rolfe will see you out.'

'Of course,' said Jennifer, shaking his hand. 'And thank you again for your time.'

'Not at all. And I hope that we'll meet again, Mr Kirk.' Tom nodded as he in turn shook Van Simson's hand. They weaved their way through the display cases towards the blindingly bright rectangle of light of the vault entrance until, just as they were about to step out into the corridor, Van Simson called after them.

'You know, this is where I plan to be buried, one day.' His arms extended to take in the room in front of him. 'Down here, sealed inside with my collection. Then I will have them all to myself for ever.'

Through the suspended glass sheets Tom could see that Van Simson had stepped up onto the raised platform. Illuminated by a single spotlight directly over his head, his eyes had sunk into dark pools of shadow.

THIRTY-NINE

3:51pm
Rolfe's achromatic stare vanished with a shudder as the heavy wooden door swung shut behind them.

'So, what do you think?' said Jennifer as they crossed the street and walked back towards the Place des Vôsges and the car.

'About what?'

Tom buried his hands in his trouser pockets.

'About what we just saw.'

'You're the detective, not me.'

She stopped and turned to face him, annoyed. It was one thing to be unfriendly. To be honest, she didn't expect anything less. But being deliberately obstructive was not part of their deal.

'We're meant to be helping each other, remember. This is going to be a lot easier on both of us if you play along.'

'I don't think cop, okay.'

'Fine.' She shrugged in frustration and set off again, shaking her head at his obstinence. 'I'll think cop for both of us then, shall I? We learnt that his coin is safe and sound. In fact it would take a small army to get to it. And . . .'

'And?'

'And I think we learnt that he already knew there was another coin. He acted surprised when I told him about it but his eyes barely flickered.' Tom nodded, stepping aside to let past a mother pushing a large baby buggy. 'He certainly didn't seem as surprised as I would have guessed he would be.'

'Yeah, but that could mean anything. Like Harry said, Van Simson is well plugged-in. It doesn't prove he was involved in taking them and even if he was, we don't know how. Or what the link was between him and the priest?'

'Ranieri?'

'Yeah. Where does he fit into Van Simson's world?'

'I've told you what I know. He stole money from the Vatican Bank and then surfaced here a year ago and set himself up as a fence. He was a small-time player.'

'Exactly. So what was he doing handling an eight million dollar coin? That was way out of his league. So what we need to find out is who gave him the coin to sell on in the first place?'

'We could go and check out his apartment?' Jennifer suggested brightly.

'Where did he live?'

'Porte de Cling . . . something.' She reached into her bag for her notebook.

'Porte de Clignancourt. That figures. I hardly expected him to be off the Champs Elysées. Haven't the police been all over it?'

'Yeah, but how closely do you think they looked?' If there was one lesson she'd learnt over the years it was to trust the evidence of her own eyes over the assurances of others, especially local cops. 'They probably couldn't wait to close the file. As far as they were concerned someone had just saved them the trouble of taking another scumbag off the streets. We might notice something they didn't.'

They were back at the car now and Tom slid behind the wheel and started the engine.

'It's your call,' he said as Jennifer got in. 'I'll drive us there if you want to go and take a look. But if you ask me it's a waste of time.'

'Lucky I didn't ask you, then,' Jennifer snapped back, again finding his attitude frustrating. She took her notebook out of her bag and leafed through it. 'Rue du Ruisseau, number seventeen. You know it?'

Tom nodded.

'Right next to the flea market. But I'm telling you, it's a waste of time.'

He pulled out and accelerated down the street, the tyres drumming over the worn and rounded cobbles.

Behind him, a dark blue car pulled out from where it had been half-hidden behind a white van and followed them, the passenger talking into his phone.

FORTY

Porte de Clignancourt, 18th Arrondissement, Paris
4:17pm

They stopped the car and looked around warily before getting out. The trees that had once lined the handsome street had long since gone, strangled by the thick air and stale light. The graffiti, loud markings of despair and hate, had been sprayed up to head height across the high ashen walls like the inside of a prison cell. The washing hanging at half-mast out of the windows above them flapped limply in the breeze.

They approached number Seventeen and pressed the buzzer. A few seconds later a torrent of indecipherable French crackled out from the intercom.

Tom said just one word.

'Police.'

There was a pause and then the door buzzed

open. Tom gave Jennifer a smile but she just pushed past him with an angry shake of her head.

'Impersonating a police officer?'

'Got us in, didn't it?'

They made their way inside, their footsteps echoing in the smooth vaulted passage that had once sheltered horse-drawn carriages, but now housed instead two large green wheelie-bins that gave off the sickly-sweet smell of rotting food. The concierge was standing at the foot of the stairs to meet them, a white haired old woman, her face aged into deep vertical furrows, the gameshow on her TV flickering through the open door behind her.

'We would like to look around Father Ranieri's apartment,' said Tom, his French faultless.

'You the Police?' Her voice was frail and brittle.

'That's right.'

'Got a badge?'

'Yes.'

'Let's see it?' Her hands were clasped, her thin wrists swollen by arthritis, each gnarled finger buckled and deformed into two sets of rigid claws.

'Don't give me any trouble, old woman.'

The concierge paused and looked Tom and then Jennifer up and down, mumbling under her breath about procedure and bullying.

'What floor?'

'Top. Room B.'

'Is there an elevator?'

'No.' The concierge jerked her thumb behind

her into the courtyard. 'Stairs.' Tom nodded and led Jennifer past the concierge, into the courtyard.

They clambered up the stairs until five minutes later their footsteps began to echo back down towards them off the domed glass roof that covered the top of the staircase. They reached the landing and saw that six pallid doors all led off a long cheerless corridor.

'This must be it,' Jennifer said as they arrived at the end of the corridor. The door on the left was sealed with blue and white police tape and an official-looking sign had been stapled to the door. Tom nodded.

'I'll get us in.'

'No need,' said Jennifer, producing a small lock-pick from her bag and bending down. 'I can manage.' She fiddled quietly with the lock before gently turning the handle and pushing the door open. The tape ripped away.

They stepped into a small room, the only light coming from a smeared and curtainless window. A narrow bed ran down one wall, its mattress propped up on the wall next to it. A small refrigerator hummed, the door open but the light clearly broken. Clothes had been pulled out of the dresser and wardrobe and lay strewn across the bed and the floor.

A chipped white sink stood in the far left-hand corner, while next to it a single gas ring, connected to a bright blue gas bottle, had been balanced on a cheap laminate table. Tom tried the light switch, but the bulb was missing. Cobwebs weaved across the ceiling.

'What a shithole!' she exclaimed.

'What were you expecting?' Tom asked.

'I don't know . . . more than this anyway.'

'This was your idea, don't forget.'

'Well, we're here now, so we might as well take a look around.'

Tom shrugged and began to work his way round the room, tapping the walls and examining the floor. Jennifer did the same, looking behind the wardrobe and moving the bed out from the wall. It wasn't long before they had covered the whole room and met back in the middle.

'So much for that,' said Tom, glaring reproachfully at the room around him. 'There's nothing here.'

'It was worth a try.'

'Was it?'

'Maybe the French police aren't as careless as I thought. Maybe . . .'

'Hold on.' Tom interrupted her. 'There really *is* nothing here.'

'What do you mean?'

'Well there are some clothes, a bed, a stove, even some books.' He kicked one across the floor and it buried itself under a bright red shirt. 'But I can't believe he was living like this. No food, no photos. I mean, there's not even a curtain.'

'No curtain?' Jennifer gave a short laugh. 'So what?'

'Have you ever tried sleeping in a room without a curtain? It's hard unless you want to wake up at four in the morning. You would have expected him to fix something up, even if it was just a sheet or a towel or something.'

She shrugged, silently conceding that he had a point. It was definitely unusual. Meanwhile, Tom had approached the window and was staring through the filthy glass at the jumble of roofs, TV aerials, windows and chimney pots that stretched out before him. He shook his head and looked down. A chair was on the floor that had presumably been overturned during the police search.

He righted it, pushing it back to what he guessed was its regular spot under the window, judging from the dirty line where its back had rubbed against the paintwork over the years. Then, just as he was about to turn away, he caught sight of the brown material that covered the chair's seat. It was covered in dusty footprints.

'That's strange.' He crouched down next to it for a closer look.

'What is it? What have you found?' Jennifer stepped forward.

'I wonder if . . .' He opened the window and stood on the chair, before stepping up and out on to the roof into a wide gully and heading to his right.

Jennifer jumped up after him and followed him along the gully as it traced the perimeter of the building, stepping up slightly as she crossed over on to the roof of the adjacent building.

Here a swirling wind was whistling in and out of the chimney pots and she soon found herself wishing that she was wearing flat shoes as she negotiated the cables and lengths of electric flex that had been untidily laid across the roof like trip wires, carefully lifting her feet over each one.

But then, just as she was stepping over the last set of cables, a particularly vicious gust threw her slightly off balance. Instinctively she put her foot down, only for her long heel to catch on one of the wires. Almost as if it was in slow motion, she felt herself falling, her hands grabbing at the air, her feet disappearing from under her, until she fell hard against the roof and began to slide down the slope towards the courtyard.

'Tom!' She screamed, somehow grabbing on to a piece of flex that brought her to a shuddering halt, although the way the wire had cracked and frayed suggested it would only provide a temporary reprieve.

'Tom!' she called again, scrabbling with her knees and feet to stop herself from sliding any further down the steep roof. Her left shoe came off and cartwheeled down the slope, stopping inches from the edge.

Tom suddenly appeared and threw himself to his stomach, straining with his hand to get to her. She reached up, her fingers desperately trying to grab his hand but remaining, agonisingly, inches apart.

'Put your foot there,' Tom called out urgently. 'Now push up.' She found the small ridge that Tom was pointing at and set her foot against it, but still she couldn't reach him. 'Don't move.'

Jennifer nodded dumbly, too terrified to speak, the flex increasingly slippery in her perspiring palms. Tom disappeared. The seconds ticked agonisingly by.

'Where are you?' she called as cramp began to set in to her hand where she was gripping the flex. 'Tom?'

Silence.

Slowly a terrifying possibility dawned on her. She screwed her eyes tight and tried not to think about it, but it just wouldn't go away – the possibility that Tom had deliberately lured her up onto this roof. Had he left her there, taking the opportunity to make his escape once and for all?

Then, just as the cramp was spreading to her legs and she thought she couldn't hold on any longer, a thick black cable, its end freshly cut, slid down the roof next to her.

'Grab onto that.' Tom had reappeared just over the crest of the roofline. Gratefully, she reached across and gripped the cable. Tom hauled her up until she was able to bring her knee up over the ridge and roll over onto her back, her chest heaving.

'Shit.' She gasped with relief.

'You're welcome.'

'I thought you were going to leave me there.'

'You really don't have much faith in people, do you?' Tom sat down next to her, rubbing his arm where he seemed to have strained it pulling her clear.

'My shoe,' she suddenly exclaimed, scrambling to her feet. 'I need to get it.'

'Well, I'm not going down there.' Tom stood up and brushed his trousers down.

'I can't leave it. They cost me five hundred bucks.'

'Five hundred. Jesus.'

'Shoes is sort of what I do for fun,' she said defensively.

'Fine. Give me the other shoe.'

'What?'

'Do you want it back or not?'

'Yes.' She slipped the other shoe off her foot and handed it to him, a suspicious look on her face. Without saying a word, Tom aimed and then threw it, catching the trapped shoe full on and sending them both tailspinning off the roof down to the courtyard. Jennifer could barely believe it. He'd just played marbles with a pair of five-hundred-dollar shoes.

'You bastard!' she shouted.

'You can pick them up when we've finished,' said Tom, and she was certain that he turned away from her just in time to conceal a smile.

Still fuming, she followed him along the gully for another few yards, treading carefully through the bird mess that pockmarked the silvery roof now that she was barefoot. It eventually ended at another window, this one covered with dark red curtains. Tom pushed against it, but it seemed to be locked firmly shut from the inside.

'What are we doing up here anyhow?' Jennifer asked, now wishing that she hadn't suggested they visit Ranieri's place at all.

'Clutching at straws,' said Tom, examining the smooth slope of the roof around the window before turning his attention to the window frame itself. He ran his fingers slowly around its flaking edges until, underneath the sill, he felt the outline of a small button. He pressed it and although it made no noise, this time when he tried the windows, they opened easily into the room, pushing the red curtains aside. Jennifer stood wide-eyed behind him, her anger suddenly forgotten.

'Okay. I forgive you for the shoes.'

'A dummy entrance is a fairly common trick if you're trying to avoid people dropping in on you unannounced. From what you've told me of Ranieri, he wasn't exactly short of people who might have liked a quick word. Anyway,' he lowered himself into the dark room, 'let's see what we find before you forgive me.'

FORTY-ONE

4:36pm

They had stepped into the bedroom, and the contrast with the apartment they had just come could not have been more marked. It was immaculately arranged, the dark blue bedspread coordinating perfectly with the elaborate Chinese wallpaper and the cream rug on the polished wooden floor. A few framed photographs had been arranged on the bedside table and the mirrored doors that ran down the far wall opened to reveal a wardrobe of suits, shirts, shoes and ties, all sorted by colour, alongside the paraphernalia of Ranieri's ecclesiastical dress. Clearly whatever he did, it paid well.

The bedroom led onto a large kitchen, with the front door set into the right-hand wall. An archway opposite gave onto an office with a large desk at one end. Here, the darkness was lifted by a synthetic red glow as the late afternoon sun filtered in through the closed curtains. Tom and Jennifer stood on the threshold and peered inside.

'Here you go,' said Jennifer. She had found a switch beside the entrance and turned it on.

'Let's see what we've got.'

Tom made his way to the desk and began leafing through the papers on it before moving onto the drawers. There was nothing there. Invoices, faxes, orders. It seemed that Ranieri had been running some sort of wine importing business as a cover.

In a way, he was surprised he was bothering at all, given his natural aversion to working with any sort of cop, especially a Fed – although Jennifer was clearly not the thick-skulled flatfoot that he was used to dealing with. Quite the opposite, in fact. But Tom was also the sort of person who liked a challenge. And, if truth be known, he was also rather intrigued by these coins and how they had found their way from Fort Knox into Ranieri's hands, although he would never say as much to Jennifer.

'This is what we need,' said Jennifer picking up an electrical cable that led from the desk to a socket. 'His laptop. Maybe someone else has been here before us and taken it?'

'Maybe it's been hidden somewhere here?'

'I'll go and take a look in the bedroom,' she volunteered.

Tom sat down heavily in one of the chairs and let his eyes play over the room, looking for something, anything that could help. It was an uncompromisingly modern room. The coffee table and desk matched, smoked glass laid on a brushed steel frame. The black leather sofa and chairs were stiff and stubby, their backs set at a steep, uncomfortable angle that pushed Tom's knees up to his chest. The walls were white and punctuated by a series of black and white photographs of New York landmarks. The triangular wedge of the Flatiron Building, the streamlined chrome of the Chrysler Building, the granite thrust of the Empire State.

Faced with the monochromatic masculinity of the room, Tom's eyes were irresistibly drawn to the red waste-paper basket that nestled in the curve of the desk's legs. He picked it up distractedly, noting its ragged and chipped surface that suggested an old and familiar possession, still pressed into loyal service despite its bold variance to the overall colour scheme.

Reaching in, he pulled out a newspaper. Nothing strange in that. Except . . . maybe the date?

'When did you say Ranieri was killed?' he called through to Jennifer.

'The 16th. Why?' her voice echoed back through the silent apartment.

'I might have something here.'

Jennifer walked back into the room, her face expectant.

'I just found this paper. It's dated the 20th.

That's four days after Ranieri was killed. Someone else *has* been here.'

'And probably destroyed or taken anything useful,' she said, her voice disappointed.

'Except . . .' Tom, indicated the room around them. 'Take a look at this place. It's not been trashed like the decoy apartment, has it?'

'Meaning?'

'That whoever it was, they knew this place and didn't need to tear it apart. They knew how to get in, where things were kept, everything. Whoever was here had been here before, possibly with Ranieri.'

'Maybe he had a partner?' Jennifer grimaced at the unforgiving rigidity of the chair as she sat down opposite Tom.

'Someone German, perhaps?' Tom suggested, holding up the paper he had retrieved from the trash. 'Our mystery guest reads the Frankfurter Allgemeine Zeitung. In fact . . .' Tom examined it more carefully, 'don't you think it looks like he folded it open at this article in particular?'

The paper had been neatly folded into four, forming a large rectangle that opened much like a book. One article dominated the middle of the front page, while the other pages were dissected and broken by competing articles, ads and photos.

'What does the headline say?' Jennifer got up and moved over to Tom, sitting next to him on the arm of the sofa.

'*Suche geht weiter für Schiphol Flughafen-Diebe,*'
Tom read out. 'Search continues for Schiphol
airport thieves,' he translated.

'Schiphol? Schiphol in Holland?'

'You know another?' asked Tom.

'Cute,' Jennifer pulled a face. She extracted her
phone from her purse and dialled a number.

'Max Springer, please.' There was a pause.
'Max, it's Jen. Fine, thanks. Are you at your desk?
Great. I want you to check something out for me.
Can you see what you've got about a theft from
Schiphol airport a few weeks ago. Yes, of course
Schiphol in Amsterdam. You know another?' She
winked at Tom.

'What are you thinking?' Tom asked. She
cupped her hand over the mouthpiece.

'We get daily crime reports from Interpol.
They're filed into our databases. Whatever
happened at Schiphol should be in there somewhere.' She snatched her hand away from the
mouthpiece. 'Yeah, hi, I'm still here. You found
something? Okay, great. Run me through it.
Slowly.' She jotted down some notes on a scrap
of paper that she grabbed from the desk. 'Okay
. . . Okay. Is that it? Great. What's that? I can't
talk to him right now.' Her eyes flicked to Tom
and then back down to the ground. 'Tell him I'll
call him tonight. Thanks, Max.' She hung up.

'So?'

'There was an armed robbery from the customs

warehouse at Schiphol airport on 11th July. Three guys snatched a fortune in vintage wine and jewellery in a hijacked UPS van. Killed two guards. Then ten days later on the 21st, a man was stabbed in a phone box in Amsterdam. Dutch police identified the victim as Karl Steiner,' Jennifer looked down at her scribbled notes as she spoke, 'an East German with a record as long as your arm for armed robbery and handling stolen goods. When they got to his place they found several cases of vintage wine and what was left of the jewellery.'

'In other words he pulled the airport job,' said Tom, standing up.

'It gets better. It turns out he was arrested on the 14th. In Paris. Apparently he'd started a fight outside a nightclub. Guess who bailed him out the next morning?'

'Ranieri?' His tone was more hopeful than questioning.

'You got it.' Jennifer smiled triumphantly.

Tom rubbed his right temple, his forehead creased in thought.

'Well, that's it, then. You've been trying to work out how Ranieri got the coin, haven't you? How this carefully constructed Fort Knox robbery went wrong. Now we know.'

'We do?'

'Amsterdam's a major trade hub. All sorts of valuable merchandise comes through there, some of it legally, some not. Let's say Steiner decided to help himself to a piece of the action. He knocks off the airport and steals a van load of wine and jewels. But what if he got lucky? What if when he unpacked it all, he found the coins hidden in one of the boxes?'

'You mean it was all just an accident? Months of planning, hundreds of thousands of dollars of investment ruined because some hood got lucky?'

'Why not? A courier would have been too risky, given how tight airport security has been recently. Cargo was a much safer option since most of it never even gets unpacked. I should know, I've used it myself. Steiner probably had people lined up to take the wine and the gems off him. But the coins – they were unusual. He needed help for those.'

'Right.' Jennifer could see where Tom was heading. 'So Steiner came to Paris to see his old friend Ranieri. Maybe gave him one of the coins as a taster. But before Ranieri could sell it, someone tracked him down and killed him. When Steiner heard what had happened he came back here, grabbed his stuff, threw his newspaper in the trash and ran back to Amsterdam, presumably with the other coins.'

'And wound up dead a few days later himself. Stabbed, just like Ranieri.'

'Didn't Harry say that there were only a small number of people in the world who would be interested or able to buy coins like these?'

'What's your point?'

'That it's just possible that both Steiner and Ranieri ended up trying to sell them back to the same people who'd had them stolen in the first place?'

Before Tom could answer, the edges of the newspaper fluttered, the pages lifting and then settling again with a faint rustle. Jennifer's eyes snapped to the open doorway.

'Did you shut the window behind you?' she whispered.

'I think so, yes,' Tom whispered back.

He slid off the sofa and flicked the switch, plunging the room back into darkness before stepping towards the doorway, pressing his back to the wall, Jennifer standing behind him.

They waited and listened, the silence strangely amplifying the sounds drifting in over the rooftops. A distant siren, a window slamming, a squeal of brakes, a baby crying. But then, through all these, a different noise. A faint creak, followed a few seconds later by another. Noises that could only be coming from inside the flat itself. From someone treading on the floorboards.

The footsteps drew irresistibly towards them like the steady beat of a muffled drum, only accompanied now, so close were they, by a faint rustle of fabric. Then, just as suddenly, they stopped and Tom knew that whoever it was must be standing just the other side of the doorway. Readying themselves.

A gun barrel edged into the room, black and polished and snub-nosed. And then a man's hand, white and podgy, with sovereign rings on each of the fingers and a spider's web tattooed onto the soft mound of skin between the thumb and the forefinger.

Without hesitating, Tom reached forward and grabbed the man's wrist, locking his fingers over the top of the man's thumb and tightening his own thumb over the lower wrist joint. In the same movement, he spun the man's hand round so that it went through 180 degrees and then snapped it back up towards his body. Tom immediately felt the connective tendons and ligaments rupturing and snapping all along the wrist joint as the gun dropped from the man's fingers to the sound of his screaming. Tom loosened his grip on his wrist and scooped the gun off the floor. The man, whose face neither of them had yet seen, leapt back from the entrance howling in pain.

'I'll shoot the next person that tries to come into this room,' Tom shouted.

There was silence and then the sound of retreating footsteps and then two muffled voices which seemed to be coming from the bedroom.

'They're probably deciding which is worse,' Tom whispered. 'Trying to take us on in here or going back empty-handed to whoever sent them.'

The doorbell suddenly rang out, a shrill medley of electronic chimes that flooded the apartment with noise. In the deep silence that followed, they heard the sound of running feet fading away across the rooftops.

FORTY-TWO

5:06pm

The bell rang again, more insistently this time. Tom crept out into the kitchen and then, keeping close to the wall, made his way to the front door. Again the sound of the bell rolled through the empty flat, only this time it was accompanied by the dull thud of someone banging a fist against the wood. Tom edged his eye towards the chrome peephole that had been drilled into the middle of the door.

'Shit,' he whispered through his teeth. 'Shit, shit, shit.' He screwed his eyes tightly shut and leaned his head against the door, shaking it slowly. This was the last thing he needed.

'Who is it?' Jennifer mouthed, still standing in the doorway to the living room, a curious look on her face. Without answering, Tom slipped the gun in his pocket, reached down, unbolted the door and opened it. The light from the corridor billowed into the room like a dense fog and made him squint.

'*Ah, Felix, mon ami*. I hope we did not disturb you?' A broad man with a cheery face and long curls of oily hair that were tied into a thick black ponytail peered into the darkness of the room, his arm extended. Jennifer recognised *Felix* as the name that Piper had claimed Kirk had operated under for the last ten years.

'*Bonjour, Jean-Pierre*. You'd better come in,' said Tom grudgingly, shaking his hand. The man signalled at the two policemen standing either side of him to wait. Jennifer flicked the lights back on as Tom shut the door behind the man. 'Jennifer, this is Jean-Pierre Dumas, from the DST – the French domestic Secret Service. Jean-Pierre, meet Special Agent Jennifer Browne of the FBI.'

'*Enchanté*.' Dumas shook Jennifer's hand, his breath pure Lucky Strike. 'These must be yours.' He glanced at her still-naked feet and held up her shoes in his left hand.

'Thank you.' Jennifer glared at Tom as she brushed the dirt and dust off each of her feet before slipping the shoes back on.

'Do you have any papers, Mademoiselle?' Dumas asked when she stood up.

Jennifer reached into her jacket pocket, pulled out her FBI badge and handed it to him. He wedged his cigarette in his mouth and examined it sceptically, his eyebrows raised in surprise.

'So, Felix really is working for the FBI. *Maintenant j'ai vraiment tout vu.*'

'I'm not working for the FBI,' Tom said tersely. 'We're co-operating, that's all.'

'That's right,' Jennifer interjected. 'Mr Kirk is here as a private citizen. Nothing more.'

'He always is,' Dumas said with a wave of his hand. 'Come. Let's sit down and we can discuss all this properly.'

He led them through to the sitting-room and sat down reluctantly on one of the sofas, his weight barely depressing the cushion's stiff springs, while Tom and Jennifer sat opposite. Dumas was dressed in a new pair of jeans, blue shirt over a white T-shirt and a heavy black leather jacket. He looked strong, although not particularly fit or fast. His brown eyes twinkled above his large, blunt nose, his face slack from alcohol and nicotine.

'So, my friend.' He turned to Tom. 'What brings you back to Paris?'

'You two are friends?'

'Well, maybe not friends,' Dumas agreed. 'Tom never likes to get too close to anyone, do you? But we have an understanding that is as close to friendship as I expect Tom will ever get.' Dumas smiled.

'I want you to tell her, J-P,' Tom said insistently. 'Tell her how we met.'

'Are you sure?' Dumas looked uncertain but

Tom gave a firm nod of his head. Shrugging, Dumas continued. 'Felix was having some problems a few years ago now. He had become, how you say, surplus to your government's requirements. He came to me and we helped him disappear on the understanding that he would help us recover an item of national importance.'

'So you *were* telling the truth about that?' Jennifer said softly with a shake of her head.

Dumas turned back to face Tom, his face suddenly serious. 'But now you are in trouble again, yes?'

'Why, what have you heard?'

'Do you know a Detective Sergeant Clarke? He certainly seems to know you.'

'That bastard,' said Tom darkly. 'Does he know I'm here?'

'No. And don't worry. I won't tell him.'

'Thanks, J-P.' Tom smiled gratefully.

'Anyway, when I heard that he wanted you for murder, I knew it was a mistake. Self-defence is one thing, but you are no killer.'

'How did you find us?' Tom asked.

'We have been watching your friend Van Simson for several months now. We suspect him of involvement in money laundering, bribery, blackmail, maybe even murder . . . he's a dangerous person to know.'

'So you followed us from there?'

'*Oui*. I put someone on it. But you surprised us

all when you came here. Nearly as much as when Mademoiselle's shoes fell out of the sky and just missed my head.'

Tom held his hand up.

'My fault. Sorry.'

Dumas waved it away.

'The gendarmes have been staking this place out for about ten days now. They are investigating the murder of an Italian priest. But I expect you already knew that.'

'They know about this apartment?' asked Tom in surprise, secretly impressed that they had found it too.

'They are not complete idiots,' said Dumas, his smile contradicting him.

'Well, we're not the only people to have been here. Someone's already been and taken anything that might have been useful.' Tom indicated the laptop cable dangling from the desk. Dumas rolled his eyes.

'*Plus ça change*. They probably wouldn't have seen you come in either if we hadn't told them to look out for you both. Which leaves the question.' He turned his gaze to Jennifer. 'What *are* you doing here?'

'Mr Kirk is assisting the FBI with an enquiry that we are conducting.'

Dumas' jaw set firm.

'And that gives you the right to break into a private apartment, does it? To impersonate a police officer? To contaminate a crime scene?' Jennifer was silent. 'Let me ask, Agent Browne, has your embassy requested assistance from the *Ministre de L'Intérieur*?'

'I would have to check with Washington.'

'Well, let me save you the trouble. They haven't. So effectively, you are here as a private citizen too. An illegal immigrant, in fact, since my colleagues in Customs don't seem to have any record of you entering the country.'

'I can assure you . . .' Jennifer began but Dumas cut her off.

'There is a French word for that sort of behaviour that I think translates well. *Espionage*. You may think the rest of the world is yours to do as you like, but here in France, we do not appreciate foreign agents operating unofficially. A small matter of national security.' Dumas' eyes flashed and as far as he could while sitting down, he had pushed his chest out and straightened his back to emphasise his point.

'Mr Dumas, I apologise for any offence caused.' Jennifer was respectful but firm. 'My visit here was unplanned and so I was unable to go through the usual channels. However I am sure that the American Ambassador would be able to vouch for me and allay any concerns you might have about my intentions here.'

Dumas snorted.

'I'm sure he will. Meanwhile, I want to know

why you're interested in Ranieri? And what he's got to do with Van Simson?'

Jennifer smiled and shook her head.

'That's classified information which I'm afraid I'm not at liberty to disclose to you.'

'He's a very dangerous man.'

'When I want to be patronised, I'll let you know.' Jennifer's response was terse. 'Believe me, I've dealt with far worse. I can look after myself.'

'Then there are two ways of doing this, Agent Browne,' Dumas said slowly. 'Either you share what you've got with me and I'll do the same in return. Or I let the two gendarmes who are waiting outside arrest you.'

'We both know that my Embassy would have me released in hours,' Jennifer said with a shrug. 'It would achieve nothing.'

'Maybe not. But I can assure you that I would see to it that the incident attracted widespread media coverage. Your picture splashed over the newspapers. Your superiors in Washington compromised. It's a situation that I expect is in everyone's interest to avoid unless you wish your investigation to end early.'

There was an awkward pause, during which Jennifer and Dumas stared stubbornly at each other until Tom broke the silence.

'Ranieri was found in possession of a valuable coin, which was stolen from the US government.'

His interjection earned him a furious look from Jennifer.

'Drop it, Tom,' she exploded. 'That's not for you to reveal and you know it.'

'I don't think any of us have got time to play games. Jean-Pierre is not the sort of person to go shooting his mouth off and none of us can afford to have our asses dragged through the press. So why don't you just tell him what you know?'

'If it helps,' Dumas said with a shrug, 'I know of this coin. This Double Eagle.' Jennifer didn't react. 'Don't forget that it was the French police who handed the coin over to the FBI in the first place.'

This time Jennifer glanced at Tom who nodded his encouragement.

'He's on your side. He already knows about the coin. Hell, he might even be able to help you. What have you got to lose?'

'You think that Ranieri was fencing the coins for whoever stole them?' Dumas prompted her gently.

'Yes.' She nodded, her voice initially hesitant but growing in fluency. 'And we're interested in Darius Van Simson because he's a major collector of gold coins. In fact, he even owns a Double Eagle. I wanted to establish whether he knew anything about the theft or the current where-abouts of the coin.'

Dumas smiled.

'Let me guess. Mr Van Simson knew nothing about either. He never does. It is like a religion with him.'

'Yeah, I did kind of get that impression,' Jennifer agreed.

'He did take us down to his vault, though,' Tom reminded her. 'Showed us his collection and his coin.'

'Then you got further than most,' said Dumas, raising his eyebrows. 'From what I hear he never takes anyone down there.'

Dumas' radio frazzled loudly and he reached into his pocket with annoyance to turn the volume down.

'Patron?' The muffled voice vibrated from inside his jacket. Dumas rolled his eyes, took the radio out and pressed it to his mouth.

'Oui.'

'Patron. On les a pincés en bas.'

'J'arrive.'

Dumas replaced the radio in his pocket and smiled at Tom.

'It seems my men have bumped into some friends of yours downstairs.'

'Oh, them.' Tom smiled. 'You know who they are?'

'They followed you here from outside Van Simson's. Of course he'll deny having sent or even seen them before.'

'One of them dropped this on his way out.

Perhaps you could return it to him.' Tom retrieved the gun from his pocket and placed it in Dumas's outstretched hand. He accepted it with a nod.

'*Bon*. There is nothing more we can do here,' Dumas said standing up, arching his back as he made his way to the door. He hadn't noticed the newspaper lying on the coffee table and Tom managed to snatch it and slip it under his jacket before he turned round.

'Where are you two staying tonight?'

Tom shook his head.

'We're not sure yet.'

'I'll book you something.'

'That's not necessary,' said Jennifer. 'We can take care of ourselves.'

'*J'insiste*,' said Dumas without smiling. 'And if you want any further cooperation from the French authorities,' he held her FBI badge up in one hand, 'then I suggest you go through the official channels. Otherwise, tomorrow, I expect you both out of the country.' With a flick of his wrist he tossed her badge towards her and she snatched it out of the air.

'Go over to the Hotel St Merri in the Fourth,' said Dumas as they emerged onto the street. 'Tell them I sent you. They'll give you a couple of rooms.'

'*Merci*, Jean-Pierre,' said Tom shaking his hand firmly as Jennifer got into the car.

'*De rien, mon ami*. It's good to have you back.'

Then in a quieter voice. 'What are you doing mixed up in all this Felix? The FBI? *C'est pas ton style.*'

'Like I said before, it's a short-term gig. She gets her coin back, I get whoever killed Harry Renwick. That's it.'

Dumas nodded and looked at Tom, then at Jennifer, then back to Tom.

'Be careful.'

'What? Of Van Simson? Don't worry, if those two were the best he's got, I'll be fine.'

'No . . . I mean of her.' Dumas winked. 'A woman like that can be dangerous. Make you do things you shouldn't. Don't forget how they treated you last time.'

Tom somehow mustered a smile.

FORTY-THREE

**Hôtel St Merri, 4th Arrondissement, Paris
7:26pm**

Tom threw his head back under the shower's massaging pulse and closed his eyes, letting it run through his hair. The water flooded his ears, blocking them, and as he listened to his suddenly amplified breathing and the strangely distant sound of the water splashing all around him, the dull throb in his head subsided a little. It was only then that he realized how tired he was.

He slid the cubicle door back a bit and a thin cloud of steam escaped through the narrow gap into the bathroom, fogging the mirror. He reached out, his eyes blinking as they fought against the water running in rivulets off his head, towards the sink and closed his fingers around the small complimentary bar of soap and bottle of shampoo that the hotel had thoughtfully provided.

He rubbed the soap all over himself, rinsed it

off and then washed his hair. He reached towards the sink again and located the small razor that had also been provided, somehow managing not to cut himself as he shaved. Then he stood there, his hands leaning against the chipped tiles and flaking grout, the water thudding onto the base of his neck, sluicing over his shoulders and down his back. He turned the temperature up a little.

How had he ended up here? He'd almost forgotten now. Uncle Harry. That was it. He'd wanted to find Harry's killers. To make them pay.

And to help himself. He couldn't deny it. Jennifer's deal offered him a real chance. His file wiped, the CIA off his back, Clarke warned off. Could he trust them, though? Could he trust her? He still wasn't sure.

He flicked the water off and grabbed first one, then another towel off the rail over the bath. He dried himself, the rough cloth rasping over his skin like sandpaper, smoothing his hair into shape with his hand. Then he pulled on clean underwear, a pair of jeans and a T-shirt, all in the bag of clothes provided by the ever-efficient FBI. Finally he laced up the trainers that he'd shoved on that morning when the police had first shown up. He stepped out into the bedroom and then made his way down the narrow staircase to Jennifer's room on the floor below. He knocked.

'Come in.'

'I'm just going down to see about getting us a table next door.'

Jennifer nodded.

'Okay. I've got to make a phone call anyway. I'm going to suggest that we go to Amsterdam and follow up on this Steiner angle.'

'Fine. But don't forget our agreement. Unless you get my deal confirmed, you'll be going on your own.'

'Understood,' she agreed.

'I'll be back in ten minutes.'

'Sure.'

She stepped into the bathroom and Tom noticed the smooth muscle of her neck as it curved into her perfect brown back. He shook his head ruefully. That was exactly what Jean-Pierre had meant about her being dangerous.

A few moments later he emerged onto the street below. The pale buildings glowed a deep yellow as the sun melted into the horizon and the stone began to radiate an intense baked-in heat. The streets were already alive with people and the noisy cafés and restaurants spilled their eager customers out onto the street under an array of brightly coloured umbrellas, lit from underneath like lanterns. Innumerable conversations ducked under the buzz of scooters and climbed over the growl of traffic on the nearby Rue de Rivoli.

The area was notorious for prostitutes, and looking up Tom noticed that one of them had already opened her window and placed a small red towel over her balcony. It was the usual signal. She was open for business.

'Tom. Over here.' At the sound of his name Tom spun round to face the table he had just walked past.

'All right?' came the voice again, this time accompanied by a wave.

Archie was virtually unrecognisable. A baseball cap, T-shirt and shorts formed an effective camouflage amidst the crowds of tourists. The camera hanging round his neck and the backpack at his feet completed the image. A pair of sunglasses sat on his face, his stubble rougher than before. It seemed to be some sort of disguise, although for what purpose Tom couldn't say. In any case, he was too surprised to comment.

'What the hell are you doing here?'

'Have you been inside? There's an art deco mirror behind the bar. Saw one like it sell for ten grand a few months ago.'

Tom grabbed him by his T-shirt and lifted him right out of his chair.

'What are you doing here? What are you playing at?'

'Easy, tiger,' said Archie, his sunglasses half off his face.

'How did you find me?' Tom snapped.

'Jean-Pierre called me this afternoon,' Archie croaked as his T-shirt pressed against his throat.

'He was just returning a favour, that's all. Honest, mate.'

Tom relaxed his grip slightly.

'What did he say?'

'That you were in Paris. I dusted off my passport, jumped on the next Eurostar and gave him a bell when I arrived. He told me he'd sent you here.'

'He didn't tell me that he'd called you when I saw him,' Tom's voice was edged with suspicion.

'Maybe he wanted it to be a surprise, I don't know. Anyway, I'm here now.'

Tom stared at Archie for a few seconds before letting him go so that he slumped back into his chrome seat. Archie pushed his sunglasses back on his nose as Tom sat heavily in the chair opposite him.

'What do you want, Archie?'

'We need to talk. There's all sorts of shit flying around. None of it good. It's a real dog's breakfast.'

'Why, what have you heard?'

'Word is you clipped old man Renwick. It looks bad.'

'Do you think I did it?'

'Don't be daft.'

Tom leant back, sighed and rubbed his eyes. He signalled to the waiter who came over and took their order.

'Bloody foreigners,' Archie grumbled. 'Never

serve proper beer, just this fizzy shit.' He eventually settled with a grunt on the lager he deemed least offensive. Tom, predictably, ordered a vodka tonic.

'I've been set up, Archie. I had dinner with Harry last night. Next thing I know, Clarke tries to nail me for whacking him. Says that my prints are everywhere.'

'Why would someone try to set you up?'

'That's what I'd like to know.'

'Is it anything to do with the bird?' asked Archie, his eyes flicking back towards the hotel doorway.

'How do you know about her?' Tom snapped back.

'Keep your hair on.' Archie looked around nervously at the people on the neighbouring tables. 'Jean-Pierre told me you were with a bird, that's all. Seemed to think she might be giving you a spot of aggro.'

The waiter returned and deposited their drinks on the shiny table, slipping the bill under the edge of the blue Pernod ashtray. Archie reached into his backpack and pulled out two phones, checking each of their screens for messages or missed calls and then placing them on the table, their colour screens reflecting rainbows in the sinking sunlight.

'You could say that. She works for the FBI.'

Archie half stood up.

'The FBI! Are you taking the piss?'

Tom motioned at him to sit down again.

'I wish I was. Apparently they got a DNA match from the New York job. The only reason they haven't picked me up is because they think I knocked off Fort Knox and want to try and cut some sort of deal with me.'

'Fort *Knox*? What are they on?'

'I'm in it up to my neck, Archie, and they've got me by the balls. They can prove I had nothing to do with Harry's death, but won't unless I help them recover what was stolen from Fort Knox. If I do, then they've promised to wipe my file clean too.'

'And you believe them?'

Tom nodded and Archie gave a short laugh. He took the phone nearest to him, checked the screen again and then began to spin the phone around on the table in front of him with a flick of his fingers. Every so often his gold bracelet clinked against the edge of the table.

'They're all the same these coppers, mate, whatever fancy initials they give themselves. To them, people like you and me are the enemy. If they can milk us for a while they will, but when the time comes, they'll do us over just like that.' Archie clicked his fingers. 'You should know that better than anyone.'

'I do.' He hesitated for a few seconds. 'And I know it's stupid, but I don't think she's like that.'

'Oh, do me a favour! You barely know her.'

'No, but I know people. And I think she's being straight with me.' Tom was surprised at the confidence in his voice.

'She can promise you anything she bloody well likes but it's the people telling *her* what to do you need to be worried about. They haven't promised you shit.'

Tom nodded.

'Not yet, but what . . .'

'Anyway, how can she prove that you had nothing to do with Renwick's murder?'

Archie picked up his second phone and checked the screen with a quick glance before replacing it and resuming the spinning of his other phone.

'Because she was at the dinner with me. Apparently Harry did some work for the FBI a few years back and they wanted some more help on this Fort Knox thing. She saw me leave and that Harry was alive when I did. She had agents watching me all night who can vouch for the fact that I didn't leave my house or call anyone.'

'And then the next morning she shows up like Mother fucking Teresa offering you a deal?'

'That's about it.'

'Wake up, Tom. She's a Federal agent, not your fairy godmother. What do you think fires her up most, you or her job? Christ, I wouldn't be surprised if she'd had Harry whacked in the first place just so you'd help her.'

Tom had a sudden chilling thought. Jennifer

had known where to find him. The plane in Kent, the car and the clothes in Deauville, it had all been so smooth, so efficient. So convenient. Was Archie right? Was he missing something?

'What happens when these witnesses disappear rather than back up your story in a few weeks time?' Archie continued, his sceptical tone unrelenting. 'What happens when Clarke turns up and suddenly she isn't around anymore to help out like she promised? What happens when another CIA assassin tries to stick a bullet in the back of your head to finish the job once and for all?' He glanced at the screen of both phones again.

'You got any other suggestions?' Tom drained his glass.

'Yeah. You get up from this table right now and you walk away and you take your chances on the run. At least there you'll see them coming rather than get knifed in the back by people you thought you could trust. You've done it before.'

'That was different. I had something to trade with the French. The CIA thought I was dead and stopped looking for me. That trick only works once.'

'I can help you,' Archie pleaded, his hands gripping the side of the table. 'Come and do this job for me. Get the other Egg. I've got it all nailed down in Amsterdam. The money for that will set you up somewhere else. I've been thinking about a change of scenery myself. Maybe we could go together. Hong Kong? Buenos Aires? You choose.'

'Is that what this has been all about? This fucking job? Do you ever think about anything other than money?'

'I think about staying alive. So should you. I can have your gear ready by tomorrow, latest. The Egg's in a private collection. You know that one we looked at a few years ago and called off. Two, maybe three guards, max. It'll be easy as pie.' Archie clicked his fingers to emphasise his point. One of his phones rang and he snatched it off the table.

'Yeah . . . well you can tell him from me that he's . . .' Tom grabbed the phone out of his hand and dropped it into Archie's largely untouched beer.

'Are you listening to me now? I've told you no. I won't do it.' Tom raised his voice as he said this, his finger stabbing towards Archie. With an angry look, Archie rescued his phone from his glass, wiping it on a paper napkin. The screen had gone blank.

'Are you listening to yourself? You're going to put all your trust in the same people who betrayed you ten years ago. And you're going to blow out this job and have Cassius after you too. It's not just bad odds, it's bloody suicide. At least if you walk away and do the job, you'll only have the Old Bill to worry about. And we both know you can deal with them.'

'You just don't get it, do you? Tom stood up

and leant down towards Archie, his fists resting on the table between them. 'If I do what you're suggesting, I'll be on the run for the rest of my life. Always looking over my shoulder, unable to trust anyone, running away from shadows. That's not a life worth living. Yes, it's risky, but what she's offering me is the best chance I've got of getting out clean. If there's even the smallest chance that could happen, I've got to go for it.'

Archie shook his head and took the back off his dripping phone. A trickle of beer fell onto the table as the plastic cover was released. He looked up at Tom reproachfully.

'And Cassius?'

'Cassius? I don't know. I'll just have to deal with him when I see him. If I see him.'

'So you're not even going to think about it, then?'

'Okay, I'll think about it if that's what you want me to say. But you need to think about finding someone else to do that job and soon.'

Archie shook his head, the dying embers of the sun reflecting off first one sunglass lens then the other.

'If you make the wrong decision Tom, it's going to cost us both. I guarantee it.'

He picked his remaining working phone off the table, checked the screen, stood up, adjusted his glasses on his head and melted away into the evening.

FORTY-FOUR

Hôtel St Merri, 4th Arrondissement, Paris
8:01pm
Jennifer's hair was wet and her shoulders still glistened with hundreds of dew-like water droplets as she slipped her panties on and fastened her black lace bra. Then she sat on the edge of the narrow bed and stepped into her black jeans, manoeuvring them up her long legs, lying back and lifting her hips up in the air as they slipped around her waist.

She was still hot from the shower and stepped to the window to let some air in, only remembering at the last minute to hide from the street below behind the net curtains that alternately rose and fell in the slight breeze. Her silvery flip-top phone began to vibrate frantically on the dresser. She paused for a few seconds before answering it, knowing who it would be, wanting to make sure that she was fully composed and had all her facts in order. She knew that the conversation she was about to have might be a difficult one.

'Hello.'

'Browne? It's Bob Corbett.' The clipped, rapid-fire intonation immediately confirmed her suspicions. Jennifer kept her own answers short and to the point, as she knew Corbett preferred them.

'Yes, sir.'

'How are you getting on? Tell me you've got some good news. Christ knows I need some.' He sounded tired and anxious and she guessed that Piper and the others must have been giving him a real hard time since Renwick's murder and the loss of the coin.

'We're making some progress.'

'Good.' He sounded relieved. 'What have you got?'

'We went to see Van Simson as agreed. His coin's still there. But we—I mean, I,' she corrected herself quickly, knowing that Corbett was the sort of person to read all sorts of implications into that sort of slip of the tongue, 'sensed that he knew more than he let on. He acted surprised, but maybe not surprised enough. I think he already knew about the coins.'

'Anything else?' He didn't sound impressed, although she knew he rarely did.

'We went to Ranieri's apartment but it was a decoy. Kirk found his real apartment and a German newspaper, dated a few days after

Ranieri's murder, which had an article mentioning a robbery from Schiphol airport.'

'Oh, yeah?' Corbett sounded more interested now.

'I got Max to look into it. Apparently, a few weeks after this Schiphol robbery a German wound up dead in Amsterdam, stabbed in the chest just like Ranieri.'

'What's the link?'

'When the Dutch police went to this guy's apartment, they found some of the gear taken in the airport job.'

'I don't follow.' She could sense a slight tension in his voice, as always when his patience ran low.

'His name was Karl Steiner. And guess who bailed him out of jail a few days before he got killed.'

'Ranieri?'

'Exactly.'

'So what are you saying?'

'It's just a theory but what if whoever stole the coins from Fort Knox tried to smuggle the coins back to Europe by hiding them in a freight shipment? Then this German guy, Steiner, got lucky at the airport and one of the packages he stole had the coins in it. Steiner knew Ranieri and so came to Paris to ask him to fence one of the coins for him. Then when Ranieri got killed, Steiner went back to Holland, leaving the newspaper we found behind. A few days later, he got killed too.'

'And your conclusion is . . . ?'

'That the same person killed both Ranieri and Steiner,' Jennifer said firmly. 'That this person was probably someone they were trying to sell the coins to. And given the small universe of people who would actually be interested in the coins, it's even possible that Ranieri and Steiner tried to sell them back to the same person who'd had them stolen in the first place.'

There was a pause until Corbett spoke again and although she felt confident about what she'd just said, the silence was still an uncomfortable one.

'It makes sense,' he said eventually, to her relief. 'In any case, it will give me enough to keep Piper and Green happy and buy you a few days. But you need to get to Amsterdam. Soon.'

'I was planning to drive there tomorrow.'

'Good. Meanwhile, I'll see what else I can dig up about the airport robbery and the murder and get it to you. That reminds me by the way, we got Renwick's phone records. He made two calls that night, both to cell phones.'

'And?'

'They were both taken out in dummy names. One in the UK, one in Holland.'

'Holland? So there might be a link to Steiner?'

'No way of knowing. The numbers are dead now. Maybe he was calling round to try and generate a bit of interest himself.'

'Well, clearly one of the calls hit home. Problem is we don't know which one or who it was to.' There was a pause. 'What do you want to do about Kirk?' She tried to ask the question casually, not wanting him to think she was especially bothered.

'What do you mean?'

'I mean did Secretary Young go for the deal or do we need to cut him loose?'

'Oh, that. Yes, I think we can live with that. As long as he keeps his side of the bargain and buries this whole Centaur thing.'

'Good.' Almost immediately she wished she had allowed herself at least a brief pause before answering to signal her indifference to Tom's fate.

'Don't get too friendly, Browne.'

'I won't.'

She shook her head ruefully. She wasn't losing perspective, of that she was sure. But there were certain things that didn't add up and she wanted them explained.

'You need to watch out for Kirk,' Corbett continued.

'I know. It's just . . .'

'Just what?'

'I don't think that Piper gave us the whole story about Kirk.'

'You mean he didn't murder his handler?'

'No – he admits he did that. But he says that he was double-crossed. That the CIA tried to have him killed and that he only acted in self-defence.'

'And you believed him?'

'Of course not,' Jennifer shot back. 'At least, not at first. The thing is the French Secret Service confirmed his story.'

'The what?' Real concern in Corbett's voice now. Jennifer shook her head, annoyed with herself. This wasn't coming out like she'd wanted it to.

'They caught up with us in Ranieri's apartment. Followed us there from Van Simson's who apparently they've had under surveillance for months. They know Kirk. Told me that his story checked out. All of it.'

'The truth is, Browne, that we can't be sure what happened back then. But even I'd sooner take Piper's word than the word of someone who has spent his whole life lying to people. At the end of the day he's a crook, plain and simple.'

'I don't deny he's a thief. But what if he's right? What if Piper trained him up and then cut him off? Wouldn't that make us at least partly responsible for what he's become? I'm not sure what choices we'd left him.'

'Okay, Browne, I take your point,' Corbett conceded. 'Maybe there is more to this than Piper's let on. But we can deal with that when this is over. Believe me, I'll be the first one to stick it right up Piper's ass if I find out he's lied to us. But in the meantime you just gotta drop it. Kirk is not your problem. Getting the coins back and whoever took them is.'

'I know that.'

'You gotta stay sharp and alert. Focused on the job at hand. If you're not, I'll pull you out right now. No questions asked.'

She could tell from his tone that he wasn't joking. And she could see Corbett's point. Raking this whole thing up wasn't going to help her solve this case. And certainly the last thing she wanted was to be pulled off it. Better just to tell Corbett what he wanted to hear and keep her thoughts to herself for now.

'No, I'm good. You can count on me to do whatever it takes to get a result. My only interest in Kirk is that I think he can help solve the case. Other than that I don't care.'

'You're doing a great job, Browne. Keep it going.'

The line went dead.

A few moments later there was a faint knock at the door. She grabbed a thin black sweatshirt from the back of the chair and slipped it on.

'Come in.' She was still standing by the window, her phone in her hand, as Tom entered.

'Everything okay?' she asked.

'Sure.' She thought she might be imagining it but she detected a slightly hostile tinge to his voice. 'I've booked us a table at the place next door.'

'Great.' She tossed her phone onto the bed. 'Let's go.'

FORTY-FIVE

Restaurant Le Pavé, 4th Arrondissement, Paris
8:26pm

The restaurant was old-fashioned and busy, smoke lazily rising from between gesticulating fingers, dented cutlery chiming against the dull glaze of white china. Their table was at the back of the room, a slab of cold marble on cast iron legs, a chair on one side and a bench on the other, its red velvet covering worn and stained. Tom chose the bench, Jennifer took the chair.

A waiter appeared and handed them both menus before lighting the candle that had been jammed into an old wine bottle, its neck thickened by layer upon layer of melted wax. The wick sputtered into life, the flame teasing and dancing as it grew, until its pale glow soared and reflected off the mirrored ceiling back down on to them.

Jennifer looked up from the menu and glanced at the room around her.

'Great place.'

'You can tell it's good because it's full of locals,' Tom nodded at the tables around them. A young couple, wedding bands freshly minted. A solitary old woman, wire wool hair drawn back into a chignon, cracked face caked in white foundation, feeding surreptitious scraps to the Shih-Tzu lurking in the depths of her handbag. A middle-aged man, arm ostentatiously draped around the shoulders of his handsome young male lover, revelling in the jealous glances from the two single women at the neighbouring table.

'Has it been here long?'

Tom's head snapped back round to face her.

'Years. Since the 1930s at least. The Germans used to come here all the time during the occupation and if nothing else they were always good judges of restaurants. The rest of Europe at war and this place was making a fortune.'

The waiter reappeared and took their order. Green salads to start and then steak for Tom and lamb for Jennifer accompanied by a bottle of Burgundy. The wine appeared almost immediately and Tom tasted it before nodding his approval. Two glasses were poured and the bottle was deposited on the table between them. The salads arrived, big green leaves coated in a thick, mustardy vinaigrette. They ate in an awkward silence, Jennifer's mind drifting over her conversation with Corbett until Tom spoke, his question coinciding with her own thoughts.

'So is our deal still on?'

Jennifer nodded as she swallowed her mouthful.

'You help us, we help you. The deal stays the same. And when this thing is over, you bury Centaur. Otherwise they'll come after you with everything they've got.'

'And you believe them?'

'Why shouldn't I? They're not interested in you anymore. They just want the coins.'

'What if they don't get the coins back? What if they change their mind? I've got no guarantees, have I?'

'Look, I give you my word on this.' Her eyes met his as she said this and she saw the same suspicion there that she had seen when they had first met. A suspicion that had faded during the day, but now seemed to have returned stronger than ever.

'Your word?'

'If you knew me, you'd know it was worth having.'

The waiter swooped down, carrying off their empty plates with a flurry of his black apron. Jennifer helped herself to another glass of wine, the alcohol helping to soothe her frayed nerves.

'So why the Bureau?' Tom asked after a long silence.

Jennifer smiled, glad for the opportunity to discuss something different.

'It's in the blood. My father, Uncle Ronnie, Grandpa George, they were all cops. I guess the Bureau was just a small step on from that.'

'And you enjoy it?'

'It's like any job; there are good times and bad times. But I guess I get a kick from feeling that I'm making a difference.'

'And that's important to you, is it? Making a difference?'

'Isn't it to everyone? Otherwise why bother?'

Tom nodded and again she got the sense he wasn't actually that interested in her replies, that he was just making conversation. She guessed that he was probably finding their unlikely cooperation as hard as her to reconcile with a lifetime of prejudices.

'So what do you do when you're not working?'

'Sleep, mainly.'

'Oh,' Tom's mouth curled into a mocking smile. 'Not seeing anyone then?'

'No.' She shot back, immediately defensive.

'But there was someone?'

'Yes.'

'What happened?'

'He died.' As soon as she said this she wished she hadn't. This was the one thing she'd buried deep, far away from her own penetrating gaze, let alone that of others.

'How?'

'I don't want to talk about it.' She drained her glass and filled it up again, feeling a little light-headed now, the candle smoke irritating her eyes.

They continued eating in silence, the restaurant quieter as a few of the tables emptied. Their plates were cleared away and Tom ordered an espresso, Jennifer preferring to finish the last of the wine. When the coffee came, Tom stirred it a few times, the creamy film on the surface melting into the black liquid beneath.

'So where are you from, Jennifer?'

She was relieved that he seemed to have moved on.

'Do you know Tarrytown? Westchester County?' Tom shook his head. 'Upstate New York. It's a nice place. Shaded streets, craft stores, shiny red fire engine, active Little League. Safe.'

'And your family?'

'Mom's a hairdresser. Worked at the same salon all her life. Just retired this year. All she wants is for me to get married so she can have grandchildren.'

Tom smiled.

'Dad's just the opposite. Very quiet but also real funny. I think he wanted a boy but he got two girls instead so he just always made us do boy things.'

'Is that why you drive so fast?'

'It's the only way I know.' She grinned.

'Anyway, he left the force five years ago now. My sister Rachel's just finished at Johns Hopkins. She wants to be a doctor.'

'You get on well with them all?'

'We have our moments like everyone. But yeah, sure. I don't see them as much as I should, though.'

There was a pause.

'They must be . . . very proud of you,' said Tom.

Perhaps it was the sudden sadness in Tom's voice that hinted at his own loss, or the smoke from the candle, or even the sharp pain of Jennifer's unspoken guilt. Whichever it was, she suddenly felt incredibly sad.

They were both silent as the waiters pirouetted around their table, suffocating the candles between their saliva-coated fingers with a sharp hiss.

FORTY-SIX

**Gare du Nord, 10th Arrondissement, Paris
9:13pm**
Archie walked up the Rue Denain towards the
station's main entrance, checking the screen of
his one remaining phone every so often. Under
the street lights, he could see that the wide area
under the building's neo-Corinthian façade was
still busy with Algerian taxi drivers and pick-
pockets cruising for their next victim. Romanian
gypsies, babies carefully positioned in the folds
of their brightly coloured skirts, begged, their
hands dark with henna tattoos and covered in
gold rings.

He sensed the car before he saw it, its head-
lights staining the road yellow, its tyres sucking
onto the tarmac as it drew up alongside him. It
stopped when the rear window drew level with
him, the smoked glass glinting. Archie's eyes
narrowed with suspicion as the window dropped

an inch. The dry scent of air conditioning seeped out onto the street.

'Going somewhere?'

'Do I know you?' Archie's tone was cautious.

'Yes, and yet no.'

'I haven't got time for riddles.'

'No. You're almost right out of time.'

'Cassius?' Archie gasped, his heart leaping in his chest.

'You came highly recommended. I have to say, so far you have done little to suggest that reputation is deserved. Late on the first Egg. Now, with two days to go, no sign of the second.' Archie swallowed, wished he had chosen not to walk.

'I know, but it's been difficult. More difficult than we thought.' As he spoke he tried to peer through the gap in the window. 'Perhaps if I had a bit more time . . .'

'That, unfortunately, is the one thing I cannot give you. I've paid you handsomely. Now I expect you to deliver. You know the consequences if you fail.'

Archie stammered out an answer.

'It's not my fault. It's Felix. I'm still working on him.'

'That is not my concern.'

'But I've got it all planned out.' Archie tried to sound confident.

'Where?'

'You know I can't tell you that.'

'Where?' The voice insisted, the single word dripping with menace.

'Amsterdam,' Archie muttered, his eyes dropping to the road.

'Good.' The voice was more relaxed now. 'I will be in touch. Don't fail me.'

The window whirred back into its frame and the car eased away from the kerb and out into the street. A few seconds later, it had gone.

PART III

All the gold which is under or upon the earth is not enough to give in exchange for virtue.

Plato – Laws (Book 5)

FORTY-SEVEN

Seven Bridges Hotel, Amsterdam, Holland
28th July – 2:37pm

Jennifer flopped onto the bed, her shoes slipping off her feet and dropping noiselessly onto the worn brown carpet. She had not slept well the previous night, even though they had taken turns during the drive from Paris. She felt drained, exhausted by the events of the past few days. She knew that this was partly due to the jet-lag, partly due to the intensity of her investigation and subsequent reconstruction of the Fort Knox robbery, days of worry and lost sleep that she was still recovering from.

And of course, the last few days had hardly been easy. An innocent man murdered, the coin that had been entrusted to her safekeeping stolen, a hasty and unauthorised flight to France with her prime suspect riding shotgun. And still so many questions. Who had ordered the Fort Knox break-in? Was Tom involved? How had one of the coins ended up in the stomach of a murdered priest/fence? Who was behind Renwick's murder? What was Van Simson's involvement, if any? Where did Steiner and his murder fit in, and where were the coins now?

Try as she might to dismiss it, she was also forced to recognise that part of her exhaustion stemmed from the emotional burden of the mismatch between the Tom Kirk portrayed by Piper and Corbett and the evidence of her own eyes and ears. The same burden that had led, her headache had poundingly reminded her that morning, to drink too much the previous night.

In Tom she had seen someone who was resourceful, intelligent and fiercely loyal. Someone who had, if you believed him, his own unarguable reasons for being who he was, for becoming what he had. She had realized that morning in the car that she had come to a cross-roads. To trust him or not to trust him? To believe what she saw, or what people told her?

In the end, she wasn't sure she had any choice. Without Tom, she never would have found Ranieri's hideout or the newspaper and made the connection to Steiner. And he'd saved her life on that roof, she was sure of it. As for the Fort Knox job, she had looked into his eyes and seen – in that instance at least – the unblinking passion of an innocent man. No, she was quite clear in her own mind. Tom Kirk deserved a second chance. The question was whether Corbett would see it the same way?

'What are you doing?' She opened one eye, then the other as she heard Tom struggling to hook a sheet around the corners of the large mirror that dominated the right-hand wall.

'People sometimes use this room to make porn movies.' Tom explained without turning round, still trying to secure the right-hand corner of the rug over the mirror's chipped frame. 'I'm pretty sure this is two-way glass, for hiding a camera behind. I figured you wouldn't want to take any chances.'

Jennifer sat upright, fully awake now.

'You've taken me to a brothel?' She slid off the bed and held her hands in front of her, scared of brushing against any surface that could have been soiled by the room's previous occupants.

'It's not a brothel. Just a place people go some-times. Anyway, I know the owner. It's clean, safe and no one will come looking for us here. Sorry they only had the one room, though. Don't worry, I'll take the floor.'

'Fine.' Unhappy but not prepared to argue further, Jennifer sat back down. She reached down the side of the bed to grab the thick padded envelope that Corbett had sent over to the hotel as promised. She opened it and summarised the first few pages out loud, her left hand brushing hair back behind each ear as she spoke.

'Karl Steiner. East German. 46 years old. A former border guard. Suspected Stasi informer. Did time for armed robbery, handling stolen goods, usual stuff. Was implicated in several murders in Germany but they could never make anything stick. Moved to Holland three years ago apparently to better serve his heroin addiction.'

Tom gave a short laugh.

'Well, he came to the right place. What about the murder? What does it say about that?'

Jennifer turned over a few more pages in the file before answering.

'Not a lot.' She looked up at Tom over the top of the brown folder and shrugged. 'Exactly the same injury as Ranieri, though. He was on the phone when it happened. The call was traced to another phone box in London. His wallet and keys were still on him, so even the Dutch police worked out it wasn't a random mugging. They think it was probably drug related. Happens all the time apparently.'

Tom pinched his nose in thought.

'Well, we know different at least. We're dealing with professionals here, trained assassins. They killed Ranieri and then made their move on Steiner. Probably counted on the fact that no one would link the two. The only question is whether they got what they wanted.' Jennifer nodded slowly.

'You mean the coins?'

'Yeah.'

She consulted another typed page.

'I don't believe it!'

'What?'

Jennifer, amazed, looked up at him.

'Apparently there's a video of the whole thing.'

'A video? What do you mean a video? A video-tape?' It was Tom's turn to look surprised. Jennifer nodded.

'Seems a couple of tourists caught the whole thing on camera. There should be a copy here somewhere.' Jennifer rummaged in the envelope until she triumphantly produced a cassette, a hastily scrawled label on the top side identifying it as 'Steiner – Video Footage' in red ink.

Tom snatched it out of her hand and prodded the TV into action, its sleek black shape strangely out of place amidst the stained and ripped floral wallpaper and the laminate furniture, painted many years before in various shades of dark green. The built-in video player hungrily swallowed the tape with a low mechanical moan.

FORTY-EIGHT

van Rijn Hotel, Amsterdam, Holland
2:49pm

The hotel room was dingy and dirty. Stained green curtains clinging onto the rail by a few loose threads hung over a grimy window that had been nailed shut. The floor and the walls were lined in the same brown corduroy-effect material, no doubt the height of fashion when it had been laid in the 1970s, but now balding and flecked with the offal of its many occupants over the years.

The bed sagged in the middle like an abandoned trampoline, the bruised white headboard and pockmarked melamine side cabinets screwed to the wall. A Gideon bible in the left-hand drawer had had several pages torn out, the few black crumbs trapped between the Gospels of Mark and Luke and the heady smell of the remaining pages suggesting that they had been smoked one night out of desperation for a cigarette paper.

The ceiling had ripened to a watery yellow colour, its sickly appearance hardly helped by the blotchy glow that emerged from the ripped and torn paper shade that engulfed the single forty-watt bulb in the middle of the ceiling.

But it served its purpose. People came and went without any questions being asked. Rooms were rented by the hour, by the day, by the week even – cash up front. It was easy to be anonymous there, to blend into the shadows, to slip in and out unobtrusively, unobserved. So he fitted in fine.

But he'd been there seven days now and was packed and ready to leave. He'd smoked himself silly, fucked four hookers, all of whom had reminded him of his sister and woken up each morning hugging an empty bottle of Jack and nursing a hangover. He'd almost proved to himself that you *could* have too much of a good thing. The mutilated bible still bothered him though. That was not right. That was not respectful.

His phone vibrated in his pocket. He pulled it out and pressed it to his face, the warm plastic nestling against his straggly blond beard.

'This is Foster.' His voice hinted at azaleas and whispering pines draped in Spanish moss, of long suffocating nights and alligator-infested swamps.

'Are you still in Amsterdam?' The voice was clipped, to the point. As always.

'Sure am.'

'Good. Stay put. There's another little job I'd like you to do. Usual fee. I'll call you in an hour.'

The line went dead.

Sighing, the man tossed the phone down onto the bed. The loose sheets swallowed it whole. He popped the catches of his suitcase and threw it open, lifting out neatly folded shirts and trousers from the lower half and placing them on the bed.

He reached into the case again, his hands pausing over the silky fabric that lined the inside of the plastic shell, before pulling it towards him. The velcro holding the lining in place gave way with a reluctant rip and he folded it back, exposing the foam-filled compartment it had concealed within the lid.

The black Teflon sheen of his dismembered Remington M24 sniper rifle gazed back at him.

FORTY-NINE

Seven Bridges Hotel, Amsterdam, Holland
2:49pm

The screen glowed into life, darkness fading to light, the image jerking from the unsteady camera-work.

A beatific sun smiled down through diaphanous clouds. The soothing hum of the tour guide's harmless chatter and the swish of the water against the boat echoed in the background. The sights and sounds of the city, its bridges and canals and long narrow houses, drifted lazily in front of them.

Abruptly the mood changed. The sun disappeared, blotted out behind a tall building. The boat was plunged into shadow, the picture cold, the sky angry and portentous. And then, initially on the right-hand side but his face soon occupying the whole screen in terrifying detail, Tom and Jennifer saw Steiner. Saw his murder.

It was so quick. A man in a phone box, two men silently approaching, the phone tumbling from his hand, swinging gracefully down and crashing against the phone's metal base, the moulded plastic shattering. Then the tell-tale flash of steel, a body lying crumpled on the pavement. In the background, the guide chanted her sing-song commentary obliviously. A few seconds later and the tape ended. The screen was dark once again. A life extinguished.

They swapped a guilty glance, Tom shifting awkwardly on the edge of the bed, Jennifer swallowing nervously. He had been transfixed by the images, unable to look away as the knife dropped, as Steiner's heart had stopped beating, as his life had spilled out onto the street. He could tell she had felt the same. That voyeuristic compulsion now hung over them like some terrible secret, a shared fetish that they were at once repulsed by and attracted to.

'Shall we have another look?' Tom was almost reluctant to suggest it, but it seemed unavoidable. Jennifer nodded silently.

He rewound the tape, pressed play and sat back down on the edge of the bed, trying to focus more objectively on what he was seeing. Steiner was easily recognisable from the mug shots and photo composites in his file. However, there was no way of identifying the murderers. The camera was never on the right side of them and by the time it was, they had both gone. Equally it was impossible to see if the two men had removed anything from Steiner. At the crucial moment, when they had both been crouching over the body, the boat had passed under a bridge.

What was clear was that Steiner had recognised the threat as soon as they appeared. With good reason. They had murdered him in cold blood and in broad daylight in full view of a boat packed with tourists. It was a miracle no one else had seen them. In fact, if anything, it was almost as if they'd wanted to be seen. Either that, or they had been unwilling to risk missing him. They just took Steiner down at the first opportunity, whatever the consequences. These were desperate, dedicated men. Dangerous men.

Tom played the tape again, moving closer to the screen as if he was going to climb into the picture and walk right up to them all. A thought suddenly occurred to him. He stood up and rewound the tape again, pausing it just before Steiner had looked up and noticed the two men. Tom tilted his head first one way and then the other, as if he was trying to see round the side of the image.

'What are you doing, Karl?' he asked slowly, more to himself than to Jennifer.

'What do you mean?'

'Well, look at him,' he walked right up to the screen and pointed at Steiner's back. 'Just before he notices the two guys. He's facing the back of the phone box, away from us. He's bent slightly forward, his left arm leaning against the back wall, the phone jammed between his head and his left shoulder. What's he doing?'

'Yeah I see.' Jennifer got up and moved next to Tom. 'It's like he's reading something. Or maybe leaning on the top of the phone with his right hand. Hey, I wonder if they found a pen on him?'

Jennifer flicked through the crime scene report again, her eyes scanning the pages for the relevant section.

'Here we go.' She nodded. 'Not on him, but there was one on the ground next to him. The cops think it must have fallen out of his pocket when the two men went through them.'

'You're thinking he was writing something down, aren't you?'

She nodded. 'Yeah, but what was he writing on?' She motioned to Tom to play the film again, advancing it frame by frame.

'You see,' she continued, 'he definitely doesn't put anything in his pockets or back in his wallet before the killers showed up and they then just stabbed him, searched him and disappeared.'

'Meaning that if he was writing something down and the police didn't find anything on him, then it might well still be down there,' said Tom, nodding in understanding. 'Where's the phone box?'

'You must be kidding. It was nearly a week ago now.'

'Believe me, the Amsterdam police are not well known for their efficiency. They've got a lot on their plate here. Let's just go and have a look.'

'Are you serious?' Tom nodded. 'Okay, fine,' Jennifer conceded with a shrug. 'It's on Prinse . . . I don't know. How do you pronounce this?'

'Prinsegracht,' said Tom glancing at the file. 'Near the Hotel Pulitzer. It's only about a fifteen-minute walk.'

FIFTY

3:21pm

They walked past the buzzing open-air cafés and ten dollar caricaturists on Rembrandtplein, the air reverberating to faded Beatles songs and South American pipe music played by groups of itinerant buskers. Then they cut across onto Singel, a human statue dressed as the Tin Man standing at the corner, his body shifting robotically every time change was thrown into the bowl at his feet. Finally they made their way up Raadhuisstraat onto Prinsegracht.

Jennifer read the names aloud off the street signs fixed high above their heads, contorting her tongue around the clearly unfamiliar spelling and pronunciation. And all around them, the canal sparkled in the sunlight like a dew-covered spider's web.

Amsterdam's crescent-shaped city centre was laid out in the 17th century, its canals originally a defence from invasion. As its importance as a trading port grew, so did the network of narrow streets and canals that fan out from this crescent, a series of concentric circles that end in squares where the city gates would have stood and been locked every night. Those gates were long gone now, and many canals had been filled in with the advent of the motor car and the desire to make the city more accessible to traffic. But the city remained unique; the Venice of the North as it is often called. Four hundred stone bridges still cross over one hundred kilometres of canal, a delicate skeleton of water that binds the city together.

It was nearly five years since Tom had last been in Amsterdam. He'd been casing a job, of course. He'd taken the time back then to commit the city to memory as he did whenever he was planning a job in a new place. Its streets and landmarks, its short-cuts, its bars and restaurants, its idioms and idiosyncrasies. Its secrets. From his perspective, it was all about minimising the risks, about getting the job done and getting away safely. Now that knowledge was rapidly being excavated from the archive of his mind.

It was obvious where the murder had taken place. A large white plastic tent had been hastily erected on the pavement, covering the phone box and an area of about five feet around it like a temporary shrine – shielding it from curious eyes. The irony of that played around the edges of Tom's mind. Steiner's actual death caught on video, the scene of his death zealously guarded. Surely, if anything, it should have been the other way round.

The tent was itself encircled by a series of steel barriers, their thick metal bars interwoven with a series of white signs shouting 'Politie' in large blue letters. Blue and white crime scene tape snapped in the wind like the ribbons on a kite.

They approached the barrier and checked the street in both directions, but no-one seemed to be guarding the tent, certainly not the police. Tom called out to make sure, but there was no answer from inside. Two girls, studs driven into their lower lips and noses, angry tattoos snaking across their midriffs and emblazoned up their backs, approached them, arguing. As they walked past, Tom casually checked his wrist as if they were waiting for someone who was late, before realising that he'd left his watch back at the hotel. The girls didn't seem to notice and when the sound of their voices had faded away he nodded at Jennifer. Almost as one, they vaulted the metal barrier and slipped under the entrance flap to the tent.

Inside, the late afternoon sun fought its way through the thick white plastic with a sickly glow. The air was heavy and wet, like a neglected greenhouse. On the floor, sawdust, now dried into thick black clods, had been scattered to soak up Steiner's blood. The raw, sordid smell of death crawled over everything.

As all over Amsterdam, the back wall of the phone box had been decorated with a collage of garish and explicit cards advertising strip shows, sex lines and prostitutes. 'Naughty Schoolgirl Needs Spanking', one claimed; 'Leather Lover Likes Licking', another promised. It was a smorgasbord of sex, each girl pictured more attractive and with bigger breasts than the next. Every whim catered for, every fantasy only a phone call away.

Stepping right into the phone box, the shattered handset still dangling from its cable, Tom studied each of them carefully.

'Are you that bored?' Jennifer joked, the hollow echo of her voice throbbing in the deadened stillness of the tent. The hot air slopped over them both like the backwash from a jet engine and Tom felt sticky and uncomfortable.

'Not exactly,' he replied without looking up. 'I'm just thinking that if he wrote something down, he might have just grabbed the nearest available piece of paper. There's nothing on any of these though.' He examined each one in turn. 'But look. There's a card missing here.' He pointed to where the back of the phone box was showing through the dense patchwork of cards, a solitary island of black plastic amidst a sea of naked flesh. 'Are you sure they didn't find a card or something on the floor?'

'The file would have said.'

'Well . . . that's it then,' his voice conceded defeat. 'If he did write on one of these it must have blown away. Maybe he wasn't writing at all. I guess we need to look somewhere else.'

He looked away, his face creased in disappointment. But then something caught his eye. A small flash of white, nothing more than a fleck. Stepping closer, he could see that it was the corner of a card that had fallen down the back of the phone.

He took his sunglasses off his head and using one of the rubberised arms, teased the corner out until he was able to pinch it between his thumb and forefinger. He drew it up into the open, the paper slick between his perspiring fingers.

It featured a blonde girl wearing nothing but cowboy boots and hat, her breasts partially concealed by the invitation to 'Ride Me Cowboy!' Tom held the card up to the gap on the phone box wall. It fitted perfectly.

'I think we just got lucky.' He smiled.

'What does it say?' Jennifer stepped towards him.

She squinted at what had had been hastily scrawled in the top left corner of the card. Numbers of some sort. Tom read them out.

'0090212'

'What do you think it means?'

'I'm not sure.' Tom fluttered the front of his

shirt to try and get some air to circulate against his skin. The plastic tent was trapping the heat like a sauna.

'An address, or a zip code?' she suggested eagerly. 'Or a safe deposit box number?'

'Perhaps.' Tom was hesitant. 'But . . . you know, in Europe 00 is the International Access Code, not 011 like in the States. It could be a phone number.'

'So what's 90 and 212?'

'Well, 212 is New York, isn't it? But the country code for the US is 1, not 90, so that doesn't make sense.'

'Isn't that a list of country codes there?' Jennifer pointed at a laminated poster to the left of the phone. 'She ran her finger down the list, muttering under her breath every so often.

'It's only got the major countries here, so it might not have it. China 86 . . . India 91 . . . Mexico 52 . . . Here we go. Turkey 90. It's Turkey.'

'Of course.' Tom snapped his fingers and grimaced in frustration.

'What?'

'I'd forgotten. 212 is the city code for Istanbul.'

'So what are you saying? That maybe Steiner was in the middle of writing someone's number down when he got killed?'

Tom agreed with a nod.

'Could be.'

'Maybe he was still searching for a buyer.

Maybe he'd found someone there that was interested.'

Tom shrugged, his voice sceptical.

'In Istanbul? It's possible, I guess. But it's not an obvious place.'

'Well, can't we find out who the most likely buyers are out there? If there isn't a big list it should make it easier.'

'I guess so.'

A shadow fell over the tent, a dark silhouette projected against the white plastic that grew smaller as its owner drew closer.

'*Wie is Daar*?' the shadow barked.

'Shit.' Tom slipped the card in his pocket and quickly searched for a way out. There was none. The tent had been firmly anchored to the ground, its skirt flush to the pavement.

A large gloved hand slipped through the doorway and gripped the entrance flap. Tom knew that this was not good. They'd used Jennifer's contacts to bypass customs, taking a small rarely patrolled road over the border. Technically, as in France, they had entered the country illegally.

What's more, Tom had ensured that they did not have to fill out a registration card at the hotel, normally mandatory for all guests, the details uploaded onto national police databases every night. That was also illegal. Neither of them could afford a run-in with the law, not at this stage. The list of possible options ran through his head. In the end, only one was practical.

He grabbed Jennifer and kissed her.

FIFTY-ONE

van Rijn Hotel, Amsterdam, Holland
3:39pm

Kyle Foster could not remember a time when he had been without a gun. His fifth birthday present had been a gas-operated BB gun and his eight-eenth a Magnum .45 with a specially engraved back-up clip slipped to him lovingly by his mother. From that day on she'd not slapped him once, told him that he was a man now, that her work was done.

By the time he was twenty he'd tried just about every handgun, machine gun, sniper, hunting and assault rifle on the market and quite a few that weren't. At least not legally.

It wasn't just that he was a good shot, which he was, having served almost twenty years with the US Army Rangers in their elite sniping unit. It wasn't just that he enjoyed killing, which he did. It was the hunt.

He still got that same feeling, that tightness in his chest, the butterflies in his stomach. He had first tasted the rush when out with his father hunting deer around the lakes near their farm in Mississippi. First revelled in the euphoria of the chase when he had had his face ritually smeared in blood from his first kill, still warm as it bubbled noisily from the deer's throat.

The ultimate killer; that's how he liked to think of himself now. Totally focused, totally in control and totally lethal. When he was hunting he was stronger, fitter, smarter than normal human beings. With his body, with all his senses working together in perfect harmony, bent to the kill, he could see further, hear clearer, smell more acutely.

Of course he had got better. Of that there was no doubt. The rifle had given way to the gun. The gun to the knife. That was his favourite, now. That required real skill, real planning. Getting in close, seeing the look of surprise, of shock, of questioning in their eyes as the polished blade sliced into them.

He took the Gideon bible out of the drawer and replaced it with the new one he had bought at the bookstore round the corner. It wasn't his favourite version, but at least all the pages were there. That had to count for something.

He'd make tonight count, too. No opportunity to use the knife this time, he'd be too far away.

It wasn't that sort of job. No, tonight he'd be hunting with the rifle.

It was just like being out with his father again.

FIFTY-TWO

Prinzegracht, Amsterdam, Holland
3:40pm

Jennifer gasped in surprise, her eyes wide open. Her arms, trapped against his chest, tried to push him away from her. And yet her eyes fluttered shut, her lips parted. It was three years since she'd last been kissed like that.

An angry-looking policeman stepped into the tent, his pale blue shirt stained under the arms, the sweat trickling down the side of his head from under the edge of his peaked hat, its thin black visor rippling in the heat like tarmac in the desert.

'*Stoppen*,' he ordered. 'Stop,' he shouted again when they ignored him. Jennifer looked up and squinted into the late afternoon sun.

'This is forbidden area,' he said in halting English. Jennifer stared at the ground, hot waves of embarrassment washing over her. 'Not for tourists.'

'Sorry,' Tom apologised. 'It's a mistake.' The policeman eyed them, his top lip quivering with suspicion, looking beyond them to see if they had moved or touched anything.

'You go now, yes.'

He held the flap open and they both stooped under his arm and vaulted the metal barriers back out onto the street. She could feel the policeman's eyes burning into her back until they turned the corner.

They retraced their steps towards the hotel in funereal silence. Eventually Tom coughed out an apology.

'I'm sorry.'

'Don't mention it.' Jennifer tried to sound casual, concentrating on her breathing, on trying to settle her stomach that was still turning over. In a way she wasn't that surprised. After three years, a kiss, any kiss, was bound to make her feel strange. What did surprise her though was what she was *not* feeling. What she would have expected to feel. Guilty.

'No, really. I *am* sorry. It was just . . . well, you know. It was the only thing I could think of. I thought it would make us look less suspicious.'

'I'm not sure how much more suspicious we could have looked,' she shot back, hoping that manufactured anger would help disguise the tremor in her voice.

Tom raised his eyebrows.

'Well, you were pretty convincing.'

'Like I had a choice?' she retorted.

There was a pause. A bicycle thrummed past, black and old-fashioned with a wicker basket hanging off the front and lights powered by a small generator that hugged the rear rubber tyre with a low pitched whirr. They stepped out of its way, the rider signalling his gratitude with a ring of his bell.

'Jesus, it was just a kiss. Get over it.'

Jennifer stared defiantly into the distance as she walked, her heart still thudding in her chest.

'Listen.' She stopped, hands on her hips. 'You know when I said that I used to see someone, that they left me, that they died. Well, I think you should know. I killed him.'

'Oh.' She could see from Tom's face that for once he was lost for words.

'So for me, there's no such thing as just a kiss. Not any more. So just drop it, okay?'

'Fine.'

She wasn't sure why she had told him this, perhaps to warn him off, perhaps to explain why she had reacted as strongly as she had. One thing was for certain, though. She felt a lot better for it.

FIFTY-THREE

Centraal Station, Amsterdam, Holland
5:32pm

The phone, moist where the moulded plastic had been pressed against his skin, trilled hypnotically in Tom's ear. On the other side of the street, a man was selling sweets, weighing them out into small paper bags for the children clamouring around his cart.

Ring-ring, ring-ring

He shut his eyes as he waited, resting his head against the phone box's glass wall.

Ring-ring, ring-ring

Unseen to him, the flow of people heading out of Centraal Station thickened briefly as a newly arrived train spewed out its passengers, then thinned out again.

Ring-ring, ring – click

Tom's eyes snapped open. As ever, there was silence from the other end. Archie always waited for the person calling him to speak first. It was his own primitive call-screening system.

'Archie, it's Fel . . . it's Tom.'

'Tom, thank God it's you. I've been trying to call since last night. Where the hell are you staying?'

Tom, sensing the panic in his voice, ignored the question.

'What's happened?'

'He found me last night.'

'Who?'

'Cassius.'

Tom's response was instantaneous.

'Bullshit. You don't know that. No one's ever seen him.' But his tone was also hopeful. He wanted Archie to be wrong. Needed him to be wrong.

'I didn't say I *saw* him. But it was him all the same. He told me that we only had a day left. That if you didn't deliver he'd find me. Then you.'

'Shit.' Tom hissed, his voice muffled by the handset. His eyes flicked absently over the woman gesticulating in the phone box next to him, her high-pitched voice vibrating through the glass. She seemed to be upset about something.

'You still with that FBI bird?'

'Yeah.'

'What are you playing at?'

'I told you. They think I broke into Fort Knox. I'm trying to sort this mess out.'

'And took what exactly?'

'Some coins. Expensive coins.' Tom sighed heavily. 'I think they're being sold to someone in Istanbul but don't know who to.'

'Istanbul? That's easy.'

'What do you mean?'

'It's where Cassius is having his off-site tomorrow night. It's what these Eggs are for.'

'So he wants the coins and the Eggs for the same gig,' Tom breathed.

'That's why he's set the deadline. I told you before, the rumour is that he had some deal go sour on him and he's lost a lot of money. He's scraping together what he can, even throwing in some of his own stuff and calling in a lot of old favours to make sure it goes well. If he hasn't got enough lots he'll have to call the whole bloody thing off. I don't imagine that would do his credibility any good.'

'Where?'

'It's very hush-hush. Strictly invitation only. All I know is that it's tomorrow night in Istanbul.'

Tom closed his eyes. The woman in the adjacent booth was crying now, small tears springing from her eyes, dropping to the galvanised floor.

'So are you up for this job or not?' Archie asked again, his tone more insistent now.

'I'm still thinking about it.'

'It's not a definite no then?' He sounded encouraged.

'It was. Now I'm not so sure.' Tom breathed in deeply and leant back against the glass door. The woman in the adjacent cabin had left now, her place taken by a blind man who had set his white stick to one side and was feeling his way round the Braille characters set onto each of the keys. Tom didn't say anything for a few seconds. When he did, his voice was thoughtful, questioning even.

'You know, when I got back to the hotel last night, after I met you, I overheard Jennifer on the phone to her boss.'

'What was she saying?'

'It was just the tail-end of the conversation. But basically that he could count on her to do whatever it took to get a result. That she doesn't care what happens to me after this.'

'You see.' Archie was triumphant. 'I told you. You can't trust these people.'

'I know, but it doesn't make any sense.'

'It makes perfect sense. It's who she is.'

'I can't just up and leave and do the job.'

'Why not?'

'All sorts of reasons. I've left my watch back at the hotel for a start.'

'It's just a watch. I'll buy you another one.'

'My mother gave it to me.'

'Well, go back and get it then. You've got time.'

'What about my kit?' Tom was searching for excuses like a drowning man fighting to keep his head above the surface.

'Everything's at the usual place. I sent it over last night.'

'How did you know I would need it?' Tom almost whispered, his mouth suddenly dry.

'Because I know you, Tom. And I know you're one of the good guys. I knew that you wouldn't just abandon me.'

Tom pressed the receiver against his head. What choice did he have? He could probably look after himself but could he really just abandon Archie to Cassius's attack dogs? And how long before they caught up with him, too?

'I'm sorry, mate,' Archie continued. 'I would have liked to believe her offer was real. That you had a real shot to get out clean. But you heard what she said. We're on our own. We always have been. We have to do what's right for us.'

'Okay.' Tom's voice was ice. 'You win. I'll get Cassius his Egg. Then we bail.'

FIFTY-FOUR

FBI Headquarters, Washington DC
28th July – 1:42pm

Bob Corbett leant towards the speakerphone, his white shirt collar pulling at his smooth tanned neck as he strained to catch Jennifer's voice.

'Say that again.'

'I said he's out.' Jennifer's voice floated into the room like expensive perfume. 'I told him I had to do some stuff and to amuse himself for a few hours. We're sharing a room, so he understood.'

'Okay Browne, thanks. We'll see what we can come up with on that Istanbul lead at our end. Call in again later.' Corbett pressed the button on the speakerphone and the line went dead.

'Sharing a room?' John Piper snarled, his face red. 'What the fuck's she thinking? Three days ago Kirk was our number one suspect. Now she's sharing a room with him? What sort of a show are you running, Bob?'

'It's called a cover, John,' Corbett hissed. He wasn't sure what she was thinking either, but there was no way he was going to let Piper score points from it. 'I thought you used to be in the field? You don't always get to choose where you stay and who you stay with.'

He swivelled round in his chair and turned to face the other people seated opposite him. The early afternoon sun slanted through the metal slates of the blind, projecting black stripes across the far wall and the polished wooden surface of the round table.

'So. What do you think?'

FBI Director Green was the first to speak, his grey suit creasing round his shoulders.

'It seems to me like Kirk is really trying to help. The link to Amsterdam and now this Istanbul thing. It's good work. Maybe we should offer him his old job back!' The other men around the table laughed. Everyone except for John Piper.

'Oh, yeah!' he said sarcastically. 'He's fucking great. Ever since Kirk's been on the scene we've lost an eight million dollar coin, wound up with a stiff in London and narrowly avoided a major diplomatic incident with the French. Let's get real here. The guy's outta control.'

Corbett drummed his fingers on the desk.

'Well it was your idea to cut him a deal,' he reminded Piper in a low voice. Piper's eyes blazed but Green cut in before he could speak.

'Calm down, John. Listen, no one knows what really happened in London yet, nor whose fault it was. As for the French, they always turn everything into a diplomatic incident. Makes them feel more important. I still say Kirk has surprised us all. His are not the actions of a guilty man.'

The noise of Corbett's nails hitting the glossy wood grew louder.

'How do we even know what's really going on?' Piper insisted. 'I told you Browne was not up to this case. I know this guy – nothing's ever what it seems with him. Now he's got her believing he's got nothing to do with all this. And let's not forget he can still finger the President. We need him under lock and key now.'

Corbett halted his desktop tattoo.

'For once, John and I agree on something,' he said. 'Kirk is a criminal. He can't be trusted. He had the means and the motive to pull the Fort Knox job. If he's helping Browne now, it's because he wants something. When he gets the chance, he'll make his move. Then he'll probably leak the Operation Centaur story just for the hell of it.'

Piper nodded at him. Corbett raised his eyebrows at this unexpected show of solidarity.

'You may well be right,' said Director Green slowly. 'But given where we are, what other options have we got? Are you saying we should just pull her out? I still think that we have more chance of locating the coins and who took them with Kirk's help than without it.'

'I'm not disagreeing with that,' Corbett nodded. 'And I still think Browne will come through for us. She can't afford to fail and she knows it. All I'm saying is that Kirk needs watching.'

'Ah want to cover all the bases here.'

Treasury Secretary Young leant into the table and spoke for the first time since they had sat down, his bald head shining like a mirror, stubby fingers gripping a thick Mont Blanc ink pen.

'Let's see what else they dig up together. You never know, they might get lucky. If Kirk becomes a problem then we remove him from the equation. Simple. Frankly when this is over, Ah don't care what happens to him. From what you've told us, John, he's a dangerous man with a lot of dangerous secrets. If he's behind the Fort Knox break-in, then let's nail him for that. If not, then Ah'm sure you can find something else to pin on him. Centaur's far less likely to leak out if he's inside anyway.'

Corbett nodded.

'Meantime, we need to make sure that Browne has back-up. John, you arrange for one of our Consulate guys to get over to their hotel and keep tabs on them both. And Bob,' Young locked eyes with Corbett, 'Ah want you to get a bag packed and a team ready. If your girl needs help, Ah want you on the next plane out there. We don't leave our people swinging in the wind. Never have. Never will.'

FIFTY-FIVE

**Seven Bridges Hotel, Amsterdam, Holland
9:33pm**

It was dark before Jennifer heard footsteps outside the room followed by a knock at the door. Tom had been out well over three hours. She'd taken the time to relax, have a bath, shave her legs and under her arms, pluck her eyebrows and moisturise herself from top to toe until her skin radiated pHC neutral hydration.

'Come in,' she called out.

'How did you get on?' Tom asked as he stepped into the room.

'Fine thanks. What about you?'

'Oh, I just had a walk around.' Tom poured himself a glass of iced water from the jug on top of the dresser. 'It's hot out there.'

'Tell me about it. Haven't they heard of A/C in Europe?'

'Oh, they've heard of it. Just don't believe in it.'

'Any news?'

'I called a friend of mine to see whether he knew anything about this Istanbul link.'

'And?'

Tom disappeared into the bathroom and his muffled voice echoed out into the room.

'He said he didn't know.'

He re-emerged fastening his watch onto his wrist and made for the door.

'You going somewhere?' Jennifer's voice registered surprise. 'You just got back?'

'Yeah. It's just this thing I've got to do.'

'What?' She took a step towards him, put a questioning hand on his arm.

'I won't be long.' He moved to leave but Jennifer sprang to the door, pressing herself against it.

'You're not leaving without me. Not with everything that's going on. Not unless you tell me what the hell you're up to.'

'This is personal. This has got nothing to do with you or the coin.'

'I don't care. You're not going.'

'I'll be back in a few hours. And I *am* going.' This time Tom returned her gaze without looking away.

Reluctantly, she stepped away from the door. What else could she do, tie him to a chair?

'Just remember,' she said as he reached for the door handle. 'You and me, we've got a deal. You screw up, we both go down.'

He gave her a quick smile.

'Don't worry. The deal means as much to me as it does to you.'

FIFTY-SIX

As soon as the door had closed and the echo of Tom's footsteps had faded into silence, Jennifer slipped a black sweater over her silk top, swapped her heels for some trainers, grabbed the room key and flew down the stairs and out onto the street.

She looked first one way and then the other, peering into the darkness, but the street was silent and empty. She was too late. Only a retreating bicycle light flickered in the distance like a buoy.

And then she saw him – a dark figure momentarily silhouetted against the red brickwork as a car turned the corner in the distance. It was Tom.

Jennifer held back, hugging the side of the street, catching a glimpse of the back of his head and shoulders every so often as he walked under a streetlight or past the blue glare of a TV in someone's front room. She followed him over the bridge, past the serrated brickwork of the Waag on Nieuwmarkt Square and the dancing lights of the open-air restaurants dotted around it, until the unmistakeable glow from the approaching shop fronts confirmed where he was headed. *De Wallen*. The red light district.

A few hundred yards later, Tom knelt as if to tie his shoelaces, and then suddenly darted into a side alley. Jennifer broke into a run. She knew that if she lost him in these labyrinthine side streets she would never find him again. Her heart was pounding, her mind bubbling over with questions. Where was he going? Why now? And why couldn't he tell her?

As the alley loomed closer she slowed to walking pace, flattened her back to the wall and edged her head around the corner.

About five feet in, the alley widened into a small square, with another alley on the opposite side leading out onto a street running parallel to the one Jennifer was now on. Three identical glass-fronted shops, their lights staining the cobblestones outside them a dark red, dominated the left side of the square. Opposite them, a dark concrete wall loomed up into the darkness of the night sky like a church steeple, the faded and peeling remains of an abstract mural dedicated to a long-forgotten World Aids Day the only relief from its grimy blankness.

Tom was standing outside the middle shop talking through the open door to its current occupant, a pretty young girl with sky-high cheekbones, tent-pole waist and freshly minted silicone breasts. Her short blonde hair bobbed playfully around her face as she talked, lips painted Chinese red, her bright blue bra, panties, stockings and garters smouldering against her milky white skin.

Tom bent towards the girl, who had stepped forward and was now leaning seductively against the door frame and whispered in her ear. She laughed, her voice pealing up the alley like a glass bell, her head thrown back so that her hair kissed the tops of her shoulders. As she laughed, Tom handed her what looked like several hundred Euro, discreetly folded so that she could quickly close her delicate hand around the clean, crisp notes. More than enough, in these streets, for sex.

Still giggling, the girl stepped aside and Tom brushed gently against her as he entered the shop. She followed him inside, closed the door and pulled the thick red curtains shut. A thin ribbon of light danced tauntingly around the window's edge.

FIFTY-SEVEN

9:56pm

Jennifer walked unsteadily back onto the street.

'You bastard.' She mouthed the words, closed her eyes, pushed the back of her head against the wall, her stomach churning. She knew that really she had no right to be upset or even surprised. Tom was, after all, a thief. Why should she have expected him to behave any differently from all the other sleaze-bags she'd come across over the years?

And yet she did feel upset. Upset with him because the little she had found out about him had made her hope for better. Upset with herself that, much as she hated to admit it, her instinctive response on seeing him go inside had been jealousy, not anger. She dismissed it immediately. But the feeling nevertheless remained, an uncomfortable ache in her stomach that she couldn't quite get rid of.

'Hashish? Ecstasy? Co-ca-ine?' Jennifer looked up in surprise at the dreadlocked Rastafarian. In the darkness, she could only make out his wide, staring eyes and the fragrant smell of the joint that hung down from the corner of his mouth.

'No, thank you.'

'It's good sheeeet.' He stretched the word, flexing it playfully between his teeth. And then, as if to prove his point, he took a long drag on the joint, his eyes rolling back in his head as he held the smoke in his lungs before gently exhaling through his nose, a dizzy smile on his face.

'*No*, thank you,' she whispered firmly.

Muttering and shrugging his shoulders, the man shuffled off down the street, the reflective heels of his white trainers winking in the street lights every time he lifted his feet.

Shaking her head, Jennifer peered round the corner again and gasped. The curtains of the shop that Tom had disappeared into only moments before had been drawn back. The blonde girl, her blue underwear dyed purple by the red lights, had lit a cigarette and was sitting on a steel and leather stool in the middle of the front room. Ready, it seemed, for her next customer. What the hell had just happened?

Jennifer turned down the alley and walked slowly into the square. As she drew level with the middle shop, the girl smiled at her lazily, the smoke coiling around her coquettish head.

Beyond her, in the rear room, the carefully folded white sheets lay undisturbed at the foot of the bed. The room was empty.

Jennifer sprinted across the rest of the square and down the opposite alleyway, emerging onto the street. There was no sign of Tom. He certainly hadn't come back the other way past her. How had she missed him?

She retreated across the square, past the blonde girl who was already in the middle of a negotiation with another potential client, back up the alley and onto the main street. What now, she asked herself. In the end she knew that she only had one option. Head back to the hotel and confront him there when he returned. If he returned.

'*Hoe veel?*'

'What?' asked Jennifer, startled by the large man who had suddenly appeared out of the darkness in front of her.

'How much?' he asked in accented English this time, lowering his face to hers so that his warm breath, laden with beer, washed over her face.

'What do you mean?' Jennifer took a step back.

'For a suck and a fuck. How much?' He gave her a toothy smile.

'No,' she said through clenched jaws. 'You want to try down there.' She jerked her head back towards the alley just behind her.

'You know what they say. You're not a man till

you've had some tan!' He gave a wide laugh and grabbed her around the waist, lifting her a few inches off the ground. Jennifer knew that a punch with the heel of her right hand against the man's exposed throat would bring him down as if he'd been shot. But she didn't hit him. Something she saw over the man's right shoulder stopped her. A figure had emerged at the top of the steps of a house about fifteen feet away from her, the light from the hallway swirling out onto the street.

It was Tom.

Her brain clicked. The hooker's shop must have had a connecting door at the rear that led to this house, presumably allowing people to enter or exit unobserved. But why had Tom used it? What was he doing there?

'Three hundred Euro,' Jennifer said to the man. He dropped her as if he had been bitten, his broad shoulders concealing Jennifer from Tom's eyes as he looked up and down the street and set off.

'How much?' he asked faintly.

'Three hundred. Or back there, fifty.' The important thing was to stay out of sight until she could see where Tom was going. In front of her, the man was rocking uncertainly on his heels, his eyes darting from Jennifer, to the alley, back to Jennifer. With a sheepish nod he stumbled past her towards the alley and the girl in the blue underwear.

Tom was already fifty yards in front of her now.

He seemed to be heading back towards the hotel. She could see that he had changed and was now dressed in black, with a large backpack slung across one of his shoulders that he hadn't had before.

It was only then, when Tom veered off to the left, that she noticed him. A shape slipping between the shadows ahead of her. A shape that was following Tom.

FIFTY-EIGHT

10:16pm

Typically, he would have spent several months planning a job like this. Getting to know the layout of the rooms, what systems were in place, where they were housed, how they were controlled and maintained. And also the guards – their names, their routines, their quirks, their weaknesses.

Tonight, he did not have that luxury. At any other time this would have been an unacceptable risk. But this was different. Five years ago he'd spent two months in Amsterdam planning a job at the same place he was going to hit tonight. That time, his target had been a small Dürer sketch. He'd planned out the whole job, covered every angle, every eventuality. But then Archie had called it off. Apparently the buyer had been murdered by pirates while sailing up the Amazon.

Tom had never known how Archie did what he did. How he seemed able to come up with blueprints and technical drawings and specifications for alarm systems. But he always did. In fact, Tom had never known Archie to be wrong when it came to a job. That was why Tom was willing to take the risk now. Archie said that the systems had not been changed since Tom had planned the job five years ago. He said that although the guards had changed, their routine hadn't. And Tom trusted Archie.

Besides, what he had seen that evening when he had nipped in just before closing time had confirmed Archie's view. Apart from the refurbished ticketing area and the installation of an extra set of fire doors on the second floor, everything looked the same.

It was more of a private collection than a museum really, housed within four slender 18th century houses that had been knocked together behind their picture book façade to create several large lateral galleries. Collected over the last fifty years by Maximillian Schenck, the sole heir of Holland's largest retailing family, it was an eclectic but immensely valuable collection of Impressionist and Old Master paintings, modern sculpture, antique furniture and objets d'art.

And one of the highlights was unquestionably the Fabergé Egg that Tom was about to steal.

FIFTY-NINE

10:27pm
The man was definitely following Tom.

For a few minutes Jennifer had thought that she might be imagining it, that he was just walking the same way. But as he darted between cars and behind trees, his head low, turning where Tom turned, stopping when Tom stopped, that possibility rapidly evaporated.

So Jennifer held back, careful to stay fifty yards or so behind as she tracked the two men in front of her, watching where she stepped, controlling her breathing, tacking from shadow to shadow like a small boat racing upwind. The instructors back at Quantico had taught her well.

They walked on, past cars that lined each side of the canal like a multicoloured metal wall. And everywhere bikes, so many bikes, chained to trees and railings and lampposts and street signs. Even to each other. Every so often they would step past a bar or a basement peepshow and the barrel-chested bouncer standing outside would ask them if they wanted to come in as they each walked past – first Tom, then the man and finally Jennifer, as if they were all part of some bizarre extended conga.

As they walked deeper into the city, the dull bass of the live bands playing in the depths of innumerable sweaty bars and the laughter of travelling students staggering from coffee shops gradually faded into the distance. Instead Jennifer's constant companion was the canal, flowing thickly alongside her, its surface dark and coagulated by the night.

Ahead of her, first Tom, then the man, turned right. Jennifer made her way slowly to the end of the street, wary of Tom turning back on himself, or running into the back of the man who might have stopped ahead of her. She edged to the street corner and looked cautiously around it.

But both men had disappeared.

SIXTY

10:59pm
At their lowest part, where the gabled rooflines angled down to meet the red bricked façade, the buildings on this street were four stories high. The large black iron cranes set into the top of each gable were the only evidence of their former lives as a series of merchant's houses where grain would have been hauled out of barges on the canal into the store rooms on the upper floors.

A ground floor entry into the Schenck Museum was always going to be out of the question. The windows were too exposed and besides it was too close to the control room where the three guards gathered at night, one eye on the closed circuit TV monitors and the other on the TV. A succession of gaudy quiz shows and translated American sitcoms filled the minutes between the patrol that two of them made through the building every forty-five minutes.

Tom knew it had to be the roof, but getting up there was almost as difficult as going in through the main entrance. He could, potentially, have used a compressed-air grappling hook, but that was risky. Unlike in the movies, there was never any guarantee it would grip onto anything and he certainly couldn't afford to have a titanium hook come crashing down onto the sidewalk from four floors up.

It only left one option. The old-fashioned way. The hard way. He had to climb up. Tom settled his heavy backpack squarely onto his shoulders. He checked again that the street was empty and started up the far right-hand side of the building, well away from the video camera which was trained on the museum entrance.

To most people, the building's sheer façade would have represented an impassable obstacle, but Tom knew that the building was old and the cracked and crumbling mortar gave a climber of his ability a succession of firm hand and toe holds.

He moved smoothly up the front of the building, his fingers searching for first one hold, then another, his feet driving him upwards as they locked onto faint ridges in the brickwork. Every so often a decorative course of white bricks had been laid slightly proud of the main wall and the narrow ledges allowed him a temporary relief.

Once he was about fifteen feet off the ground, he traversed a few feet across the side of the building until he reached a thick metal drainpipe that emerged at that point out of the brickwork and led up to the roof.

Below him a police car swung onto the street and made its way slowly past the museum entrance. Tom pressed himself flat against the wall, the brickwork scraping against his cheek, his left foot jammed between the drainpipe and the wall. The car drove by, paused momentarily and then turned right over a bridge and down another street. Peeling himself away from the wall Tom gripped the drainpipe and started up towards the roof.

Two minutes later he swung his right arm, then his right leg over the parapet and dragged himself onto the roof. He lay there for a few moments, fighting to catch his breath, his mouth dry and sour as his muscles leaked lactic acid. Overhead, the stars sparkled, brilliant jewels laid on a black velvet cushion. Just for a moment, Tom allowed himself to think again about what he was doing. He'd fought against this hard, but in the end Archie had probably been right. Much as he wanted to believe Jennifer's promise of a fresh start he couldn't trust anyone but himself.

His watch beeped and snapped his mind back into focus. He was right on time.

Rolling to his feet, he grabbed a long black rope out of his bag. Securing it quickly to the parapet, he dropped it down the side of the building, the thin nylon cord nestling in the shadow cast by a neighbouring tree. From the street it was almost invisible but it gave him a quick way down. Just in case.

Behind the gabled façade the roof was flat, the original triangular roofline having been removed in the 1960s in favour of a starker, more modern look for the galleries below. As part of these works, a series of large skylights had also been set into the flat roof to allow natural light in. Tom padded over to the window set into the very middle of the building and crouched down next to it.

On cue, two guards appeared at the doorway of the large room beneath him and looked in, running their flashlights around the room. Then, as they withdrew, one of them suddenly flashed his flashlight up towards the skylights overhead. The powerful beam leapt up from the floor below and shone up through the glass like a spotlight. Tom jumped back from the opening and set the timer on his watch. He had forty-five minutes exactly until they came back.

He removed a small axle grinder from the front pocket of his pack. It was battery-powered and had been specially modified by him to silence the sound of the electric motor. With a faint buzzing noise, he cut into the glass's smooth surface, scoring the outline of a large square.

Replacing the axle grinder, Tom produced two Anver suction hand cups, aluminium handles with two large circular rubber sucker pads at each end of them designed to carry about 66 pounds of load each. Placing these against the glass, he eased down the black plastic lever at the centre of each pad, creating a vacuum.

This was the moment of truth. Get it wrong, and the window would shatter into a thousand pieces. He jerked his hands and with a loud cracking noise the section of glass snapped cleanly out of the frame.

He was in.

SIXTY-ONE

11:31pm

On the roof of the building opposite the one he'd just seen Kirk climb up, Kyle Foster unpacked his M24 from his bag and began to assemble it. Just for fun, he did it with his eyes closed, like they'd been trained to back at Fort Benning in Georgia.

First slip the barrel assembly into the stock. Then insert and tighten the action screws, locking in the trigger guard assembly. Then clip on the scope by using the half inch combination wrench to tighten the front and rear mounting ring nuts. Finally insert the bolt assembly. Magazine in. Safety off. Good to go.

Foster preferred the M24's bolt action to the PSG-1 or the M21's semi-automatic mechanisms that spat shell casings all over the place. It was light too, featuring a HS Precision stock made of a Kevlar, graphite and fibreglass composite bound together with epoxy resins. Empty, without a scope, it weighed just five and a half kilos and had an effective range of about eight hundred metres. More than enough for tonight's job.

He'd swapped the normal Leupold M3A 10x42 day optic scope for a Litton Aquila x6 night vision device. And just to make sure, he'd also clipped on a Harris bipod and an under-barrel laser pointer. Double-bagging it, as his old staff sergeant used to say.

His only real complaint with the whole package, apart from the well known limitations of the M118 round which used to drive everyone in his unit nuts, was the long action which had been known to cause feeding problems if the rounds were not pushed all the way to the rear of the magazine. But as he grasped its familiar shape, the butt nestling snugly against his shoulder, his eye pressed up to the scope, such minor considerations faded into insignificance. He was only going to need one shot anyway.

Instead the memories surged.

'El Angel Negro.'

The Dark Angel, that's what the locals had taken to calling him in Columbia. Not that they ever knew who he was, or even if he was human. Some said he was a ghost, carrying their children and brothers and sisters and parents into the forest never to be seen alive again, their mutilated bodies only found months later buried in a shallow grave or strung high above them in the dark branches of the forest canopy.

'Why?', their innocent eyes had asked as he leant over them.

'Because I can,' he had whispered. 'Because I've been told to.'

Just like he'd been told tonight. The usual phone call, the clipped voice rasping its instructions.

'Follow Kirk. Stay close. Take up a position opposite. And don't miss.'

SIXTY-TWO

11:32pm

Tom placed the sheet of glass down a few feet away, loosened the suction pads and replaced them in his pack. Then he stood up and walked over to the chattering air conditioning vent that sat just behind the skylight, a small pool of water at its base where the moisture extracted from the room below had condensed and dripped to the ground.

Kneeling down, Tom lifted a small remote-controlled Ramsey ATV winch out of his pack and secured it in place by looping a rope around the vent's thick neck and then clipping it onto each side of the winch. Although designed to be powered by a car engine, Tom had adapted it for battery power. It wouldn't last long, but it would be more than enough for what he had planned tonight. He flicked the winch on and fed out several feet of slack from its drum, the narrow steel cable glinting like barbed wire.

Standing at the edge of the skylight, he put his pack on back to front, so the main compartment sat on his chest and clipped the cable onto the abseiling harness that he wore over his black overalls, the metal buckles, clips and hoops wrapped in black tape to minimise noise and cut out reflective glare. Finally he slipped on a black ski mask, the material moulding itself to his face with familiar intimacy. He was ready.

Crouching, he levered himself through the hole he had cut, until his legs were suspended in the room below, the winch taking his weight. He slid a small piece of hardened rubber under the wire to stop it rubbing against the frame. Pressing the remote control, he was silently lowered into the room.

The gallery floor lay about 20 feet below him, with the room itself measuring about 30 feet square. The only doorway into the gallery led out to a wide corridor with access to the other rooms and the main staircase down to the lower floors. There were also three cameras in the room. One static camera was covering the doorway and two tracking cameras in opposing corners were covering approximately half the room each.

The white gallery walls glowed eerily in the moonlight, the semi-darkness broken regularly by the periodic flashing of the small red lights that indicated that the three cameras were all functioning properly.

The gallery had been daringly hung with a mix of artists from across the centuries. Rothko next to Rembrandt. Modigliani next to Monet. On the left-hand wall, he could just about make out the outline of the Dürer sketch that he had been planning to steal all those years before.

Through the open doorway, Tom could also make out a faint green glow. He knew from Archie's schematics that this was the control panel for the grid of infrared tripwires that would trigger if anything touched the floor. But the floor was irrelevant; he had no intention of touching it. So too was the static camera trained on the doorway, since he wouldn't be going near that.

But the other two tracking cameras, their glass eyes sweeping rhythmically backwards and forwards across the room every ten seconds or so, they would have to be dealt with. Both cameras had been deliberately angled down towards the lower parts of the surrounding walls and the floor, their relentless gaze directed, understandably, at the actual paintings and sculptures and display cabinets that they were protecting. This meant that they took in perhaps only ten feet of vertical height at the most. Suspended just below the skylight in the middle of the room, therefore, Tom was out of the cameras' field of vision and would remain so as long as he stayed high and kept his legs up.

Tom reached into the backpack and took out a

small spear gun. Usually kept on life rafts, the great advantage of the JBL Mini Carbine was its compact size, being only twenty-seven inches from tip to butt. Underwater it had an effective range of 9 feet, but on land and with a few modifications, Tom had increased it to 20. He judged the distance from him to the wall over the top of the left hand camera to be about 15 feet, well within range. He took aim carefully a few feet above the camera, knowing that if he missed, the spear would crash down to the floor and set the alarm off.

He felt the familiar taste of carbon on his tongue, dry and metallic. This was common to most art galleries, the carbon filters installed to remove fumes and odours but most importantly the sulphur dioxide generated by the exhalation of gallery visitors that could severely damage the paintings if left unchecked.

Swallowing, Tom squeezed the trigger and the spear flashed across the room, spooling a thin nylon rope out behind it as it slammed into the wall, burying its nickel-plated steel tip about five inches deep. Without pausing he reloaded the gun, turned and fired another spear above the other camera in the opposite corner.

With both spears in place, he fed the ends of the thin nylon ropes that were attached to the ends of both spears through a metal tightener. Winding the small handle on the side of the tightener drew the ropes together until they were taut. He checked his watch. Thirty-five minutes left.

Tom attached himself to the nylon cord that was now stretched diagonally across the room and unclipped himself from the steel cable. Crossing his ankles over the cord, his back to the floor, he pulled himself across the room, the metal clip fizzing against the rope like a zip wire, until he was directly above the right-hand camera.

Reaching down, he clipped a small black box to the wire that carried the video signal back down to the control room on the ground floor. Once activated, this stored two minutes of video footage onto its small memory chip before switching into playback mode, overriding the input signal and transmitting its recorded images again and again until the batteries died about an hour later. He'd be long gone by then.

Tom switched the device on, waited the two minutes for the playback to start and then hauled himself back over to the camera on the other side of the room where he repeated the same procedure. Two minutes later and the room was effectively invisible to the guards downstairs. Twenty-five minutes left.

Tom heaved himself back along the nylon cord and stopped in the middle of the room. Looking down over his shoulder towards the floor, the square display case beneath him stared back. Through its glass top, the gold filigree that embraced the Fabergé Egg's green surface winked at him in the half light, urging him on. Tom grinned. He hated to admit it, but he was enjoying himself. The buzz was still there.

He clipped himself back onto the steel wire dangling down from the roof and pressing the remote, lowered himself face down until he was right above the display case, his breath gently clouding the glass surface before instantly evaporating. The case rested on an elegant brushed-steel column that widened into a large square base which, ziggurat-like, cascaded down to the floor through a series of narrow steps and ledges, each about two inches wide.

Tom pressed the remote again and lowered himself below the level of the glass display cabinet, examining the sides of the metal column until he was only a few feet above the floor, his legs bent back to avoid brushing against its polished wooden surface. Right at the bottom of the column, just before the base widened out, Tom finally found the metal panel that he was looking for – it was set flush to the surface and secured in each corner with four small screws. He checked his watch. Fifteen minutes left.

Slipping a slim electric screwdriver out from inside his jacket he carefully unscrewed the plate, each screw sticking resolutely to the magnetised tip of the screwdriver as they came free, before he deposited them safely on the top step of the column's base. The last screw came loose and Tom trapped the panel with his left hand to stop it falling out.

But the sudden movement must have caused his right hand to shake a little, because the screw dropped from the screwdriver, hit the base of the platform with a metallic ping and then rolled, with agonising lethargy, down each of its narrow ledges towards the floor.

SIXTY-THREE

11:50pm

Tom looked on in horrified fascination as the tiny silver screw tripped and skipped its way from step to step, flirting with the final edge that would have sent it spinning to the ground and the alarm being triggered.

But it did not fall.

Instead it hesitated, its shiny head peeking over the edge into oblivion, before gently coming to a rest. Tom blew through his masked lips in relief.

He reached towards the screw with the magnetised tip of the screwdriver, picked it up and deposited it safely. Looking into the small hole revealed by the panel he had just removed he could just make out two wires. As Archie had predicted, it looked like the supply to a fairly basic pressure switch that would trigger if the Egg was lifted out of the case.

He snapped a small metal clip between the

two wires that cut down through the insulation to the bare wires underneath. Easy enough to deal with.

He pressed the remote control, and the winch drew him back up over the top of the display case. Reaching into his overalls again, he produced a small diamond cutter with which he etched a large round circle into the glass directly beneath him. Replacing the cutter in his pocket, he struck the circle smartly with the heel of his hand. It snapped free, dropping into the case and bouncing off the top of the Egg.

Tom reached into the case and clamped his gloved fingers around the Egg's silky surface. Hesitating momentarily, he lifted it out of the cabinet, a gentle click resonating inside the glass case as he pulled it clear. But the alarm stayed silent. Although the switch had been tripped, the circuit flowed uninterrupted through the secondary circuit that he had fixed to the wires.

Forty minutes gone. Five minutes left. Just enough time to get out.

He slipped the Egg inside his jacket and then pressing the remote, was hauled back up towards the roof. As his head and shoulders emerged through the space in the skylight, he stopped the winch and used his arms to help pull himself through.

That was when he noticed it. A small red dot flush in the middle of his chest. Tom stiffened, transfixed. He knew what it was immediately. The laser pointer of a high-powered rifle.

The red dot slid up to his face, flashing briefly into his left eye and making him blink. The dot then danced around his lips, tumbled down his arm, skidded across his gloved hand until it finally settled on the winch's motor. Whoever it was, they were on the roof of the building on the other side of the canal. Playing with him.

There was a single shot. The motor sheared apart in an eruption of hot metal and sparks and the cable spooled free, sending Tom flying backwards through the gap into the room below.

Instinctively he reached out and somehow hooked the taut nylon cord that he had run across the room under his left hand arm. It brought him up short and hard, wrenching his shoulder in its socket. He clung onto the cord, locking his arm into place by grabbing his elbow with his other arm, panting in fear and pain. What the hell was going on? Who was out there? How had they known he would be there?

The cord dropped a few inches. Jolted by the sudden impact, the left hand spear had been torn from the wall. As Tom watched, its barbed tip slowly worked its way through the wood and plaster, the cord sinking inexorably lower. He held his breath. Five seconds. Ten seconds.

The spear abruptly ripped free and Tom plummeted to the alarmed floor.

The room exploded into life on impact. The lights burst on, their damning glare blinding Tom as he lay on the floor. The alarm detonated, a sonic boom of high pitched sirens and bells that swept across the room in a wave of sound.

He staggered to his feet, reached helplessly for the doorway, but a huge steel door slammed down in front of it, sealing the only realistic exit from the room. With the skylight twenty feet above him, he knew that there was no way in or out.

He was trapped.

SIXTY-FOUR

12:04am

The sight of the red dot on the opposite roof had suddenly explained to Jennifer where the man following Tom had vanished to. And yet it had still taken a few more seconds for her, crouching on the museum roof where she had climbed using the rope Tom had left dangling down the side of the building, to realise what the red dot actually was.

Even so, when it actually came only moments later, the sound of the shot had momentarily paralysed her. It was only the strident sound of the alarm from the gallery below that had finally prodded her to her feet and sent her scrambling towards the skylight where she now stood, hands on hips, looking down at Tom through the hole in the glass.

'Having fun?' Her voice was like cracked stone.

'You?' Tom's voice registered his surprise, but it was soon gone. 'Quick, get me out of here.'

'I don't think so.'

'Look, it's not what it seems.'

She took in the alarm, the shattered display case, the masked figure below her. It was exactly what it seemed. Exactly what she'd been warned by Corbett to expect. How could she have been so stupid to think that everyone else might have got it wrong?

'Oh no?' She laughed coldly. 'What is it, then?'

Tom ripped the ski mask from his head, his hair damp and ruffled. She could see his eyes, big and dark and perhaps even a little frightened.

'I have about 90 seconds before the guards get here,' he motioned anxiously towards the steel door. 'I'll explain later.'

'No, you'll explain now.' Her voice was firm, unyielding. She didn't even know for sure why she was listening – why she hadn't just gone straight to the police when she found the rope dangling down the side of the museum wall. But part of her wanted a reason.

'There's no time.' Tom pleaded.

'I've got plenty.'

Tom shook his head, looked away, then back up at her.

'The Fabergé Egg I stole in New York was for Cassius. Do you know who he is?' Cassius? The name was familiar, but she couldn't think where from. Then it came to her. Cassius was the Captain Nemo figure that Corbett had mentioned in the meeting with Secretary Young. The criminal mastermind he believed was behind a coordinated spate of high-end art thefts. She nodded. 'Right, so you know what I'm up against. The job was for two Eggs but I backed out of taking the second. You see, I wasn't lying when I said that I'd decided to get out. But Cassius wouldn't have it. He threatened to kill me and a guy I work with if I don't get it by tomorrow.'

She remained silent. How could she believe him? The steel shutter rose an inch from the floor as it was jacked open by the guards outside, their excited voices echoing through the gap.

'Why didn't you just tell me?'

'Would that have made a difference? Would you have let me do this job?'

'No.'

'Then what choice did I have? Do nothing and get myself and someone else killed?'

'We had a deal. You should have trusted me. I could have protected you.' Her eyes flashed coldly but she was more uncertain now. Despite herself, despite everything, she wanted to believe him.

Tom shook his head with a sad smile.

'I heard you the other night, Jennifer. On the phone to your boss. Saying that he could count on you to do whatever it took to get a result. That you didn't care what happened to me. I have to look after myself. I can't rely on you or anyone else to protect me. I never have.'

Jennifer flushed as she heard her own words played back to her. Suddenly the reason for Tom being so cold over dinner in Paris made sense.

'What I meant was that my only interest in you is my belief that you can help solve this case and that's true. I'm not interested in who's done what to who in the past. As far as I'm concerned we have a deal, and I intend to stick to it as long as you do.'

The steel shutter was three inches off the ground now and she could see the metal toecaps of the guards' boots under the gap.

'Maybe that's what you think now. But when the time comes, things might not be so clear. You'll have your career to think about. I couldn't take the risk of being betrayed a second time.'

'So what were you planning to do? Steal the Egg and then disappear? Where to?'

'It's for an off-site that Cassius is holding tomorrow night in Istanbul.' Tom was throwing increasingly nervous glances towards the slowly rising steel door. 'I was planning to go to there and try and settle this once and for all. For Harry.'

'Istanbul?' Despite everything, she couldn't hide the sudden interest in her voice. Istanbul was a link to the coins. Perhaps a chance to get them back and the people who'd taken them. 'Why didn't you say so before?'

'That's why Steiner had begun to write the number down on that card when he was killed.

Cassius was clearly lining up the coins for his off-site. He may have even had them stolen specially for it. The coins and the two Fabergé Eggs are probably the star lots.'

'So what happens if Cassius doesn't get the second Egg?'

'He can't afford to have people show up to the off-site and then not produce the items he's promised them will be there. He'll probably just cancel it.'

Jennifer's mind was racing. If the off-site was cancelled, she'd lose her best chance of catching up with the coins. The chances of ever catching up with them all again after that were small. She needed the off-site to go ahead.

'Grab this.'

Jennifer threw her rope down to him, the heavy cord whistling through the air as it uncoiled. The steel shutter was almost a foot off the ground now and she could see someone struggling to slide under it sideways.

Tom grabbed the rope, heaving himself out of the room as the steel security door rose another three inches. His feet flicked through the hole in the skylight just as the first guard slid into the room and jumped to his feet, gun out.

Tom leant forward on his knees, sucking air. He looked up at Jennifer, his voice like sand on glass.

'Next time, just throw the rope down, will you. We can chat later.'

'There won't be a next time. There wasn't meant to be a *this* time.' She pulled him to his feet. 'Let's get out of here.'

They made their escape along the roofs of the adjacent buildings, abseiling down to the street and then retracing their steps to the hotel. The two-tone sound of police sirens and a growing swarm of flashing blue lights faded into the distance, a faint echo in the still night air.

They were followed all the way though by a single, incredulous, pair of eyes. As they disappeared into the hotel's entrance, he pulled his phone from his suit pocket. He spoke as soon as it was answered the other end.

'It's Jones, sir . . . It's a goddamned circus out here . . . Kirk just broke into a museum and then some crazy tried to take him out on the roof with a rifle . . . No he missed. Browne? I'm sorry, sir, but it looks like she helped Kirk escape.'

SIXTY-FIVE

Seven Bridges Hotel, Amsterdam, Holland
12:36am

'Let me see it. Let me have a look.' Jennifer's voice was strained, excited even. The adrenaline was still coursing through their bloodstreams, their hearts beating fast, their brains fizzing as they arrived back in their room.

'Are you sure?' Tom eyed her uncertainly. 'You're in deep enough already. Maybe it would be better if you just left it at that.'

'I've helped you escape from a crime scene. How much deeper can I get?'

Tom nodded, then flashed her an awkward look.

'You know, I really appreciate what you did for me back there.'

'I must be crazy,' she whispered, almost to herself. 'If anyone finds out, it will finish me. You know that, don't you?' Her large round eyes glistened as she spoke.

'Yeah.' He paused. 'So why did you do it?'

'No Egg, no off-site. No off-site, no coins.'

'So purely business then?' Tom almost sounded disappointed.

'Just business.' She hoped he didn't notice the hesitation in her voice. Because there had been another factor running through her mind when she threw down that rope, a factor that she barely wanted to admit to herself, let alone Tom. That part of her had needed him to believe that he could trust her. That they were in this together. Because she knew what it was like not to be trusted, to have people always doubting your motives and your actions. Because she was determined to give him the second chance that so few people, until Corbett, had been willing to give her.

Tom smiled, his twinkling eyes suggesting that he knew she hadn't told him everything, although he didn't press the point.

'Well – whatever the reason, it was the right one. We're going to finish this together. Now, hold your hands out.'

He reached into his jacket and gently placed the small Egg in her cupped hands.

'Oh my God. It's beautiful,' she breathed, stroking the Egg's smooth green surface, her fingers tracing the gilded flowers that snaked up its side from the twisted roots that served as its base. 'What's it called?'

'The Pansy Egg. It's one of my favourites.'

'Why?'

'I'll show you.'

He opened the Egg and revealed a removable golden heart-shaped shield with eleven tiny doors, mounted on a delicately crafted easel.

'Each door opens to reveal miniature portraits of different members of the Imperial family.' He opened a few of the doors. Sombre, pale faces stared back. 'I've always thought they look very sad, as if they knew what was going to happen to them.'

'You're talking about the Russian Revolution?'

'I'm talking about the Bolsheviks murdering them, confiscating the collection and selling it to finance Stalin's army. For me, this one piece tells me more about the history of Russia than a thousand text books. It's all here. The glory and the horror.'

'How many eggs are there in all?'

'Fabergé only made fifty. Eight have been lost. The Armory Museum in the Kremlin still has ten and a Russian billionaire recently bought nine from the Forbes family. The rest are in the hands of other museums and private collectors.'

'Haven't you ever been tempted to keep all these things you've taken over the years for yourself?'

'Never.' Tom smiled. 'It's one of the first rules you learn. You do the job and then you move on. You can't afford to fall in love with whatever it is

you're taking.' He held out his hand and reluctantly she handed the Egg and the shield back.

Tom wrapped the Egg up and put it down on
the side. 'Let's check in with Archie.'

'Who?'

'A . . . colleague.' She sat down on the bed next
to him as he dialled. 'It's me.' He said when the
phone was answered.

'Are you all right, mate? Is there a problem?'
Archie's concerned voice filtered back down the
phone.

'No I'm fine. I've got it.'

'You've got it. Oh, thank fucking God. Well
done, mate. Well done.'

'Thanks,' said Tom, smiling at his friend's relief.

'Any problems?' Archie had calmed down now
and his tone was more businesslike. Tom gave a
short laugh.

'You could say that. Archie, did you let
anyone know that I was going to hit that place
tonight?'

'Of course not. What do you take me for?'

'Okay, okay.'

'Why, what happened?'

'Well, as I was coming out . . .'

'Oh, screw me!' Archie interrupted. 'I did
mention it to someone. Not where you were going
to hit exactly but the city it was in.'

'Who?'

'The other night. Cassius.'

'Cassius?' Jennifer started in surprise. 'For Christ's sake, Archie. Whose side are you on here?'

'I know, I'm sorry. He caught me by surprise. Why what happened?'

'Someone shot my winch out to try and get me caught.'

'Why the hell would Cassius get you to half-inch something, then make sure you got pinched nicking it? It doesn't make any sense. It must be someone else.'

'Maybe.'

'How did you get out?'

'Jennifer.'

'The Fed? You having me on?'

'No.'

'What's her game? She must want something.'

'Maybe.' Tom eyed Jennifer who was listening to his side of the conversation avidly. 'I'm not sure of anything anymore. We'll talk about it later. Anyway, I'll leave the Egg with Fleure in the morning together with my kit. You can take it from there.'

'No problem. Oh . . . and Tom?'

'Yeah.'

'Cheers.'

'Don't mention it.'

The line went dead. Tom turned to face Jennifer.

'Did you get all that?'

She nodded, her face serious.

'Archie, who I'm assuming is your fence, told Cassius about this job.' Tom nodded. 'Now you think Cassius deliberately tried to have you trapped in that museum. And you don't know why.'

'Do you?'

'The answer's in Istanbul. It must be. I'll get us down there in the morning,' she said calmly. 'Max will take care of the tickets.'

'Don't you need to call your boss, let him know what's happening?'

'I will. But for now, we should both get some rest.' She paused, looked him in the eye. 'By the way, who was that girl?'

'What girl?'

'Back there. The blonde one with the Victoria's Secret dress sense.'

'That's Fleure, the girl I've got to deliver the Egg to in the morning. She's just someone I know. Someone I can rely on. Why? You jealous?' Tom asked with a grin.

'You wish!' She shrugged the question away. 'Do you want to flip a coin for who gets the floor?'

'No need,' Tom said generously. 'The bed's all yours.'

SIXTY-SIX

Istanbul, Turkey
29th July – 5:43pm

The İlesam Lokall tea garden lies just off the Divan Yolu, the ancient Road to the Imperial Council that stretches from the ruins of the Roman Hippodrome, where chariots once raced and gladiators fought to the cheer of the baying crowds, right up to the Cannon Gate in the old city walls.

Behind the garden's thick walls the clattering of the trams, the incessant sounding of car horns and the fierce cries of the street traders gave way to a cool, stony stillness and the gentle rattle of dice on large and elaborately inlaid backgammon boards. Several enterprising locals had arranged brightly-covered cushions and kilims on the benches and hung rugs from the walls. These were subtle traps, designed to tempt a few of the garden's many guests into one of the stalls that had been set up in the small cells that had served as classrooms when the garden still housed the Medrese, or Islamic school, of the neighbouring mosque.

As always, the air was thick with smoke from the water pipes – a sickly sweet concoction of apple-flavoured tobacco laid on top of an endless supply of red-hot coals dispensed by a leathered old man who shuffled between the tables with sepulchral resignation. As the tobacco smoke was drawn down through the clear water, the gentle rumble of bursting bubbles rippled through the air like a large purring cat.

'Why do they do that?' asked Jennifer, as they sat down in the far corner of the garden, waving away the rug sellers who had immediately homed in on them as likely buyers of 'genuine' Turkish kilims.

'It cleans the smoke. Cools it down,' Tom explained.

'You've been here before?'

'I spent some time here once,' said Tom, trying to attract the waiter's attention.

'You've spent time in a lot of places,' Jennifer observed.

'More than is healthy,' Tom agreed. 'What do you want? Apple tea or coffee? Just so you know, the apple tea is so sweet that it makes your teeth feel like they're about to fall out. But, on the other hand, the coffee is so bitter that it will make you grind your teeth together.'

'Oh my, what a choice.' She rolled her eyes. 'The coffee I think.' Tom ordered a tea and a coffee and they appeared moments later, the tea steaming in a small curved glass, the viscous coffee bubbling like molten lead in its porcelain crucible.

'So why are we here?' asked Jennifer, sipping her coffee and looking around her, gratefully feeling the hard slap of the caffeine hit her brain. The garden was busy, but far from full and she was aware of suspicious glances from the small groups of Turks who had gathered around the low tables to drink and smoke.

'Because we need information and this is the place to get it,' Tom explained, stretching his feet out on the bench.

Jennifer had called Corbett first thing that morning, insisting that the call was patched through to his house even though it was about three am. She'd told him what Tom had found out. That there was an illegal auction taking place in Istanbul and that they were both headed out there in case the coins surfaced. He had agreed with her plans and told her to be careful.

They had caught an eleven am flight out from Amsterdam that morning. It had been an awkward journey, both of them aware that what had happened at the museum had changed the relationship between them, yet neither of them quite yet able to understand how.

There was a sudden commotion near the garden

entrance. Two large men clad in mirrored sunglasses and shiny grey suits, the material embroidered with silvery specks, strode into the garden and quickly scanned its occupants. Seemingly satisfied, they looked over their shoulders and nodded.

In swept a little barrel of a man that Jennifer took to be their boss. His face was almost entirely taken up by a thick bulbous nose and a wild black beard that matched his wavy jet black hair. She thought they both looked dyed. His eyes were hidden under thick rimmed tortoiseshell Ray Bans, the maker's logo printed on the corner of the left hand lens so that their designer pedigree could not be doubted. He wore a heavy black leather jacket, the top three buttons of his black silk shirt left undone, his wrists and open-shirted neck glinting with thick knots of gold chains.

Two more men followed him in, each taking up strategic positions around him, their left armpits bulging tellingly. The waiter fussed nervously around their boss, showing him to the largest, most shaded table and unceremoniously shooing its objecting occupants across the floor, a well-aimed kick sending one of the more vocal protesters sprawling.

'Who's that?' Jennifer hissed.

'Amin Madhavy. A liar and a thief,' said Tom quietly.

'Friend of yours then?'

'How did you guess?' Tom winked. 'Come on. We're on.'

SIXTY-SEVEN

5:52pm
The bodyguards, too busy ordering their own drinks, did not see Tom until he was only a few feet away.

'Madhavy-bey.' Tom used the respectful epithet that Turks reserved for formal greetings. 'Have you returned for another lesson?'

A frown flickered across the man's face. He did not look up, instead stirring first one, then two, then three spoons of sugar into his coffee.

'Kirk-bey,' he said eventually, mirroring the polite greeting, his high-pitched voice heavily accented. He looked up and the frown melted into a smile. 'Welcome.'

The bodyguards, who had spun round at the unexpected sound of Tom's voice, reaching inside their jackets, relaxed. Madhavy waved them away contemptuously.

'It's too late now, you incompetent fools.' He

snarled. 'I would already be dead if he'd wanted to kill me.' He relaxed into a smile again. 'I don't know why I bother.' He shrugged, indicating the padded bench opposite him to Tom. 'Come. Join me.'

He eyed Tom carefully as he sat down, his coffee cup dwarfed by his thick brown hands, gold rings glittering on each finger like expensive armour.

'So what brings you back to Istanbul?' He took his sunglasses off and his dark brown eyes twinkled mischievously. 'Which poor soul will have the misfortune of your visit this time around?' Tom shook his head.

'Haven't you heard? I've retired.'

'Ha! You must think me a fool.'

'I'm serious.'

'What are you doing here, then?'

'Actually, I'm looking for something. Well, some*where* really.'

'Ah!' Understanding flashed across Madhavy's face. 'And you need my help.'

'This is your city, Amin. Who else can I ask?' Madhavy nodded his agreement, his eyebrows rising.

'This is true.'

'Do you know anything about a sale that is taking place tonight? An auction of art.' Tom leant forward. 'Expensive art.'

Madhavy set his cup down.

'So.' He rested his hands on his wide stomach.

'That is what brings you back. I know of it, of course, but the location is secret. Very secret. No one really knows where it is taking place. Not even I.' He clasped his hand to his chest to illustrate his hurt. 'I would love to be able to help you, old friend, but . . .' He shrugged his shoulders. Tom knew Madhavy well enough to see where this was leading.

'Okay, *old friend*. What do you want? Name your price.'

'My price! You think that Amin Madhavy can be bought?' He raised his voice and looked around him in indignation. Satisfied that enough people had heard him, he leant forward and whispered. 'A re-match.'

Madhavy's tone had an urgent edge now and he shuffled forward to the edge of his seat.

'Last time, I couldn't show my face for months. People were laughing at me. At *me*.' Madhavy flashed an incredulous look around the garden. 'This time you will not be so lucky.'

Madhavy motioned with his hand and a large backgammon board appeared from nowhere and was placed on the low table between them. Tom smiled.

'Very well. First to five points given I'm in a hurry. I win, you tell me the location. You win and . . . what happens if you win?'

Madhavy pointed at Tom's wrist.

'I win, I get your watch.'

Tom hesitated. His watch. The watch his mother had left him. But what choice did he have? The auction was that evening, only hours away.

'Fine.' Tom conceded.

As they had been talking Jennifer had drawn close to the table and the bodyguards, clearly stung by Madhavy's earlier criticism, responded this time with drawn weapons and loud shouts.

'She's with me,' said Tom without looking up, as he quickly arranged his pieces on the board. Madhavy grunted a few words and the bodyguards let Jennifer through to the table.

'Thanks for nothing,' she said reproachfully to Tom.

Madhavy laughed at her obvious annoyance.

'Woman trouble?' he asked, his voice tinged with mock concern. 'I hope you won't get distracted.'

'Don't get your hopes up. It'll take more than that for you to beat me. Let's play.'

SIXTY-EIGHT

6:00pm

An eerie quiet had descended around them as the game started. The bodyguards, sensing Madhavy's tension, had drawn closer to the table, trying to keep one eye on the game and one eye on the rest of the garden.

They both played in the Arab style, violently flicking the tiny dice with their thumbs across the board, flashing the pieces around before most people would have had a chance to even see what they had rolled, let alone work out the best move.

Backgammon, or Shesh Besh as the Arabs call it, is one of the world's oldest board games. To the inexperienced player, it is a game of luck, the dice cruelly dictating your moves, strategy a hostage to fortune. But to a player like Tom, the role of chance was relegated to that of willing accomplice. Where Tom drew his tactical advantage was by allying his mathematical mind and his understanding of probability with his ability to bluff.

The modern game is played with a doubling dice, allowing you to double the stake or points in play. Failure to bear off any pieces by the time your opponent has finished is known as a Gammon and further doubles whatever has been staked on the game. Leaving a piece on the bar by the time your opponent has finished is known as a Backgammon and triples the stake. Knowing when to accept, reject or even double back, the equivalent in poker to raising, is as important as the positioning of your pieces. If not more so.

Madhavy started well, rolling a six and a one to form a vital point just outside his home board. Then on his next throw he got a double six, the double entitling him to four moves of six rather than the usual two, allowing him to move his two pieces out of Tom's home board and close off another point.

Given Madhavy's strong start, Tom was not surprised when he doubled him on his next turn. Normally, he would probably have refused the double, preferring to lose the one point rather than risk two. But this wasn't a normal game.

To Madhavy's thinly-concealed delight, therefore, he accepted the double and a few moves later Tom lost the game. Normally each game was worth a point, but with Tom having accepted the double this one was worth two.

'I win,' crowed Madhavy, punching the air. 'Two points. You have lost your touch.'

'You were lucky,' said Tom, swiftly rearranging his pieces. 'It's first to five, don't forget.'

Madhavy bent his head back down towards the board and his earlier jubilation seemed to evaporate as a swift exchange of pieces raised the excited murmur of the growing crowd of onlookers. Mindful of how the game was evolving, Tom quickly settled on a back-game, placing his pieces in blocking positions and then waiting for an opportunity to hit Madhavy as he tried to bear off. It was a risky but potentially devastating strategy.

As Tom had planned, it wasn't long before Madhavy, cursing his misfortune in rapid-fire Turkish, was forced to leave a piece exposed. Sensing his opportunity, Tom doubled him, but Madhavy, clearly fancying his odds, immediately doubled Tom back. In a few seconds it had gone from a one point to a four point game.

Tom stared Madhavy in the eye as he flicked the dice, not bothering to look down to see what he had rolled. The gasps from the enthralled crowd and Jennifer's low whistle were sufficient. He had hit him.

With Tom having blocked all the points in his home board, Madhavy was now frozen out of the game, his piece stranded on the bar. All he could do was watch stonily as Tom swiftly bore off almost half his pieces before he was able to get back on the board and begin to bear off himself. He angrily conceded the game.

Four two to Tom.

SIXTY-NINE

6:17pm

Madhavy snarled out an order for another coffee and snapped at one of his bodyguards for talking. Tom knew now that Madhavy couldn't afford to make a single mistake or he had lost. And, according to the rules, there was no opportunity to use the doubling dice any more, with Tom being only one point from victory. Madhavy had no choice but to win three games in a row. No wonder he looked rattled.

The muttering onlookers, crowded round them in a tight, jostling circle, were feeding hungrily on the tension. Tom studied Madhavy's face thoughtfully, took in his bulging eyes, the nervous fidgeting with his beard, the oily slick of sweat on his forehead, the continuous wetting of his lips. Madhavy looked up and returned Tom's stare, smiling apprehensively. Tom could see that Madhavy was on show here, in front of his own people. He had to play this very carefully.

The next game started with a balanced exchange of moves between the two players, no real advantage accruing to either of them. About four rolls in, though, a succession of poor throws forced Tom to change his strategy to an all out blitz of Madhavy's pieces. Death or glory.

Madhavy reacted well, striking Tom back and with a few doubles closing out most of the points in his home board. Tom suddenly found himself in a very difficult position, his pieces strung out over the board like a ragged necklace and two pieces on the bar.

Three rolls later and Tom was in the same position Madhavy had faced in the previous game, frozen out, except that he had three pieces off the board while Madhavy had only had the one. Madhavy swiftly bore off his pieces, Tom eventually getting one, then another piece back on. With only four pieces left to bear off, Madhavy's anxious face relaxed into a grin. He rolled. Boxcars – a double six.

He purposefully took the final four pieces off the board and looked up at Tom, smiling. Tom still had one piece on the bar. Backgammon. Three points to Madhavy and therefore the match.

The small crowd around them erupted into applause and Madhavy energetically shook Tom's hand, all smiles now. His bodyguards slapped him on the back, the tea garden manager fussed round him appreciatively and he waved regally at the chattering crowd who nodded their appreciation back. Tom Kirk beaten. It would be the talk of the town.

'Well done,' said Tom.

'Better luck next time, Kirk-bey.' Madhavy didn't bother to mask his elation. Tom loosened the watch strap from his wrist, took a last regretful look at it and handed it over to Madhavy. He accepted the watch with both hands and then held it over his head like a small trophy. Again the small crowd clapped and cheered.

'Come on. Let's go,' Tom whispered to Jennifer.

'Go? Is that it? We didn't even . . .' she tailed off as she caught Tom's glare.

'But we didn't find anything out.' She hissed into Tom's ear as they stood up. 'What about the off-site?' Tom didn't say anything, steering her instead towards the exit with a firm hand on her elbow. But just as they were about to leave, Madhavy called after them.

'Kirk-Bey, wait.'

He walked up to them, leaving his admirers chatting excitedly in the middle of the garden.

'Come, let us part as friends.' He held his hands out and gave Tom a long hug, his head over Tom's left shoulder, his arms around his waist, before shaking his hand again.

'Until next time,' Madhavy called after them as they walked out into late afternoon heat.

'What the hell was all that about?' Jennifer asked as they immersed themselves into the street's clamouring tumult. The older men were clad in suits and neatly trimmed moustaches, the youngsters clean-shaven and wearing designer jeans and shirts. The women were smart, dressed in this year's Italian fashions and last year's Hollywood haircuts. Mobile phones were on show everywhere, clipped to belts or hung round necks like expensive necklaces.

'Have you ever heard of the Cistern of Theodosius?' Tom asked her, an amused look on his face. He swerved past a marble block, the remnant of some ancient temple or pillar that had been left to rot at the side of the road.

'The Cistern of what?' She screwed her face up in confusion. 'Wait a minute. Is that where it's happening? Did he tell you?'

Tom nodded.

'He whispered it when he said goodbye.'

'Even though he won?' Tom nodded. 'Why?'

'I guess he was being gracious in victory.'

'You mean you lost deliberately?'

'The last time I played him, I won twenty games in a row. Ended up with his Mercedes. I heard he didn't play for two years after that. I just figured he would be more likely to tell me if I lost convincingly than if I beat him again. Especially with all his people looking on. It wouldn't look good to lose face twice.'

'But what about your watch? Didn't you say your mother gave you that?'

'Oh, it was in a good cause. Besides,' Tom reached into his jacket pocket. 'I don't think I'll miss it.' Grinning, he held his watch out.

Jennifer held her hands up in disbelief.

'How?' was all she could muster.

'Amin Madhavy started out as a pickpocket before he hit the big time,' he explained as he strapped the watch back on. 'I guess that makes him as good at putting stuff back into pockets as taking them out. If I know Amin, while he was happy to take the win, his sense of honour wouldn't let him keep the watch without winning it fair and square. You see, despite what you might think, not all thieves are robbers.'

SEVENTY

Galata Tower, Istanbul, Turkey
8:20pm

The dark waters of the Golden Horn, the wide harbour that separates Europe on one side from Asia on the other, East from West, Christianity from Islam, were stained pink by the setting sun. And a lone, chanting voice rose clearly through the thin air.

'Allahu Akbar, Allahu Akbar . . . Ash-hadu alla ilaha illa-llah . . . Ash-hadu anna Muhammadar-Rasulullah.'

The words fell from the neighbouring minaret only to be buffeted joyfully across the jagged rooftops as first one, then another, then another voice took up the same chant. The haunting sound of the muezzins calling the faithful to prayer spread and rose over the city like a forest fire fanned by a hot summer wind.

'How long are we going to wait here?' Jennifer asked.

'Not long. Just until it's dark.'

They were both sitting in the dark blue BMW that they had rented at the airport. Outside, the light was beginning to fade and the last few stragglers were hurrying to their nearest mosque.

'So, what is the Cistern of Theodosius?' Jennifer settled back into her seat and turned the air conditioning up a notch.

'When the Romans were here they built huge aqueducts to bring fresh water to the city,' Tom explained. 'The cisterns were underground reservoirs, built to store the water once it had got here. There are several of them all over the city, although they're all disused now.'

Jennifer nodded thoughtfully. They were both silent as the sun finally sank below the horizon and the water was plunged into blackness, its surface oily and dark. A small white bird landed on the front of the car and hopped about on the smooth blue metallic surface as if it were a shallow puddle.

'Tom, there's something I want to tell you.' Her eyes were full, her voice unsteady. 'Something I think you might understand. I'd rather you heard it from me than anyone else. I just don't know how to begin.'

Tom turned round to face her, pulling one of his legs up underneath him, his face suddenly serious.

'You know, the Byzantines closed the mouth

of the Golden Horn with a thick chain to stop anyone invading by sea. But when the Arabs got here they just took their boats out of the water and moved them overland on rollers and slides before launching them back into the water on the other side. A few years later and the city was theirs.' She was silent. 'You see, sometimes, the largest obstacles can be easily overcome if you just don't approach them head on,' Tom added gently.

She smiled and nodded, then took a deep breath.

'You remember I told you that there used to be someone. That he'd died. That I'd killed him. I wasn't joking, you know.'

Tom said nothing.

'His name was Greg. I met him at the Academy. He came to give a talk about a case he'd worked. I'll never forget when he came into the classroom. He was so confident and determined and strong.'

Jennifer spoke quickly. Although she sounded excited, her eyes were dead. They looked straight ahead as she talked, absently tracking the small white bird as it bounced along the paintwork. Tom listened in silence.

'A few weeks later, he came to find me. Asked me out.' She flashed Tom a look as she said this. 'We started dating. It was good. He made me feel good.' Now the images came back thick and fast; images that she tried not to think about. Greg smiling across a restaurant table. Greg laughing as he slipped an ice cube down her back. Greg lying in a pool of his own blood.

'Then I got assigned to work with him. It was just dumb luck, really. No one else knew we were seeing each other. If they had, they never would have allowed it. But we got a bit of a thrill from it all.'

Her voice now was hard and unfeeling. The white bird stretched its wings and flitted off into the night.

'One day we got called out on a raid of a warehouse. Some bullshit joint op with the DEA over in Maryland. We'd all fanned out through the building. Suddenly a door burst open and there was a guy there with a gun. I didn't think. It was just instinctive. He was dead before he hit the floor . . . I killed him . . . I shot him.'

She looked at Tom, gave him an awkward shrug, then turned away again. 'I can't even cry about it anymore. I ran out of tears a long time ago. Now, mostly, I just feel numb.'

'What happened? After?'

'There was an inquiry, of course. A special investigation team went through every second of that day a hundred times. And it came out that we were seeing each other. It's funny, but I think that freaked them more than the fact I'd shot him. So they looked into whether we'd been fighting or split up. Whether this was some sort of revenge killing or lovers' quarrel. You know, whether I'd murdered him.'

She gave a joyless laugh.

'But in the end, they concluded that it wasn't my fault. That Greg had wandered ahead of everyone else and not kept up radio contact. That he shouldn't have been where he was. That under the circumstances any other agent would have done the same. But I could tell that they didn't entirely believe it. Not all of them, anyway. I could see it in their eyes, that suspicion that I was guilty of something, even if they didn't quite know what. When they posted me down to Atlanta they said it was in my interest to keep a low profile until it had all blown over. Really, it was for theirs. Because it was easier for them to keep me out of sight than accept what had happened.'

There was a long silence and outside the car, for the first time since they had been there, nothing seemed to move or speak or shout or bang. The city paused. Expectant.

'I don't know what to say,' Tom said eventually.

'There's nothing to say.'

'Only . . . I understand what it is to lose someone you love.'

And she knew that he really did understand.

'And I understand what it feels like to be rejected, to be viewed as a terrible accident that needs to be hidden away. I understand that it never gets any easier. That no matter how much others blame you, you blame yourself even more.' She gave a barely perceptible nod of her head and there was a long pause before Tom spoke again. 'He was a good guy?'

'A great guy. And a good agent.'

'In that order?' Tom asked smiling.

'Yeah.' She laughed.

'It was a mistake, Jen.' Tom's voice was gentle and this time she found the use of her pet name strangely comforting. 'That's all. A mistake, an accident. You didn't do anything wrong.'

'I killed the man I was in love with. My best friend. Now it's like I have to live up to his expectations as well as my own.'

A stream of people, filtering home from their evening prayers, parted around them like water around a stone.

'So this case . . . ?'

'Is my first real break in years. It took a lot of hard work to earn this chance. That's why I don't want to blow it. I owe it to myself. I owe it to my family. I owe it to Greg.'

'But you know solving this case won't bring Greg back. Won't stop the hurt.'

She nodded.

'I know that. But it might just help me to stop hating myself.'

SEVENTY-ONE

Çemberlitaş, Istanbul, Turkey
9:37pm

Night had settled with a thick, dusty cloak. The air was dry and the choking smell of rotting drains and stale exhaust fumes drifted through the narrow streets, pooling in doorways and under the streetlights' sodium glow like a thick fog. In some places, old newspapers had been placed over the drain covers and wetted down to try and contain the warm flush of decay oozing up from the sewers.

From the rooftop vantage point that Tom had led them to, they could count at least five men, all of them heavily armed, guarding the cistern entrance. It was an ugly concrete shed entered through a single metal door about a hundred yards in front of them. Cars arrived and accelerated away. Faces were checked against computer printouts with flashlights. People spoke in low, urgent voices.

'How are we going to get past them?' whispered Jennifer as she squinted through the rubberised binoculars that Tom had handed her.

'We're not.' Tom smiled. 'We're going to go under them.' He crawled over to the other side of the roof, dodging the washing lines that had been strung across its satellite dish encrusted surface like bunting. 'Through there.'

He pointed to the square on the other side of the street. Lit by a tawdry neon sign, a narrow passage nestled between a spice shop on one side and a carpet shop on the other. The spices were fluorescent reds and yellows and oranges, laid out in a small mountain range of conical piles like sand at the bottom of an hourglass. The carpets, by contrast, were dark-muddy reds and browns occasionally lifted by a dirty white or yellow. The shop was so full, the carpets piled so high, that the windows seemed to be bowing out, the glass stretching and straining.

'If you say so.'

'Are you ready?' Tom was worried that Jennifer was not feeling one hundred per cent, that the cathartic effort of her earlier unburdening had taken its unavoidable emotional and physical toll. But he knew it was pointless to suggest she stay behind. She would never agree.

'Yeah.' She nodded, her face set into a determined half smile, as if she sensed Tom's concern and wanted to reassure him.

They made their way off the roof and down the staircase that led out to the street. From there it was a two minute walk to the narrow passage, the intermittent blinking of the neon illuminating their way.

Tom led them under the sign and into the passage. About half way down, on the right hand side, a circular window had been roughly hacked into the wall and behind it sat a bearded Turk, his face caving in on itself with age. Tom handed over a few dirty notes. A wet, minty heat blew up the passage towards them.

'What is this place?' asked Jennifer as they continued down the passage, the ragged concrete floor and walls giving way abruptly to a rich and dense white marble.

'A hammam. You know, a Turkish bath. It's one of the oldest in the city, built over four hundred years ago by Sinan. Men that way. Women that way.' He nodded at the corridor to his right that led to another wooden door, identical to the one they were facing now.

'Are we splitting up?' asked Jennifer with surprise.

'No, we're heading this way. To the basement.' Tom indicated a narrow wooden door recessed into the far left hand wall. It opened onto a spiral staircase, the steep stone steps winding down into tenebrous nothingness.

At the bottom, the staircase gave onto a low,

stone flagged room, lit by a prancing light that seeped under a door at the far end.

'This is where all the water for the baths upstairs is heated,' Tom explained.

The demonic roar of the gas-fired water heaters grew as they neared the door. The heat became more and more intense with each step, until, almost without them realising it, their clothes were soaked, the sweat seeming to bubble up and out of their skin.

'These baths used to be supplied with water from the main aqueduct.'

Tom's voice sounded weak through the scalding thunder as they stepped into the sulphurous depths of the main boiler room. It was a mass of metal and fire, a hissing nest of pipes snaking out from two huge cauldrons, their roasting bellies glowing through thick glass inspection panels like a pair of malevolent eyes.

'The water came here via the Cistern of Theodosius.' He had to shout to be heard. 'Now the water is piped in from a modern ring main, but the old water tunnels are still here. Look.' He pointed at a large square opening about six feet up the wall that had been crudely boarded over. 'Here, give me a hand.'

He grabbed a thick metal pipe off the floor and rammed it into a narrow gap between two of the boards. Pulling down on the pipe they levered off first one, then another two boards, the dry, brittle wood splintering, the rusty nails snapping. Soon there was enough space for them to crawl through.

Tom slipped a black Maglite out of his trousers and flicked it on before clamping it firmly between his teeth. Pulling himself up to the hole, he dragged himself in. Jennifer followed right behind him.

After about three minutes of slow progress, their elbows and knees raw and tender where they had drawn them raspingly over the tunnel's rough stone surface, the narrow space widened out enough to allow them to almost stand. The flashlight flickered over the dry walls around them. In the darkness ahead, dim lights appeared and then vanished as they approached. Rats, Tom guessed with a grimace.

A hundred and fifty yards further on, their clothes filthy, the dark passage grew lighter and the faint murmur of voices echoed towards them. Tom snapped the flashlight off and tiptoed towards the noise.

The tunnel mouth was sealed by a large rusty metal grille. They approached it carefully, crouching down when they reached it. Peering through, they could see that the tunnel emerged about ten feet off the cistern floor and four feet below the ceiling.

Thick stone columns, their sides pale and worn smooth, stretched the length and breadth of the cistern, supporting the roof at regular intervals. Originally, the entire room would have been flooded and the columns totally submerged. But now, with only a few inches of water covering the floor, they disappeared into the distance, reflecting off the surface like the bleached ribs of an enormous whale.

Below and to the left of them, about twenty feet away, a large wooden platform had been erected next to a brick staircase that Tom assumed ran up to street level and the concrete shed they had observed before. Chairs had been arranged in neat rows in front of a low podium on the wooden platform.

Arc lights had been lashed to the corners of the platform, revealing a kaleidoscope of shapes and colours as people moved across its wooden surface, a shifting human mosaic. Tom counted perhaps thirty people in all and their voices filtered up to him – French, Russian, Italian, English – a babble of sound accompanying nervous handshakes and half smiles.

Abruptly, the lights dimmed and an expectant silence fell over the assembled guests as they took to their seats.

SEVENTY-TWO

10:00pm

A man stepped up onto the small podium, his heavily gelled black hair gleaming like a polished helmet.

'Ladies and Gentlemen. Thank you for coming here tonight and as usual, our apologies for the late notice and the enthusiastic search by my colleagues upstairs.' His sallow, acne-scared face twisted into a toothless smile, the nostrils on his thin nose flaring, his white lips pinched tight. His audience laughed nervously.

'We have thirty lots to get through tonight, so I anticipate we will be done by about midnight.' The man continued, his voice echoing eerily off the stone walls up to where Tom and Jennifer were crouching. Tom recognised the flat open vowels and harsh consonants of an Afrikaner, his pronunciation battle-hardened by 350 years of struggle against the native South Africans, the English and nature.

'All bids are to be made in US dollars and must be settled immediately either in cash or by confirmed electronic transfer. Bids are binding and there is no appeal, so think twice before coughing.' Again the audience laughed apprehensively. This time, the man did not smile.

'If there are no questions, then I will begin.'

The assembled buyers remained silent and with a slight nod from the man who was clearly acting as the auctioneer for the evening, a small door set into the wall to the side of the platform opened. Two muscled figures emerged holding a gilt-framed painting, which they set down on an easel to the left of the auctioneer's podium. With a theatrical flourish one of them threw back the green cloth that had been laid over the canvas. Tom breathed in sharply.

'What is it?' asked Jennifer.

'Vermeer,' whispered Tom. 'Stolen in the Isabella Stewart Gardner job. I'd heard it had been destroyed. Cassius must be selling off his best stuff.'

'The Concert by Jan Vermeer, painted in 1665 to '66. The bidding will start at three million dollars. Can anyone give me three million. Thank you sir. Three million two hundred thousand . . . ?'

The bidding was fast and uncomplicated. There were no mobile phones or computer screens, no delays or deliberations, no live links to New York and Tokyo. The buyers had clearly come with detailed instructions from their employers on what to buy and how much to bid. The Vermeer went for just over six million dollars. A Rembrandt that Tom identified as Storm on the Sea of Galilee taken in the same job as the Vermeer, for eight million dollars. A Giacommetti sculpture recently stolen from a museum in Hamburg and replaced with a wooden replica under the noses of the guards for three hundred thousand.

'This could be us,' hissed Tom suddenly.

One of the auctioneer's assistants had stepped onto the platform holding a slim metallic case about ten inches long by three inches wide.

'And now, ladies and gentlemen, an extremely rare item.' The auctioneer surveyed his expectant audience as the man holding the silvery case opened it and angled it to the light so they could see its contents.

'There are only eight surviving examples of the 450,000 Double Eagles minted by the US Treasury in 1933 and then destroyed in 1937 by Presidential decree. Five of them are offered here. I'm going to start the bidding at twenty million dollars. Do I hear twenty million?'

Four hands shot into the air just as a deafening boom thundered through the cistern and a section of the roof collapsed into the water below.

SEVENTY-THREE

10:33pm

The door at the top of the stairs exploded open, the force of the charge laid next to it ripping it from its hinges and sending it pirouetting down onto the platform where it narrowly missed the front row of seats.

Through the smoke five masked men burst into the room, firing silenced machine guns over their heads, the bullets spitting into the brickwork and showering the bewildered people below with shards of hot stone, spent shells coughing out and hitting the water with a hiss. Two ropes spiralled down through the gaping hole in the roof and four more men slid down into the room, their heavy boots splashing down noisily on the cistern floor. Within seconds, the dazed people on the platform had been surrounded and the auctioneer and his two assistants disarmed without anyone putting up a struggle.

Jennifer jumped to her feet but Tom dragged her back.

'Stay down.'

Tom raised his binoculars and studied the unfolding scene below. The men were well drilled, probably ex-military, moving deliberately and in close coordination. They were heavily-armed, grenades hanging off their webbing, their hands clutching Heckler and Koch MP5SD6s, the silenced version of the weapon of choice for the world's elite military and paramilitary units.

Their commander stood at the foot of the stairs, barking instructions, his shoulders broad as the side of a small car. As Tom watched, he smashed the butt of his gun into the small of someone's back who had not knelt down quickly enough.

Another figure, also masked and dressed in black, appeared through the swirling dust and smoke at the top of the stairs. He made his way silently down to the auctioneer's assistant, now on his knees, but still holding the metallic coin case in his left hand. The man took the case from him, opened it to check its contents, then slipped it inside his jacket.

He nodded to the commander, turned and walked back up the stairs. The auctioneer began to scream hysterically.

'You are all dead men! You don't know who you're fucking with! Nobody steals from Cassius!'

The man stopped at the top of the stairs and

looked back over his shoulder at the kneeling figure, his gelled hair dusty and dishevelled, his face chiselled with hate. The auctioneer spat in the man's direction, the gelatinous glob hitting the side of the brick staircase and snailing down to the floor. The man turned and made his way back down to the auctioneer.

Without saying a word, he slipped a shiny silver Sig P228 out of his holster and pressed it against the auctioneer's mouth. He levered it between his lips, rattling the smooth muzzle against his teeth, cutting into his gums as he tried to force it in, until the blood was dripping out of the corner of the auctioneer's mouth onto the floor. Still the auctioneer kept his jaws clamped firmly shut, his eyes staring defiantly ahead, until with a stomach-churning crunch, he lost his two front teeth. He screamed and as his mouth opened in agony the man slid the gun in, penetrating him until the trigger guard was jammed against his lips.

The auctioneer started to gag on the barrel, his body convulsing as the cold metal pressed against the back of his throat. Then a single, muffled shot rang out, the noise deadened by the auctioneer's skull. The back of his head exploded as he slumped at the man's feet, his jaw hanging off on one side from the force of the explosion. One of his eyes had burst down his lifeless cheek.

Tom surveyed the macabre scene through his binoculars, a grim look on his face. For as the man had pulled the trigger, the sleeve on his black flak jacket had ridden up onto his wrist. Tom had instantly recognised the watch he was wearing.

It had a black face and a pink gold case, one of only fifteen like it in the world. It was a Lange & Söhne. It was the same watch that Van Simson wore.

SEVENTY-FOUR

10:41pm

Indifferent to the execution that they had just witnessed, the armed men started to edge towards the staircase, still covering their cowering captives with their guns. A thick red cloud billowed in the water beneath the platform as the auctioneer leaked blood.

'They're getting away,' said Jennifer, rising to her feet. 'We've got to stop them.'

'Wait. We can get them later. I know who it is.'

He grabbed Jennifer by the shoulder but her momentum knocked him off balance and he tripped, falling heavily against the grille. Years of corrosion had clearly taken their toll. The grille gave way under Tom's weight and he plunged head first down into the cistern.

At the noise the three men still at the foot of the stairs spun round and opened fire blindly in

Tom's direction, the bullets fizzing overhead and slamming into the wall behind him.

'Hold your fire.' The man had reappeared at the top of the stairs, his silver gun still drawn and flecked with blood, skin and pieces of the auctioneer's teeth.

'I want him alive,' he barked. 'Bring him with us.'

The three armed men vaulted over the platform's low rail and splashed down into the cistern and over to Tom, dragging him to his feet. He seemed confused, his legs unable to support his own weight, as if he had hit his head on the way down.

Above them, Jennifer's mind was racing. She had recognised the man's voice. It was Van Simson.

'Oh, and clean that hole out.' Van Simson shouted. 'He might still be with that meddling FBI bitch.'

Jennifer was already on her way. She had to get out and follow them. They had Tom. They had the coins. She couldn't lose them now.

Behind her she heard a gentle metallic ping and then the unmistakable sound of metal striking stone, first once, then again, the echo bouncing and bobbling down the tunnel like large marbles. Grenades.

She scrabbled along as quickly as she could until she was fifty, sixty, eighty yards from the opening into the cistern. Silently she counted down the seconds. Five, Four, Three, Two. Jennifer flattened herself to the floor, shut her eyes and covered her ears. One.

Nothing could have prepared her for the deafening explosion of sound and heat that rolled over her, an inhuman roar that pressed her to the ground, driving the air from her lungs. As she gasped for breath, a second explosion rocked through the tunnel, the force of it lifting her several inches off the ground before dumping her back down again like a sack of coal.

She struggled back to her feet, shaking the debris from her hair, her eyes streaming in the smoke and dust. She coughed hoarsely, her mouth dry with fear, as blood seeped from a gash on her chin. She had to get out. Fast.

A few minutes later she jumped down into the Hammam's boiler room. A surprised, bare-chested Turk, his dark and hairy body glowing red and covered in an oily slick of sweat and grime, leapt backwards in surprise before firing machine-gun Turkish at her retreating back.

Out of the room, up the stairs, through the corridor, back into the square where they had parked the car in the forbidding shadow of the ancient Çemberlitaş column, its metal hoops gleaming like manacles.

She slipped behind the wheel and fired up the engine just as two blue vans sped down the street in front of her. She knew she had to stop them, do something, before they got away.

She swung the car onto Divan Yolu, the tyres squealing reluctantly over its polished cobble stones. It had long been closed to car traffic, given over instead to trams running in both directions down the middle of the road, a low kerb separating the tram lines from the pavements on either side which were, as ever, full of people.

She mounted the kerb, the car's suspension groaning as it slammed down the other side onto the metal tramlines. Ahead of her, the two vans seemed to be trapped behind a tram but as she accelerated up to them, they both managed to slip out from behind it and roar past. She accelerated up to the tram and then wrenched the wheel sideways to follow them, the left front wing dipping as gravity and aerodynamic pressures took over.

Her windscreen was immediately swallowed by the looming headlights of an onrushing tram.

'Shit.'

She stamped on the brakes, the car weaving unsteadily as she tucked it back in, the tram flashing past in a blur of lights and bells, warm air flooding through the open window.

'Shit.'

As soon as it was safely past, she dropped the car into second gear, the engine screaming in protest as the rev counter flicked to the right, and overtook the tram.

The delay had cost her valuable time. The vans were already over at the far end of the Hippodrome to her right and she gunned the motor hard as she launched herself off the tram-lines and after them. The rubber bit into the cracked tarmac.

Up to fourth, then fifth; she was doing nearly seventy miles an hour as Aya Sofya and then the Blue Mosque sped past, their massed walls dyed white in the floodlights, their minarets reaching into the sky like bony fingers. Her headlights flashing, she leaned on the horn, pedestrians scattering in her wake, the car jigging round the seemingly insomniac postcard-sellers that littered the city.

'Get out the way!' she screamed over the whine of the engine, catching sight of her wild hair and dust-caked face in the rear-view mirror. Long, dirty tear stains tumbled from the corner of her eyes even though she couldn't remember crying. The acrid smell of her burning clutch filled the car, making her cough.

At the end of the Hippodrome, the road banked sharply downhill and towards the left. Jennifer saw the turn late, but instinct took over. She dropped into second again and lifted the hand brake as she turned the wheel, sending the car into a screeching sideways skid, the suspension yawing violently.

Her foot instantly back on the accelerator, she

massaged the engine speed, turning first into the skid and then, as she sensed some faint traction returning to the blistering tyres, back the other way as she goosed the gas. The car flicked obediently out of the skid, rounded the corner and plunged down the hill like a rollercoaster jack-knifing through a turn.

She could see the vans down below her now, heading down to the water's edge, but a police car leapt out of a side street to her left, siren blaring and blue lights flashing. She yanked the wheel to the right to avoid clipping its front wing and then back to the left, the car carving across the cobbles like an ice-skater doing a figure of eight. Above her, she caught a glimpse of the tiered foundations of the Hippodrome's banked seating, the silent ghosts of the bloodthirsty crowds cheering her on.

She turned to follow the vans down a narrow side street but was immediately confronted by another police car speeding towards her, its lights on full beam. Blinded, she threw her arm up to her face. The front right tyre hit the kerb and snatched the wheel out of her hand. The car jumped sideways and ploughed into the side of an apartment block, the metal chewing into the crumbling stone in a blaze of sparks.

Panting, she gripped the wheel, her knuckles white. The police car's passenger door flew open and a familiar figure emerged into the beam of her one remaining headlight. Jennifer tumbled out of the car.

'It's Van Simson, sir. He's got the coins. And he's got Tom.'

SEVENTY-FIVE

Paris, France
30th July – 11:02am
The smell of chloroform hung about Tom's clothes like cheap aftershave, its burning sweet taste clinging to his dry and cracked lips. He remembered falling, being dragged out of the cistern and then tossed roughly into the depths of a van. But then nothing.

He was alive, at least. Given the cold-blooded way that Van Simson had disposed of the auctioneer, that was something. Although it did raise the question, of course, as to what exactly Van Simson was planning to do with him.

He tentatively rolled over onto his front and tried to stand up, his eyes still adjusting to the light. He collapsed almost immediately, vomiting noisily over the stone floor. Gasping, he rolled onto his back and fought back the waves of nausea, focusing on his breathing to try and calm his racing heart and pounding head.

Van Simson? Was he Cassius? It didn't make sense to Tom. He couldn't be – why would he have stolen coins from his own auction? But he could still have been behind the Fort Knox job and then had the misfortune of Steiner stealing them from Schiphol airport. Maybe he'd murdered Harry and hit the off-site to take back what he deemed to be rightfully his.

Either way, Van Simson was deeply involved in the whole mess and Tom had fallen straight into his lap. Literally. And what about Jennifer? Had she been able to get away? How would she know where Tom was when he didn't even know himself for sure?

The nausea subsiding, Tom allowed himself to study the room around him. It was twelve feet square, lit by a single bulb housed under an industrial-looking glass dome. There were no windows and the only way in or out was through a single steel door. An untouched tray of grey rice and yellowing chicken lay at Tom's feet.

He would have guessed that the room was an old wine cellar or some similar type of underground storeroom, if it hadn't been for the items that had been theatrically arranged throughout the cell. In the far corner, he recognised the unmistakeable shape of an iron maiden, so called because of the unsmiling female face that decorated its exterior, unkempt hair trailing, some said, like a Gorgon.

Shaped like an upright sarcophagus and standing about six feet tall, it opened down the middle to reveal an inside filled with iron spikes. Its unfortunate victim would be placed inside and the two doors shut so as to impale them. In a sadistic refinement, the spikes were carefully positioned to avoid vital organs and so prolong the agony.

The walls were studded with similarly grotesque items. A blunt looking Heretic's Fork, large thumb screws and some rusty cat's paws were just some of the items Tom recognised. Suspended from the ceiling, the thick chains of a Judas Cradle swung gently in an unseen breeze.

The sound of approaching footsteps broke into his thoughts and he snapped his eyes towards the door as it gently eased open.

Darius Van Simson strode into the room followed by two men, one wiry and thin, the other short and square. All three were still dressed in black combat fatigues. Clearly they had not been back long.

'Tom, Tom, Tom.' Van Simson shook his head and tutted like a disappointed parent as he looked from the pool of vomit to Tom still huddled on the floor. 'I'm sorry, really I am. That it should come to this. It's not what I wanted.'

'Spare me your sympathy, Darius,' said Tom

weakly. 'By the way, nice place you've got down here.'

Van Simson smiled stonily.

'I'm reliably informed that this is the original torture chamber of the gaol that stood on this site in the fifteenth century, before they knocked it down and built my house.'

So they were in Paris, Tom now knew. That was a five hour flight from Istanbul even in Van Simson's private jet. With a car journey at each end, that meant that at least six or seven hours must have passed since he'd been caught.

'I discovered it during the restoration work and thought I would re-commission it. For historical reasons, of course. The items you see displayed here are all authentic.'

'What are you playing at, Darius? If the FBI aren't on to you yet they soon will be. And you've got Cassius to contend with now.' At Cassius' name, Van Simson's back had stiffened slightly. Quickly he relaxed into another grudging smile.

'I see you share your father's fighting spirit,' he observed.

'You leave my father out of this.' Tom snapped.

'And you also share his inability to mind your own fucking business.' The spittle flew from Van Simson's mouth as he spoke, momentarily staining the floor black where it landed on the dusty flag-stones.

'You made it my business when you killed

Harry,' Tom yelled back, his strength returning to him.

'Harry? Harry Renwick? Is that what this is about? Oh, you should have said – we could have avoided all this unpleasantness. That was nothing to do with me. All I wanted was the coins. All I've ever wanted was the coins. I let that slimy bastard Ranieri slip through my fingers, but when I heard all five were going to be sold off I made my move. You should have kept out of it. It was a private party and you weren't invited.'

'And you were?' Tom gave a short laugh.

'You think I'm worried? By Jean-Pierre Dumas's eager little helpers scuttling around outside my house? They've got nothing. But the FBI? Well, that's why you're still alive, Tom. When they find out that Agent Browne's dead and that the coins have disappeared for good, I think they're going to be pretty interested in talking to you. I'm going to gift wrap you and hand you over myself. I might even tell them I caught you trying to break in here just to spice it up some more.' Van Simson's mouth twisted into a cruel smile at the look on Tom's face. 'Oh, I'm sorry. You didn't know, did you? I flushed out your little rabbit hole. I'm afraid she's gone. Along with any alibi you might have had.'

With a sudden cry of fury Tom lunged at Van Simson. But before he could cover the few feet between them, he was overpowered by the two guards who leapt onto him. The two men pinned Tom's arms to his side and sat him up with his back to the wall.

'You will have to excuse me, Tom, but I am expecting someone,' said Van Simson as he reached up and unhooked a large metal object off the wall.

Tom recognised what he was holding. A scold's bridle. A large cage made to lock around its victim's head and prevent its unfortunate wearer from speaking by jamming a metal protrusion into their mouth.

'Husbands used to put these on their nagging wives,' said Van Simson as the two guards forced the cage over Tom's head. 'Let's see if it cools your tongue. And your temper.' The lock clicked shut as he turned the key.

Tom tried to shout as Van Simson and his two guards left the room, but the thick metal tongue piece dug sharply into the back of his throat and he began to gag.

One thing was clear to Tom. He had to get out – and he had to get out fast, before Van Simson changed his mind and returned to try out any more of his sadistic toys.

Running both hands around his neck, he soon found the lock positioned on the right hand side of the cage. He felt a glimmer of hope. Van Simson, in his commitment to authenticity, had not replaced the original, rather rudimentary lock with a more modern one. Grabbing the metal fork off the tray of congealed food on the floor next to him, he bent one of its prongs out and then back in on itself to make a small hook.

Inserting the bent prong into the lock opening, Tom moved it carefully around, feeling his way through the springs and levers until with a sudden click, the mechanism popped open. He lifted the cage off his head with relief, massaging his jaw and moving his tongue around in his mouth to get the circulation back, spitting flecks of paint and rusty metal out onto the floor.

Struggling to his feet, he made his way over to the door. This was not so hopeful. Here Van Simson had not compromised, fitting a complex electronic lock that would require specialist equipment to open. Equipment that Tom didn't have. Across the room, half lost in the semi-darkness, the iron maiden leered at him pitilessly.

SEVENTY-SIX

11:34am

The banging from the cell resonated down the corridor. At first the guard, the shorter, squatter one of the two men who had accompanied Van Simson, ignored it, burying his nose deeper into the newspaper. But as the incessant bone-jarring crashing of metal upon metal grew louder and louder, he threw increasingly angry glances towards the cell.

Finally, a renewed barrage caught him unawares and made him spill his coffee down his front, the scalding liquid soaking into his black combat trousers. He swore, swung his feet down off his narrow desk, threw the paper down on his seat and stomped towards the cell.

The crashing abruptly stopped and the guard smiled, loosening his new IMI Barak combat handgun from his under-arm holster. He had been around long enough to know when people were trying it on. But that was fine. If they wanted to play games, he'd show them a good time. He knew how to party.

He turned a key in the lock and as it clicked open he kicked the cell door open with the heel of his foot. The heavy steel door flew back on its hinges and slammed into the wall with a shuddering crash. That would take care of anyone hiding behind the door. He wasn't falling for that old trick.

The light bulb had been unscrewed and he flicked on the small under-barrel flashlight on his Barak. Through the open doorway, the beam picked out the cage that only minutes before he had helped fix onto the prisoner's head. It had been placed in the middle of the room. He ran the flashlight around the rest of the cell. It was eerily quiet after the incessant banging. And it was also empty.

Or was it?

In the far corner, barely visible even in the bright beam of his flashlight, he saw that the doors of the iron maiden were ajar. Not much, but perhaps enough to allow someone to hide very carefully inside without being impaled. Smiling at his perceptiveness, he crept towards the large metallic object, his finger on the trigger.

'Come out!' he shouted from only a few feet away. But the iron maiden stayed silent.

'Come out! I know you're in there.'

Nothing.

He cursed and leant forward, placing his left hand on one door and the barrel of his gun on the other, before throwing them open in a quick movement.

It was empty.

Crouching in the corner, Tom pushed back as hard as he could, driving his legs against the stone wall. The iron maiden teetered onto its front edge and then crashed to the floor, the spikes on its open doors impaling the guard underneath it and snapping his back like a twig.

SEVENTY-SEVEN

12:02pm

Tom snatched up the guard's gun and swallowed hard at the sight of his bloody and twisted face. It wasn't the first time that he'd had to kill someone, but that never made it any easier.

He slipped out of the room and along the vaulted corridor, past dark rooms piled high with the debris of Van Simson's life. Crates of wine, neatly catalogued archive boxes full of paper and files, sporting equipment arranged in specially constructed steel racks.

The gun's rubberised grip felt like raw meat in Tom's sweaty hands, wet and slippery. He paused at the foot of a narrow stone staircase to catch his breath and wipe his palms against his trousers. He didn't really have a plan and he knew that was dangerous. He also knew that he was angry and upset and that that could make him careless. But despite all that he knew that he owed it to Harry and Jennifer to get to Van Simson. He owed it to himself. At that moment, that single desire informed his every movement, his every decision.

Tom edged open the door at the top of the stairs to reveal a limestone-floored corridor. The sound of approaching footsteps, metal-tipped heels rhythmically clipping the stone floor, forced him to pull it shut, leaving only a tiny sliver of light that cut into the darkness and cast a thin white line down the middle of Tom's face.

The footsteps grew louder and then carried on past. Through the crack Tom recognised Rolfe, the albino who had frisked him and Jennifer at the entrance gate on their previous visit. Jennifer. Gone. He bit his lip, shook her image from his mind again. He couldn't think about that now.

He eased the door open and crept up behind Rolfe who had paused in front of the door at the end of the corridor to locate something in his pocket. He brought the butt of his gun crashing down on the base of his neck and the man fell grunting to the floor. It took another blow, though, Tom's gun slapping into his temple, before he rolled over onto his side, unconscious.

He dragged Rolfe's body back to the staircase and pushed him down the first few steps. Then, stepping back into the corridor and shutting the door behind him, he walked along it until he emerged into the familiar surroundings of the huge ground-floor entrance hall. Ahead of him, he knew, was the elevator. The one sure way up to Van Simson's office and down to the vault.

He tried to force the elevator doors open but he could only push them a few inches apart before they sprang shut with a violent metallic crash. Looking around him, Tom noticed a thin bronze sculpture nestling in the shadows next to the staircase. He grabbed it, a determined look on his face. Jamming the sculpture between the two lift doors, he pried them apart as it slipped into the gap. Gradually, the doors slid further and further open, until, when they were about a foot apart, they gave up their struggle and retracted noiselessly into the wall.

Tom placed the bronze on the floor, stepped forward and looked up and then down the elevator shaft. The top of the cabin reflected dully in the gloom beneath him. A plan formed in his mind – he would surprise Van Simson when he returned to the lift by leaping on him through the access hatch.

Reaching into the darkness, Tom grabbed the steel cable that ran down from the lift motor somewhere in the roof to the top of the elevator. Locking the greasy cable between his legs and arms, he slid down it, landing gently on the elevator roof.

He crouched and listened. A strange noise seemed to be emanating from underneath him, a rhythmical mechanical clunking, as if a machine had been programmed into some monotonous, repetitive cycle. Tom cautiously lifted the edge of the hatch. There was blood all over the elevator wall.

Opening the hatch fully, Tom recognised the wiry guard who had just accompanied Van Simson to his cell, slumped in the corner, a single gunshot wound to his head. The elevator doors were opening and shutting again and again on his outstretched legs.

Tom swung down into the elevator and stepped over the body. He peeked into the brightly-lit concrete corridor that led down to the vault. It was empty. But the steel gate had been raised and beyond it he could see that the vault door was wide open. Tom crept along the corridor, keeping to the wall, gripping the Barak with both hands. The video cameras gazed blindly at him, their lenses smashed.

The vault was as he remembered it, black rubberised floor meandering maze-like between twenty or so display cases, a shallow trench flanking the base of each wall. Over the top of the display cases he could see Van Simson hunched over the desk that dominated the small raised platform at the rear of the room. Tom dropped to his knees and picked his way through the cases, careful to always keep at least one between himself and the platform so that he could not be seen.

Eventually only one case separated him from Van Simson. It was now or never. Taking a deep breath and checking that the safety was off, Tom spun out from the side of the case and aimed the gun at Van Simson's head.

'Don't move, Darius.'

Van Simson barely reacted, slowly raising his eyes to Tom's.

'I hope you didn't kill Rolfe.' He seemed distracted, sad even. 'He's a good boy. Very capable.'

'Where are the coins?' Tom demanded, stepping up onto the platform, Van Simson still firmly within his sights.

'The coins? Here. Take them.' Van Simson slapped the same slim metallic case he'd snatched in Istanbul down onto the table. A muffled echo. 'You think you've won? You've won nothing. We've all lost.'

'No, you've lost.' Tom reached forward to pick the case up. 'And as you said before, I'm not sure you've left me many options.' He raised his gun as his fingers closed around the case, Jennifer's image flooding his mind now. He owed her what he was about to do.

But a familiar voice rang out before he could pull the trigger.

'Not so fast, Thomas.'

SEVENTY-EIGHT

12:26pm

The voice tore into Tom like a blunt blade. He swivelled round. A figure stepped out of the shadows and advanced into the light, his Glock 19, his gloved hand, then his outstretched arm slowly coming into view.

'Harry?' Tom croaked as the light finally fell on the man's face.

'Put the gun down, would you, there's a good chap,' said Renwick. It was hard to believe this was the same, slightly dishevelled man that Tom had hugged goodbye just a few days ago. He looked immaculate in a dark blue suit, crisp white shirt and bright blue Hermès tie. His hair was cropped neatly into his head, his face smooth and pink, his eyes burning with a strange intensity that Tom had not seen before. Only the squat gold signet ring remained of the man Tom had known for years.

Tom lowered his gun and trance-like, gazed at it as if he couldn't work out how it had come to be in his hand in the first place. He went to put it on the table, but Renwick's voice snapped out.

'Don't be an idiot, Thomas! On the floor. Kick it towards me.' There was no hint of warmth or kindness in Renwick's voice. Instead it drilled into Tom, familiar and yet foreign at the same time.

Tom bent down, placed the gun on the floor and kicked it over. Renwick adjusted his grip on his own gun and kept it firmly pointed at Tom as he stooped to pick it up and then slipped it into his pocket.

'Harry? I don't understand. How? Why?'

Renwick laughed.

'There's the American in you. Always so keen to understand *why*. To find a reason. To blame some childhood trauma or unloving sibling. Well, it's not that easy. You're not meant to understand people like me, just accept them.'

'But I thought you were dead.' Tom was almost whispering now, his head spinning.

'Why? Because some incompetent policeman found a body in my house? Because Agent Browne says she saw me die? All she saw was two blanks get fired and me go down. By the time she came to, I'd swapped the bodies.'

'Who with?'

'A nobody. Someone who was no longer important to me. Someone who did me a greater service by dying than he ever did when he was alive. After that, it was a simple matter of changing the dental records. How else were they going to identify a burnt corpse? They fell for it, of course, as I knew they would. The police are so wonderfully predictable. I'm surprised *you* did, though, given that you employed a similar trick a few years ago when escaping your CIA masters.'

'You know about that?'

'Oh, there's not much I don't know about you, Thomas.'

'I'm only here because of you. To get the people who killed you.'

'How wonderfully loyal of you. I'm almost touched.'

'Who the hell *are* you?' asked Tom, repelled and yet fascinated by Renwick's dispassionate tone.

'Can't you guess?'

There was a long silence.

'Cassius.' Tom breathed. 'You're Cassius.'

Renwick smiled.

'Some people call me that.'

'After all this time, it's you.' Tom took a step towards Renwick who raised his gun and narrowed his eyes.

'Be careful, Thomas,' he said gently. 'Be very careful.'

'It was all you, wasn't it?' Tom's brain was struggling to re-order the past few days' events in his mind. 'You had the coins stolen. Then you got me to do that job in New York so that I'd be in the US at the same time.'

Renwick shrugged.

'I had simply planned to tip off the police but you kindly obliged by dropping a hair at the scene for the NYPD to find. An uncharacteristic oversight. In any event, it all worked out rather well in the end, although at one stage I was concerned that you were taking too long to steal the first Egg.'

'And then, what? You lost the coins. Steiner stole them from you and gave one to Ranieri to sell.'

Renwick's face darkened.

'A minor inconvenience. Those responsible paid the price for their interference. Their mistake was to try and sell them back to one of my people.'

'So you got four coins back off Steiner and then bumped into me at Sotheby's and invited me to dinner with Agent Browne who just handed over the one coin you didn't have.'

Renwick gave a short laugh.

'It was rather amusing. The coin showing up in my house, of all places. I'd been thinking about killing Harry Renwick off for a while. He was becoming rather depressing. It was too good an opportunity to miss.' There was no feeling in Renwick's voice as he spoke, just a sense of relentless, ruthless efficiency.

'But I have to admit you impressed me, Thomas. Even I, who have followed your career so closely over the years, was surprised by your ability to wriggle out of trouble. First you slip out from under the murder charges that I had pinned on you in London. Then you somehow convinced Agent Browne that you had nothing to do with the Fort Knox robbery. Finally, you even escaped from the museum in Amsterdam after I had generously instructed my sniper not to hurt you but just to make sure you got caught.'

'You should have had him kill me when you had the chance.'

'Of course, I considered it. But you know, a live suspect is so much more satisfying for the police than a dead one. It stops them having to look for his killers. Closes the circle. The British, the Americans, they would all have believed that they had their man. And in any case I'm not a complete monster. I owed you that much at least.'

'And him?' Tom nodded towards Van Simson, who had remained silent during the entire exchange, his face slack and grey.

'Darius?' Renwick's voice rose again as he glanced at Van Simson. 'He should have stuck to bribing politicians and murdering his business rivals. By the way, I don't know what he told you, but Agent Browne's very much alive. I'm so glad. She seemed a charming young lady.'

Tom's heart jumped and his eyes pressed shut

momentarily. She was alive. That was one thing at least.

'But you, Thomas – unlike Darius here – have a choice. It's not too late. Not yet.'

'What do you mean?'

Renwick took a step towards him, his hand outstretched. 'You could join me. You'd be amazed at what we could accomplish together. As a team. As a family. We'd be unstoppable.' For the first time since Renwick had appeared, Tom detected just a hint of pleading in Renwick's voice, sensed an unspoken need in his eyes.

Tom laughed.

'You really are mad. You took away the only real family I had left when you killed Harry Renwick. And now you offer it back at the point of a gun? I have no idea who you are anymore.'

'Then you're about to find out.'

Renwick reached into his pocket, took out the gun that Tom had kicked over to him, aimed it at Van Simson's chest and fired.

SEVENTY-NINE

12:32pm

The bullet lifted Van Simson clean out of his chair and he thudded to the floor, limp. Sensing his opportunity, Tom dived to his left, rolling off the platform and running into the middle of the vault. Renwick reacted instantly, firing off three shots in the blink of an eye as he tracked Tom across the room. But the bullets smashed harmlessly into the bullet-proof glass sheets suspended over each of the display cases, the glass cracking but holding firm. As Tom had remembered they would.

'A pointless gesture, Thomas,' Renwick shouted coldly, the echo of the shots still pinballing around the room. 'Come out now and I'll spare you. Of course, they'll probably send you to prison for killing poor old Darius here when they find your prints all over the murder weapon, but at least you'll be alive.'

The room was silent.

'So be it.' Renwick muttered. He stepped off the platform and, steeling himself, leapt round the side of the case where Tom had rolled only seconds before, gun gripped in both outstretched hands.

There was no one there.

'Stop playing games,' Renwick hissed.

Nothing.

His anger was replaced by a look of grim determination. Working methodically, he moved through the room, checking behind every display case as he went, his gun leading him round the corner of each case in a series of tightly choreographed steps, the soles of his shoes squeaking against the floor like sneakers on a basketball court. Suddenly a smile flickered across his lips. Ahead of him, barely visible, he could just see the tip of a shoe poking out from the cabinet in front of him.

He crouched and then pounced, firing two shots in quick succession before Tom could do or say anything. But the bullets just buried themselves harmlessly into the floor. There was no-one there. Just two shoes neatly arranged one next to the other. Renwick knelt down to feel them. They were still warm.

Tom jumped out from behind the neighbouring cabinet and launched himself at Renwick, bringing his shoulder crashing against his side. The impact slammed Renwick into the side of the case and sent his gun skidding across the room and into the trench at the base of the far wall. Renwick collapsed to his knees, clutching his chest as Tom scrambled on all fours to retrieve the gun.

'You bastard!' Renwick shouted after him.

He was interrupted by a bright red light flashing over the vault door. Tom's eyes immediately snapped towards the platform. Van Simson had dragged himself over to the keyboard on the desk. He looked up into Tom's eyes and as he smiled Tom understood. He was going to lock them all in.

Renwick, hauled himself to his feet and sprinted towards the closing vault door. Tom, however, realized that from where he had crawled to retrieve Renwick's gun, there was no way he was going to be able to reach the door before it shut. Then, suddenly remembering something that Van Simson had shown them on their last visit, he bent down to open the third drawer in the display case nearest to him. The dull sheen of Nazi bullion smouldered in the darkness. Grabbing an ingot, Tom swivelled round on the balls of his feet and in one fluid movement threw it at Renwick as hard as he could. The ingot flashed through the air like a heavy blade, climbing slowly on its upper trajectory and then accelerating fast as gravity powered it home.

It struck Renwick hard between his shoulder blades. The impact caused him to stumble and he lurched unsteadily towards the shrinking gap as the door swung shut. He put his arm out to stop himself from falling and only just slipped through the narrow opening in time. But his sleeve caught on the door frame and before he could free it, the heavy steel door crashed shut. Renwick's hand was severed just above the wrist.

His screams were only silenced as the locking bolts slid home and the vault's air-tight seal was activated.

The vault had become a tomb.

EIGHTY

12:36pm

A new sound now.

Running water.

Looking down, Tom realized that his feet were already submerged as water bubbled up from the trenches at the foot of the walls and surged across the floor. Van Simson's voice echoed in his head. What had he called it? Another little precaution?

He leapt onto the top of the nearest display cabinet just as a powerful electric charge was run through the water which had levelled off at a depth of about three inches. Near the vault door, Renwick's hand twitched spasmodically as it floated into the darkness.

Tom knew that his best chance of escape was to try and get back to the platform and see if he could get the vault opened again from there. Problem was, of course, that he was a good fifteen feet away.

He judged the distance to the nearest display case at about six feet. If he could get onto that, then he could see a path through to the platform by jumping from case to case.

He manoeuvred himself to the edge of the display case and stood up. This was not going to be easy. The low ceiling and the suspended glass screens made getting any sort of momentum into his jump difficult and he was barefoot, his shoes sloshing around somewhere on the floor beneath him.

He took several deep breaths, swinging his arms forward with every breath as he timed his jump. One, two, three.

He propelled himself across the void and landed heavily on the cabinet. He groaned in pain as his chest crashed down on the glass surface, his thighs and knees slamming into the steel drawers on its side. Almost immediately he began to slip, his hands sliding across the polished surface, scrabbling for grip, his nails squeaking as his knees sank lower and lower.

He stopped, his feet only inches above the water. Slowly he hauled himself forward until he was able to hook his left knee over the edge and pull himself up to safety. He stood up and breathed a sigh of relief.

From there it was easy. Five relatively short jumps took him over to the platform and Van Simson who had slumped back into his chair.

'Darius. Wake up.' Tom shook him by the shoulder. 'Stay with me. Come on, wake up.'

Van Simson's eyelids fluttered.

'Darius, listen to me,' said Tom. 'Renwick's escaped. He got out. Open the door. Let me go after him. Let me get some help for you.'

Van Simson shook his head.

'No,' he whispered. 'It's too late.' His eyes shut again, until Tom shook him roughly by the shoulder.

'It's not too late.'

Tom ripped Van Simson's shirt open and studied the wound. A small hole in the upper right side of his chest was bubbling with bright red blood. He pressed his ear against Van Simson's chest, his cheek staining red.

'You've got a punctured lung,' Tom explained, scrabbling around on the desk for something that he could use. 'Every time you breathe in, you're drawing air into your chest cavity through the bullet hole. That's making it harder and harder for you to breathe as the air pressure builds up and crushes your lung.'

Tom found what he was looking for. A plastic document folder and some tape.

'You'll live if we get help fast.' He ripped a small three-inch square out of the folder and placed it over the bullet hole. 'But you have to open the door, Darius. You have to let us out.'

Using the sellotape, he stuck down three sides

of the plastic square to Van Simson's skin, leaving the fourth side free. It was a simple valve, allowing air to escape as he breathed out through the unstuck side, but sealing itself back to the skin when he breathed in. Within a few minutes, Van Simson's breathing eased and his eyes opened again. Tom spoke gently now.

'Darius, you don't have to die here. You don't have to die now. Open the door. I'll get help, I promise. And then I'll get Renwick. I'll get him for both of us. This isn't over.'

Van Simson stared at Tom and then nodded. He reached forward towards the keyboard in front of him. Pausing every few seconds to summon his strength, he slowly tapped out a long sequence of numbers before fainting back into the chair.

The vault door began to swing open.

EIGHTY-ONE

12:51pm

Armed French police swarmed into the room, the plastic visors on their sinister black helmets glinting like huge eyes, their radios spitting.

'Les mains sur la tête.' The instructions were shouted and tense. Tom clasped his hands around the back of his head and called back.

'Il me faut un médécin.'

The policemen fanned out through the vault, cautiously making their way towards the platform, guns raised.

'A terre.' Came another barked order. Tom struggled down onto one knee and then the other, his arms still raised. Two policemen approached the platform, one covering Tom, the other stepping forward to examine Van Simson. He was still unconscious, his breathing shallow and strained.

'Une ambulance, vite,' called the policeman.

'Tom,' Jennifer called out as she ran into the

room, dodging between the policemen and the display cabinets. 'Are you okay? I saw the blood outside and . . . oh, you're fine.'

'You sound disappointed,' Tom joked. The police backed off, shouldered their weapons, muttered under their breath.

'No – it's just that . . .'

'I've been drugged, kidnapped and nearly electrocuted. What does a guy need to do to get a little sympathy round here?'

'Get shot,' she said with a smile, catching sight of Van Simson over Tom's shoulder. 'Is he going to be okay?' Two paramedics had arrived. They checked Van Simson's vital signs before fixing him to a drip and hoisting him onto a stretcher.

'He'll live. Any sign of Renwick?'

'Who?'

'It was Harry, Jen, Harry all along. He organised the Fort Knox job. He had Ranieri and Steiner killed when they chanced upon the coins. Then when you showed up with the last coin he faked his own death and tried to pin everything on me.'

Jennifer shook her head, her forehead creased in confusion.

'Harry? I don't believe it.'

'Neither did I.' Tom's voice was sad, hurt even. 'But it was him all along, he admitted the whole thing.'

'I'm so sorry, Tom.' She squeezed his hand. 'I know how much he meant to you.'

The familiar shape of Jean-Pierre Dumas appeared in the vault doorway. He waved at Tom from across the room before buttonholing two policemen and shouting some orders. Tom shaped his eyebrows into a question mark.

'I recognised Van Simson's voice in the Cistern but this time I figured we could do with some back-up. Jean-Pierre arranged all this.' She waved at the small army buzzing around them. 'We came in as soon as we knew for sure that Van Simson was in the building.'

'Well done.' A powerful voice cut through the noise as a tall man strode into the room and up to the platform, his hand extended, pristine white shirt nestling under an immaculate double-breasted suit. 'My name's Bob Corbett. I'm the agent in charge of this investigation. You've done a great job here. A great job.' He continued, shaking Tom's hand vigorously. 'I have to admit I had my doubts, given your past history. But Agent Browne has made it clear that if it wasn't for you we'd be nowhere. The US government is very grateful.'

'It was Renwick, sir,' said Jennifer urgently. 'He was behind the whole thing.'

Corbett frowned in confusion.

'Harry Renwick?' The question was almost laughed, as if the possibility was so remote as to be faintly ridiculous.

Tom nodded firmly.

'He's been playing us off against each other all along.'

Corbett's eyes narrowed as disbelief turned to hard faced determination. 'Tell us what you can and I'll get on it. He can't have gotten far.' Corbett turned to face two of his men and rattled off a series of instructions in a low voice before turning back to them, a purposeful look in his eye.

'These are yours, I believe.' Tom slid the slim metallic case off the desk and handed it to Corbett.

'Thank you.' Corbett pressed the catch and looked up gratefully. 'Let's just see if we can hang onto them this time.'

EIGHTY-TWO

Hôtel St Merri, 4th Arrondissement, Paris
30th July – 8:42pm

The hotel windows were open and the same intoxicating blend of laughter, Vespa engines and tinkling crockery soared up to his room as it had two nights before. He was alone now, though, Jennifer having joined Corbett at the George V or wherever it was that the FBI saw fit to house its agents.

He didn't blame her for going back there with them. No doubt she had to be debriefed and Corbett would want to know the ins and outs of everything that had happened for the past few days. At least he trusted her to tell his side of the story and argue his case for him. He'd followed through on his part of the deal, Amsterdam aside; but he knew she wouldn't mention that.

There was a knock on the door. He crossed the room, the wooden floor sloping towards the middle of the building where the beams had settled over the centuries, and opened it. It was Jennifer. He stood staring at her blankly for a few moments before she spoke.

'Can I come in?'

'Yes. Yes of course, sorry.' He opened the door and she stepped inside. The bed was the only piece of furniture solid enough to sit on and she perched on the end of it. 'I just wasn't expecting you, that's all. How's it going?' He remained standing near the door. 'I'm surprised they let you out.'

'Well, they didn't really, but they were driving me nuts asking the same questions over and over again. So I thought I'd come and find a familiar face.'

'I'm glad you did. How's Corbett?'

'Oh, he's fine. Mad as hell that he was the one that arranged for me to have dinner at Renwick's, but fine. He's got Renwick firmly in his sights now though. He's even talking of a Federal taskforce to track him down. Oh . . . and he wants to see you in the morning to discuss your deal and how it's going to happen. He said that he guessed you'd rather not do it at the US Embassy, so he suggested a place called Les Invalides. Said you'd know it.'

Tom nodded but didn't move from the door.

'Will you be there?'

'Sure.'

'It's an interesting place. Well worth a visit. You should get a guide book.'

She nodded and there was an awkward pause.

'You know, you didn't need to come all the way over to tell me that.' Tom said. 'You could have called.'

'I know, but I wanted to come.'

Tom flashed her an amused grin.

'Agent Browne, did you actually miss me?'

Her eyes dipped to the floor.

'A little, maybe.'

Tom reached down and locked the door. At the sound of the key turning, she raised her eyes to his and smiled. Tom felt his pulse quickening.

EIGHTY-THREE

Les Invalides, Paris, France
31st July – 1:22pm
A thick heat had settled on the city by the lunchtime of the following day. Jennifer was glad to walk out of the haze of exhaust fumes, through the vaulted entrance arch, into the coolness of the Hôtel des Invalides' vast stone courtyard. She was a little early for her meeting with Bob and Tom, but then she hated being late.

The thought of Tom brought warm memories from the long, lazy night they'd spent together. She surprised herself by how much she'd wanted him. How much she'd needed that release. But she was also realistic. She knew that it was unlikely to last. That he was not the sort of man to be pinned down by anyone, even though she sensed that was perhaps what he thought he wanted.

She looked up at the weather-stained building

around her and flicked to the relevant page in the guide book she'd brought from the hotel's gift shop that morning.

'The Hôtel des Invalides', she read, *'comprises the largest single complex of monuments in Paris. It was founded in 1670 as a military hospital and barracks by Louis XIV, the Sun King. Today it houses the Musée de l'Armée and the remains of Emperor Napoleon Bonaparte, transferred from St Helena in 1840 and housed under the magnificent gilded dome of the Eglise St Louis, one of Paris's most well known landmarks. No expense was spared for the tomb and Napoleon's body lies within six separate coffins – iron, mahogany, two of lead, ebony and red porphyry – the whole resting on a green-granite pedestal.'*

She looked up and smiled. Half of the cobblestone courtyard was bathed in light, the other cloaked in shadow, as the sun made its way over the sloping roof. Windows had been set into the grey slate, each one carved to look like a medieval knight's helmet, while the rounded windows of the floor below echoed the swooping arches of the raised cloister that ran all the way around the courtyard. She stepped up into the cloister, walked past the rusting and scarred hulks of captured cannons that had been strapped to the wall or laid on wooden blocks, her nose buried in the guide book again.

'When the Eglise St Louis was built, in 1676, state protocol forbade soldiers from using the same entrance

as the King and his Court when attending Mass. The
unusual solution was a double church with a shared
altar in the middle of the building, the soldiers entering
from the courtyard on the North side and the King
entering from the South side under the dome.'

Without warning, Tom stepped out from behind
a column. He grabbed her by the arm and marched
her into the shadows in the far left corner of the
courtyard.

'What the fuck is going on?' Tom hissed into
her ear as they walked.

'Get off. You're hurting me.' Jennifer struggled
under his rough grasp. He pushed her away from
him, Jennifer only just managing to remain on
her feet as she tottered across the slippery stone
slabs.

'I should have known,' Tom took a step towards
her. 'Archie was right, you're all the same.'

'What the hell are you talking about?' Her back
was against a First World War tank, one of the
permanent exhibits on show there.

'Don't tell me you don't know . . .'

'Know what?'

'What's *he* doing here?' He jerked his thumb
over his shoulder.

'Who?'

'Clarke. The British police. There are four of
them out there waiting to pick me up. You've sold
me out.'

'What?' Jennifer's eyes widened. 'Tom – listen

to me.' She stepped towards him, her voice low and serious. 'I don't know anything about this, you've got to believe me. It must be a mistake or something.'

Tom glared at her as she took another step forward.

'Look,' she continued. 'You stay here. I'll go and find Bob. I'll try and find out what's going on. I'm sure it's just a mix-up. After what you've done for us, you've got nothing to worry about. Believe me.'

She took a final step and placed her hand on his arm. Tom nodded reluctantly.

'I'll give you ten minutes. If you're not back by then, you'll never see or hear from me again. That's a promise.'

'Ten minutes. Fine.'

Signs pointed the way to the Tomb in five different languages. She followed them down a dark corridor, emerging onto a gravelled area at the side of the church. Large metal barriers had been drawn across the path and again translated signs told her that the Tomb was temporarily closed and apologised for any inconvenience. Seeing no one around, she vaulted over the barrier and walked round to the front of the church. Low, honey-coloured steps led up to the entrance.

She paused at the top of the steps and looked out at the gardens around her. They were empty and in a few places the sprinklers were on, rainbows of water glittering in the midday sun as they arced twenty feet over the grass and bushes.

She could see the men that Tom had meant now, on the other side of the railings that encircled the gardens. Four of them in all, two in a car, one on a bench pretending to read a paper, the other pacing up and down. They were obviously watching the church entrance. One of them looked especially agitated, his suit jacket hanging listlessly off his thin, hunched shoulders. She turned to the entrance and stepped inside, the city vanishing as the glass vestibule door shut behind her.

She found herself swallowed by a deadened hush, the air still, the light muted and restrained, the marbled floor and stone walls frozen in respectful awe. Above her soared the dome, its interior an ecstatic communion of reds and oranges and blues. The painted figures represented the Apostles, her guide book had told her.

There were four side chapels and here the light that filtered in was dyed by their stained glass windows, one green, the other blue, another yellow, the last one orange – small islands of colour that glowed in each corner of the room like fires. A solitary tomb dominated the middle of each chapel, smaller monuments and memorials mounted on and against the walls. She whispered their names as she walked past.

'Foch, Vauban, Bertrand, Lyautey, Duroc.'

Names she didn't know but that sounded appropriately impressive and heroic. More than Browne certainly. Or Corbett for that matter. She frowned. Where was he? It wasn't like him to be late.

A huge black marble and gold leaf altar stood at the far end of the room and behind it a glass wall glittered, separating what was now a tomb from what had been the soldier's side of the double church. A low circular marble balustrade lay directly beneath the dome. As she approached it she could see that here the floor had been removed. In its place, rising from what had once been the crypt floor, was an enormous coffin, a spectacular scrolled mass of red stone resting on a green pedestal.

She leant on the balustrade and looked down. The floor around the coffin had been inlaid with the names of Napoleon's greatest victories with the whole encircled by a white marble colonnade. And then, as her eyes adjusted to the light, she could just about make out a shape in the shadows cast by the columns.

The sole of a shoe. A man's leg.

She jumped up and ran towards the altar at the rear of the church, flew down the steps behind it that led to the lower level. Max, her CIA contact from London, lay slumped on the floor in the narrow corridor that led from the stairs to the colonnade, his shirt stained red. She opened his eyelids, saw that he was dead, stepped over him, her heart racing.

And then she saw Corbett on the other side of the colonnade, stretched out on the floor, his head covered in blood, still and silent.

EIGHTY-FOUR

1:36pm

With a small cry Jennifer sprang towards Corbett and turned him over, pressing her fingers against his carotid artery, feeling for a pulse.

He was still alive. Thank God. He had a deep cut down the right side of his head, but he was still alive.

'Sir. Sir, can you hear me? It's Browne.'

At the sound of Jennifer's voice, Corbett's eyes fluttered open. He groaned and she bent her head down to listen, her ear hovering over his mouth.

'The coins. He took the coins.'

He was lying half in and half out of a small chamber that gave off the colonnade. The chamber was dominated by a towering marble statue of Napoleon dressed in all his Imperial finery. On the floor in front of this, on a white marbled tombstone engraved with the name 'Napoleon II', was a small vase of flowers. Jennifer tipped some of the water from it onto her handkerchief and handed it to Corbett. He had dragged himself upright and was sitting against the door frame. He accepted the wet cloth gratefully, placing it against the wound to staunch the blood.

'What happened?' Jennifer asked gently, crouching down on the floor opposite him. He shook his head in confusion, his voice weak, his face ashen. Jennifer was suddenly struck by how old he looked.

'I don't know. It all happened so fast. I thought I'd have a look around while I was waiting for you guys. He hit me from behind. I just got a glimpse of his face as I fell. It was Renwick.'

'Renwick? Are you sure?'

He nodded.

'I recognised him. No question.' He began to cough, his body convulsing as he fought to clear his lungs. Jennifer waited until he had settled.

'And the coins?'

'They were in my pocket.' He patted his jacket. 'They're gone.' His voice cracked with disappointment. 'I figured if I had Max, I'd be okay. I never thought someone would . . .'

'Don't worry about that now. I'll get a doctor down here, get you checked out.' Jennifer stood up. 'Okay?'

Corbett nodded feebly.

Jennifer took her mobile out of her purse, flipped it open, but paused before dialling.

'By the way, why's Clarke here?'

'Who?' She couldn't see Corbett's face, the handkerchief was masking it, but she sensed him frowning.

'Clarke. British cop. I saw him outside. Did you call him?' Corbett lowered the cloth from his head and narrowed his eyes, his voice suddenly firmer.

'Stay out of that, Jennifer. It's way over your head. It's straight from the top.'

'Stay out of what? What the hell's going on?'

'It's for the best.'

Her eyes widened.

'You're turning him in? He helps us and you just hand him over? He's done nothing wrong. He's innocent.' Her eyes flashed with indignation. Corbett gave her a watery smile.

'Innocent? Of what? Maybe he didn't kill Renwick. Maybe he didn't steal the coins. But he's done plenty of other jobs. He's a crook, Browne, a two-bit thief who deserves to be inside.'

'That's bullshit!' she shouted angrily.

'You think we can have a guy like that running around knowing what he knows? It would just be a matter of time before he spilt his guts, and then what? A diplomatic shit-storm that would set our foreign policy back twenty years.'

'We had a deal. He helped us and promised to keep quiet and in return we wiped his slate clean. He trusted me. I gave him my word.'

'And you believed him? Hah!' Corbett snorted.

'I told you not to get too close, that he was dangerous. There's more riding on this than your word. As far as the Brits are concerned, Renwick's been murdered and Kirk's their man. This way we get to go after Renwick and Kirk gets taken off the street and his silence is guaranteed.'

'Screw that.' Jennifer's voice shook with anger. 'You're betraying him for what? So the President doesn't get asked a few awkward questions. So the CIA doesn't have to face up to its own mistakes? So you can stick another collar on your resumé?'

'Wake up, Jennifer.' Corbett snapped back, using her name for the first time. 'This is the real world and sometimes it gets ugly.' His voice was rough and unfeeling. 'This is about getting the right result. For all of us. It's cut bait time and you know it.'

'This is exactly the sort of bullshit you told me you hate. If you think I'm going to stand by and just let this happen, you're wrong. Dead wrong.'

'Hold it right there.' Corbett snapped. There was a pause. 'You need to think about your next step very carefully,' Corbett's voice was edged with menace. 'And I'm telling you this because I care about you.' He paused. 'You see, back home we've been a little worried that you were getting too close to Kirk. That you might be in danger. So Piper got one of our guys in Amsterdam to keep an eye on you both; you know, sort of watch your back.'

Jennifer swallowed, not daring to break eye-contact.

'I've got a sworn statement saying he followed two people back from a museum to your hotel three nights ago. Turns out the museum was robbed the same night.'

He paused again.

'It would be a goddamned shame if he was to identify you as one of the people he saw. You know, I'm not even sure what would happen.' His voice had a carefree tone now. 'You'd do time, for sure. The Bureau hates its own agents crossing over to the other side. It's not good for morale.'

'You bastard.' She spat the words out but knew he had her. He would place her at the scene and she would go down for it. Five, seven years inside. There'd be no going back.

'You bastard,' she said again, hearing the uncertainty in her voice.

'It hurts now,' said Corbett soothingly. 'But in time you'll see it's for the best. It ain't pretty, but this is how the system works. Sometimes, you gotta take some shortcuts. There's no reason anyone should know what happened in Amsterdam. That's between me and you now. I know you only did it for the right reasons. You play your cards right and you're going all the way in the Bureau. I guarantee it.'

Jennifer didn't answer, staring instead at the floor. She wanted to hit him.

'Why don't you clean up,' he said, pointing at her blood covered fingers, 'and then we can talk some more.'

Jennifer went into the small chamber and picked up the vase from the floor, emptying its contents into her cupped left hand. Then she put the vase down and rubbed her hands together, the water splashing and dripping onto the floor, the white marble blushing red. She looked up, tears of rage and frustration in her eyes, at the statue.

Was this it, she found herself wondering as she gazed into the statue's unseeing and proud eyes? Was this what it was all about? Using and discarding people – was that the secret of Bob Corbett's success? Is that what she would have to do if she was going to make it herself?

And all for what? They had nothing. The coins gone. Cassius vanished. Tom betrayed. But what could she do? Whatever she said they'd still put Tom away for the Amsterdam job. It was pointless.

She rubbed her hands down the sides of her skirt, the black material soft and absorbent, preparing herself to turn round and face Corbett's smug smile. She checked to make sure all the blood had gone from under her nails and the sight of her fingers made the memory of Renwick's severed hand flash into her head – a bloody stump dropped callously into a clear plastic evidence bag and then carried off to some lab or evidence room. His right hand.

Her brain snapped into focus. His right hand.

What was it that Finch had told her back in Louisville after Short's autopsy? Something about an old forensic trick. About how right handed people would tend to strike down on the right side of their victim's head because otherwise they can't get any real force into the blow. Corbett had a gash down the right hand side of his head. How could Renwick have done that if he was missing his right hand?

'Bob, I'm going to go and get you a doctor.' She tried to keep her voice casual, her eyes steady. 'Let's talk about all this later.'

There was no reply.

She turned round and saw Corbett almost standing on top of her. He had his gun out and brought it crashing into the side of her jaw. She collapsed to the floor, blood pouring from her mouth.

'Move.' Corbett barked. 'Back in there.' He kicked her in the ribs as she half crawled, half dragged herself into the depths of the small chamber, shielding her face from Corbett's immaculately polished black shoes.

'I'm sorry, Jennifer. Really I am. I never thought it would come to this.' He reached into his pocket and took out a thick silencer that he screwed carefully onto the end of his standard issue Beretta as he spoke.

'It's Kirk's fault I'm going to have to kill you.' There was an almost hysterical edge to his voice as he spoke. He pulled back on the Beretta, the gun giving a distinctive metallic click as a bullet was loaded into the chamber.

'What are you doing, Bob?' Jennifer croaked. She coughed, swallowed the blood in her mouth, felt her back against the cool marble of the statue's pedestal.

'I would have thought that was obvious.'

EIGHTY-FIVE

1:51pm

Once Jennifer had left him, Tom had slipped through the soldier's entrance of the Eglise St Louis from the courtyard of the main building. Despite what he'd said about disappearing he wanted to know what was really going on for himself – whether Jennifer had betrayed him or if it really was all a mistake.

Inside the church, banks of dark wooden seats stretched in front of him across the limestone floor. High above, where the massive walls met the delicately barrelled roof, regimental and captured enemy flags extended along the length of the nave, flutering gently, their battle-ravaged and blood-stained colours still vibrant. At the far end was an altar.

Tom had walked to the altar and then made his way behind it. There, set into the glass wall, he had found the small connecting door between the two halves of the church he was looking for. Tom's hand was on the door handle, poised to open it, when he heard raised voices on the other side. Then it fell quiet again. Instinctively, he knew something was wrong. Very wrong.

He tried the handle and the door opened noise-lessly onto the small half-landing that led down to the colonnaded walkway around the base of the sarcophagus. Crouching, he could see Max on the floor, clearly dead.

He turned to his right and walked silently up the stairs to the ground floor level, making his way over to the low marble balustrade. He could hear voices again now, talking beneath him.

'Tell me, how did you know?' He recognised Corbett's voice. 'I'm interested.'

'Your wound.' Jennifer's voice sounded strange. 'Renwick couldn't have done that with his right hand missing.'

'Very clever. As always. Maybe I'll just have to pretend Kirk did it, just before he took my gun and shot you.'

Corbett's voice got louder as Tom made his way around the balustrade, suggesting that he was moving closer to him. Jennifer's voice was weaker and Tom guessed that she was in the small chamber that he knew lay over at this side of the coffin.

'Why are you doing this? Why now? For the money?' Corbett laughed, and Tom could tell that he must be right below him now. Without hesitating Tom slipped over the balustrade and crouched on the narrow rim at its base.

EIGHTY-SIX

1:56pm

'I'll almost miss you Browne,' said Corbett as he raised his gun. He paused just for a second as he tightened his grip, his finger toying with the trigger's tightness as he steeled himself for the shot.

With a final push, Tom swung down off the ledge and hit Corbett square in his back with the flat of his feet. Corbett slammed into the wall, his nose breaking against the marble, the gun spinning out of his hand and into the chamber where it struck the statue's pedestal before dropping to the floor. Tom landed heavily on his back, his hands breaking his fall enough to stop him cracking his coccyx.

Corbett turned round snarling, fists clenched, poised to leap on Tom, but Jennifer stepped between them, gripping his gun.

'I will shoot you if I have to, sir.' She tilted her

head to one side and raised the gun to his chest. 'We both know I've done it before.'

Corbett's eyes narrowed, the blood filtering through his fingers from his nose and his voice muffled as he cupped his face.

'You talk a big game, Browne, but you and I both know you're bluffing. You can't kill me, not after what you did to Greg. They'll just lock you away this time.'

'Maybe they will, maybe they won't. But sometimes you got to take some shortcuts if you want to get the right result; isn't that true?'

Something in her tone seemed to make Corbett hesitate.

'You won't do it.' He snarled eventually.

'Well, I will then,' said Tom, stepping forward and taking the gun from her grasp. 'So I suggest you shut the hell up.'

Corbett began to laugh, his blood forming large bubbles from his nose that burst before re-forming again.

'What's funny?'

'You two. What a team. We never planned on that.'

'We?' said Jennifer, taking a step forward. 'What we?' Corbett didn't answer, his laugh melting into a thick cough as some blood flowed back down his throat.

'Cassius,' said Tom suddenly. 'You've been working with Cassius, haven't you?' Corbett pressed his back heavily against the wall as his cough subsided. Tom glanced at Jennifer. 'That's how he knew that you were still alive. That's how he knew the NYPD got a DNA match on me in New York.' He looked back at Corbett. 'Because you told him.' Corbett remained silent.

'But I don't understand,' said Jennifer, turning to Tom. 'How could he have been involved with Renwick? I was working with him all along.'

'Because he only let you see what he wanted,' Tom countered. 'After Steiner got lucky at Schiphol airport, Renwick tracked him and Ranieri down and had them both killed. The only problem was that Ranieri had swallowed the fifth coin and it ended back with you guys in Washington. So they arranged for both of us to meet for dinner at Renwick's house. That gave them the opportunity to grab the coin back, get rid of Harry Renwick once and for all and incriminate me so that I'd be blamed for everything. Only they didn't count on you doing such a good job of pinning down my movements all night.'

'You still don't get who he is, do you? The genius of the man. What he's capable of,' Corbett spat, his voice getting stronger now. 'You're both as dumb as the rest of them. Piper, Green, Young – they all fell for it.'

'What do you mean, fell for it? Fell for what?' Tom asked.

'Oh my God,' Jennifer gasped. 'Of course. None of it ever happened, did it?'

Corbett began to clap slowly, his face twisted and hateful.

'What are you talking about?' asked Tom.

'You were right, Tom.' She turned and spewed words at him as her mouth strained to catch up with her brain. 'You said it was all too convenient. That they'd wanted us to discover the faked suicide and the container. Well, that's why. None of it ever happened. Corbett was the one who suggested going through the personnel files. He knew I'd find out sooner or later that Short had been murdered and focus the investigation there. He knew I'd find the container out the back of his house and the money in his bank account. The whole thing was a set-up.'

'Short was so fucking bored,' Corbett dabbed his nose with his sleeve. 'So desperate to be a cop again, to get a bit of the old buzz back. So when I flashed my badge and told him that we needed his help on a secret government project, he couldn't do enough to help. Dumb fuck didn't even want to get paid. Told me he was proud enough to be doing something for his country again. Can you believe that?'

'So there was no gold shipment?' Tom asked.

'Oh, the container turned up all right. Short did the inventory himself so no one else would get a good look at it. Then he saw to it that it was put downstairs and that all the paperwork checked out and screwed around with the generator so I could sell my computer virus theory. But there was nobody inside the container. The whole thing was Renwick's idea. To set up a robbery that never actually happened. So that if anyone came looking, they'd have something to investigate.' He locked eyes with Tom and smiled. 'Some*one* to investigate.'

'But if no one was in the container, how did you get into the vault? How did you get the coins out?' Jennifer asked, frowning in confusion.

Tom nodded in sudden understanding.

'Because this wasn't a set-up. It was a cover-up. All this was to cover up an earlier crime, wasn't it? Because you already had the coins. You just needed to make sure that someone else took the fall. Me.'

There was a pause as Jennifer looked from Tom to Corbett, and then back to Tom in confusion.

'Ten years,' said Corbett slowly, breaking the silence. 'Ten years they've been sitting in a safety deposit box. Waiting. Millions of dollars and I couldn't touch it. Until Renwick offered me a way out.'

'But how did you get them?' Jennifer asked. 'How did you do it?'

'Didn't you get taught to check back?' Corbett flicked his eyes to hers. 'FBI 101, Jennifer. Always check back. You were more interested in following the obvious clues I'd left you than do your basic homework.' He gave a short laugh. 'But then that's why I chose you. I knew you'd be so desperate to do well, to impress, to earn another shot at the big time, that you'd go for the story I'd carefully laid out for you. If you'd looked properly, you'd have noticed my name as the officer in charge when the coins were moved from Philadelphia back to Fort Knox ten years ago.'

Jennifer felt suddenly hot. He was right. She had followed the obvious clues, even when she'd sensed that something was wrong. She'd got carried away by her hunger to succeed.

'There I was, two weeks after Martha left me for some guy she met in her yoga class, sitting in the back of a van with five coins worth millions of dollars handcuffed to my wrist. So I just opened the case and took them. When we got down to Fort Knox, no one checked that the coins were there. They just signed the case in and took it straight down to the vault, empty. Everyone trusted good old Bob Corbett. They always have. It was too easy.' He smiled at them triumphantly.

'And then what? Smuggle the coins back to Europe and auction them off? What was your cut?' Tom asked.

'Half the proceeds.'

'I've heard enough,' said Jennifer, her face wrinkled in disgust. 'Give me the coins.'

Corbett reached inside his jacket and removed the polished metal case.

'You'd better call for some back-up,' said Tom

as he took it from Corbett and gave it to Jennifer.
She opened it to check the coins were there and
then snapped it shut again.

'You leave first.'

'No way. Not till he's been dealt with.'

'I'm serious. I can take it from here.' She held
her hand out for the gun. 'Until all this has been
cleared up, you shouldn't risk getting caught.'

'You sure?'

An unfamiliar voice echoed across the tomb's
empty space before she could answer.

'What the bloody hell is going on here?'

A man was standing in the corridor's half
shadow, gazing at Max's outstretched body. Tom
turned to Jennifer.

'It's Clarke.'

EIGHTY-SEVEN

2:10pm

As Tom turned, Corbett kicked out and caught his hand with the side of his shoe. The gun flew through the air and landed with a noisy rattle on the floor behind him. In the same movement Corbett turned on his heel and sprinted towards the stairs.

'Ah, Corbett,' said Clarke when he saw him running towards him. 'I thought I heard someone down here.' He pointed at Max's body. 'Is this Kirk's work?'

Corbett elbowed him out the way without breaking his stride and Clarke's head hit the marble wall with a thump. He slumped to the floor.

'Quick,' said Tom. 'Give me a leg up.'

Jennifer cupped her hands and Tom stepped up onto them until he could reach the rim of the balustrade above. He hauled himself up and

crouched there until he heard the clatter of
Corbett's heels reaching the top of the stairs. Tom
jumped up onto the balustrade as Corbett came
past and threw himself at him, his arms wrap-
ping around Corbett's waist and then sliding
down to his ankles, toppling him like a rolled up
carpet.

Corbett was up in a flash, catching Tom on the
side of his face with a heavy blow that made his
face sting. Tom rolled to his feet, adrenaline
pumping, blood trickling from the side of his
mouth, and placed himself between Corbett and
the exit. Corbett stood, fists raised, his eyes flicking
uncertainly between Tom and the door, clearly
trying to assess how likely he was to get past him.

'Be my guest,' said Tom.

With a roar, Corbett launched himself at Tom,
lashing out with a series of well-aimed kicks and
punches that Tom blocked with his arms before
striking out himself and catching Corbett on the
left cheekbone, sending him sprawling. On his
hands and knees now, Corbett lifted his head
towards Tom, his eyes ablaze.

He stood up and took several steps back. Tom
realized too late what he was doing as he
unclipped the red rope from one of the mobile
barriers that had been pushed up against the wall
behind him and picked one of its brass poles up.
With a triumphant sneer he walked towards Tom,
swinging the heavy brass pole in front of him with

both hands, the thick square base swishing menacingly through the air.

Tom backed away and Corbett broke into a run, swinging the pole around his head like a claymore. Tom dodged the first two sweeps, one to his right, one to his left, but the third took him by surprise, a low sweep that caught him just behind the left knee and flipped him onto his back. Corbett immediately raised the pole above his head and brought it crashing down. Tom rolled one way and then the other just in time as the heavy brass base struck the marble twice, sending large chunks of the polished stone spinning through the air. He kicked out and caught Corbett in the stomach, momentarily winding him and sending him staggering back.

Tom scrambled to his feet and ran to the other pole, unclipping the rope from it and picking it up, flipping it between his hands as he tried to get used to the weight. The two men circled each other warily, both looking for an opening.

Corbett made the first move, taking a wild swing at Tom's head. Tom parried the blow, the two brass poles crashing together with a metallic clang that echoed back off the painted dome like a bell. He immediately struck back, catching Corbett on his arm. Corbett shouted with pain; he stumbled backwards and then charged again, swinging the pole backwards and forwards. Tom defended himself desperately as he was driven back towards the marble balustrade, the brass poles clashing again and again and again, until his hands were numb from the vibrations.

Sensing the balustrade behind him, Tom jumped up onto it and Corbett leapt forward, swinging at Tom's legs. Tom jumped up, the pole swinging harmlessly under his feet and then again as it came back the other way. But the momentum of the second swing seemed to throw Corbett slightly off balance and Tom kicked out, catching him across his already bloodied and broken nose. Corbett shrieked with pain and dropped his pole as his hands flew to his face. Tom jumped down and booted the pole across the room, then threw his own after it.

Corbett looked up at him, eyes streaming, hair wild, blood dripping from his nose, his suit ripped and dirty. With a final, desperate roar, Corbett propelled himself across the few feet that separated them. Tom threw himself sideways and tripped him as he came past, Corbett's face flicking from hate to surprise as he fell heavily.

Tom was on his back immediately and wrapped his arm around his neck in a choke hold. He tightened his grip as Corbett began to cough, slapping Tom's forearm like a capitulating wrestler as he struggled to get his breath.

Tom slowly lifted Corbett's head back towards him, felt his struggling get more desperate as the ligaments in his neck began to stretch and tear and the vertebrae grind against each other, crushing his spinal column.

Some faint memory from his CIA training flashed into his head – it only requires 6 pounds of pressure to break a human neck.

EIGHTY-EIGHT

2:23pm

'Don't do it, Tom.' He felt Jennifer's gentle touch on his shoulder. 'He's not worth it.'

He held Corbett still, his mind on fire, the pounding in his head drowning everything out. Again her voice came, gentle and calm.

'Let him go. Don't prove him right.'

Slowly Tom loosened his grip, until he suddenly snatched his arm away and jumped up, leaving Corbett writhing on the floor, coughing and gasping. Jennifer smiled at him.

'Well done.'

'Right, nobody move.' Clarke emerged from behind the altar and walked towards them, Corbett's gun in his hand. 'Nobody's going anywhere until I find out exactly what's going on here.' He was rubbing the back of his head and still looked dazed.

'It's very simple,' said Jennifer, stepping towards

him and then stopping when Clarke waggled the gun at her. 'Bob Corbett is suspected of complicity in a criminal conspiracy. I have just placed him under arrest.'

Clarke raised his eyebrows.

'What, one of your own bloody agents? What are you Yanks playing at?'

'It's complicated,' said Jennifer, throwing him a quick smile.

'It's a bloody shambles, that's what it is. Normally is with you lot. Anyway, that's your business. I'm here for him.' He turned to face Tom, his voice unsteady but strengthening. 'I told you I'd catch up with you eventually.' He gave a thin smile.

'I hate to dissapoint you, but Tom has been working for us,' said Jennifer gently, taking another step towards him.

'Kirk? Working for the FBI? Pull the other one. He's a killer.'

'You mean Harry Renwick?'

Clarke nodded.

'Too bloody right I do.'

Jennifer took another step forward and was now standing just a few feet from Clarke.

'Harry Renwick's still alive and I can prove it.'

Clarke looked at each of them disbelievingly, the colour rising in his face, a muscle in his neck throbbing violently under his pale skin.

'Bollocks. You're protecting him. You think I

was born yesterday?' There was a desperate tone to his voice now.

'I'm not and the Bureau will back me up.'

'Oh, I get it!' Clarke's worried face lifted into a triumphant sneer. 'You're working with him, aren't you. You're both in this together. It's some sort of scam. Well, I'll have you both.' He reached into his pocket and pulled out a shiny set of handcuffs.

'Tom Kirk,' he began. 'I'm arresting you for the murder of . . .'

Tom shot a glance at Jennifer.

'Do you mind?' he asked.

'Let me.'

'. . . Henry Julius Renwick,' Clarke continued. 'Anything you say . . .'

Jennifer drew her right hand back and punched Clarke on the point of his chin. He gave a wheezy cough and then collapsed onto the floor like a puppet that had had its strings cut.

EIGHTY-NINE

Charles de Gaulle Airport, France
1st August – 6:30pm
The announcer's tinny voice echoed through the departure lounge, first in French, then in English.

'Final call for Air France flight number 9074 for Washington, DC. Would all remaining passengers please make their way immediately to gate number five.'

'I guess that's my flight,' sighed Jennifer.

'I guess it is,' said Tom.

'Listen. I want to say thank you,' Jennifer said awkwardly. 'You know, for everything.'

'No, thank *you*. For trusting me. It meant a lot. Still does.'

Jennifer blushed and looked down at her feet.

'Well, if you're ever in the States . . .'

Tom smiled.

'Don't worry, I will. If you have time now you're so important.'

'Oh, you heard about that.' She blushed again.

'You deserve it. I'm sure Corbett would have approved. How is he, by the way?'

'Jean-Pierre smoothed things over with the local authorities here. Now he's under escort until he gets back to DC. Then we'll see. Like he told me, the Bureau has a thing about rogue agents. My guess is it'll be a long, long time before they let him out!'

'Good. He's earned it.'

'And what about you? What will you do now?'

'Oh, I don't know. I've got my shop opening soon. There's still a lot to do for that. I guess I haven't really thought about it. I've never had time to think about it before.'

'And you're sure that you don't want any protection in case Renwick makes a move.'

'Oh no, I'll be fine. I have a feeling I'll see him again soon – but I'll be ready.'

'Well, we'll be looking for him too.' Jennifer picked her bag up. 'I'll let you know if we find him.' A pause. 'I'd better go.'

'I know,' said Tom. He kissed her on the forehead, then the lips and they hugged each other tightly.

'Take care,' she whispered into his ear as they parted.

'Oh, and by the way,' she said as she turned towards the gate, 'your friend Piper has resigned. The Treasury Secretary didn't take too kindly to being lied to about what happened. And as long as you keep quiet about Centaur, our deal stands. When you get home your friend Clarke will give you the full red carpet treatment.'

'That's great.' Somehow Tom doubted it.

'The Secretary even suggested some sort of reward or something for you, but then I remembered that you didn't really like working for the government, so probably wouldn't want anything.'

Tom smiled.

'Just the memories.'

'Bye, Tom,' she said, her eyes twinkling.

'Don't you mean *au revoir*?' he whispered to himself as she disappeared through the gate.

NINETY

6:39pm

'So that's put the kibosh on that, then?' Archie's familiar voice broke into Tom's thoughts. 'Thank God!'

Tom shook his head in smiling disbelief.

'Just happened to be passing, did you?' He kept his eyes fixed on the spot where he had last seen Jennifer. Archie stepped forward and rested his back against the low steel rail that Tom was leaning on. He wore a suit and tie, a briefcase in one hand and the *Financial Times* under the other arm, blending in seamlessly with the hordes of businessmen making their way through the terminal.

'Someone's got to watch your back.' His words were muffled as he took another bite of the sandwich that he was clutching in his right hand. The yellow wrapper matched his Ferragamo tie.

'Last time you were watching my back you

signed me up to do a job for Cassius and nearly got me shot,' Tom said sarcastically.

Archie looked mortified.

'Oh, that hurts, mate. That really hurts.'

'What are you really doing here?'

'Making sure you didn't do something you might regret. Like get on that plane.'

'Would that have been such a bad idea?' asked Tom thoughtfully.

'Er . . . yes!' Archie slurped on his drink. 'First she's a Fed. That's generally bad news if you're a thief. Second, she lives in America. That's a long way from home. Third, she's far too hot for the likes of a muppet like you.'

'You're probably right,' said Tom laughing.

He stood up straight and turned round, leaning against the rail next to Archie, and shoved his hands into his jacket pockets. Nestling at the bottom of his left hand pocket, he felt an unfamiliar shape. He slipped it out into the open.

It was a stainless steel 1934 Rolex Prince, its case glinting brightly. The one Jennifer had pointed out to him in the shop window on the morning they had first met. The one she must have slipped into his pocket when they had hugged goodbye. A little trick she seemed to have picked up from Amin Madhavy back in Istanbul.

'Nice piece,' said Archie, peering in for a closer look. 'I know someone who'll take that off your hands if you want to shift it.'

'No, thanks,' said Tom, following Jennifer's plane as it taxied out onto the runway, imagining her knuckles glowing white as they gripped the arm rests in anticipation of take-off. 'I think I'll hang onto this one.'

There was a silence and the airport throbbed around them, children screaming, baggage trolleys squeaking, phones ringing.

Archie coughed and straightened his tie.

'Actually, Tom, there's another reason I'm here.'

'Here we go.' Tom rolled his eyes. 'What have you done now?'

'Nothing. It's just that I've had this great idea. Think about it. You and me. Kirk and Connolly. In business together.' Tom sighed and began to walk towards the exit.

'Where are you going?' Archie ran after him. 'Your skills and my connections – we'd be unstoppable! Think about it.'

'Archie I've told you. No more jobs.'

'No, that's my point. A proper business. All kosher and above board. You know, buying stuff here, selling it there, helping people get stuff back. We could make a fortune. We could be the good guys for a change.'

'Archie,' said Tom as he threw his arm around his shoulders. 'If you're involved, how can we ever be the good guys?'

Archie stopped in his tracks, his expression pained.

'Oh, that hurts, mate. That really hurts.'
Tom laughed.
'Maybe a pint will help you get over it.'
'As long as it's none of this foreign muck.'

EPILOGUE

The only thing we have to fear is fear itself.

President Franklin D Roosevelt –
Inaugural Address, 4th March 1933

Epilogue

Near Lyon, France
Two weeks later – 10:07pm
'Please remove any metallic objects from your pockets. Keys, coins, mobile phone, glasses. Place them in the containers before stepping through the detector. Thank you.'

The noisy queue snaked back on itself several times, like the entrance to a ride at an amusement park. Most of the people in it, returning from their holidays judging from the raw redness of their skin, chose to ignore the security guard until they were almost through the metal detector and X-ray machines, only then scrabbling to empty their pockets of any offending items.

It was this that marked the tall man out in particular. Not his immaculate black suit and dog collar amidst the sea of fluorescent T-shirts and sandals, but the fact that well before the gate he had carefully separated all his metallic objects into one hand.

Not that the security guards noticed. The airport had only recently been given a new lease of life, plucked from obscurity by an enterprising low-cost airline and re-christened with the name of a large city 30 miles to the north of it. It was why he'd chosen it. The security was not as tight as at one of the major airports; the quality of the personnel not as high. He had done this before when he needed to slip out of a country un-noticed.

He smiled at the guard as he carefully deposited a small pile of loose change and some keys into one of the grey plastic containers placed at the end of the X-ray machines. Just enough to look normal. He then walked through the machine. It beeped loudly. As he knew it would.

'Any other metal objects on you, Father?' asked the guard in French as he directed the man back through the detector. He patted his pockets and shook his head.

'No,' he answered.

'Okay. Step back through the gate, please.' He did as he was told but the machine beeped again.

'Please stand over here, Father. Move your legs apart a little. Thank you.' The guard ran a hand-held scanner over his black suit. It screamed loudly as it passed over his gloved right hand.

'Can I see?' the guard said pointing suspiciously.

'Oh, of course.' The man shook his head. 'How foolish of me. After all this time I forget all about it.' He had thought this part through carefully. The key was to make it look like he'd been this way for years. It mustn't seem a recent injury; they might be on the lookout for that.

'Forget what?'

'My hand,' he said, pulling off the glove and revealing a pink prosthetic hand attached to his arm. Some girls in the queue behind him tittered at the sight of it.

'I'm sorry, sir,' said the guard blushing, clearly embarrassed for him by their laughter.

'No, not at all, it's my fault,' he said. 'It happens all the time. I should have remembered.'

'Thank you, Father. Sorry, Father. Where are you going?'

'Geneva.'

'Well, at least the plane should be leaving on time. We've had so many delays recently with all the extra security checks.'

'I'm in no hurry,' the man said, retrieving his coins and keys. 'Believe me, I've got plenty to think about.'

'Have a pleasant flight.'

'Bless you. Bless you, my son,' said Cassius.

The security guard watched the one-handed man walk into the departure lounge.

Out of habit, he made the sign of the cross in the direction of his retreating back.

The Black Sun
HIGH ADVENTURE.
MIND-BLOWING SUSPENSE.
TOM KIRK IS BACK

In London, an Auschwitz survivor is murdered in his hospital bed, his killers making off with a macabre trophy-his severed left arm.

In Fort Mead, Maryland, a vicious gang breaks into the NSA museum and steals a second world war Enigma machine, lynching the guard who happens to cross their path.

Meanwhile, in Prague, a frenzied and mindless anti-Semitic attack on a Synagogue culminates in the theft of a seemingly worthless painting by a little known Czech artist called Karel Bellak.

A year has passed since Tom Kirk, the world's greatest art thief, decided to put his criminal past behind him and embark on a new career, on the right side of the law. Then three major thefts occur, and suddenly Tom is confronted with a deadly mystery and a sinister face from the past.

ISBN 0-00-719016-6